Kindling

Skye Malone

Kindling

Book One of the Kindling Trilogy
Previously Published as The Children and the Blood Trilogy

Cover design by Karri Klawiter
www.artbykarri.com

ISBN-10: 1-940617-35-9
ISBN-13: 978-1-940617-35-0

Join Skye Malone's mailing list to hear about new releases!
www.skyemalone.com/mailinglist

For Avery

Prologue

———◆———

Blood dripped from his hands to stain the carpet, handcuffs clinked on his wrists as the car swerved, and Howard Bartlow knew he was going to die.

Other than that, nothing was certain.

"You'll let them go, right?" he asked again, hating how tentative his voice sounded in the darkness. "They'll be safe after this?"

"We've given you our word, Mr. Bartlow," said the suit-clad giant next to him, his voice calm as he flipped through the contents of Howard's wallet. Though his weight shifted slightly as the car whipped around another turn on the gravel road, the man's eyes didn't leave the wrinkled family photograph he pulled from between the credit cards. "Our goal is simply to end this. We have no interest in murder."

Howard looked away, unable to stand the sight of the man holding the picture of his wife and child. And as for the rest, that wasn't really true, was it? The monsters around him might not consider what they were about to do as murder, but Howard knew otherwise.

So many would be killed. If they were lucky, a few in hiding might survive. But everything he and the others had worked and bled and died for these past eight years would mean absolutely nothing. Rage swelled at the thought, building till he was sure it would explode from his body and swallow everyone in the car in flame.

And then it drained, just as it had every other time in these past six hours of hell. The monsters had Missy. They had his beloved Tanya. They had the only reasons Howard had suffered through these eight horrific years, and they would kill them both if he didn't do exactly as they said. Everything was pointless without his wife and little girl. The hiding. The running. The living in buildings abandoned so long ago that even the rats had gone to find other places to stay. He'd left his home. He'd left his career. This whole mess was the fault of those now holding his wife and daughter captive, and with his help, they were going to destroy everything.

But Missy and Tanya wouldn't die.

He squeezed his eyes shut, furious tears trying to break past his resolve. They hadn't known it, none of them. These bastards had been killing people off one by one, secretly and without the slightest chance of detection. They were invisible, seemingly invincible, and so much stronger than he'd ever believed anyone could be. It hurt to think of how many of his friends had fought and died, never knowing these monsters existed, and never knowing how pointless their own battles would be in the end.

The car slammed to a stop, jerking him forward into the driver's headrest and then back against his seat.

"Is that it?" asked the giant, glancing out the smoked window.

Howard couldn't look. A last, irrational urge to lie swept over him. He could tell them the house was elsewhere. He could tell them the family had moved. He could say anything, and somehow, everything would still be alright.

His eyes fell to the photograph in the man's hand and the impulse withered away. Guiltily, his gaze climbed to the pastoral tableau beyond the darkened glass.

Moonlight silvered the rolling hills surrounding the old, three-story farmhouse, while radiant security lights illuminated the yard. Near the attic, a single lamp spilled golden light out into the darkness, though every other window was black. From Howard's perch on the gravel road emerging from the mountains, he could see dense forests cresting the hills behind the farmhouse and the barn, shielding the buildings from the horizon. A sleepy little ranch house nestled in the shadow of the mountains to the west, and hillocks ran along the edge of the whole property, blocking the farmland from view of the road. Beyond the next rise and farther down the gravel lane, he could just make out the porch light of a cottage – the only other neighbor for miles, and too far away to wake at the sound of anything to come.

"Yes," he whispered.

The car raced down into the valley.

"Out," the giant ordered as the sedan came to a stop. The men in front left the vehicle immediately. A heartbeat later, the rear door was thrown open, and they hauled Howard into the darkness and threw him to the ground. In the wake of the sedan, other cars pulled up, swiftly discharging their black-clad occupants.

"You know what to do," the giant said.

The men disappeared over the embankment.

Minutes passed in silence.

One of the men appeared atop the rise. He nodded. The giant nodded once in return.

Howard closed his eyes.

"Will you let them go now?" he asked, barely noticing how

tenuous his voice sounded in the night.

The giant sighed. "Honestly, Mr. Bartlow, that won't be necessary. I would assume your family remains safely ensconced in whatever hole they're currently hiding in, same as they were when we intercepted you."

Howard stared at him.

"Arranging a girl to pretend to be your daughter wasn't difficult. A static-filled phone call is simple enough to reproduce, and the little actress screaming on the other end just thought she was auditioning for a movie. Your fears did the rest."

The giant gave him a mildly ironic look. "I told you we had no interest in murder."

His feet pulled him toward the farmhouse before Howard realized he was running. His bound hands hit the dirt, scrabbling at the roots and weeds to drag him over the rise. He gathered his strength for a desperate attempt at a warning, and then choked as pain exploded in his back.

The bullets tore through his spine and chest, throwing him to the ground, while only making popping sounds as they left the silenced gun.

A heartbeat passed. The giant bent down next to him, regarding him with the same dispassionate gaze to which he treated everything else. "No interest," he repeated. "Unless we have no choice."

He gave Howard a last glance, and then rose. His footsteps disappeared over the embankment, leaving Howard alone.

A wet gurgle of breath escaped him. His hands clawed uselessly at the grass, and all around him, the silver night was fading. Tears slid down his cheek, wetting the dirt pressed against his face.

"God forgive me," he whispered as he died.

——————— ◆ ———————

Mason Brogan tucked the gun beneath his jacket and regarded the farmhouse. Light from a security lamp spread a circle on the grass, ending only inches from his black Italian shoes. The farmland was silent around him, his men making no sound as they secured the grounds.

But he would have expected nothing less.

He drew a slim satellite phone from a pocket and flipped it open, hitting the first speed dial. Eyes still on the house, he raised the phone to his ear, unsurprised when the recipient picked up before the end of the initial ring.

"We found them," he said.

The phone flipped closed.

Fire lit the sky.

Beyond the circle of the security light, Brogan's lips pulled back in the closest he ever came to a genuine smile.

Chapter One

———◆———

Ten Hours Ago

"How's that?" Ashley called, twisting carefully atop the rickety porch railing to see her little sister on the lawn below.

Lily glanced away from the pile of crafts by her knees and squinted into the late afternoon sunlight. Tightening her hold on the porch column, Ashley waited as the petite eight-year-old considered the position of the wind chimes dangling from the eaves.

Biting her lip, Lily turned, scrutinizing the other decorations of her own creation dotting the large yard. Bird feeders made of empty milk cartons shared space with pinwheels and streamers fashioned from every scrap of fabric the girl could get her hands on. Painted flower pots lined the weathered steps in multihued splendor, framed by equally brilliant painted rocks. The world around the old gray farmhouse was a cacophony of color, into which the wind chimes had to be placed just right.

"A little to the left," Lily replied.

Adjusting her grip, Ashley unhooked the chimes, stretched a few inches more and then attached them to the eaves again.

"Perfect," Lily announced, satisfied.

Exhaling in silent relief, Ashley climbed down from the railing and jumped to the lawn.

"Okay," she said, brushing her hands on her jeans as she checked the remaining crafts. "Looks like we've just got the pinwheels for the vegetable garden, and then we'll be–"

"We forgot the birdhouses!" Lily exclaimed. Shoving away from the grass, she raced across the yard and up the steps, letting the screen door slam as she dashed inside.

Ashley smiled, shaking her head. Ever since she was four years old, Lily had insisted on placing birdhouses in the yard, regardless of how they both knew it would turn out. Acres of forest surrounded their farm, with miles of western Montana's hills and mountain ranges beyond. Given such plentiful places to nest, birds were a rare sight on their property. But Lily was nothing if not stubborn, and prior disappointment did nothing to dissuade her from putting out fresh houses each spring.

Bending down, Ashley collected the multicolored pinwheels from the grass. It was an annual tradition, replacing the older decorations with new ones. Every year called for different color schemes and arrangements, according to Lily, who worked through the winter creating her latest designs for spring. And despite the occasional danger of tripping over a painted rock or fallen streamer, all the farmhands swore to the little girl that the place just wouldn't seem right without her hard work.

In the distance, Ashley heard a door close and she looked up to see her dad coming out of the farmhands' house with Jonathan, the head caretaker of her father's property. Spotting her at the heart of the new decorations, Patrick waved and then bid a quick goodbye to the old farmer before heading her way.

"Wow," he said, running a hand through his gray-flecked brown hair as he surveyed the yard. "You two really outdid yourselves."

Ashley shrugged. "It's Lily's work. I'm just the slave labor. You wouldn't believe how upset she gets if I don't help put everything in place."

He chuckled as he took a pinwheel from her and spun it, watching the bright colors blur. His humor faded. "I'd forgotten you girls did this."

She scoffed. "It's not a big deal, Dad."

For a moment, Patrick regarded the pinwheel and then drew a breath. "So…"

Ashley braced herself, reading his tone. She'd expected this. She always expected it from the moment he arrived. "You've got to go."

"A job called."

"Where this time?" she asked, burying her disappointment so he wouldn't see. It wasn't his fault he'd miss her birthday. Again. As a freelance researcher, he had to take what jobs he could get in order to keep their family afloat.

No matter how badly timed those jobs always seemed to be.

"Here, there, back again," he replied dryly. "You know, the usual."

She grinned. "Ah, frequent flyer miles."

A laugh escaped him, and then his gaze went to the farmhouse.

"Lily'll be fine, Dad," Ashley said, trying to preempt the worry she saw rising in his eyes. "When are you heading out?"

"Tomorrow afternoon, I think." His brow furrowed, and then he looked back at her, pushing the expression away. "I'm sorry I couldn't stay longer. You know I hate being away from the two of you."

She shrugged. "It's okay. Pays the bills, right?"

He gave her a wry smile.

"When are you going to tell Lily?"

Patrick took a breath, his eyebrows shrugging expressively.

The screen door slammed as the little girl came outside, her arms loaded with precariously balanced birdhouses. Leaving the question unanswered, Patrick hurried to help, catching one of the houses before it fell.

Watching him go, Ashley sighed. Lily would be upset when he left, of course, but the girl was growing up. Almost a year had gone by since his last visit, with nearly six months between the one before that. While the three weeks he'd spent with them this spring had been wonderful, both she and Lily had known it would end. And like Ashley before her, the little girl was learning to accept their father's sudden departures, and the long absences that followed.

Arms full of birdhouses, Patrick called for her to come help, and Ashley pushed a smile back onto her face as she jogged toward them. When she was a child, he'd often said that once he'd saved enough money, he'd leave research and come here to stay. She'd clung to those words when she was nine. Now, at nearly seventeen, she held a soft place in her heart for that hope, but knew that even if the money had been there, the love her father had for his work was too deeply ingrained for him to ever walk away.

In short order, pinwheels filled the vegetable garden, each dutifully placed in locations approved by Lily. At the girl's direction, Patrick and Ashley tackled the birdhouses next, and by the time Jonathan called them for dinner, the decorating was complete.

"It'll do," Lily stated, hands on her hips as she studied the yard.

Patrick glanced to Ashley. She smothered a laugh.

"Everything looks wonderful, Lilybud," he told the girl. "Now come on. Sun's setting; there's not much more you can do today."

Still frowning at her creations, Lily nevertheless allowed him to lead her toward the house. With a grin, Ashley followed.

Warm light filled the entryway and spilled into the room to their right where Jonathan and his wife Rose had slept till an unexpected freeze burst a pipe and drove them to stay at the farmhands' house. At the end of the hall, pots clanked behind the kitchen door, providing arrhythmic accompaniment to the music of one of Rose's classic rock albums.

"Hey, Patrick," Jonathan said, rising from the living room sofa and setting aside his dog-eared copy of the almanac. "Quick question."

"Go help Rose," Patrick told Lily.

Immediately, the little girl glanced back at the front door.

Turning her gently, Patrick gave her a nudge toward the kitchen. "I mean it, kiddo. No more crafts tonight. I'll join you in a minute."

He cast a glance to Ashley and she nodded. Herding Lily before her, she drove the girl down the hall, leaving Jonathan to pull Patrick aside.

Pushing open the swinging door, Lily started into the kitchen, only to have a glass bowl of salad shoved into her arms.

"Put that on the table, would you, Ashley?" Rose asked distractedly, whirling back to the chaos of the kitchen. Pots bubbled on the stove, garlic bread lay half-cut on the chopping board, and a block of cheese waited beside the grater. Humidity from the boiling water turned the woman's hair into a cloud of graying curls and made her face glisten the color of her namesake.

"Rose?" Ashley called, grabbing the bowl to help Lily balance as the door swung back to hit them both.

"What? I– oh, Lily!" She rushed over to steady the dish. "I'm so sorry, sweetie! From the corner of my eye, you just..." She looked between the sisters and then smiled at the little girl. "Sorry."

Lily nodded with relief as Rose handed the salad to Ashley.

"Come on," Rose said, ruffling Lily's hair affectionately. "Help me with the bread."

Ashley headed for the dining room. As she set the salad on the long table, she caught sight of Jonathan and her father coming down the hall, though they barely made it through the kitchen door before Rose assigned them tasks as well. Shoving dishes and silverware into their hands, Rose admonished them for leaving the girls all the work and, with chastened expressions sufficient to satisfy the woman, the two men made quick work of the remaining setup.

"So," Patrick said after everyone sat down. "Cause for celebration soon, eh?"

Ashley glanced to him as she took a piece of garlic bread. "Huh?"

"Your birthday," he supplied, a grin deepening the faint wrinkles around his dark eyes. "It's still in three days, right? You didn't move it?"

She faltered, and Lily laughed at her silence. "Silly, of course it is!" the girl cried. "And this one's the best yet, because Daddy's here."

Ashley picked up her fork and looked to her plate, unsure what to say. Even without her dad, her birthday would be fine. It always was.

She just hadn't expected him to actually bring it up.

Oblivious, Lily turned her smile on the rest of the table. "We're gonna make a big cake like last year, right?"

Rose smiled. "Of course," she said, the slight tension in her voice hinting that she knew Patrick would be leaving the next day.

"Chocolate," Ashley volunteered tightly. Gratitude showed in Rose's eyes.

"Well, how about we start the celebration tomorrow?" Patrick suggested. "No rule saying we have to wait, right?"

Ashley looked up. "Really? But what about–"

She cut off, remembering Lily. Blinking, she dropped her gaze to her plate again, but not before she saw his pleasure at her reaction.

"Yeah," Lily agreed happily. "A whole week of parties, and then it'll be Mom's birthday too, and we can do it all over again."

The clink of silverware echoed in the dining room.

"What?" the little girl asked, looking around the table at the silence.

Patrick swallowed. "I-I didn't realize you celebrated that," he said, his voice a rough semblance of normalcy. His eyes went to Rose and Jonathan, who both shifted awkwardly.

"Lily wanted to," Ashley explained quietly.

"You said it was a good idea!" Lily protested. Confusion clouded her face as she turned to the others. "What's wrong?"

Patrick cleared his throat. "Nothing, Lilybud," he said, reaching over to squeeze her hand. "Just took me by surprise, that's all."

Looking unconvinced, Lily hesitated. "Is it okay?"

He smiled. "Of course."

Brow still furrowed, Lily went back to her salad.

Ashley risked a glance in her father's direction. His eyes closed briefly, and then he drove any trace of expression from his face and returned to his dinner as though nothing had happened.

She took a bite of her food as the joy of the moment before slunk from the room. It didn't matter what he tried to pretend. She knew he was thinking about Rebecca and everyone else lost that night.

They all were.

Snow had been falling the night their worlds changed. She remembered it so clearly, if only through the lens of all that followed. But Patrick said, as the white flakes drifted through the lights of the grocery store parking lot, that she'd told him they were inside a snow globe. And at the memory of her words, he always smiled.

It was Christmas Eve and eight-year-old Ashley had gone with her father on a run for soda from the local store. The family had been holding a party. Uncles, aunts and cousins had all gathered to celebrate the holiday at her grandparents' house, and no one had wanted to leave. But Ashley adored the snow, and so when Patrick finally volunteered to pick up more drinks, he said she'd jumped at the chance to go.

One little moment. She couldn't remember it, but she'd wondered at it as the years went by.

The firemen said it might've been a gas main, or someone pulling a prank that went horribly wrong. In Patrick's recollection, a fireball lit the night sky as he pulled away from the grocery store, and he'd known – just known – that it was his parents' home. He'd driven back at top speed, and screeched to a halt in the middle of a nightmare.

In all the years since, it was the only time she'd seen her father cry.

Doctors told Patrick that the trauma must have damaged her somehow. The shock of such tremendous loss must have overwhelmed her, causing her to pass out and retreat inside her own mind for protection. And later, whenever she tried to push beyond the moment of waking in the car that night, to recall anything prior to the sight of the house in flames and her father's tears, not a single memory remained. Not her mother's laugh or her favorite toys, the color of her bedroom or the name of a single friend. Everything was gone as though it had never been.

For Ashley, life began with fire.

Half the block had been destroyed. Beyond her grandparents' house, other homes were burning, and shivering people crowded the sidewalks while hoses rained water on the flames. Christmas lights still dangled from porches and windows farther down the street, sparkling in surreal relief against the orange sky.

And overhead, ash drifted down, mingling with the snow.

Of her grandparents' home, almost nothing was left. The blast had ripped through the building, gutting it and leaving the houses across the backyard visible through the hole. Only two walls remained, one on either side, though they were bowed and burning and beginning to crumble before her eyes. Emergency crews crawled through the wreckage, their forms little more than shifting apparitions in the smoke.

Patrick held her, crushing her to him as the police kept him from coming closer to the house. As the bodies began to be pulled from the debris, he'd buried her face in his side, trying to spare her the sight.

It hadn't mattered. She'd known whenever they brought someone out; his hands clenched tighter around her every time.

Rebecca was the last. Furthest from the blast, she must've seen the disaster coming and known she wouldn't survive. But in her final moments, she'd done what she could, and thrown herself over her baby girl, who was only one month old that day.

The EMTs found Lily buried beneath her mother and sobbing, her little body unscathed by the destruction. They'd called her a miracle baby, and when they carried her out, even the fire crews paused in disbelief.

Patrick had choked as they brought her to him. With shaking hands, he'd released Ashley and taken Lily, his gaze running over the child as though he'd never seen anything like her in his life. He'd crouched then, cradling the baby in one arm and wrapping the other around Ashley as he cried.

Other people came as time slid by. Friends to console and care, though each struggled to know what to say. Every face was like an image blurred by water for Ashley, and she could never remember any of their names. After a while, Patrick left to attend to the police, and to answer questions he said no child should ever have to hear. With her fingers clutching those of a tall black man in a trench coat smelling of vanilla and cedar, she'd sat on a park bench around the corner and held Lily, who had long since fallen asleep.

They'd moved in the days that followed.

She suspected another planet would've felt closer than Montana, because although she couldn't remember much of the city, she'd still instantly felt every ounce of her unfamiliarity with farms. But Jonathan and Rose met them at the driveway of their new home, and embraced them as though they were long-lost friends come to stay. Routines and chores soon followed and, though she'd resented them at the time, when she looked back now, she realized the couple had just been trying to give the grieving children every shred of normalcy they could spare.

Patrick tried to settle into farm life for the sake of his daughters, for whom he'd felt the need to move away from anyone who might ever endanger them again. Vandals could've been responsible for the tragedy as easily as a broken gas main. The ambiguity was more than he could stand, and only by leaving his girls in rural obscurity could he let himself believe they might be safe. The isolation wore on him, though, and jobs constantly called. Any given day could find him pacing the house, one hand grasping the phone and the other raking through his hair as he tried to figure out how to live in two places at once. Finally, with no choice but bankruptcy or insanity, he returned to work and left his girls on the farm with the promise he'd come back soon.

They'd seen him barely a dozen times since, and as she picked at her dinner, Ashley tried not to think of the many things he'd missed over the years, beyond simple traditions like celebrating their mother's birthday. Lily's first steps. The girl's first words. Missing teeth and the identity of the tooth fairy. He'd missed so much of their lives, and sometimes, when she let herself, she could feel the hurt of that fact simmering deep down inside.

Dinner ended in silence and, with worried eyes, Lily left the table before anyone else. Regret clouded Patrick's face as he watched her go, but wordlessly, he just helped the others take the dishes away.

"Chocolate?" he asked Ashley as they walked into the kitchen. "I thought you liked carrot cake best?"

She slid the plates into the soapy water of the sink and then glanced to him, hiding her pity. Beneath his thinly veiled attempt at seeming casual, she could see he was struggling. "I do, Dad. Chocolate is Lily's favorite."

Taking a breath, he nodded. One memory was accurate, at least.

"Just give it a few minutes, then go upstairs and play with her," Ashley advised quietly. "She'll be fine."

He looked at her, and she could see the thoughts warring behind his dark brown eyes. Accepting guidance from his teenage daughter clashed with the idea of being her parent, but after a moment, he settled on giving her a small nod and then headed for the living room to wait.

She returned to washing the dishes.

Rose came in and set the bowls by the sink. Wordlessly, the woman placed a hand on Ashley's shoulder, squeezing briefly before returning to the dining room.

Ashley sighed.

A crash echoed up from the basement. Dropping a plate into the sink, she spun, heart pounding.

"What the hell–" Patrick said as he raced from the living room, his body tensed as though ready to grab the nearest heavy object within reach.

Jonathan strode around him and yanked open the basement door. "Damn cats," he growled. Glancing back to Patrick, he held up a hand. "It's fine."

Muttering under his breath, the old man disappeared down the darkened stairway. Yowling was followed by a crash, and then another. Rose winced at every sound, and Ashley could see her imagining the objects breaking as the chase continued.

The basement went silent and then Jonathan emerged, scratches on his arms and a furious expression on his face. By the scruff of its neck, a flailing cat twisted in his fist.

At the sight of Rose, the cat renewed its struggles, catching its captor across the back of his arm with its claws. Jonathan yelped and released the animal, sending it plummeting to the floor. Paws scrambling on the hardwood, the cat propelled itself past Patrick and sped beneath a chair in the furthest corner of the living room.

Rose snatched a napkin from the table and rushed to Jonathan's aid, covering his bleeding scratches. She glanced at Ashley.

"Got it," Ashley said with a nod.

Patrick looked between them as she walked past.

"Thelma's cats don't like Rose or Jonathan much," she told her father dryly.

One brow raised, he eyed the couple and then followed her into the living room.

In the shadows, the cat's eyes flashed. Dark stripes like a tiger ran down its frantically heaving sides and, as she crouched in front of the chair, the creature hissed and batted at her.

She sank onto her heels to wait.

"This happen a lot?" Patrick asked. Watching her, he leaned on the hallway wall.

"All the time. Rose grows valerian and catnip for her teas. She stores the herbs in the basement and, well… " She tossed him a grin before she returned her gaze to the cat.

Gradually, the animal seemed to realize none of the humans besides Ashley and Patrick were following it into the room. Though clearly still on edge, the cat lowered itself onto its haunches and began cleaning a paw with an almost theatrical display of calm.

Ashley scoffed. "Yeah, right," she murmured, gingerly reaching her hand between the legs of the chair. "Here, kitty." A look of mild disdain surfaced amid the creature's residual nervousness, but after a few moment's consideration, it condescended to allow her to pull it out.

Bundling the cat into her arms, she grinned at her father. "Be back in a few minutes."

"Where are you going?"

"To bring the cat back to Thelma. It's fine; she's just down the road."

For a moment, he seemed torn by the protective urge to go with her, and she smiled. "Really, Dad." She jerked her head toward the stairs. "Go take care of Lily. She'll be worried about all the noise down here."

Still looking reluctant, he nodded. "Be careful."

She smiled as she scooped up Jonathan's heavy-duty flashlight from beside the coat rack. "I will," she assured him, and then let the screen door swing shut behind her.

Darkness surrounded her as she left the island of light around the farmhouse. Stars carpeted the sky, taking full advantage of the new moon and the cloudless night. Crickets ceased their chirping as she passed, and tree frogs grew silent, only to start singing again once she was gone. The cat twisted at the sounds, teased by the idea of chasing all the tiny, invisible things moving in the grass. Shifting the animal in her arms and quietly threatening it with dire consequences if it scratched her, she continued toward the bungalow half a mile away.

A bare light bulb dangled from the rafters of the weathered porch, and moths danced around it madly. The splintered steps bowed beneath her feet as she climbed, and she winced, fully expecting that this time, one of them would finally give way. Swatting ineffectually at the bugs with the bulky flashlight, she ducked low and then rapped on the wooden screen door. A chorus of discordant meows greeted her, and the cat struggled to escape her grasp at the noise.

Moments passed and the meowing faded, but no one came to the door. Flinching away from a kamikaze moth diving toward her head, Ashley bit her lip indecisively. She could leave the cat on the porch, but odds were it would return immediately to the basement and she'd just have to bring it back again. The stupid animals never learned.

Grimacing, she raised her hand to knock again.

With a creak of rusty hinges, the door behind the screen inched open, revealing nothing but darkness beyond.

"Thelma?"

"Ooh," came a voice from behind the narrow opening.

"Thelma, one of your cats got into our basement again," she called, telling herself to be patient. Thelma kept things interesting, the farmhands said. She just hoped the old woman was lucid enough tonight to see the cat in front of her. Or the person, for that matter.

The crack widened and a frail hand emerged to push at the screen door. A pause followed, punctuated by renewed meows from within the house, and then Thelma slipped through the narrow space and stepped onto the porch as though emerging onto a stage. A cloud of gray hair surrounded her thin, wrinkled face and too-bright eyes darted between Ashley, the cat and the darkness. Her razor-thin lips parted, revealing yellowed teeth in what passed for a smile. "Ashley, Ashley, burning bright…" she whispered fondly.

Glancing from the glowing flashlight to the tiger-striped cat, Ashley tried not to sigh. Poetry tonight. Last week, Thelma had spoken only in metaphors from children's stories. At least this time the comment had a vague connection to reality.

"That's right," she said. "Now, could you please take your cat?"

Thelma paused, examining the animal as if evaluating whether she'd seen it before. Finally, with the air of coming to a difficult decision, she sighed mightily and reached out, folding her fingers around the creature's middle and then curling it into her wiry arms.

"Thank you," Ashley said, hurrying to escape the bug-infested porch.

Thelma had already forgotten her. Chastising the cat with snippets of poetry, the old woman slipped back into her cottage, letting in a score of moths as she went. The chorus of meows grew louder for a moment, and then faded behind the shut door.

Shaking her head, Ashley jogged up the gravel road, the beam of her flashlight bouncing wildly as she went. Six months after her family moved to their property, Thelma arrived at the decrepit bungalow they'd all believed to be condemned. Apparently abandoned by her children for being too much of a handful, the old woman had been gifted the house as a last gesture of nominal support from distant and uninvolved relations – or so the story went. In truth, she seemed to scarcely remember her family and what information they managed to get out of her made so little sense, it could as easily have been fantasy as reality.

She caught the screen door to keep it from slamming as she returned to the house, and then grinned at Jonathan as he glanced up from his almanac. Beneath the buttery light of the living room lamp, the old farmer sat in his customary position on the worn leather sofa, one leg propped atop his knee and his reading glasses perched on his nose. Down the hall, dishes clinked to the melody of a softly playing ballad as Rose finished the washing.

"All taken care of?" he asked.

"Same as always."

Beneath his bushy white brows, his blue eyes twinkled. "So we'll see the cat tomorrow."

"Probably."

He grinned. "You headed to bed?"

She shrugged and he gave her a knowing look. "Don't stay up too late, bookworm."

"When have I ever done that?" she replied innocently.

He scoffed. "Upstairs with you. And, Ashley Rebecca, if I see that light of yours on…"

Fighting to keep a straight face, she nodded. "Yes sir."

She could hear him chuckling as she ran up the stairs.

Past the landing, the second floor hallway was dim, though the light spilling from Lily's room and beneath the door to Patrick's study softened the gloom. With easy familiarity, she swung around the wood banister and headed for the end of the hall, where the stairway to her attic bedroom was a black opening in the shadows.

"Hey, Ashley," Lily called as she passed the little girl's room.

She caught herself on the doorframe. Her brow furrowed. "Where's Dad?" she asked, looking around. Multicolored scraps of paper carpeted the floor, and boxes filled with crayons, markers, scissors and glue were stacked in every available corner.

"Work called."

Ashley glanced across the hallway. Beneath the doorway, she could see his shadow block the light intermittently as he paced. His muffled voice carried through the wood, harried and intense, but unintelligible.

She bit her lip. Tomorrow afternoon might be too long for him to wait before leaving.

Forcibly pushing the disquiet aside, she turned back to Lily with a smile. "What's up?"

"I-I'm sorry I ruined things earlier."

Ashley rolled her eyes. "You didn't ruin anything. Just get to sleep, okay?"

Shoving off the door, she grinned and then started toward the stairs again.

"Ashe?"

She stopped. Lily rarely used the nickname she'd given her sister when she was too young to pronounce words correctly. And though it was a common enough derivative of her own name, Ashley had never known anyone else to use it.

The name belonged to Lily. Rose and the others seemed to understand that.

She stepped back into the doorway.

"I didn't," Lily repeated.

With a sigh, Ashley crossed the room and sank down into the middle of the craft paper. Gently, she took Lily's hand.

"Lil," she said, responding in kind with her own nickname for the girl. "You didn't ruin anything. I swear. Dad just misses Mom."

The girl's gaze went to the door. "I think he's going to leave soon."

Ashley studied the paper beneath her knees. "You need to go to sleep, kiddo."

Lily paused, watching her sister. "It's really soon, isn't it?"

"Tomorrow," Ashley admitted.

A small breath escaped Lily. The little girl closed her eyes, her brow furrowing.

"At least there'll be a birthday party first, right?" Ashley offered.

Expression unchanged, Lily nodded.

Ashley put a hand on her sister's shoulder. A heartbeat passed, and then Lily leaned against it.

"Come on," Ashley said. "Let's get you to sleep."

Lily let Ashley help her stand, and then followed her to the cluttered bed. Stuffed animals crowded every inch of the surface, barely allowing a glimpse of the patchwork quilt beneath them. Carefully pushing the animals closer to the wall, Ashley made space for Lily to burrow beneath the quilts. A few months before, Rose had tried to remove them, saying Lily was too grown up for toys. While Lily held the dolls and cried, Ashley had refused to allow Rose through the door.

No one would take anything from Lily until the little girl was ready. Not if Ashley had anything to say about it.

Bending down, she pecked her sister on the head with a kiss as Lily pulled the blankets up beneath her chin. "Sleep well."

The girl nodded.

Navigating the piles of paper, Ashley crossed the room and then flipped off the light.

"I hate when he leaves," Lily said quietly.

In the darkness, Ashley glanced back. Lily's pale face shone in the light from the lamps outside.

"Me too," Ashley told her.

She left the bedroom door cracked slightly and then headed for the attic stairs. The steps squeaked beneath her feet and she automatically skipped the loose seventh step entirely. Slipping past the door, she crossed the room and flicked on the bedside lamp. Instantly, an enormous moth fled the bulb and barreled at her face, making her shriek in surprise.

Grabbing a pillow from her desk chair, she herded the frantic bug toward the window. Yanking the lower pane up, she drove the creature out to join its innumerable relatives dancing around the security lights, and then slammed the window down.

In the yard, one of the farmhands looked up from his patrol, startled by the sound. Heart pounding, she gave him a casual wave, and then shuddered furiously once he turned away. Of all the rooms in the house, the moths only seemed to enjoy her own, a fact which drove her to distraction. Tossing the pillow across the room and then scanning the ceiling for any other invaders, she sank into the window seat, twitching every few seconds as her skin crawled.

Like small stars orbiting the house, the farmhands circled the property, their flashlights bright points in the night. Coyotes were a constant nuisance this close to the mountains and, after such a cold winter, the animals became more of a problem than usual. But even in a good year, the hungry creatures chased everything from children to cats, and after a few close calls when the girls first arrived, Jonathan had ordered the men to stand guard at night.

Taking a deep breath, Ashley watched them, while the rumble of freight trains on the tracks beyond the forest carried through the darkness. Every so often, the farmhands would pause at a random noise, only to continue circling a moment later, and though she knew they traded off from time to time to allow each other sleep, Jonathan's orders would keep the lights crossing the fields till morning.

A soft knock sounded behind her. Blinking after the darkness of the stairway, Patrick pushed open the door and then smiled. "Can I come in?"

She nodded.

He glanced around as he stepped inside, and she saw his eyebrow rise at the piles of books in her room. In addition to the dozen teetering on her dresser, more lined the walls while smaller stacks crowded beneath the bed.

Ashley glared in mock threat at his surprise and he grinned.

"I came to say I'm sorry about dinner," he said, sinking onto the bed next to the window seat.

"It's nobody's fault."

Patrick grimaced, seeming unconvinced as he looked away. His eyes came to rest on the nightstand between them, and the photograph sitting there.

"You look like her, you know," he said after a moment. "More all the time."

Ashley glanced at the photo. From Rebecca's arms, Ashley's smiling three-year-old self beamed out at the world. Under the blazing summer sun, Rebecca's black hair glistened and her aquamarine eyes sparkled. Ashley knew her father must have been behind the camera that day, because surely only he could have brought out the joy she saw in her mother's eyes.

"Lily does more than me."

"She has her eyes," he countered, bending to catch Ashley's deep brown gaze. "You have her smile."

The words brought a hesitant smile to her lips and she tried to push it away, feeling awkward.

He grinned. "I have a present for you." He pulled a small package from his back pocket and handed it to her.

For a moment, she stared at the rudimentary wrapping, complete with a tangled blue ribbon tied around the middle. Her eyes rose to meet his.

"Yeah, okay, so I wrapped it myself," he said. "Do you want it or not?"

"You're leaving, aren't you? Sooner than you planned."

The humor in his expression dissipated. "The powers-that-be want me on the east coast by noon," he admitted.

She struggled not to gape. "But… you'll have to leave like…"

"I know." He jerked his chin toward the present. "But I didn't want to miss something of your birthday."

Trying to regroup, she looked down at the package. Brow

furrowing at the urge to continue protesting, no matter how pointless she knew it would be, she picked off the wrapping paper and then froze.

The pocket knife was pale steel, but the mother-of-pearl in its handle was kaleidoscopic in the light. With a flick of her thumb, the blade snapped out, small but wickedly sharp.

She looked up at him, baffled.

"Jonathan said you liked to help him around the farm," he explained with a shrug. "And he mentioned how you needed a pocket knife. I know it's not the most practical one in the world, but I thought you might like it anyway."

"I love it," she said, starting to grin.

Relief spread over his features. "Good. I just wasn't sure if—"

Ashley dropped the knife to the cushions and jumped up, throwing her arms around him. Taken back, he hesitated and then returned the hug.

"I'm sorry I have to go, honey," he said.

She nodded into his shoulder. Patrick squeezed her tighter.

A moment went by, and then she straightened and returned to the window seat.

He smiled. "Get some sleep, okay?"

Ashley chuckled, hearing her own words to Lily repeated back. "I will," she promised.

He rose and patted her shoulder. "I'll see you in the morning." Crossing the room, he paused by the door and then glanced back. "I love you, kiddo."

"Love you too, Dad."

Nodding again, he hesitated another moment, and then let the door shut behind him as he left the room.

Ashley's gaze returned to the knife. Picking it up carefully, she turned it over in her hand, watching the mother-of-pearl shimmer in the light. A smile crossed her face as she flicked it closed and then slid it into her pocket. Practical wasn't everything, but she wasn't sure she'd ever risk damaging her father's gift by using it for anything as rough as working with Jonathan.

Her questing hand found the paperback book where she'd left it beneath the window seat pillow. With a small grin for Jonathan's admonishments, she settled herself deeper into the cushions, flipped to her bookmark, and began to read.

Chapter Two

—•◆•—

Eight Hours Ago

"**D**ude, your parents are going to be so pissed," Travis laughed, tossing his empty beer can deep into the junkyard. "I mean… *damn*. You know if the tow truck brought it back to the house yet?"

Cole didn't answer. His friend's amusement was starting to grate on him. Travis could laugh. Travis still had a truck. He hadn't smashed his only means of transportation into a tree in an attempt to impress the head cheerleader by challenging her quarterback boyfriend to a race.

Travis wouldn't be the laughingstock of the school tomorrow.

Leaning back on the hood of his custom-painted truck, the other boy grinned at the stars. "Classic."

Taking a breath, Cole shoved up from the hood and hopped to the ground, wincing as his muscles protested the motion.

"You're leaving?" Travis called.

"Might as well get it over with," Cole replied tiredly. "See you when they let me out in a year."

"Or ten," Travis agreed, popping open another beer.

"Right," Cole muttered as he slid through the gap in the junk-yard fence and stepped onto the street.

Stoplights glared painfully as he crossed the empty intersection and started toward home. His head still ached from the accident, but it wasn't anything a few aspirin couldn't stop. The shouts he knew were coming, on the other hand, promised to go on for quite some time.

The neighborhoods grew in affluence as he walked, like an archi-tectural timeline brought to life. Old homes in formerly coveted zip codes gave way to crisp new developments with only shreds of personality in their design, and then even those surrendered to eccen-tric residential monstrosities advertising money with every line.

He kept going. The houses fell behind him and the sidewalks disappeared. In the distance, small orbs of light perched ten feet off the ground, affixed to a concrete wall with fashionably twisted iron spikes and petite security cameras on top. A metal gate brought the road to an irrefutable halt, and roadside signs warned the unwary that access was restricted to residents only. To one side of the gate, the blue-green bubble of the guard station held one of the inter-changeable rent-a-cops idly watching a basketball game. The man barely glanced up as Cole swiped his pass card and then slipped through the pedestrian access set into the wall.

Flawless lawns in keeping with the homeowner's association's specifications fronted the equally flawless homes on either side of the street, and identical lampposts glowed in each yard. Tiredly, he continued down the road, avoiding the grass. He didn't need to give anyone else cause to yell at him tonight.

Too soon, the gray house was in front of him, its neutral shutters and roof rendering it indistinguishable from every other home on the street. A rigidly straight sidewalk led from the curb to the door, and not even a brightly colored flower threatened to differentiate the yard from its neighbors.

Ignoring the walkway, he circled to the back door, hoping Robert and Melissa wouldn't spot him. As he passed the garage, he caught a glimpse through the window of his truck draped by a tarp and safely concealed from the sight of any passerby.

He rolled his eyes. Motion-sensitive security lights flared to life as he came near the back door, making him wince. Shielding his eyes, he climbed the steps and then reached for the silver handle.

The door whipped open.

"Where have you been?" Melissa demanded. Her gaze swept the drive, searching for the prying eyes of the eternally curious neighbors. "Get in here."

Without waiting for him to respond, she grabbed his arm, trying to drag him through the door. Shrugging her off, he eyed her askance as he continued inside. Scanning the yard again, she scowled and then firmly shut the door.

"Give me that," she snapped, turning to snatch the gate pass from his pocket. "How dare you run off without telling me?"

Fuming, she busied herself with burying the card in a drawer.

Ignoring the display, he walked through the pristine kitchen, his reflection following him as he passed the gleaming metal appliances. In the living room, Robert was sullenly polishing the chrome coffee table, while behind him the muted television scrolled images of the latest crime spree in a distant city. A carefully organized bucket of cleaning supplies sat near the man's knee, and around the rest of the room, every nondescript pillow and decoration had been ruthlessly straightened.

"What's going on?" Cole asked.

"Your uncle Edmund is coming over," Melissa said, pushing past him and then snatching the polishing rag from Robert's hand. Wordlessly, the man glared at her back before heading to the kitchen for another cloth.

"You called *Vaughn*?" Cole asked, incredulous despite belatedly feeling that he should have anticipated this. As one of the cadre of therapists paid to keep Cole in Melissa Smith's idea of perfection, 'uncle' Edmund Vaughn had become a recurrent visitor over the years – summoned every time she felt her adopted son needed a bit of tweaking. The sight of the truck would have sent her to DEFCON One. He was surprised the man wasn't installed in the living room already.

"What did you expect?" she snapped as Robert returned and silently began cleaning the console table by the stairway. "The school called about your little adventure today. They took care of the police, you'll be happy to know. It won't go on your record. But we couldn't exactly let something like that go unaddressed, could we? Now go upstairs and get changed. He'll be here any minute."

She attacked the chrome table with a vengeance, and from across the room, he could hear the polishing cloth squeak as it waged war on the microscopic tarnish.

He shoved his annoyance down, knowing any display of emotion would only provoke later retribution. Jaw muscles jumping, he headed for the stairs, ignoring Robert as he passed.

Robert's hand shot out, snagging Cole's arm. The man's nose twitched and fury rose in his eyes. "Have you been drinking again?" he growled quietly.

Cole jerked his arm, trying to break the other man's grip. Robert's fingers tightened painfully.

"Is that what happened today?" Robert asked. "You were *drunk?* Do you have *any* idea the trouble you could cause if–"

Seething, the man cut off, his gaze snapping to Melissa. Caught up in exorcising the demons of dirt and dust, the woman was momentarily ignoring them. Robert hesitated, and in his eyes, Cole could see the man weighing the factors. Melissa's hysteria. Uncle Edmund's bill. His own desire to return to the relative safety of his study and his firearm memorabilia as soon as possible.

With a small shove, Robert released Cole's arm. "We'll discuss this later," he muttered.

Trying not to scoff, Cole continued up the stairs. Behind him, Melissa snapped at Robert, who instantly retaliated by flipping the television audio back on. A heated argument ensued, unintelligible beneath the sound of a reporter telling of yet another apartment fire dozens of miles away.

As he reached the second floor, he sighed, grateful for even this limited distance from the couple. To his left, Melissa's door was closed, though a few steps farther down the hall, the light in Robert's room had been left on. Neither of them had slept in the same bedroom since the year after they adopted Cole, a fact which was guarded fanatically from anyone outside their four walls.

Ignoring the basket of laundry left by his room, Cole shut the door behind him and rested his head against the surface, willing the throbbing in his temples to stop. Cracking one eye open, he glanced at the dresser, and then snatched the bottle of aspirin off it gratefully. Gulping two pills down, he crossed to his bed and lay back on the rumpled covers.

Melissa's voice echoed from the front room, rising in angry

incoherence over the sound of the television before fading again. Cole groaned, dragging the pillow from beneath his head and then smothering his face in attempt to block her out.

Perfection was one of the woman's two religions, the other being what he dubbed 'neighborly fear'. As lottery winners the year before they adopted him, the couple had moved up in the world with lightning speed, a fact which left Robert initially thrilled, and took Melissa's already rampant insecurities to a whole new level. Ill-equipped for her sudden wealth and petrified those of equal riches might think her low class, the woman committed herself to creating an identity safe from ridicule by the old money she both worshipped and feared.

A neighborhood sheltered from undesirable influence was required, complete with a modestly elaborate home and well-maintained yard. Two midsize sedans of understated elegance came next, and then a pristine wardrobe of expensively muted clothes.

Exterior factors addressed, the necessity of a picture-perfect marriage became priority. Unable to have their own children and with her image of domestic perfection in jeopardy, Melissa demanded they adopt. Growing steadily more cowed by the day, Robert agreed, and ten-year-old Cole entered their world. He met her standard, which Cole suspected was the sole factor in his selection. His brown hair matched her own. In other respects, his build and features were similar to those of Robert. Without being told, no one would suspect Cole wasn't their son – a fact he was certain had been her motivation all along.

The perfect school was next, and the private institution they found couldn't have been more ideal. Accustomed to handling the needs of the influential and the affluent, Brighton Modisett Prep

School made common practice of keeping from public and legal notice any indiscretions which might later affect their students' potentially lucrative political or business careers. Blatant mention of Cole's adopted status was duly eschewed in their records, and thus – short of occasional correction – Melissa's world was complete.

Maintenance came in the form of counselors. In ordinary conversation, Melissa and Robert referred to them as Cole's 'uncles', and sometimes even paid the men extra to arrive by night. No cost was too great to keep the neighbors from suspecting the Smiths' world possessed any flaws. Edmund Vaughn was the youngest member of the army of psychological alteration Melissa commanded and, with his obsequious manner and tone, he had continuously retained his position as Cole's most hated therapist of all.

The drone of the television disappeared, and the thud of footsteps on the stairs made him pull the pillow away from his face. His bedroom door opened, and Melissa poked her head inside, taking in the situation with a glance.

"What are you–" she hissed. "I told you to get changed!"

Incredulity at his disobedience in her eyes, she slipped into the room and closed the door. Making a beeline to his closet, she began sorting through his clothes frantically, and then yanked a shirt from the chaos.

"Here," she snapped, tossing it at him.

Cole caught it, eyeing the hideously striped polo shirt. "This is stupid," he said flatly. "Vaughn won't care if I'm–"

"Get changed!" Her voice broke as she shrieked.

He pulled off his sweatshirt and changed into the polo. From his dresser, she tugged out a pair of clean khakis and threw those at him as well.

Cole paused, his brow furrowing as he looked between her and the pants. "Um…"

Rolling her eyes in infuriated impatience, she slipped out the door.

Pants changed, he left the room to find her pacing the confines of the hall. As his door opened, she spun and ran her eyes over him quickly. Apparently satisfied, she grabbed his hand, half-dragging him down the hallway and then the stairs. At the last turn of the staircase, she paused, dropping his hand to straighten her hair. Taking a deep breath, she pasted on a cheery smile and trotted down to the first floor.

"Here we are," she announced brightly to Robert and the other occupant of the room. Standing by the pale sofa, the counselor seemed to blend with the furniture around him. Dressed in khakis and a beige button-down, with a slightly darker brown sports coat on top, the man appeared in every way unremarkable. His hair matched his jacket, and his eyes too. When he smiled, his flaccid lips revealed teeth only a shade lighter than his clothes.

Crossing gracefully to her husband's side, Melissa simpered a little as Robert slid an arm around her waist. "Well, have a seat everybody," she continued, smiling at Vaughn and then turning the expression on Cole with the addition of sugary daggers in her eyes. "Can I get anyone a drink?"

Cole met her gaze without expression, realizing the source of the couple's earlier disagreement. Tonight was going to be fun. The only question was whether she chose to get Vaughn involved in the argumentative festivities.

"Oh, you needn't trouble yourself, Mrs. Smith," the counselor said blithely. "Though the offer really is too kind."

He motioned for her to join them, and then turned to Cole, waiting patiently till he lowered himself onto the couch as well. A cloyingly understanding look taking up residence on his face, Vaughn thumbed open his pocket notebook and then drew out a pen from his brown sports coat. "So… it's been a while since we've seen each other, hasn't it?"

Cole didn't answer. It'd only been two months, and not remotely long enough.

Undeterred, Vaughn continued. "How's school going?"

Silence greeted the question.

"Sweetheart," Melissa admonished lovingly. "We didn't bring Dr. Vaughn all this way for you to ignore him. Come on. He wants to help you."

Paternally, Robert nodded, playing his part with a dedication born of knowing the consequences for any other behavior. "Go ahead, son. We're all here for you."

A scoff evaluated the benefits of emerging, and then reconsidered.

"School's fine."

Vaughn beamed. "Oh, good. And friends? I know your mom mentioned you'd had some trouble staying connected to a good crowd. How's that been going?"

"Fine," Cole replied, barely keeping the dry note from his voice.

Pleased, the counselor nodded. "I'm very glad to hear that." Thumbing to a new page in his notebook, he took a deep breath. "So, Cole. Can you tell me about what happened today?"

A list of potential responses ran through his head, ranging from the sarcastic to the downright rude. Melissa would make him pay for any of them, and after a moment's further reflection, he dropped them all as pointless.

"Wrecked my truck," he said, settling for facts.

"I can see that," Vaughn chuckled.

Fondly, Melissa cocked her head and raised an eyebrow in encouragement.

"Tried to impress a girl," Cole elaborated flatly. "Didn't work."

"Pretty dangerous way to get her attention, wouldn't you say?" Vaughn replied, mildly chastising.

Cole didn't bother responding.

"And you're feeling alright? Not too shaken up, I hope?"

"I'm fine."

Vaughn paused, jotting down a few notes. "And what did your friends think of what you did?"

Cole hesitated. "What did my friends think?"

"Well, the school reported you left with friends," Vaughn explained. "We're just trying to assess if they put you up to anything. If they're a bad element, you see. Were they the ones you were hanging out with this evening?"

His skin crawling, Cole glanced to Melissa before he could stop himself. *That's* what this was about? Learning the identities of his friends, as much as any concern his actions might've stemmed from some inherent flaw?

Struggling to keep his anger from showing, he tried to decide what to say. Any answer could cause trouble, but the truth would be worst. The perfect crowd was as much a priority to the woman as anything, but her quest for elitism left her isolated, and so she targeted his friends' families as a way of ingratiating herself with the 'right people'. Over the years, he'd lost more friends than he cared to count to her overeager interest, and he knew it would happen again. Though Travis practically made laziness an art form, his family had been rich and successful for generations. He'd known since he met the guy that the Brauns would be prime targets for his adoptive mother's crusade.

"Yeah," he said, aware an answer was expected. "But they didn't put me up to anything."

"Do they have names?" Vaughn teased lightly.

He hesitated. "Tom and Owen. They're new to school."

The friendly expression on Vaughn's face flickered. "Ah," he said, placid smile snapping back into place. Swiftly, he scribbled down the names. "Well, we should probably make certain Tom and Owen know you need to be home before dark from now on. If you're going to keep doing well in school, you have to get to bed at a decent hour. Speaking of which…"

He glanced to the couple stationed on the loveseat.

Melissa rose quickly. "Dr. Vaughn is *so* right," she agreed happily. "Off to bed, dear. School day tomorrow." She bustled into the kitchen, returning a moment later with a steaming mug of cocoa. "And here you go, sweetheart," she said, handing it to Cole. "Just the way you like it."

Cole rose, his gaze meeting hers as he took the mug. Melissa's smile took on an acidic cast, and it required every ounce of willpower he possessed to keep from tossing the liquid onto her flawless carpet.

"Oh, is that your special cocoa recipe I've heard so much about, Mrs. Smith?" Vaughn asked, oblivious to the exchange. At her happy nod, he continued. "The other counselors simply *rave* about it. I'd love to try some one of these days, if it wouldn't be too much trouble."

Cole left them fawning at each other and headed back upstairs, the ridiculous mug of cocoa clutched in one hand. As he reached his bedroom, he could still hear them, cheerfully discussing his sanity from the dubious comfort of the couch.

He set the cocoa on the dresser and shut the door. Stripping off the garish polo and stiff khakis, he tossed the costume into a corner and then retrieved his jeans, t-shirt, and hooded sweatshirt from the pile of clothes on the floor.

Slowly, he exhaled, his muscles trembling. Sinking down onto the bed, he closed his eyes and then gradually crushed handfuls of the bedspread inside his fists.

Nights like these were when he missed his parents most of all.

In the eight years since he'd been selected by Robert and Melissa Smith, he'd tried not to think too much about the circumstances leading to his life in this upper-class hell. The conclusion always overshadowed any pleasant memory, but when the Smiths' act became too much to take, sometimes the remembered horrors faded away.

Victor and Clara Jamison had been good parents, for all that Melissa disparaged them constantly for having been poor. In truth, as inheritance babies, the Jamisons could have had money beyond the woman's wildest dreams. But when their parents disapproved of their marriage, Clara and Victor had renounced their legacies and chosen to make their own way in the world – a fact that, in this place, always made Cole proud.

As a family they'd done the best they could, and by the time Cole was ten, they'd moved to a nice apartment on the edge of a seedy neighborhood and were working hard to create a good future for their only son. Clara was a school nurse, healing the scrapes and wiping the tears of toddlers at a local nursery school. Victor was a banker, educated at the finest institutions by his wealthy father but struggling in the recession economy to find work. But in spite of their hardships, Clara and Victor forged a happy life with what they had, buying quality if not quantity and teaching their son about being content.

But due to greed or envy, others had taken notice, and one Christmas Eve night, they'd done something about the little family living quietly on the apartment building's third floor.

Of the actual break in, he remembered only pieces. His mother had sent him to his room early, joking that Santa couldn't arrive till he was asleep. He'd hurried to bed, only to wake to their apartment door bursting open and his mother screaming. To his bleary mind, fireworks seemed to be going off, though later he'd learned they were guns. Hooded men stormed his room, knocking over his toys and stuffing into bags anything of value they could grab. Through the open doorway, he saw his mother lying on the floor, and as he'd run for her, something heavy hit his head from behind.

When next he woke, he was curled in the back of a social worker's car with a bandage on his head. Dizzy and confused, he'd asked for his mother, only to receive a sympathetic glance from the man in the driver's seat. His mother and father couldn't come right now, the man explained. Cole was going to stay with some friends for a while.

In the following days, Cole learned they'd shot his father in the hallway, taking him from behind and using his key to get into the apartment. His mother had been next, and if not for the cops arriving swiftly to a neighbor's frantic 9-1-1 call, Cole would have been third.

And for all that the police had rushed to the scene, they'd never captured the ones responsible. Fingerprints led nowhere. The thieves used the fire escape to slip away unseen, and no tips gave clues to the criminals' identities. For most of the world, it became just one more cold case in a long list of violent tragedies, regrettably forgotten.

No relatives came to take him from the office of Child and Family Services, though he knew he was the only grandchild on either family's side. Not a single one even bothered to call. And to his ten-year-old self, the message had been clear: in their eyes, Cole may as well have also died.

Eight years drifted by, and in the midst of this zealously maintained world, everything from his life before took on the quality of a pleasant dream. Deep inside, some part of him clung to the memory of his father's voice and the smell of his mother's hair, because except for his memories, nothing of Clara or Victor Jamison remained. Due to being collected as evidence, every item from his past life had been taken from him. Years later, they still sat rotting in a police archive, inaccessible in case they were needed someday for a trial.

Opening his eyes, Cole sighed. Ignoring the fact that propping his tennis shoes on the blankets would make Melissa scream, he lay back on his bed and tried to put the dark thoughts behind him. In a few more months, it would all be over. Graduation was drawing near, and if he could just hold out that long, he could start working on a life that would have made his parents proud. Whether or not the Smiths approved of college, they couldn't stop him from applying. And with scholarships and grants, or loans or anything, he would find a way to pay for the educational ticket that meant he'd never have to come back here again.

A shout from the living room made him sit up in alarm. Accustomed to the racket of the Smiths' fights, he could tell neither of them had made the sound. Brow furrowing, he hesitated and then crossed the room silently and cracked open the door.

Angry voices, speaking too low and fast to understand, rose from downstairs. Confusion growing, he slipped into the hallway and crept to the top of the stairwell.

"–and you are losing control of him," Vaughn snarled, all semblance of toadying gone. "Drinking? Getting into car accidents? You have one job to do, just *one*, and you cannot even accomplish that."

"We're keeping him under control," Melissa said, her pleading tone so strange it made Cole pause. "It's fine, really. The truck thing was just an aberration. It won't happen again."

"He could have *died*, you stupid girl!" Vaughn snapped, his voice rising briefly before dropping low again. "That boy is the only insurance you've got, and you just blithely let him run off and nearly get himself killed! And you have the gall to tell me it's fine. Are you tired of this life? Would you prefer we dropped you back on the streets? Because it could happen."

"Now hold on, you're not going to do that," Robert interjected hurriedly. "We've taken care of this so far. You need us."

Vaughn chuckled. "*Need* you?" he drawled, almost too softly for Cole to hear.

"I-I mean…" Robert began, real fear in his voice.

"You will keep him here," Vaughn continued. "You will have him behaved, responsive, agreeable and happy or so help me, I will *personally* kill you both. Understand?"

Silence met his words, and a moment later, Cole heard the front door shut.

The couch squeaked as one of them sat down.

"Is he–" Melissa started.

"Getting in the car," Robert said. "Talking on his cell. Not leaving."

A muffled sob followed the statement. The noise jarred Cole from his shock. Face crumpling in confusion, he stood immobile for a heartbeat, and then carefully walked downstairs.

"What's going on?"

The couple jumped as though he'd set off a bomb.

Robert recovered first. "What the hell is he doing awake?" he demanded of Melissa furiously.

"I–" she sputtered and then regrouped. "Cole, why are you not in bed?" she said, her tone lost somewhere between her usual acid and the saccharin of moments before. "I told you to drink your cocoa and go to bed like a good boy."

He stared at her, wondering fleetingly how she'd ever been under the impression he'd actually do that. "What was Vaughn talking about?" he asked cautiously, stepping farther into the living room.

Melissa looked to Robert with a tinge of desperation. Dropping his hand from the blinds, Robert stalked across the room and then snagged Cole's arm, propelling him toward the stairs.

"You heard your mother. Get back up there and get in bed now."

Ripping his arm from Robert's grasp, Cole scoffed. "And what? Forget this ever happened? What the hell is going on here?"

He stared at them both. "Who are you people?"

Robert glanced at Melissa, and she nodded. Carefully, she rose to her feet, her expression becoming conciliatory. "Cole, honey, we know you're under a lot of pressure. The truck, graduation, the fact your parents can't be there. But you've been saying things that don't make sense for a while now, darling. Seeing things that aren't there. We're worried about you."

She walked towards him, her hands making pacifying gestures. "I don't know what you think is happening here, but everything's fine, sweetheart. Just take it easy."

Eyes wide, Cole backed away, while Robert made noises of agreement and moved to circle him. Trying to keep both her and Robert in view, Cole turned, and suddenly saw something swing toward him.

With a shout, he ducked and the bookend swept over his head. Off balance, Robert caught himself on the banister as Cole stumbled back. Melissa lunged, struggling to pin his arms, while Robert hefted the bookend once again.

Shoving Melissa off him, Cole backpedalled toward the door. His eyes raked the room, searching for a phone, a weapon, anything to alert someone and keep those two away at the same time. The couple glanced at each other, and then separated, trying to herd him toward the corner.

"We just want what's best for you, Cole," Robert said, his reasonable tone belied by the look in his eyes.

Cole's gaze landed on the keys on the console table. In one motion, he snagged them and spun for the door. Ripping it open, he dashed outside as Robert bolted after him.

"Neighbors!" Melissa shrieked.

Mashing the key fob frantically, Cole grabbed at the door handle as the locks popped up. Gasping, he tumbled into the driver's seat and then yanked the door closed, locking it again hastily. Rushing up to the car, Robert hauled on the handle.

"Open the door, Cole!"

The engine kicked over easily. Robert always kept his car in such great shape, with a continually full tank of gas and all the maintenance up to date. Cole had never paid much attention, but he was desperately grateful now. Heart racing, he pulled the gearshift into reverse and floored the pedal, sending the car flying backwards.

Shouting, Robert ran after him, but he'd already thrown it into drive.

As he sped away, the last expression he saw on their faces was terror.

Darkened houses whipped past as he raced toward the guard station. Melissa wouldn't want to risk the neighbors learning of his escape, but Robert might grow enough backbone to alert the rent-a-cops. If they'd already been called, he was screwed.

The Smiths had just attacked him. The thought played back as he clutched the steering wheel. Prissy Melissa and gutless Robert had just tried to bash his brains in with a bookend.

Out of fear of the obsequious little counselor.

Up ahead, he saw Vaughn's sedan pulling into the security station. Cole swallowed hard, slowing the car as a crazed idea occurred to him. What if he just talked to the man? Whoever they were, the Smiths' covers were blown anyway. What could it cost him to just tell Cole the truth?

Through the open car window, Vaughn surrendered his visitor's pass and then waved inanely to the guard as he drove away.

Cole swore. Dropping one hand from the wheel, he patted his pockets in a panicked inventory. Cell phone. Wallet. Nothing else. The image of his pass card in the kitchen drawer arose. Hoping Robert had left his behind, Cole searched the rest of the car desperately. The console revealed only gas station receipts. The back seats were empty. Reaching over, he yanked open the glove box and then froze.

A slow breath escaped him as he stared at the handgun.

Quickly, he slammed the glove box closed. He'd forgotten Robert kept a weapon in there.

Running a shaking hand over his hair, Cole checked the streets, knowing what he'd see. No other way out of the walled neighborhood existed. And Vaughn was getting away. Without any option, he took a deep breath and pulled up next to the security booth.

"I, um… I forgot my card…" he said uncomfortably.

Radiating annoyance, the guard glanced away from his basketball game to run his eyes over Cole's face with a clear message of loathing for the lazy little rich boy in daddy's sedan. "Yeah, whatever," he said, flicking the gate switch as he returned to watching the tiny television.

Cole floored it as the gate swung wide.

Vaughn's car had reached the intersection. After coming to a brief stop, the vehicle turned away from town, heading down the country road that led to the interstate.

Drawing a steadying breath, Cole pulled after him and tried to focus. Talking to the counselor aside, Vaughn had just threatened to kill the Smiths. Vaughn was clearly not a nice man. But Vaughn knew what was going on. Hell, Vaughn was at the *heart* of whatever was going on, and Cole desperately needed answers.

So how was he going to get the guy to talk?

Of their own volition, Cole's eyes flicked toward the glove box, and he forced his gaze back to the road as his blood pressure spiked. Holding the man at gunpoint. Stupid option. Twenty-to-life would put a serious kink in his college plans.

Feeling slightly hysterical, he took another breath. It was okay. His adoptive parents had attacked him. They were in league with a guy who'd been psychologically prodding him for the past eight years. No reason to panic. He could handle this. He just needed a plan.

The taillights of the counselor's car flashed, and the sedan pulled onto the shoulder.

He had no plan.

For a fleeting moment, he considered just driving past the man. The city of Monfort in the northern reaches of Utah fronted all manner of empty places he could go.

In a stolen car. With a gun in the glove compartment. And no answers.

He pulled over.

The door of the sedan ahead of him swung open, and Vaughn climbed out, annoyance clear on his face. "Robert, what the hell is wrong with you?" he called, holding up a hand to block the glare of the headlights. "Why are you–"

Cole stepped from the car.

The man's words died. Thoughts flickered over his face, too fast to follow, and though his expression settled into something approaching pleasant confusion, the sharp look never left his eyes. "Well, this is a surprise. What's up, Cole? What brings you out here so late?"

"I heard what you said to Melissa and Robert."

Vaughn paused. "What I said to–" He chuckled as though baffled. "I'm not sure I know what you mean."

"About them having a job to do… controlling me."

He felt ridiculous saying it.

The counselor's eyebrows climbed. "*Controlling* you? Cole, you sure you're feeling alright?"

"What were you talking about?" he continued, shifting warily as the counselor walked toward him.

"I think you were having a dream. Do your parents know you're out here?"

"What were you talking about?" he insisted, heart pounding.

Vaughn came up and leaned on the car. "Cole," he sighed, pulling out his cell phone. "Why don't we discuss this tomorrow, eh? We can have another session. But right now, I think we'd better call your—"

The man cut off. A few miles away, a car turned onto the country road. "Parents," the counselor finished, not taking his eyes from the distant headlights.

Cole glanced back as a second car followed the first. "I'm not leaving till you—"

Vaughn grabbed him, shoving him backward and then pinning him against the car. With his free hand, the man yanked the handle, fighting to hold Cole and open the door at the same time.

Desperately, Cole slammed his fist into the man's gut, and then twisted out of his grasp. Stumbling backward, he rounded the trunk, trying to keep the sedan between him and the counselor.

Swiftly, Vaughn glanced between Cole and the approaching vehicles. "Get in the car, kid," he growled.

Cole threw a quick look to the road as he retreated. The cars were coming closer. Whatever was going on, they were worrying Vaughn, and right now that was all that mattered. Drawing a breath, Cole shifted his weight and braced himself to make a run for it.

Vaughn charged. Bolting from behind the car, Cole made it only a few steps before the man snagged the back of his sweatshirt, twisted him around sharply, and then hurled him through the air.

Branches stabbed him as he crashed into the overgrown ditch a dozen feet away. His head ringing horribly, Cole shoved up on one arm, blinking in shock.

He looked to the road and then froze as Vaughn drew a gun from beneath his sports coat.

"Pull up your hood and get beneath those bushes," the man

ordered, dividing his attention between Cole and the approaching cars. "Don't make a sound. You move, you're dead, understand?"

Warily, Cole complied. Eyeing him a moment longer, Vaughn slipped the weapon beneath his jacket, and then swiftly rounded the car to yank the trunk release by the driver's seat. Returning to the rear of the sedan, he lifted the trunk lid and then paused. One hand on the metal lid, Cole saw the man close his eyes and take a breath as though trying to remain calm. Drawing out the jumper cables, Vaughn slammed the trunk and then glanced back toward the other cars.

High beams blazing, the two vehicles pulled to a stop a few yards away. Vaughn raised a hand, shielding his eyes.

"No help needed, thanks!" he called cheerily, waving as though to motion them on.

A man stepped from the nearest vehicle.

Cole froze, suddenly wondering if Robert and Melissa had been right. He was seeing things. He was losing his mind.

Because the man was glowing.

"Seems you're having some car trouble," the man said with a smile. From the vehicles behind him, three other men climbed out.

A faint silvery sheen covered them, obscured by their clothes but blatantly visible on every piece of exposed skin. Cole's heart pounded as he stared at them, making his headache surge back in full force.

Clearly, he'd hit his head a whole lot harder than he thought this morning.

"Oh, it's nothing," Vaughn replied, giving no sign he noticed the surreal glow coming from the other men. "The wife's car just died. You know how it is."

The man chuckled agreeably, the humor never touching his eyes.

"Right," he said, glancing to his companions.

Metal shrieked as the driver's side door of Vaughn's sedan tore from its hinges and scythed through the air. Spinning, the counselor threw his hands in front of his face. The door rocketed into the night sky. Whirling around, Vaughn barely had time to flinch before the closest of the men slammed into him, crushing him against the trunk of Robert's car.

The counselor's head snapped sideways, propelled by nothing Cole could see. Blood dripped from his mouth, and from the bushes, Cole could hear him fighting for air against the weight of the man bearing down on him.

"What do you want?" Vaughn gasped.

Disgust twisted the man's face. "What do you think? Give us the boy."

Cole's blood went cold.

"What boy?" Vaughn asked, and then choked as the man pressed down against his throat.

"Do *not* play stupid with me, toady," the man growled. He looked to the others. "Search the area. There's a reason two cars are here." His gaze returned to Vaughn, and a humorless smile curved his mouth. "Maybe he's protecting someone."

The men fanned out, two heading for the counselor's sedan while one started down into the ditch.

Cole held his breath. Dried and crackled from the winter, every twig around him seemed like a firecracker waiting to explode. Boots crunched over the gravel, and suddenly the beam of a flashlight skewered the bushes ahead of him.

He couldn't move. His eyes fixed on the light sweeping the ground as the other men yelled that the car was empty. The beam of the flashlight swung closer.

A cell phone rang.

Cole's heart nearly climbed out of his chest.

The man paused, thumbing on his phone as the beam of his flashlight came to rest mere feet from Cole's head. "Keller here."

He listened briefly, and then flicked the phone off again. The light swung away as he scaled back up the slope of the ditch.

"Reece," he called. Vaughn's captor glanced up. "Bartlow made the deal."

"He bought it?"

Keller nodded. "Simeon wants us to drop everything and get there now. They're taking them out the minute Brogan arrives."

Seeming torn, Reece glanced to the others. "You didn't find anything in the car?"

The men shook their heads. "Picture of a woman," one volunteered. "Could be a wife."

Reece sighed. "You were telling the truth, toady?" he asked Vaughn. He shook his head in disappointment, and then took the man by the collar, pulling him upright. "Damn."

Vaughn didn't have time to scream as he flew back. His body slammed into his sedan with a crunch and blood splattered the trunk.

Cole stared. Limply, the counselor's body slid to the ground, where a dark pool spread beneath his head onto the gravel.

"Roadside accidents," Reece commented.

Keller made a noise of agreement.

"So did Simeon tell you anything else?" Reece continued, turning away from the scene.

"There's seven guards with him," Keller answered, and then he grinned. "And his two little girls."

"He's with his kids?"

"One fell swoop."

Reece exhaled. "How far?"

"Close."

Anticipation shone in Reece's eyes. "Go," he ordered. As he slid with Keller into the nearest sedan, the other men rushed for the second car.

Both vehicles sped off into the night.

Trembling, Cole crawled from the bushes and rose shakily to his feet, his gaze sliding to the body on the roadside.

His gorge rose. Blood dripped from the trunk, falling silently on the corpse below. Vaughn's corpse. After they killed him.

Spinning, Cole vomited into the bushes, heaving and choking as his stomach tried to turn itself inside out.

A minor eternity crept by. Wiping his mouth, he straightened and walked away from the bushes toward his adoptive father's car.

Robert's sedan was in good shape, all things considered. Not too many dents or scratches or anything. The keys were still in his pocket too, which was nice. It just seemed like it was taking a while for him to reach the door.

Numbly, he noticed he'd stopped walking.

He was in shock, he realized. This was what shock felt like. Because right now, the fact that four glowing men had killed the guy posing as his counselor, after having ripped the door from a car without touching it, was being hastily filed away in a tiny black box marked 'things that didn't just happen'.

People couldn't be after him. No one would ever kill to find him. He just needed to get out of here and forget about this, because

Vaughn couldn't possibly be dead, his parents couldn't have attacked him, and there was no way those superpowered figments of his imagination had just driven off to…

His thoughts skidded to a halt.

To kill two little girls.

Cole's eyes slid toward the distant taillights, watching as they raced for the horizon.

He was going crazy. He'd lost sight of the deep end an hour before and the only rational decision was to swim back now.

Two little girls.

His mother, dead on the carpet. His father, shot in the hallway. Masked men, storming his room.

And one person, calling the police to save his life.

He drew a slow breath. He couldn't call the cops without telling them where the men were heading. And he wouldn't know that unless…

Vaughn's voice echoed back to him, telling him to stay down or he'd die.

This was what shock felt like when it was breaking.

Cole ran for the car.

Chapter Three

Now

With a clunk, the book hit the ground. Ashley jerked awake.

At the sudden motion, her neck twinged and she winced. Moving gingerly, she shifted out of her awkward position against the window frame and rubbed her neck with a hand still tingling from being pinned between her body and the wall. Red imprints in the shape of the window molding marked her arm, and she suspected from the weird feeling on her face that they crossed her cheek as well.

She could just picture Jonathan's expression when he found out she'd once again fallen asleep only inches from her bed.

Rolling her shoulders to loosen them, she glanced at the clock on the nightstand and instantly regretted it. Depressingly small numbers glowed back at her, burning indelibly into her mind the math of how few hours' sleep she'd have till sunrise.

With a sigh, she reached down, retrieving the book from the floor and then tucking it beneath the window cushion. Propping herself against the nightstand, she fumbled for the lamp switch and then clicked it off.

A strange, orange glow filled the room.

Deep in her stomach, she felt herself start quivering.

With tremulous control, she pushed to her feet. Her eyes locked on the shifting shadows and light playing over the dark walls, tracing them back to the window on the far side of the room.

Orange ghosts shimmered on the casement. Her hand clutched at the rail of the footboard as she navigated around the bed, and when she came into view of the window, she forgot how to breathe.

Fire engulfed the barn.

Black silhouettes against the light, the farmhands looked tiny as they battled the towering blaze. Broken beams shifted in and out of view behind the curtains of flame, and from the ranch house, she could hear someone ringing the alarm bell, though she could already tell that the structure was a loss.

All that mattered now was getting everyone out before the embers spread the flames.

Gasping, she whirled from the window and tore across the room. The door crashed against the dresser as she threw it open, toppling books to the ground. Taking the steps two at a time, she raced to the second floor and landed with a thud at the foot of the stairs.

"Dad!" she screamed.

Not waiting for him, she dashed into Lily's room, skidding on the paper and crushing crafts beneath her feet. The little girl blinked blearily and let out a confused cry as Ashley ripped the blanket away and then yanked the child to her feet.

Ashley glanced back as Patrick's door flew open.

He took in the dark hall and his panicked daughter in a glance. "What's going on?"

"Fire. The barn."

Spinning back toward Lily, she grabbed the girl's jeans from the floor and pushed them into her sister's hands. "Come on."

Dragging the girl behind her, she headed for the door. "Jonathan and the others are out there," she called over her shoulder. "The stupid hay probably wasn't dry enough. But they're trying to put it out."

She rushed down the stairs. Pausing in the foyer, she shoved her feet into her shoes and quickly motioned for Lily to do the same. Patrick pushed past them both, heading for the back door. Glancing to her sister, Ashley tried to smile.

"It's going to be fine, Lil."

The girl nodded nervously as she pulled on her jeans and shoes.

Clutching Lily's hand, Ashley hurried after her father. Yanking open the door, he started down the concrete stairs, his daughters on his heels.

At a popping noise, Patrick stopped. Ashley jerked to a halt behind him, confused. His brow furrowed as he glanced back at her, and she couldn't understand the look in his eyes.

He tumbled down the steps to the ground.

"Daddy?" Lily cried.

Ashley stared.

Blood spread like water from the holes in his chest, dyeing his pale t-shirt red. Choking wetly, his face crumpled in bewilderment and pain as he dragged his gaze over to hers.

"Run," he gasped.

Ashley stumbled down the stairs, crashing to her knees by his side. Bubbles of blood hovered around his lips, with more frothing up every time he breathed.

This couldn't be happening.

This wasn't real.

"Jonathan!" she screamed.

She tore her gaze from her father and scanned the fields desperately. He had to be there. He would help them.

The farmhands walked away from the flames. The person on the steps dropped the bell and headed their way.

And from behind the hillocks around the farm, masked men with rifles rose to join them.

Lily whimpered, fingers digging into Ashley's arm.

"Ashley," Patrick whispered. "Run."

She looked down as his head lolled sideways to face the approaching men. Determination flickered through his eyes.

White light surrounded her and rushing air roared in her ears. Distantly, she heard Lily screaming. And then something soft crushed into her.

Gasping, she sat up. She was in the vegetable garden, Lily clutching her hand. Frantically, she scrambled to her feet, searching for her father.

Masked men surrounded him.

With a cry, she tried to run to him. Lily hauled on her arm, holding her back with terror in her eyes.

Through the circle, another man approached. Amid the ski masks and rifles, his business suit and uncovered face stood in sharp contrast. Firelight played off his dark hair, turning his eyes into shadowed pits and chiseling his face in strange relief. Several inches taller than anyone around him, he towered like a giant over her father on the ground.

In spite of everything, Patrick tried to stand. Fury surged past the pain on his face, and his hand rose as if to strike the man.

The giant scoffed, and his fingers twitched as though flicking away a fly. Patrick gasped. His back arched sharply. And then he crashed to the ground and didn't move again.

Ashley couldn't breathe.

This wasn't happening.

A smile curled the giant's mouth as he looked toward the girls in the vegetable garden.

"Get them," he ordered.

Like unleashed hunting dogs, the men charged.

The sight shattered her paralysis. Ripping her gaze from her father, Ashley spun. Yanking Lily behind her, she tore across the tilled soil, choking back a sob as the soft earth sucked at her feet, slowing her down.

She reached the edge of the garden and took off across the field with no idea of where to go. Lily clung to her, and she could hear the girl crying. Thelma's house was an eternity away, and she couldn't see the woman's porch light. The farmhands' house was dark. No one had emerged this whole time.

Tears burned her eyes.

She kept running.

Headlights surged over the rise at the edge of the property. With a shriek, Ashley tried to turn, her feet sliding from beneath her on the grass. Lily slammed into her and frantically, Ashley grabbed the girl and shoved her to the side.

Lily rolled away.

Ashley didn't have time to move.

The car roared straight at her.

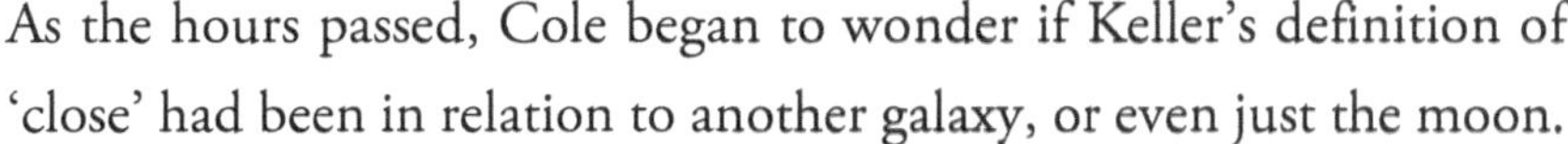

As the hours passed, Cole began to wonder if Keller's definition of 'close' had been in relation to another galaxy, or even just the moon.

He scrubbed a hand across his burning eyes, trying to stay focused on the road. An indeterminate number of miles before, they'd passed a large blue sign welcoming them to Montana, so he knew what state they were in, at least. But they'd left the highway a while ago, and had since been following circuitous mountain roads through tiny towns with little more than a street light to separate them from complete oblivion. Occasionally, the pinprick glows of distant farms would appear. Even more rarely, a sign pointed into the black abyss of an adjoining road, denoting other specks of life lost somewhere in the darkness. But town names or mile markers were infrequent at best and he couldn't make himself believe that anything he saw would guide the police to the other vehicles' destination very well.

Assuming he could call them.

And he didn't run out of gas before he got there.

Grimacing, he glanced at his cell phone for the twentieth time in as many minutes. Once they'd left the interstate, the bars of signal had dwindled, and for the past few miles, he'd only seen a tiny message politely notifying him of the utter lack of connection.

It was maddening. All his plans went out the window if he couldn't do something as simple as call the police.

Taillights flared ahead of him again. For the first hour or so, he'd expected them to notice the luxury sedan pacing them along the miles of interstate – and to make something horrible happen to him as a result. But as time passed, several other cars pulled in behind the leaders, forming a loosely connected caravan, and he realized they'd assumed he was one of them all along.

It wasn't exactly comforting, though it did mean he probably wouldn't die before they reached their destination.

Drawing a steadying breath, he shoved the fatalistic thoughts away. Up ahead, Keller's car veered onto a nearly invisible fork hidden among the trees. The other vehicles disappeared after him, and soon Cole could see glimmers of their headlights twisting down the mountainside.

And as with every other blind, unmarked turn in the past few hours, he gripped the wheel and followed them without the slightest clue where they were going.

The narrow track wound through the forest, rolling with the dips and turns of the steep descent. Trees shadowed the road, obliterating any trace of starlight. Gravel growled beneath his tires, making the sedan feel barely stable on the mountainside.

And then they came around a curve, and the valley opened up below them.

Unconsciously, he eased off the accelerator, barely noticing as the car slowed.

He was too late.

They'd already started.

Fire engulfed the barn on the far side of the valley, lighting the night sky. For the moment, the houses remained untouched, but he knew that would change. Reece and his friends were pulling up to block the drive, and in the flickering light of the flames, he could see dark figures hidden behind hillocks in the ground.

His hand fumbled for the cell phone. Thumbing it on, he cursed vehemently and then tossed the useless thing into the passenger seat.

Crushing the pedal to the floor, he sent the car careening down the mountainside.

His eyes flicked from the road to the houses below. He didn't know what he was going to do when he got there, but if he could warn them that the weird, glowing men were coming – and that the fire was a trap – maybe they'd stand a chance.

Three figures rushed from the house. One fell.

He swore, the car nearly leaving the road as he careened around another curve.

A burst of light made his gaze snap back to the farm.

The fallen one still lay on the ground, but the two others were gone. A large figure stood over the prone body, while the black-clad vultures circled.

Cole scanned the yard in confusion, and then he spotted them.

The two girls were alive, huddling several yards from where they'd been standing.

And then the men started coming for them.

He hit the gravel track bordering the property, and instantly, the embankments obscured his view. Gasping, he glanced to the road. He was running out of time.

A dead body was sprawled across the lane.

Shouting, he swerved. At full speed, the car rushed up the embankment and charged over the rise.

A girl was directly in his path.

Frantically, he hauled on the wheel and the emergency brake, sending the vehicle whirling in a tight arc around the girl and missing her by inches. Grass and dirt flew everywhere as the car spun to a halt between her and the men.

He couldn't believe he'd just done that.

Gasping, he flung himself at the passenger door, throwing it open.

"Get in!" he shouted.

The driver's side window shattered.

Lunging forward, the older girl grabbed the younger one and propelled the child into the car before tumbling in behind.

Cole's foot hit the floor, taking the gas pedal with it.

The engine roared as he whipped the car around. Dirt spewing from beneath the tires, the vehicle surged toward the far edge of the property.

He glanced over as the older girl let out a choked cry. Another house. More bodies. A bloodied floral dress and a glimpse of a dead man with white hair were all he saw before the car rushed past and left the carnage behind.

Gripping the wheel, he braced himself as the sedan flew over the embankment and crashed back down onto the path. Gravel spit furiously from beneath them as the car fishtailed.

The tires caught. The sedan righted itself with a lurch. Head-lights flooded his rearview mirror.

Reece and his friends were coming.

The car raced for the mountain road.

"Are you hurt?" he yelled over the growl of the gravel.

No response.

He looked over quickly. Eyes glazed, the older one stared at the floor. The younger had her head buried in the other girl's lap.

Drawing a breath, he checked out the window as the sedan wound up the mountainside. The other cars weren't too far behind, but the turnoff was ahead. And then the main road. And then the interstate.

If he could reach it in time.

Slowing as much as he dared, he started to turn.

Headlights surged into view. A horn blared. Hitting the brakes, he swerved madly as a pickup truck veered out of the way and smashed into the trees behind him.

With a cornering ability born of being too expensive for its own good, the sedan snapped back onto the concrete. Hanging onto the wheel with a white-knuckled grip, Cole risked a hasty glance in the rearview mirror.

The driver was getting out and shouting after him. But his truck was blocking the road Reece and the others were driving. Relief at the latter, and guilt at the former, warred inside Cole momentarily before he settled on just being glad the three of them were alive.

Except now he was going in the wrong direction.

And he couldn't believe that little roadblock would slow them for long.

"Hey," he called, looking swiftly to the older girl.

No response.

"Hey!"

The girl flinched, and then slowly, her eyes tracked over to him.

"Where's this road go?" he asked, clenching the wheel as they flew around another turn.

Incrementally, her gaze turned to the darkness, and lingered there.

He grimaced. She wasn't even seeing the road right now.

"Girl!" he called, trying to draw her back.

"I don't know," she answered numbly. She blinked a few times, and then her gaze dropped to her lap. Gently, she ran her fingers over her sister's black hair.

He looked back at the road, trying not to swear.

The road crested and then began to descend in a rapid series of dips and curves. On the left side of the car, the foliage-covered mountainside disappeared, leaving only a steep drop-off. Slender trees clung to the cliff, the only real barrier between the car, the open air, and the shimmering river a terrifyingly long distance below.

He swallowed hard, focusing on staying on the road. A bit farther downhill, a wide bridge arched across the river. Under the starlight, the open space seemed cavernous, welcoming anyone chasing them to see their car from miles away. Taking a breath, he guided the sedan into the winding curves, fighting the urge to just floor it.

The tires hit ice.

Frantically, he cranked the wheel and hit the brakes, feeling them pulse madly beneath his feet. Skidding sideways, the sedan careened through the turn and caught a tree against the rear door. The impact whipped the frontend around hard, and in an instant, they slammed into the trees.

Someone was screaming. Sluggishly, he looked around. The girls were pressed against him and the noise was the ringing in his ears. But his face was warm. With a thick hand, he reached up, smearing the blood trickling down his cheek.

A small gash. Nothing bad. Debris from the rear window was all.

Details started to play back through his mind.

Blinking slowly, he looked to the left. All the side airbags had deployed, saving him from impaling his skull on the broken window, but he couldn't see anything past the gaps between them. It was just black. And then he glanced up at the windshield.

The truth hit him like ice water.

They were resting against the trees. The tiny slivers of trees clinging to the sheer edge of the mountainside.

His head turned, though his body was afraid to move. The older girl raised her head and looked at him dazedly.

"Get out," he said, his tone meticulously calm. "Climb out the passenger side right now."

Her gaze moved to the windshield, to the trees, and then to the darkness. Already pale, her face lost every shred of color it still possessed.

Shaking her sister's shoulder, she roused the child and then motioned jerkily for the girl to climb out over her. Trembling, the child obeyed.

"Come on," the older girl said to him, her voice tense.

"Just go."

She reached over, taking his hand and pulling him with her.

The car shuddered as they moved, and if he'd had anything left in his stomach, it would've risked coming back up right then. His arms felt like lead, and his body was thoroughly engaged in hating him for all he'd put it through. At the edge of the seat, the girl paused, waiting as he scooted over the console and inched toward her.

She yanked him with her as she fled the car. Stumbling out after her, he swallowed hard, while the car sagged farther into the creaking embrace of the trees.

"Thanks," he said.

With a tiny nod, she stared at the car, and then her eyes went to the road.

He followed her gaze. A hundred yards ahead, the bridge waited, its broad expanse practically glowing beneath the starlight. It'd take forever to cross, and they'd be visible the whole time. And even if they reached the opposite side, without a car they'd still be sitting ducks for everyone chasing them down this road.

Which left heading up.

He glanced at the mountainside, his eyes tracing the treacherous path to the top. If they could reach that, and the damned cell phone started working, maybe they could hide long enough for help to arrive.

Taking a breath, he reached carefully back into the car. The girl made an incredulous noise, and then stared at him like he was insane when he eased back out.

He held up the cell phone and gun. "Come on," he said, walking past her toward the slope with much more composure than he felt.

Gripping her sister's hand, she followed.

"Who are you?" she asked quietly.

He glanced back. "Cole." It wasn't an explanation. It wasn't even much of an answer, honestly. But the truth was complicated, and he couldn't begin to think of what else to say.

Her brow furrowed. "Okay." A pause. "I'm Ashley."

They reached the side of the road and the conversation died.

Tucking the phone into his pocket and the gun into the back of his jeans, he headed for the first of the fallen rocks dotting the mountainside. Hoisting himself up, he grimaced against the protests raised by every muscle he owned. Behind him, Ashley boosted her sister onto the rocks, and then pulled herself up after them.

Moss carpeted the boulders protruding from the slope, threatening to dislodge him from every inch of height he gained. Scraggly bushes clung to scraps of soil beneath trees twisting at awkward angles toward the sky. The road grew more obscured as they climbed, and soon nothing of it was visible beyond the brush.

At the first level area, he turned and grabbed the younger girl, pulling her up to his side. Blue eyes like a moonlit pool stared up at him from beneath a mop of jet black hair, and then dropped worriedly away to find her sister. Gripping the rocks determinedly, Ashley hauled herself over the edge and then took the little girl's hand.

He glanced around. Forest surrounded them, but farther on, he could see the mountain continuing to rise. He let out a breath, energy draining at the prospect of more climbing.

Tires screeched to a halt on the road. Doors slammed. A voice, muffled and angry, snarled orders and, a heartbeat later, a car sped away.

Ashley's eyes found his, and he could see her shaking.

Rustles carried from the bushes below.

The men had split up and they were climbing. Fast.

He scooped the child into his arms and took off through the forest with Ashley a step behind.

The tree cover broke ahead of them. For fifty yards, a sparsely wooded plateau stretched across the mountainside, the product of falling rocks barreling through the forest in an old avalanche. Without pausing, he and Ashley tore across the distance, racing for the densely packed trees on the far side.

A gunshot shattered the silence.

Ashley screamed.

Skidding on the dirt, Cole turned. Ashley lay on the ground, clutching her leg as blood soaked her jeans. In his arms, the younger girl twisted, fighting to return to her sister.

His grip on the child tightened as his gaze went to the forest. Black-clad men emerged between the trees, and one of them was glowing.

He recognized Reece and his blood went cold. Keller was nowhere to be seen.

Frantically, Ashley fumbled a knife from her pocket and then flicked it open, pointing it at the men as she struggled to rise.

"Run!" she shouted at Cole.

He ignored her, yanking out the gun. "Get away from her!" he yelled, clutching the little girl with one arm as he aimed the weapon at the men.

He felt the gunshot before he heard it.

Pain tore through his shoulder. He stumbled back.

And then there was only air.

The little girl screamed as they fell into the night.

The bullet flew past her and she heard Lily scream. Spinning around, she saw the boy stumble, agony twisting his face.

And then they were gone.

Ashley stared.

Lily was gone.

She flinched as the cries cut off. With a gasp, she pushed away from the ground and ran for the cliff. Lily couldn't have fallen. Lily couldn't have...

Her leg gave out beneath her in an explosion of pain and she crashed down, hands skidding across the dirt and the knife flying away to clatter against a boulder. Eyes locked on the space where the boy had stood, she scrambled at the soil, hauling herself toward the ledge.

Hands grabbed her, dragging her backward and shoving her down till her face smashed into the dirt. Wrenching her arms behind her, they crushed a knee into her back and shouted for her to remain still.

A cry tore from her throat as she tried to fight.

Lily couldn't…

A fist came out of nowhere. Slamming her face with a dazzling display of red and white light, it drove her back to the ground, and she couldn't do anything but struggle to breathe around the pain. Tears burned in her eyes, her head rang, and her cheekbone felt shattered. Choking, she opened an eye, staring through a blurry haze toward the cliff.

Men surrounded her. At the edge of the ravine, a few stood, and amid the ringing in her ears, their words surfaced slowly.

"What the hell were you thinking?" one snapped, glaring at his burly companion.

The other man shrugged, an impatiently defensive look on his sweaty face. "What? Kid pulled a gun on me. Besides, Brogan said we only needed one."

Looking at him as though he was insane, the first man snarled disgustedly and then turned away, pulling out his cell. "Get me Brogan," he barked into the phone. He paused. "Well then, dammit, find Simeon!"

Ashley stared, their words spinning in her mind. Only needed one. Lily was… and her dad… and Jonathan… and Rose… these men had… she didn't even know why…

And all because they'd only needed one of them to survive.

As though feeling the pressure of her gaze, the burly man glanced back, and a smirk twisted his face at the sight of her. Nonchalantly, he crossed the distance to her side.

Bending down, he wrapped his fingers into her hair, pulling her head away from the ground. "You got a problem with me, brat?" he snickered. "Do something about it."

Sharply, he shoved her face deeper into the dirt, sending pain surging through her cheek. Laughing, he straightened and then clapped the man holding her on the shoulder before sauntering away.

She couldn't breathe. Trembling shook her and she couldn't stop it. Somewhere inside, emotions welled up, superseding one another in tumbling waves. Grief gave way to anguish, gave way to agony, gave way to searing pain…

Gave way to rage.

Burning, twisting, seething rage. From deep inside it rose like magma from the heart of the earth, roaring to the surface and tearing her body apart as it came.

They'd hurt Lily.

They'd destroyed everything.

Because they'd only needed one.

Just one.

Her eyes found the burly man. She watched him turn back toward her.

And then the world exploded in flame.

———•◆•———

The ground hit him hard.

Crashing onto his back on the rock, Cole felt the air rush from his chest, and pain nearly blinded him. A few inches away, the little girl slammed down, her screams ending as though severed by a knife.

Gasping, he blinked hard, trying to see the girl past the red fog in his eyes.

Her hand found his.

The haze pulled back. He glanced behind him.

He lay an inch from the abyss, on a tiny protrusion of rock barely a few feet wide. An overhang of rock covered part of the ledge, and without thinking, he gripped the girl's hand and rolled to his feet, heading for the negligible cover.

Pain went off like a firecracker inside his shoulder.

Sucking air through his teeth, he flung himself beneath the overhang, dragging the little girl with him. Together, they tumbled into the back wall, hitting rocky outcroppings and dried roots as they landed.

The girl whimpered, and quickly, he put his hand over her mouth to silence her. On the edge of the outcropping, he caught sight of his own blood, glimmering like a red beacon. Blanching, he drew his feet in as tightly as they would go and pulled the girl closer, waiting.

Pebbles scattered across the ledge, kicked down carelessly from above.

"What the hell were you thinking?"

Reece.

His teeth were clenched so tight, they were about ready to break.

"What?" came the reply. "Kid pulled a gun on me. Besides, Brogan said we only needed one."

The words made his brow furrow, jarring as they did against the idea that the men had been out to kill the girls. They didn't care if the little girl was dead. They just wanted one of them alive. He could still call the cops. Ashley might stand a chance.

He heard Reece growl something inarticulate in response, and a heartbeat later, gravel crunched as footsteps moved off. Drawing a shuddering breath, Cole tried to focus on reaching the cell phone in his pocket a million miles away.

In his grasp, the little girl twisted. Her eyes flicked toward his shoulder worriedly before turning to the rock above them as though seeing through the mountain to her sister. Gritting her teeth, she pulled away from him and started crawling from beneath the overhang.

He could barely move to stop her. His arm felt useless and probably was. The blood soaking his shoulder was like ice, and the pain made it ridiculously hard to think. Blinking, he swallowed and then struggled away from the rocks, reaching out with his good arm to draw her back.

A wave of fire blasted over the edge of the cliff.

With a shout, Cole crashed backward while trees, rocks, and screaming men flew into the night to tumble down into the river far below. Snagging the little girl with one hand, he yanked her back against him and stared.

The gout of flame died, disappearing into the sky in a cloud of black smoke. Fire crackled overhead, loud in the sudden silence.

They… he shivered, unable to form a coherent thought.

His gaze slid to the little girl.

"Ashe," she whispered.

Beyond the cave, the night grew darker. Despite the fires, the world was cold. The screaming agony in his shoulder faded away.

Rock caught his face with only a glimmer of pain.

A desperate sob escaped the girl as she spun. "No," she whimpered, shaking him.

She was a pale ghost amid the black shadows crowding him and the moonlight glowed off her skin like diamonds. He wanted to tell her it was okay, because that's what people always said in these situations. No matter what was happening, at that moment, it was okay.

"Please…" she begged, tears falling from her blue moon eyes to land on her skin so bright.

So very bright.

The pain faded away.

He opened his eyes.

They were still in the cave. The little girl was clutching his arm. And he felt fine. Better than fine. Blinking in confusion, he sat up and looked at his shoulder, and then pulled the sweatshirt up to see his chest.

Nothing. Smooth skin beneath a dark t-shirt sodden with blood.

His gaze rose to the little girl.

The little girl who was glowing.

"What–" he started, flinching back.

Glistening cheeks streaked with tears, she looked at him and then her face crumpled into a muted sob.

Brow furrowing, he hesitated and then reached out. Avoiding his blood-soaked shoulder, he pulled her close.

"It's okay," he whispered, holding her while she silently cried.

———◆———

Lily.

The thought clanged through Ashley's head, sending her surging to her feet as the pressure of the men pinning her down suddenly went away. Charging forward, she raced to the cliff, and then skidded to a halt, staring.

Smoke billowed into the sky, suffocating the stars. At the base of the ravine, the river shimmered with orange light.

And on an outcropping several feet below, blood pooled in the dirt and trailed off the ledge into the darkness.

Ashley choked.

She was gone.

Lily was actually gone.

Trembling, she fell to her knees. Tears slipped from beneath her closed lids, evaporating instantly.

A moment crept by, and slowly, her brow drew down. Blinking in numbed confusion, she looked over her shoulder.

The mountainside was on fire.

She gasped and scrambled for her feet. A wall of flame surrounded her, engulfing what was left of the underbrush and trees. Blackened trunks torn up from their roots fanned out around the clearing as though propelled by an explosion, and the men who'd held her were nowhere to be seen. Towering flames roared at the night, spreading swiftly across the mountain and clawing toward the sky.

And in the heart of it, she was standing.

Memory flickered back as she stared at the flames, and instinctively, her fingers went to her jeans, brushing the bullet hole in the fabric. Unbroken skin lay beneath. Brow furrowing in confusion, she looked down.

She choked on a scream.

Flames danced from her hands and coiled around her arms before twisting away to join the mountainside blaze. Trembling, she lifted her hands before her, unable to take her eyes from the fire shimmering over her unmarked skin.

This was a dream.

She looked up at the inferno swallowing the mountain.

This had to be a dream. The words repeated in her head, chasing themselves in circles till they descended into insensibility.

Hesitantly, she stepped forward and despite the flames twisting all around her, she was touched by nothing more than a warm breeze. Sparks and embers flew into the air and drifted down onto her skin painlessly.

She caught sight of a glimmer on the gravel and paused. A pool of metal rested at the base of a boulder, its silvery surface reflecting the fire.

Grief faded as she watched the orange light play across the pocket knife's remains.

This wasn't happening.

None of this was real.

Walking back through the fire, Ashley left the cliff behind.

———— ◆ ————

"She's stronger than we thought," Simeon commented, leaning against the stone wall of the scenic overlook while he watched the fire devouring the forest several miles away.

At his side, Brogan exhaled. "How many did we lose?"

"About a dozen, mostly recruits," Simeon answered, and then he paused. "But Reece was there. He was on the phone with me before…"

Brogan made no reply.

"He said one of the recruits shot at the targets," Simeon continued. "And as a result, that boy, whoever he was… he fell over the cliff with the younger girl."

At this, Brogan's gaze slid to meet the slender, ponytailed man's eyes. "So she could be dead," he stated flatly.

Simeon shrugged his graying eyebrows. "Or seriously injured."

Brogan looked back at the fires.

The rumble of tires on the mountain road made Simeon turn. Pulling to a stop behind them, Keller threw the car into park and then climbed out.

"The crew at the house burned it down before I got back there," he called furiously. He slammed the door and then stalked toward them. "Overeager bastards had the audacity to tell me it was standard operating procedure, putting the bodies in the basement and then torching every building on the property."

Brogan closed his eyes.

"What do you want to do?" Simeon asked.

"Besides kill them all?" Keller growled rhetorically. He tossed a look to Brogan. "They're all too impatient to end this, boss. Sloppy doesn't *begin* to cover it."

His gaze flicked to Keller and the man caught himself. "Brogan," he corrected. "Sorry."

Drawing a breath, Brogan turned from the fires and started toward his car. "We need proof the younger girl is dead. Take the survivors and check for corpses. If there are none, get back to the farmhouse. Find something to track them by."

"Damn recruits," Keller grumbled.

"Kill some as an example if necessary," Brogan called over his shoulder as he opened the car door. "But get this under control. Tear apart the property, and if there's nothing of use…"

He paused, thinking. "Pin it on the older girl. Regardless, she's still alive. Pull out your old FBI credentials if you have to, but gather what information we have and make up a cover story blaming her for the house, the bodies, all of it. The more incriminating, the better. Involve that boy and the younger girl too, just in case. And then leak it to the press and the police. I want half the country looking for them by sunrise."

"Are you sure that's a good idea?" Simeon asked. "I mean… Brogan, the cops can't help and if–"

"According to Bartlow, Patrick didn't tell them anything," Brogan said. "So if they're scared and confused enough, the police and the media might stand a chance. As for the rest, tonight wasn't subtle. They'll be coming after the girls anyway."

He glanced back at the flames. "We just have to get to them first."

Chapter Four

Heat continued to build in their tiny hollow beneath the blaze, making sweat drip down Cole's face. Embers crumbled onto the ledge every so often as the fire consumed everything it touched. At his side, the little girl hadn't stopped crying, though she never made a sound. Barely breathing and trembling hard, she huddled in a tense little ball, fists curled as though she was fighting with all her strength to hold the grief inside.

One hand on the girl's shoulder, Cole glanced down. The glow around her hadn't faded, and the more he studied it, the more disconcerted he became. Though she glistened to his eyes, the shimmer emanating from her skin cast no light on the cave walls, and did nothing for the shadows. Whatever he was seeing had no effect on the outside world, and the thought was anything but comforting.

But she'd also saved his life, despite the bullet wound and massive blood loss. And the men who'd attacked them had tossed Vaughn thirty feet through the air into the back of a sedan. Both groups glowed, and thus he was left with the inescapable conclusion that glowing people possessed superpowers.

And that he was probably insane.

Cole glanced at the cave opening as more embers scattered across the ledge. Regardless of his own estimation of his current mental stability, he knew they couldn't stay here much longer, not only because of the heat, but also because the fire could be seen for miles. And while emergency crews and police were sure to come, the truth was Keller and his cronies had to be on the way as well. They'd killed to find him in Utah, and they'd killed to find Ashley and her sister too. They only wanted one of the girls, and so the best thing he could do was keep them from learning the kid was alive and that he was here, at least until he could get the cops involved.

He shifted slightly. At the motion, the little girl flinched and then pushed away from his side. Swiping her eyes with the back of her hand, she only vaguely appeared to register he was there.

"What's your name?" he asked.

"Lily," she whispered.

He tried a smile, but the expression felt awkward and stupid against the hurt in her eyes. "I'm Cole."

Silence answered him.

The ticking of time made him glance to the ledge again. "Lily, we need to get going. Police and firemen will be here soon, but the guys who were after us might be coming too. We need to find the cops before then."

She didn't move.

"Lily."

"I want to go home."

Caught off guard, he hesitated. "Y-you can't."

Want and reality warred in her distant gaze. "Take me home," she insisted, pulling her knees to her chest and wrapping her arms around them tightly.

Cole stared at her as images of glowing men with guns raced through his mind. His own weapon had skittered away in the darkness when they fell, presumably to drown in the river below, and even though the cell phone had survived the drop, as far as signal was concerned, they may as well have been on the moon. The police were their best chance at survival, but instead, she wanted to head back to where the bad guys were almost certain to be.

She was a kid going through hell, but it was everything he could do not to scoff.

"Please?" she persisted when he didn't respond, a touch of desperation in her voice.

"Listen," he said, forcing himself to sound calm. "We can't go back to your house now. But," he continued hastily, seeing the nascent hysteria in her expression, "is there anywhere I can take you? Other family? Friends maybe?"

At his words, the hysteria faded. The vaguely catatonic look returned to her eyes.

"What?" he pressed.

She bundled herself into an even smaller ball. "I want to go home."

"We can't go there now. But the cops will be coming and they can help us. If there's someone they can contact…"

For the first time, her eyes lifted to meet his. "They're all dead," she told him tonelessly. "The fires killed them when I was little."

He faltered, staring at her distant blue gaze. Struggling to regroup, he glanced to the ledge. "Lily, we have to get out of here."

The girl looked up at the cave ceiling and shook her head. "I need to find Ashley first."

Words deserted him. He had no idea what'd happened in the mere seconds between he and Lily falling and the explosion, but there was no way Ashley's captors could've already taken her far enough away to not be caught in the blast. Men and trees had flown from the cliff like confetti, meaning the bastards had been victims of whatever they'd tried. It had to have been an accident, but for the better part of the past fifteen minutes the mountain had been an inferno.

Nothing could have survived.

Carefully, he took the girl's hand as he struggled to find a way to explain reality to a kid who looked like she couldn't be more than six years old. Nothing came to him.

"Ashley's dead, Lily," he said quietly, feeling like a monster.

The little girl ripped her hand away, staring at him in horrified disbelief.

"You're lying," she said with absolute conviction. Face furrowing angrily, she shook her head to drive away the words, and then turned to study the ledge, as though trying to determine how to climb up without being burned by the flames.

"Lily," he said painfully. "Ashley's gone."

She trembled, not turning around.

"We have to go."

"I'm going *home*."

Repressing the urge to shout at her, he looked away and forced himself to breathe. "Okay, fine. We'll go home soon," he said, lying and knowing he was a jerk for doing so. "Just… we need to get away from here first, alright?"

For several irretrievable seconds, the girl didn't move. "Really?" she asked, her voice tiny and hopeful as she turned back.

He fought a grimace. There was probably a special circle in hell for people who lied to kids like this. "Yeah. Just as soon as we can."

Eyeing him a moment more, she nodded.

Suppressing a surge of guilty relief, he crept toward the edge of the ravine. Fire roared above, making a return to the plateau a suicidal impossibility and though the cliff below them wasn't a direct drop, he still turned away sharply as vertigo hit. Rocky outcroppings protruded from the sides, and scraggly bushes clung to the scraps of dirt in between. One wrong move would send them plummeting straight to the bottom, but as he checked the steep slope one more time, he started to see a way down.

"Okay," he told the girl, working to keep the discomfort from his voice. "You climb trees much?"

She shrugged guardedly.

"Alright, well, just follow my lead, don't look down, and you'll be fine."

The girl didn't appear convinced, but he ignored it. Shifting around in a tight circle, he took a deep breath and then reached out, carefully placing a foot on the nearest ledge. Resting his weight on it slowly, he gave her an attempt at a smile and then began climbing down.

Inch by cautious inch, they descended. The prospect of falling made it hard to breathe, and the thought of Keller and his people spotting them ran circles in his head. The bottom of the canyon seemed to grow farther away as the seconds ticked by, and despite his instruction not to look down, he found himself checking their distance from the ravine floor with every move he made.

Rocks skittered beneath him as he finally arrived at the base of the mountain. Reaching up, he helped the little girl down the last few feet with arms that felt like month-old Jell-O. Breathing hard, she looked ill as he set her down, and tears leaked from the corners of her eyes.

"You okay?" he asked.

She nodded jerkily, determination flickering through her nauseated expression.

He shook his head. Tough kid. He felt like collapsing.

Drawing a breath, he checked around. Several hundred feet to the left, the bridge arched over the orange-lit water, while on the right, the river curved out of view, following a serpentine path through the mountains. On the opposite side of the water, a steep service track descended through the trees, leading from the main road to the river. Bushes crowded the base of the slopes around them, petering away a dozen feet shy of the banks to leave only gravel, dirt, and smoldering detritus from the fire.

He exhaled slowly. Beneath the firelight and what remained of the stars, they'd be easily visible near the water. But Keller and his friends were nowhere to be seen, and if the two of them moved fast and made it up the service road to the bridge, they could hide in the brush till the cops arrived.

"Come on," he said quietly. "Stay near the bushes, okay?"

He studied the river as they drew closer to the bridge, his confidence faltering. Babbling loudly, water rushed by, and sharp rocks showed amid the turbulent surface. Being seen was only part of the problem. Being swept away to drown was an equal issue.

Headlights appeared on the service road and hurriedly, he motioned for Lily to hide. Following, he crouched behind the bushes as two black SUVs crept down the hill and then pulled up by the base of the bridge.

Four men climbed from each vehicle, and Keller was one of them.

Lily let out a small whimper.

"Shh," he whispered, not taking his eyes from them.

Keller motioned toward the water. Fanning out, the men began searching the riverbank.

Feeling as though he was going to be sick, Cole watched them make their way closer and then glanced back, trying to map a course through the underbrush that would keep them from being spotted.

Lily flinched and he looked to the riverbank.

Red and blue strobe lights flashed as a police car wound down the service road. Reaching the riverbank, two cops got out of their vehicle and approached Keller and his men cautiously.

Unable to decide between relief at the police presence or fear for their safety, Cole held his breath.

One of the policemen said something, and over the rushing water, Cole couldn't hear a word. But Keller pulled his wallet from his pocket calmly, and showed it to the nearest cop without a shred of concern in his posture.

Taking it carefully, the policeman reviewed the contents, and then nodded, caution fading. The cop called back to his companion and then turned, apologetically shaking Keller's hand before walking with him toward the riverbank.

Cole stared, incoherent thoughts tumbling through his head. The cops were in league with the bad guys. It felt like a B-grade horror movie. But if he went to them now and accused their new best friends of murdering people, Keller would probably just turn around and make the police believe Cole'd actually been the one behind it all along.

Or that he was psychotic. He'd seen enough bad movies to know how that usually went. He'd be locked up and interrogated by the cops till the glowing freaks showed up and made him and the little girl disappear.

Which raised another point…

"Lily," he hissed, his voice barely audible above the rushing water. "Are any of those men, um… *glowing* to you?"

Her alarmed expression was answer enough.

"Never mind," he said, grimacing.

With a quick glance to the police, Cole pulled Lily's arm, drawing her farther into the brush. Near the base of the mountain slope, the undergrowth thinned and, keeping to the shadows, they crept away from the men on the opposite riverbank. The babbling of the water covered the small sounds of their passage, and even though he checked back repeatedly, there was no sign the others noticed them slipping away.

Cautiously, they followed the curve of the river, until the slope obscured the men completely. Orange light still reflected from the water, and overhead, the fire continued down the eastern ridge of the mountains for as far as his eyes could see.

Holding the girl's hand tightly, he left the bushes. "Run," he ordered.

They took off down the riverbank.

Gravel crunched as they ran, and his breath was desperately loud to his own ears. Clinging to his hand, Lily stumbled along without making a sound. Exhausted from climbing, his body bewailed every motion and as the minutes passed, he found his legs slowing despite his efforts to keep moving.

Breathing hard, Lily came to a stop and looked up at him questioningly. He glanced around. The men were nowhere to be seen and the fire on the eastern mountains meant they couldn't be up there waiting. The water seemed slower here too, and the slopes on the opposite side of the river didn't appear as steep.

"Okay," he said to Lily as he tugged the cell phone from his pocket to spare it a bath. "We're going to cross here. Just hang onto me, alright?"

She nodded. Taking a ragged breath, he hefted the girl up and then started into the hip-deep water.

Ice would have been warmer.

Gasping, he kept walking as the river sucked at his feet, trying to pull him from the slick rocks. In his arms, Lily whimpered as the freezing water swept around them, and the sound galvanized his tired muscles. Tightening his hold on her, he forced himself to move faster as he gritted his teeth against the bone-numbing cold.

He stumbled onto the banks, shivering uncontrollably. Quickly, he checked upriver, but the mountainside still obscured the police and Keller's men. Lowering the girl down next to him, he wrapped an arm around her and chafed her shoulder to keep her warm.

"You okay?"

She nodded, the motion barely discernible amid her shivering.

He hesitated, and then pulled off his hooded sweatshirt, distantly grateful for the dark fabric and his equally dark t-shirt beneath. The bullet hole could pass as a tear, and in the heat of the small cave, the bloodstains had mostly dried as well.

"Here," he said, handing it to her. "Put this on."

Wordlessly, she pulled the sweatshirt over her pink pajama top. His high school logo hung somewhere around her stomach, and the sleeves flopped past her hands.

"Thanks," she whispered, bundling the long sleeves into her fists and hugging them to her chest.

Nodding, he glanced away. "Come on," he said between teeth clenched to keep them from chattering. Drawing her after him, he started for the slope.

The underbrush was a mass of shadows beneath the trees, but as they came closer, he hesitated. A post protruded from the bushes, and a number was roughly carved on its wooden surface. Fatigue slowing him, he stared for a heartbeat before realizing what it was.

A trail marker.

Blinking, he looked down at the brush. A rotted log backed up against hardened gravel and dirt, and past the bushes, he could just make out another log higher up the slope.

Pushing back an incredulous laugh at the scrap of crude civilization in the midst of this nightmare, he started up the stairway.

His legs hated him when they reached the top, but he refused to listen. With a quick look to make sure Lily was still standing, he started down the overgrown path, trying to draw some comfort from the fact it didn't look like anyone had come this way in quite a while.

Their jeans slowly transitioned from ice to warm clamminess as time crept by. Gradually, the shadows thinned as the sun inched toward the eastern horizon and the morning birds filled the air with their chirping. If his legs hadn't felt ready to give way and his heart hadn't hit his throat at the slightest sound, it would have been practically relaxing.

"Where are we going?" Lily asked, her voice faint.

Cole looked down. Beneath the tangles of her black hair, her face was alarmingly pale and dark circles hung under her eyes. As she clutched his fingers, her grip trembled, and when they stopped walking, she looked ready to simply fall down.

He hesitated, not wanting to admit he had no idea what to do now. They were lost in the middle of a forest in Montana, a state with more than its fair share of empty spaces and an apparent dearth of roads. The cell phone didn't have signal, though if it had, he didn't know who he'd bother to call. The cops were cohorts of Keller's group, or at least weren't remotely suspicious of them.

And thus, he'd run out of options on how to handle the situation.

"Just a little farther," he told her, starting forward again.

Too tired to protest, she followed.

Desperation started to gnaw at him as the forest continued, unchanging. Maps from half-forgotten geography classes played through his head, showing the continental swath of the Rocky Mountain range in sharp and uncompromising relief. Even if a road was within a couple miles, he wasn't certain either of them would have the endurance to reach it.

They needed to rest till he could figure this out — and to eat something before they both starved. After everything, the stupidity of collapsing in the wilderness would've infuriated him if he'd had the energy.

A whistling noise broke the dull torpor of his thoughts and brought him to a halt. Motioning Lily to stay put, he crept forward, alertness returning as he searched for the source of the sound.

The road appeared beyond the trees, and as he came closer, he caught sight of a rusted pickup truck on the gravel shoulder. Furniture and mismatched junk filled the rear, and ropes lashed to high wooden slats on the truck's sides restrained the mess. Tarps draped in haphazard fashion over the contents, and more ropes strapped the coverings down. The cab was unoccupied, but farther along the road, he spotted the source of the tuneless whistling. A man stood just beyond the trees by the roadside, peeing into the bushes.

Cole grimaced and glanced back at the truck. He hesitated.

"Hurry," he whispered to Lily, snagging her hand as she came closer. Drawing her after him, he rushed toward the pickup. As she started to look toward the whistling, he made a cautioning noise. "Come on."

Brow furrowing in confusion, she obeyed.

At the rear of the truck, he pulled back the edge of the tarp and then hoisted Lily over the tailgate. With a quick check to make sure the man hadn't seen them, Cole climbed in after her and squeezed between the piles of junk inside.

"Stay still," he told her quietly, tugging the covering back into place.

Curled up beside him, she didn't move, her eyes on the sliver of light between the tarp and the wall.

A minute slid by. Footsteps crunched over gravel, and Cole held his breath, waiting. Hinges creaked loudly and then the truck shook as the driver's door slammed.

The engine roared to life. With a jerk, the truck shifted into gear and then started down the shoulder. Furniture shuddered as the vehicle bumped back onto the road, but restrained by the ropes, nothing fell.

Cole exhaled. "You okay?"

Lily shrugged, and then twisted to look at him. "Where are we going?"

"I'm not sure," he admitted tiredly. "Some place safer than here, I hope." He glanced down. "Get some sleep, okay?"

Her brow furrowed uncertainly and the ghosts of old protests rose in her eyes, but after a moment they faded. Twisting back around, she pillowed her head on her arm and, in only a few heartbeats, he could feel her breathing slow.

Exhaustion weighing on him, he watched the trees flash past the sliver of space between the tarp and the truck, and tried to think of what to do now.

———— ◆ ————

For a lifetime she wandered, till her feet carried her back through the forest by her home. The world flitted past in a series of broken images, disconnected and surreal, and each immersed in a numbness that reduced them to irrelevancy.

Because this wasn't happening.

A pile of smoking timbers lay where the gray farmhouse had stood. To one side, the farmhands' home still burned in fits and starts, spewing occasional sparks into the sky. On the far end of the field, the barn was a heap of smoldering rubble, and only the distant sound of popping embers broke the stillness.

Like a sleepwalker, Ashley stepped from the line of trees.

In the distance behind her, fires still raged on the mountainside, painting the sky above the forest with a patina of orange. On the horizon ahead, the first hint of sunrise fought the haze. Winds swept past her as she crossed the field, stirring her dark hair, while all around, ash drifted like snow.

But none of it was real and didn't matter anyway.

Fear and pain had been locked up long ago, imprisoned behind walls of glass like toothless predators in an archaic zoo. And sometime soon, reality would return to give them their rest. She would open her eyes to see the sun pouring through her windows, and to feel the warm blankets draped over her bed. Lily would be up already, playing with her crafts and creating new designs. Her dad would be sipping coffee, getting ready to leave while discussing the next planting season with Jonathan and Rose.

And everything would be alright.

By her feet, something clinked, and she looked down. Two thin metal tubes, their painted sides bubbled and blackened, were all that remained of the wind chimes. Gingerly, she bent and picked them up, soot staining her fingers as she turned them around in her hands.

Tears, foreign and unwanted, stung her eyes. Cautiously, she retreated from the feelings, fighting to continue keeping them at bay.

Only moments now. She would wake up. Everything would be alright.

Her gaze lifted to the wreckage of the farmhouse.

Everything would be alright…

Hand clutching the wind chimes, she waged a silent war against the tears while she waited for reality to change the destruction before her eyes.

Something brushed against her leg. She flinched and glanced down.

The tiger-striped cat meowed and looked up at her expectantly before running its side across her leg again. Ashley's gaze rose, tracing the path back to the tiny bungalow.

On the crest of the hill, Thelma stood, a sea of cats at her feet and sunrise and firelight playing off her wild gray hair. Over the distance, her eyes locked on the farmhouse debris and, cats swirling around her, she walked down from the hilltop.

"Ashley, Ashley," the woman murmured as she drew near. Her gaze moved to the wreckage, sorrow deepening the wrinkles of her face. "Where's the little flower?"

Her grip trembling on the wind chimes, Ashley couldn't find the words to reply.

Thelma shook her head and sighed. Bending down, she lifted a shattered piece of flowerpot from the ash-strewn grass. Gently, she turned it over in her hands, her bony fingers brushing the dust from the fragments of Lily's design.

"I didn't know they were firemen," the old woman said. "At least, not the bad kind. I just..."

Her brow furrowed regretfully. She bent, gently returning the scrap to the grass and then stroking it lovingly.

"There were three," Thelma offered as she straightened, her gaze on the broken piece of pottery. "At the beginning, I mean. Not just one. Two and the other... dear old Elvis." She paused, a fond smile flitting across her weathered face. "I remember Elvis. Didn't know what it was going to cost him. Though he probably would have done it anyway. But then it got all tangled. Hurtful and horrible, and so I never told anybody."

She glanced over and patted Ashley's shoulder, her expression a strange mix of consolation and apology.

Numbly, Ashley stared. It hurt. Thelma standing there. Her cats. Engaging this stupid, false reality. But she would wake up. Any moment now, it'd all just be a dream.

It had to be a dream.

"What was I supposed to say?" Thelma continued, as though in response to Ashley's expression. "If it was just going to be like last time? And he wasn't here to talk to..." She trailed off and then shook her head. "I could've tried harder. I just didn't want it to be like last time. And now..."

The old woman closed her eyes, and then she exhaled as though pushing the thoughts away. "But I told you," she said, reaching over to take Ashley's hand. "Because I want to help."

For a moment, Ashley couldn't turn from the woman's half-focused, too-bright eyes. And then of its own volition, her hand tore from Thelma's grasp.

Lily was… They took *Lily*. And her dad. And everybody.

The words tumbled past her defenses in an avalanche, obliterating everything. Searing pain howled in their wake, and all she could do was stare at the deranged old woman with cats twisting around her feet.

They'd destroyed everything.

And Thelma was here. To *help*.

She couldn't breathe. Images of Lily and her whole world bombarded her, and her fingernails bit through the skin of her palms to keep the agony of them away.

"Why you?" she whispered, her voice breaking.

Thelma's brow furrowed in confusion.

"Why everybody… and not you?"

Hurt flickered across the woman's face, and she looked down, seeming lost as she watched the cats weave between her feet.

Ashley trembled, fighting to keep from screaming.

And from deep inside, a surging, twisting core of flames began to grow. Spread. Rise.

The forest. Men screaming. She gasped, scrambling internally to stop the impossible fire rushing through her body. Heat played over her skin, making the air shimmer. Eyes wide, Thelma stumbled in retreat as the cats scattered.

Panicking, Ashley backed away, her head shaking in denial of what she was feeling.

Something crinkled beneath her feet. She looked down.

One of Lily's pinwheels lay in the grass.

A broken sob escaped her, the sight shattering her panic. She crumbled to her knees as the grief slammed the fires like a wave, crushing the blaze. Her trembling fingers reached out to touch the precise folds, and then jerked back as the residual heat from her skin made the paper begin to blacken and curl.

She wrapped her arms around her stomach, choking on sobs and squeezing her eyes shut as the heat faded from her body.

"This isn't real," she whispered desperately. "This isn't happening."

A hand rested on her shoulder. Ashley flinched and looked up at Thelma, baffled that the old woman hadn't run shrieking to the hills.

But who knew what else Thelma thought she saw every day?

Carefully, the old woman reached down, taking the pinwheel and straightening the folds tenderly. "Pretty little flower," she murmured.

Ashley nodded.

With a sad smile, the old woman sank down to the grass by her side. Crossing her legs beneath her long skirts, Thelma sat, spinning the pinwheel thoughtfully from time to time.

Embers popped in the stillness as the sun crept into the sky.

The rumble of gravel carried through the silence.

Heart picking up speed, Ashley looked back. Black sedans cruised down the mountain road, heading toward the farmhouse.

Thelma grabbed her arm. Scrambling upright, she struggled to tug Ashley with her. "Trees," she ordered.

Confused, Ashley stumbled to her feet, staring at the old woman.

"Firemen!" Thelma shrieked, propelling her toward the far side of the property. "Trees!"

Understanding hitting her like a hammer, Ashley bolted for the forest.

On the other side of the barn wreckage, she glanced back. Cars were pulling into the drive, but Thelma was blocking their path, waving her arms as she railed at them unintelligibly. A man climbed from one of the vehicles and grabbed the old woman, moving her forcibly out of the way.

Ashley kept going. Car doors slammed as she darted beneath the cover of the trees. Catching herself on a trunk, she spun and looked back again.

Half a dozen people headed to the house at the shouted command of a ponytailed man. With a sharp motion, he ordered the remaining men toward the rest of the property and swiftly, they fanned out, some of them striding toward the woods.

Panic surged through her. Shoving off the tree trunk, she raced deeper into the forest.

Branches and leaves slapped her as she ran. Unseen roots snagged her feet, sending her sprawling. Tumbling through the undergrowth, she choked as mud splattered over her. Swiping the mess from her face, she scrambled to her feet and didn't stop running.

On the crest of a hill, the trees gave way to farmland. Skidding to a halt, she scanned the open fields frantically.

Nothing moved. Half a mile to the south, the gravel road emerged from the forest to wind toward the empty horizon. Farther north, a railroad track cut through the grassland and then disappeared behind the hills. The sunrise covered the landscape in a wash of gold, growing brighter with every second.

Adrenaline shivered through her. Miles and miles of nowhere to hide. And they were coming.

Her gaze caught on a shape barely visible beyond the rolling hillsides. Stopped on the tracks, the freight train was a dull shadow in the morning light.

Trembling, she stared.

She hadn't wanted to leave.

And there was nowhere else to go.

Over her shoulder, she cast a look to the woods. Birds chirped overhead and leaves quivered in the breeze. The rubble of her home was lost in the forest, and even the smoke marking its location no longer drifted into the sky.

But the men would be coming.

Tears burning in her eyes, she dashed down the hillside.

A sea of grass separated her from the train, and only seemed to grow larger the more she ran. At any moment, she expected shouting to break out behind her, and the fear drove her heart into her throat. Muscles burning, she pushed herself to go faster as the dawn air scraped her lungs.

At the top of a hill, she fell to her knees and glanced over her shoulder, terrified of seeing the black-clad men racing after her.

Nothing. The empty fields undulated beneath the spring wind.

Gulping down a breath, she turned, studying the train through a curtain of tall prairie grass. Dozens of freight cars stretched away to her right, and a few yards to her left, the enormous engine waited. The dark wheels were utterly still, without even the tiniest shudder of potential motion.

"Dang it, Nelson!"

Ashley's head snapped toward the engine. A man's angry voice carried from the open window high on the side.

"Well, do they have any idea when we'll be allowed to go on? We've been here over an hour!" A pause. "Yes, of course I could tell the fire was huge, but I've got deadlines to make, or don't you remember those?" He scoffed. "What're we supposed to do in the meantime, huh? It's not like–" A longer pause. "Good."

Something slammed down inside the cabin. A heartbeat passed, and then the man spoke again, his voice annoyed but calmer. "Five minutes. Fire marshal's giving the all-clear now."

Silence fell. Worriedly, Ashley glanced to the other cars, and then back at the engine. She couldn't make a run for it from here; the engineer was certain to see. Inching backward, she retreated to the base of the hill, checked the prairie for pursuit one last time, and then took off.

For a hundred yards, no break appeared between the hills. Panic made her breath come in ragged gasps as she fought to run faster. The train could be leaving. She couldn't hear anything over the pounding of her heart in her ears.

A small dip appeared in the ridge separating her from the train, and she scrambled over it. Throwing a glance to the engine, she launched herself down the slope and then raced toward the side of the train.

Grain cars waited ahead of her, their angular ends sloped over small ledges with ladders framing their sides. Darting between the cars, she grabbed at the metal railing and then clambered onto the platform.

The train jerked as she landed on the filthy surface. Hands convulsing around the rail, she tried to keep breathing as the grainer vibrated beneath her.

Swallowing hard, she looked around. A space like a cubbyhole sat behind her, old rags stained with grease discarded on its floor. For a moment, she hesitated, and then scooted backward into the storage spot, keeping as far from the rags as she could. With a shudder, the train began to move. Working to ignore the stale stench of the rags, she wrapped her arms around one side of the ladder and hung on.

The wind picked up speed with the train, whipping through the cubbyhole and making her hair fly. Fading adrenaline dragged at her, and though the temperature must have been plummeting, she barely felt the cold past her own trembling. Abused for hours, her muscles absorbed themselves with the task of furiously aching, while below her, the wheels of the train churned over the tracks and filled the world with their deafening roar.

Trees appeared as the forest suddenly lined the track on both sides. Shifting warily, she drew her knees up, watching the woods.

No black-clad men lurked in the shadows. No trace of her house could be seen. From the view of the train, the sun had simply risen on another calm spring morning. No one had been murdered in the night. Nothing in the world had changed.

And tomorrow, she'd wake up. Tomorrow, this would all be a dream. She'd play with Lily, cook breakfast with Rose, and kiss her father goodbye. Patrick would come back for Christmas, and Jonathan would teach her all he knew about farming the whole summer long.

Tomorrow, everything would be alright.

The forest dropped away. Rocky outcroppings surrounded her, ash coating their sides. The remnants of the fire blazed in the distance as emergency helicopters circled the morning sky.

Closing her eyes, Ashley buried her head in her knees and cried.

———•◆•———

The phone rang.

Glancing away from his email, Brogan lifted the cell from the writing table of his hotel room.

"Report."

Simeon's hesitation was answer enough. "The younger girl's body wasn't anywhere we could see. And the house was… unhelpful. We've started leaking a story to the police, but for better or worse, there isn't much to go on."

"Did you determine their names?"

Again, the man hesitated. "No. We found photos of the girls in the debris, but no names. We're still searching the remains of the smaller house, but there's even less to go on there, and thus far, the neighbor has been unable to supply useful assistance."

"Force her."

"I tried," Simeon said, clearly struggling to keep the frustration from his tone. "She denied knowing the girls, and then refused to tell us anything about Elvis. After that, she became agitated, began threatening to kill all of our Jabberwockies, and then got distracted by her cats. We searched her house, Brogan. She had a pharmacies'-worth of prescriptions for dementia in her cupboard, all of which expired years ago."

Simeon sighed. "What do you want to do?"

A moment passed.

"Brogan? Are you there?"

"Get your men back here. Start focusing on the police; follow any leads they find."

He hung up before Simeon could say another word.

Frowning slightly, he rubbed his fingers against his temple, and as a measure of frustration, contemplated eliminating the neighbor on account of being inconveniently insane.

But there was no benefit, and it would only cause a delay.

Setting the phone aside, Brogan returned to his email.

Chapter Five

Cole woke with a start as the truck bounced over a pothole and jostled everything around him. Disoriented, he blinked, and then grimaced as memory returned.

From the cab beyond the tarp, he could hear country music blaring. Furniture strained against the ropes holding it to the wooden siding of the truck, and a basket of smelly clothes toppled from its perch between two bookshelves to scatter across his legs. Scowling, he kicked the clothing away, and then glanced down to make sure Lily was still alright.

Furrows lined her forehead and her fists were clenched. Squirming in place, she whimpered, cowering from something in her dream.

Cursing himself for falling asleep, he shook her shoulder. "Lily, wake up," he whispered.

With a gasp, her eyes flew open and she flinched back, her elbow hitting his stomach hard. He choked, struggling not to make too much noise.

She twisted around. "I'm so sorry!" she cried softly. "I didn't mean—"

He motioned for her to stop apologizing. "It's fine," he wheezed. He swallowed, trying not to let his voice belie the words. "You okay?"

She hesitated, and then nodded, lying transparently. He waited.

"Daddy," she said as though the single word was all she could bear to explain.

He squeezed her shoulder as memory supplied the rest. Three figures running down the stairs. One falling. He was fuzzy on the details, but knew in essence what she must've seen.

"They were horrible," she whispered, her gaze haunted.

"Yeah," he agreed quietly.

Her eyes met his, and after a moment, she nodded, as though his statement somehow made it more concrete. Tears slid down her cheeks, and his grip on her shoulder tightened. Minutes passed as the furniture swayed and the tires stuttered across potholes in the road.

"Why'd you ask me if those men glowed?" she asked.

He paused, reluctant to appear potentially insane. "It doesn't matter."

"But why?"

"How'd you heal me, Lily?" he asked, pretending to change the subject.

Annoyance crossed her face. "Why'd you ask me?" she persisted.

He sighed. "One of them just looked funny to me. It was probably a trick of the light."

She fidgeted nervously. "They seemed weird to me too," she admitted. "I just... I thought there was something wrong with me."

"You saw it too?" he asked, uncertain whether to feel elated or concerned.

"Not exactly..."

"What?"

"They just… when I'd look at them… they all *felt* weird. Same as anybody else, except different. Like… grayer or something." She cut off, frustration with her inability to explain clear on her face. "They were all like that, except the one in charge. He just felt like… nothing."

"You only felt this around the other guys?" Cole asked slowly.

Lily nodded, and then glanced back with a worried expression. "And then you…"

"What about me?"

"It's not there. The feeling. It's not even nothing like the leader guy. With you, something's missing."

Fearfully, her eyes rose to meet his. "Why is it missing?"

He blinked, confused beyond words. "I-I don't know."

Brow furrowing, she nodded and looked away.

Cole stared at the back of her tousled head, feeling like things had officially moved so far off the reservation, he wasn't certain how to even begin processing them anymore.

"How'd you fix my shoulder, Lily?"

Not turning around, she shrugged.

"Had you ever done anything like that before?"

She shook her head. "Made me feel funny, though."

"How?"

Biting her lip, she turned back. "Quivery. Like, if I don't really try to stop them, there's all these tiny rabbits running around crazy inside." She paused, her face tightening with concentration. "But if I think about putting them in little cages, it starts getting better."

She glanced up at him. "Do you think they came from whatever's missing, you know, in you?"

Cole hesitated. Forget the reservation. Earth would be hard to pinpoint right now.

"I'm not sure," he answered.

Apprehensively, she returned to watching the gap in the tarp.

"Am I crazy?" she asked softly.

He closed his eyes.

"Cole?"

"Only if I am too."

She looked back, confused.

"You glow when I look at you," he confessed. "Like there's diamonds sparkling in your skin. And the guy you said felt like nothing glowed too. But..." He paused, thinking back. "But not the same way. The glow didn't seem the same around him as it does you." He grimaced as her eyebrows climbed. "I don't know how to explain; I haven't seen anything like this before."

She stared at him. "I'm *glowing*?"

He shrugged a shoulder awkwardly. "A bit. At least to me. But I think it's *only* to me. The cops didn't seem to notice it on the other guy, and–" He cut off, censoring himself on the subject of Vaughn. "And neither has anybody else. But just like you healing me, I saw that guy do some pretty impossible stuff, so..."

Cole glanced to her again. "But you'd never done anything like that before," he said, half-questioning. "And you never saw anybody do something like it either?"

She shook her head. He sighed.

"So we're both crazy," Lily offered, a ghost of a smile pulling at her lips.

He paused, taken back by the attempt at a joke. "Yeah," he replied, grinning in return. "Guess so."

The tentative humor in her eyes lingered for a moment, and then faded as she looked back at the gap beneath the tarp.

"I wish Ashley was here," she whispered.

He didn't know what to say.

A bump shuddered through the truck, and then the furniture shifted as the vehicle headed along a small incline. Cole glanced up. The tops of hotel buildings sped past, and highway signs for food and gas flew by faster than he could read. With careless force, the truck rocked to a stop and then turned, leaving the off-ramp behind.

Stores and fast food restaurants zipped by, and when they reached a stoplight, he ducked lower, wary of neighboring cars. As the light switched to green, the driver whipped the truck around a corner and then came to an abrupt halt next to a gas station pump.

The music cut off sharply as the engine died, and then the door squeaked open. Still whistling the last song on the radio, the driver strolled around the front of the truck.

Cole held his breath and clenched Lily's shoulder to keep her still. He needn't have bothered; the little girl was paralyzed, her eyes locked on the space between the truck and the thin tarp covering them.

The man's flannel-covered chest came into view. With a thunk, the fuel door flipped open, and a moment later, a nozzle clattered into place. A voice over the loudspeaker instructed the driver at pump seven to pay inside when he was finished, and the man muttered sarcastically in reply.

Moments passed. Still whistling, the man yanked out the nozzle, and then swore when gas splattered his boots. Shoving the nozzle back into the pump, he strode toward the station to pay.

Rising carefully, Cole scanned the area beyond the truck. "Come on," he whispered to Lily, seeing no one. Pushing back the tarp, he swung his legs over the tailgate and then dropped to the ground. Turning, he reached for Lily.

"What in the world are you *doing*?"

The cry made him freeze. One hand suspended in startlement over her quilted purse, an elderly woman gaped at them from behind her plastic-rimmed glasses. "Don't you know that's dangerous? What are you thinking, putting a child back there?"

Drawn by the shouting, the truck's owner emerged from the station while others turned toward the commotion.

Quickly, Cole grabbed Lily under her arms and hefted her to the ground.

"What the hell?" the man yelled, racing toward them. "Get away from my stuff!"

Lily's hand crushed in his fist, Cole ran.

The old woman shrieked for someone to call the police. For a hundred yards, the driver's footsteps pounded after them, and then the man seemed to realize he was leaving the truck with his stuff. Cars flew past as the two of them tore down the sidewalk and then dashed into a strip mall parking lot. Mothers with strollers stared as he and Lily raced by, while a group of frat boys shouted encouragement for them to keep going.

Dodging around a gaggle of teenage girls outside a shoe store, Cole glanced over his shoulder. They'd run a few blocks, and no one had bothered to follow. Contrary to the old woman's demands, the cops apparently hadn't been called either.

Running a hand over his hair, he slowed and scanned their surroundings as he tried to catch his breath. Across the street, a bank clock briefly flashed the time before switching to a vague approximation of the temperature. Though the clock confirmed his suspicion that it was before noon, not a single sign on the road gave the name of the city, or even the state.

He needed to think. More than that, he needed to figure out where they were. In his gratitude at escaping the forest, he hadn't paid attention to the direction the truck traveled, and as a result, they could be anywhere.

Cole grimaced, needs and necessities running around in his mind. His head was pounding from a lack of real sleep, and his stomach was grouchily reminding him of the absence of meals since lunch yesterday. A newspaper could probably help identify where they were, but until they found one, he really had to do something about the food situation.

Rubbing his neck, he gave Lily a tired smile and started walking. The shoe store backed up against yet another strip mall, and as he circled around the edge of the building, a restaurant came into view. A local dining spot with a shingled roof and faded siding, the place didn't seem popular. The parking lot was nearly empty.

"You hungry?" he asked Lily.

She nodded, still watching the street behind them.

Echoing the motion, he checked around again and then headed for the restaurant.

A greasy smell hung in the air outside the door, and when they entered, the odor increased. Gray sunlight filtered through the blinds and sapped the color from the country décor crowding every spare inch of the walls. A television hung behind the breakfast bar near the entrance, and farther inside, empty booths and tables filled the remaining space.

From her post by the cash register, a waitress looked up as they entered, examining and dismissing them with a single glance before returning to her gossip magazine. Following the directions to find his own seat, printed on the handwritten sign taped to the door, Cole ignored her and headed for a spot with a decent view of the roads.

At a faintly sticky table, Cole pulled out his wallet and flipped it open, quickly counting the cash inside. Though still damp from the river, the bills would be sufficient to at least grant them a meal.

He looked up to see Lily eyeing him nervously. "It's okay," he told her, and then jerked his chin at the menus pinned between the ketchup and mustard bottles. "What do you want?"

Lily was still examining the menu when the waitress sauntered up with two glasses of water and set them down without a word. Wondering briefly how she kept her job, Cole skimmed the menu and then ordered a cheeseburger.

"You?" the waitress asked Lily.

"Blueberry pancakes, please."

The woman walked away.

"She hates this place," Lily murmured.

"Probably," Cole agreed. He hesitated and then continued, feeling vaguely crazy for asking. "She look okay though? Not... weird or anything?"

Lily shrugged. "Like nothing, I guess." She paused. "Like that one guy."

He could hear the wary question in her tone. "She doesn't look like him to me," he said.

Cole glanced back at the waitress, his brow furrowing. It didn't make sense, but he hoped the fact she didn't look like the glowing men or whatever Lily saw was a good thing. "You want to stay?"

"I'm pretty hungry," Lily admitted, seeming torn.

He nodded. "Me too."

Lifting his glass, he took a sip and then steadily began draining the water, thirst hitting him in full force. In moments, the liquid was gone. He set the glass back on the table, and saw Lily finishing her drink as well.

She gave him a small smile, looking slightly less pale as she put the cup down. Her gaze drifted to the condiments, and when she spotted the crayons tucked beside the menus, her eyes went wide.

He looked back to the street, working to form anything resembling a plan. Obviously, they needed somewhere to hide. Somewhere away from the cops until he could figure out the glowing men, his adoptive parents, and the little girl doodling flowers on her paper placemat. He had some cash, though it wouldn't get them far, and he knew using the family credit card wouldn't be a good idea. Not if he wanted to stay off Robert and Melissa's radar.

Travis.

His thoughts slowed, examining the idea from every angle while trying to determine if the epiphany was brilliance or suicide. Travis was an amateur anarchist in paradise, merrily damning the man from the comfort of his trust fund. His disregard for anything smacking of authority or propriety was a large part of why Cole liked him, and he'd jump at the chance to be involved in something that looked like a conspiracy of ludicrous proportions. Glowing kids? People with superpowers? Cole shook his head. Even with all that stripped away, the other details were more than juicy enough to interest the guy. Knowing Travis, he'd probably just ask for blogging rights when this was finally over, relishing the chance to broadcast the conspiracy to the world.

But Robert, Melissa, and Vaughn had all been ridiculously convincing imposters and, again with the movies, he knew how that plot line usually ran. Everyone would be in on it, and after he trusted Travis, the aliens or the secret government agency or whatever would arrive to brainwash Cole too.

He grimaced. Life wasn't a movie, and Hollywood was a poor guide to reality. He couldn't keep running with a little kid, hoping he was the only one who could see her glow and that the men who killed Vaughn didn't have any friends. They needed help, and Travis was the best – and only – option.

Exhaling, he watched the traffic, trying to think of the next move. Once he knew where they were, he could call Travis and have him come pick them up. Or a bus might be an option. And as for the risk of involving the guy, Lily apparently saw all the bad people who didn't glow and thought Cole looked weird besides. If they were careful, maybe she could tell if Travis was one of the conspirators too.

Cole struggled not to roll his eyes at himself. Crazy or not, he was certainly starting to sound that way.

He glanced to Lily, and then froze at the sight of tears sliding down her cheeks.

"Lily?"

She set down the crayon, though her other hand lingered over the flowers she had drawn. Gritting her teeth, she closed her eyes, fighting the tears.

Uncertainly, he reached across the table and rested a hand on top of hers.

A moment passed, and then the waitress arrived. Eyeing them both as he pulled his hand from the girl's, the woman deposited the plates and then walked away.

Watching the woman, Cole's mouth tightened and then he turned back, nodding to the food. Giving Lily a smile, he picked up the cheeseburger and took a bite.

Bad service or not, the food was delicious, though he realized hunger probably skewed his judgment. Forcing himself not to inhale the burger, he mentally ran through the contents of his wallet while evaluating the possibility of ordering at least two more.

Lily made a choked noise and her fork landed among her pancakes with a splat. Alarmed, he looked up, and then followed her gaze.

Surrounded by blinking headlines, a news update played across the television. The sound was muted, but the closed captioning compensated with machine-gun rapidity.

Multiple murders. Arson. Kidnapping. The words flashed beneath the images on the screen, all of which he recognized.

After all, he'd just been there.

The camera crew hovered over the farmland from the omnipotent view of their helicopter. On the ash-covered yard, emergency crews surrounded the farmhouse rubble, and near the drive, he could see coroners offloading body bags from gurneys into their vehicles.

Ashley's picture appeared in the corner of the screen, her smiling face incongruous with the horrors displayed below. Staring at it, he missed the first words of the closed captioning, glancing down only in time to catch the phrase 'police suspect'. More text followed, telling of information found at the scene, all pointing to a girl with a heavy drug habit and an increasingly paranoid mind bent on murder for the sake of saving her sister from the plot she perceived.

He stared, dumbstruck as Lily's picture replaced Ashley's. The authorities didn't seem to know either girl's name, but at the sight of her photograph, he heard Lily whimper.

The closed captioning scrolled on, becoming more damning with every inconceivable line. Police believed the older girl may have been in a relationship with her drug dealer, a young white male between the age of eighteen and twenty-five with a medium build and brown hair, who authorities considered armed and dangerous. Suspicion now pointed to the two splitting up and going into hiding, with the younger girl left in the possession of the dealer. Evidence indicated that although the elder sister suspected sexual abuse and exploitation of the little girl was the motivation for the dealer's insistence upon being the one to retain the child, she was too dependent on the drugs he provided to do more than comply.

Shaking, Cole tried and failed to tear his eyes from the screen. The newscasters listed hotlines to call if anyone sighted the suspects, and then blithely segued into a discussion of the increasing crime rate. He couldn't breathe, and he didn't know whether to throw up or break something. His hands ached and distantly, he realized his fingers were clenched on the chair back so hard his knuckles had gone white.

"Why are they saying those things?" Lily whispered.

He couldn't bring himself to look at her, not with the rage he felt on his face. If he'd had any doubt the police and the men who did this were siding together, it had just been summarily destroyed. The story was too sensational, too grotesque. In hours, if not sooner, it'd be all over the country, and then every soccer mom in America would be keeping an eye out for the little girl, all to save her from the bastard they'd seen on TV.

His gaze slid to the waitress, but the woman was still engrossed in her gossip magazine. No one else occupied the restaurant, and for the moment, the television was plastered with commercials for the latest miracle cure from the pharmaceutical industry.

They had to get out of here.

Fumbling his wallet from his pocket, he tossed a twenty on the table. "Come on," he said to Lily.

Not waiting, he headed for the exit with the girl on his heels.

"Thanks," he called to the waitress as he pushed open the door. "I left the money on the table. Keep the change."

As she glanced over to check if the cash was actually there, he hurried out into the sunlight. Circling around the restaurant, he scanned the area and then strode toward the back of another strip mall a few hundred yards away. The burger was a lump of lead in his stomach, and the news report kept looping in his mind.

Somehow, the glowing bastards must suspect Lily was alive. And since they needed one of the girls for reasons he couldn't begin to comprehend, they were doing everything they could to locate her. They hadn't found any bodies, of course. That must've been what they were looking for in the ravine. So now they doubted if Lily was dead.

And as a result, he and the kid were screwed.

Busses were out. Trains. Taxis. Everything. They had to get underground fast, and he couldn't think of another way to do it, besides calling Travis and then hiding till the guy could arrive. But that presented a problem, because everywhere was now filled with people who'd want his head on a platter, and who'd happily deliver Lily to the bastards who'd just murdered her sister.

Partway down the alley between two stores, he stopped.

They'd killed Ashley. They'd blown her up, and lost over half a dozen people in the process.

So why have the public chase someone who was dead?

The lump in his stomach wanted to rise as the realization hit him.

They didn't know who'd saved the girls, but they wanted to make sure that when the soccer moms turned him in, the authorities could claim he was as deeply implicated as anyone. And even if somehow he was cleared of the drug charges, even if someone proved he hadn't wanted to hurt the little girl, the cops could hold him forever as a material witness to everything Ashley'd allegedly done. The glowing bastards could retrieve him at their leisure, and Lily would be so long gone by then, it'd be laughable.

At which point they'd realize he was the same guy they'd killed Vaughn to find.

And then things would *really* get interesting.

Running a hand over his hair, he glanced toward the end of the alley. From the logo painted on the cinderblock walls, he could tell they were next to a grocery store. Cars and minivans lined the parking lot, and people with carts were everywhere. The store faced a busy street, across which lay another shopping center.

He sighed. They should've kept hiding in the truck.

"Okay," he said to Lily. "Do me a favor? Pull your hood up."

Lily complied, tucking her dark hair inside and then eyeing him from the oversized concealment of the sweatshirt.

He nodded. It wasn't exactly cold out, though the spring weather still had a bite. People might look at them strange because she was so bundled, but at least they wouldn't see her face and then run screaming for the cops.

"Hey kid?"

Cole nearly jumped out of his skin. Trying to hide his startlement, he turned to the man paused at the rear entrance of the alley. A businessman by his apparel, the guy lowered his cell phone, regarding them with concern.

Lily's grip on Cole's hand tightened. "Bad man," she whispered, her voice breaking in fear. "Bad, bad, bad…"

The man's gaze snapped between them with lightning speed, and though innocent bewilderment showed on his face, something almost predatory flashed through his eyes.

"You okay there, son?" the man asked, walking toward them.

Letting out a squeak, Lily retreated.

Heart pounding, Cole waved dismissively. "Yep, just fine, thanks," he called, starting toward the opposite end of the alley as his spiking blood pressure made his head start to ache.

"You don't look fine," the man said, moving a bit faster to catch up. "Just hang on a second. Are you in some kind of trouble?"

Cole took off running, Lily in tow.

Fleeing the alley, he pulled her with him as he raced into the busy parking lot. Cars skidded to a stop as the two of them darted across the lanes and horns blared in their wake. At the noise, people turned and stared, but no one moved to intervene. The sidewalk came into sight, with the road beyond, and hurriedly, Cole risked a glance over his shoulder.

The man was right behind them.

Clenching Lily's hand, Cole charged into traffic. Tires squealing, a truck swerved madly to avoid them, only to sideswipe the man coming behind. Slamming into the truck, the businessman rebounded and crashed to the ground.

Across the congested street and into a service drive, Cole ran. Garbage bins lined the wall to their right, and briefly, he considered knocking them down to block the guy's way. But there wasn't time. As he looked back, he saw the man staggering to his feet, rage twisting his face. Ignoring the baffled truck driver, the guy barreled after them.

Cole blanched and fought for extra speed as he and Lily bolted into a shopping center parking lot. Cars were everywhere, surrounded by an impenetrable wall of shops on three sides, and more stores speckled the lot like islands in the vehicular sea. Lily was panting for air behind him, her feet stumbling as she tried to keep up, and his stomach churned with nauseated adrenaline. Endless city stretched out before them, filled with nothing helpful.

Dodging through the lanes, he glanced over his shoulder again.

The man had left the service drive.

A red sports car flew between two parked minivans directly ahead and Cole skidded to a panicked stop, yanking Lily back before she could rush past him. The wind of the vehicle's passage buffeted him, the side mirror flying past only inches from his leg, and the driver didn't so much as tap the brakes as he sped by. The car whipped through the lanes and then screeched to a halt outside a café at the edge of the parking lot. Throwing the door open and leaving the engine running, the driver clambered out and then stormed into the coffee shop with a drink in hand.

Incredulously, Cole's eyes went from the driver to the car and back.

Shoving open the café door, the man marched up to the barista and then slammed the drink down, splattering coffee all over the counter. Pointing to the drink as if its existence was an affront, the man began yelling thunderously.

Cole rushed for the car.

"What're you doing?" Lily cried, her hood falling back and her sleeves flapping as he dragged her after him.

He propelled her toward the open door. "Get in!"

She scrambled across the black leather seats.

With a last glance to the customer in the coffee shop and the man racing after them, Cole jumped inside and slammed the door.

Two stolen cars in twenty-four hours.

He scoffed and threw the gearshift into drive.

Chapter Six

———◆———

The train lurched and Ashley opened her eyes. Beneath the platform at the back of the grain car, she felt the wheels shudder as the engineer applied the brakes, and the resultant squealing cut through the roar that had filled her world for hours.

She'd been sleeping. Dreams flitted through her memory, barely more than flashes of garish image and color, and hastily, she pushed them away. She didn't want to remember. It was bad enough that the world around her hadn't yet proved a dream.

Squinting into the wind whipping past the train, she wrapped her arms tighter around the ladder on the side of the small platform and looked around. Mountains dominated the eastern horizon beneath the blazing noonday sun, and beyond the train cars ahead, she could make out the beginnings of a city. The scrub-brush-covered terrain nearby was flat, though, and the city skyline looked like nothing she'd seen in any of Jonathan's travel books.

She had no idea where she was.

Fear bubbled up at the realization, with fire on its heels.

Panicking, she fought to hold the flames back, and then gasped when she felt them start to fade. Buoyed by the shred of victory over the impossible, she concentrated on bundling every scrap of them down into a tiny ball in her core, and then squished them together even harder.

The heat dissipated. The fires vanished almost entirely. Her heart pounded and trembling shook her as adrenaline drained away. She'd stopped them. A hysterical laugh threatened to emerge at the infinitesimal success, and she swallowed hard to keep herself under control. With shaking hands, she adjusted her grip on the ladder, and tried not to give into fear as the train rolled into the unknown city.

A river traced a sinuous path through the landscape, and bisected the town into lopsided halves. Bridges arched over the riverbanks and the sluggish strip of blue-brown water in between. On the eastern side, a few buildings struggled to approach skyscraper status, though most of the city petered out around five or six stories high.

Gradually, the tracks slid between older brick buildings while slowly curving to meet the river's edge. Graffiti covered some of the walls, while others bore painted logos of businesses long since gone. Through gaps between buildings and openings for dead-end streets, she could see people going about their day, paying no attention to the train creeping by.

She pulled her knees in tighter, shivering.

The buildings fell behind as the train moved on through a stretch of abandoned lots that bordered the river. Chain-link fences surrounded the overgrown concrete spaces, and garbage rolled across the ground like tumbleweeds in the breeze. Faded For Sale signs plastered a few fences, and old boxcars rested farther on, overlooking the expanse like weary guards dutifully protecting the rail yard behind them from the encroaching decay.

With a speed that felt slower than walking, the train pulled in among the other freight cars, and then inched to a stop. Carefully, Ashley leaned around the ladder, and then jerked back as the engineer and conductor climbed from the engine.

A voice called from deeper in the yard, unintelligible over the distance. Footsteps crunched over gravel, coming closer, and she scooted back on the platform as far as she could go. A barely audible conversation rose, and then gradually faded.

She hesitated, and then leaned out again. The men were gone. Biting her lip, she looked down the length of cars, wondering if she stayed, if the train would eventually make its way back to her home. But it probably didn't work that way.

Drawing a steadying breath, she worked her stiff legs around and then jumped to the gravel. Aching and tingling, her muscles nearly gave out after so long on the vibrating train, and she gripped the filthy edge of the platform to keep from collapsing.

The numbness retreated. Warily, she glanced around. The rail yard looked empty of life, and the station was quite a distance away. Her stomach grumbled, lodging its own complaint against the hours on the train. Trying to ignore the feeling, she started toward the abandoned lots, hoping to find someplace in the old boxcars to hide.

The engineer stepped from behind a train car, a man in coveralls at his side.

"Told you I saw someone hiding up there," the man told the engineer.

Ashley spun and then came to a sharp halt as the conductor popped out behind her. Glancing between them swiftly, she darted for the open space between the two groups, but the engineer cut her off.

"Hang on there," he said, holding up his hands.

She backed away, nearly tripping over the gravel before bumping against the filthy side of the train.

"Take it easy, kid," the engineer said. "We're not here to hurt you."

She stared at them. The horrible men who shot her had felt funny. Like anyone else, except shadowed somehow. The boy who'd saved them and then died had felt like something was missing in him. And these men felt like Lily, just without her warmth and everything that'd made her wonderful.

The realizations spilled through her head, incomprehensible and insane. People didn't feel like anything. They were just people. And while she'd never really met anyone outside her family and the farmhands, here she was thinking these men felt like nothing, yet like Lily at the same time.

She was losing her mind and wanted to cry.

"I promise you're not in danger from us, okay?" the engineer continued, misreading her expression. "But you can't stay here. Freight hopping's dangerous. There's lots of bad folks who'll hurt you if you stay on the streets like this."

Ashley swallowed hard, trying to keep her eyes on all of them at the same time. The engineer glanced to the other two men, appearing concerned.

"You look pretty rough, kid," he told her gently. "Are you hungry? Can we get you some food or something?"

She shivered. The kindness, the truly genuine-seeming kindness, was almost too much. It was stupid and didn't fit in this new nightmare world she couldn't seem to escape. But her stomach didn't care, and before she could stop herself, she gave him a small nod.

"Come on," he said, gesturing toward the station.

Warily, with her eyes still trying to track all three men at once, she went with them.

"My wife volunteers at a teen shelter here in town," the engineer said as they walked. Her brow furrowed, uncertain what he meant. "It's okay. The people there can help you. And they won't force you to go back to whatever you're running from. Not if you don't want to."

Her gaze dropped away.

The station door swung open, and a security guard stepped into the sunshine. Squinting in the brightness, he waved to the men and then paused to hold the door.

"Who's your friend?" the guard called.

"Oh, just a kid we found hanging out near the trains," the engineer replied. "Gonna hook her up with the wife's shelter."

"That's good of you."

The engineer shrugged. "Just what I'd want someone to do if my girl was in a bad situation."

Nodding peaceably, the guard gave her another cursory glance and then paused. His eyes traced her face. The friendly look in his gaze faded away.

"So you guys get stalled by that fire up north?" he asked, and though his cordial tone remained, it possessed an edge it hadn't before. "I hear it's stopping a lot of travel that way."

Fear quivered through her. He didn't feel like the horrible men from the cliff. And apparently, that meant nothing.

Deep inside, the fires started twisting.

The engineer chuckled. "Oh yeah, stopped for an hour at least. Nearly reached through the phone to strangle Nelson for not rerouting us too, didn't I?"

He grinned at the conductor, who shook his head with a smile.

"Huh," the guard replied.

Ashley's heart pounded, every beat feeding the flames, and her efforts at control floundered at the look in the guard's eyes.

She was going to kill them, and she couldn't stop it.

The security guard studied her. Sweat dripped down her face as she tried to breathe.

His eyes narrowed. "Sorry, Frank," he said to the engineer.

Tears burned in her eyes and fear battered her attempts to contain the heat. Frank was nice. He had a little girl.

And she was going to kill him.

"Are you going to turn yourself in, or do we have to make this difficult?"

Confusion hit her at the guard's words.

"Your friend here is wanted for crimes in Montana," he told the other men, and then looked back at her. "You going to come quietly?"

Shock rained down on the fires and, for an entirely different reason, she found herself unable to breathe.

"What?" she whispered, her voice rough from hours on the train.

His mouth tightened. Grabbing her arm, he spun her around and then yanked her wrists behind her back as he pulled out his handcuffs. She couldn't resist. Couldn't think. Numbed, she ran his words through her head again, trying to find a way in which they made sense.

The guard headed toward the station with her in tow. She stared at the ground. Crimes in Montana. Had they found out about the forest? Did they know what happened there?

She shook her head. People didn't get arrested for blowing up forests. Not like that, anyway. Nobody got arrested for that. Because it was impossible. And insane.

"Wait a minute!" Frank called. "You sure about this? I mean, she's just a kid."

"She's not a kid," the guard replied. "She murdered her whole family last night before burning the house down."

Ice shot through her, freezing everything.

No.

No, that wasn't right.

That…

Her thoughts stuttered to a halt.

Beside her, the guard thumbed on his cell, calling the police and then tugging open the door. She twisted, looking back as he pulled her inside.

Frank's baffled face met her gaze, and then the door slammed closed.

The guard took her into another room, with folding chairs lining the empty walls. Time shuddered and suddenly the police were there. Her hands hurt from the handcuffs and she couldn't think. She was being arrested for murder, and at that, reality had stalled.

Strange words floated around her, talking of rights to attorneys and other things she didn't understand. Outside the station, a police car waited, with railway employees and passersby watching from nearby. An officer pushed her head down as she climbed into the car, and then shut the door, leaving her propped awkwardly on her bound hands.

They felt like nothing. Not like the horrible, shadowed men or the dead boy from the cliff. They felt like Lily. And yet not at all.

Lily…

Streets passed in a blur, filled with colors and lights and people without faces. Emptily, she stared, barely noticing the city shift between the blinks of her eyes.

She was being arrested for the murder of…

Unbalanced, she rocked as the car came to a stop. The door opened and a policeman drew her out.

She shivered from the cold. Everything was so cold.

An enormous tan building waited beyond the curb, with metal letters reading Monfort Police Department swimming in and out of focus on its sides. Steps appeared beneath her feet, leading to the building and a green glass door like murky water.

Her eyes lingered on the surface, finding solace there. The world was murky now. And in it, she was drowning.

The silver frames of the glass doors swung wide, opening on a bustle that thundered in her numbed ears. People surrounded her and their noise came with them. Men chained to benches leered at her. Cops answered phones, hung up phones, talked into phones, while nearby officers shouted for information and files.

It was too much.

She couldn't breathe.

The cops took her down a hall. Bright lights overhead and taupe walls. Posters admonishing, guiding, and instructing. Their colors swirled. A door opened. She blinked and time shifted. Paper appeared in front of her. And ink.

With one hand holding hers, the cop rolled her fingertips over the spongy surface, and then across little meaningless boxes on the page. Documenting her. Filing her. Shutting her away in a drawer.

She blinked.

They were leaving the paper behind. Her eyes dwelled on it. This wasn't her. Not her life. This wasn't happening anymore.

Another door. She was seated at a table. The cops chained her handcuffs down. And left.

Silence reigned.

Gradually, her eyes crept up from the metal table to the gray cement walls. A mirror covered one side of the room, and in it, the sliver of barred window behind her showed only sky.

Her gaze dropped to her reflection and then turned away. A pale ghost covered in ash and dirt, with tangled hair and stained clothes, the sight of her own condition only made everything else more real.

Time drifted.

She was being arrested for murder, and she hadn't killed anyone.

But that wasn't true, was it?

A clink echoed in the room. She looked over at the door, watching it swing open. Two men came inside, feeling like nothing and she couldn't find it in herself to care. Stepping back into a corner, the older of the pair crossed his arms over his brown sports coat as he studied her, an unreadable expression in his pale blue eyes.

The younger man sat on the metal chair across from her. "Good afternoon," he said, giving her a measured smile. "My name is Detective Malden. This is Detective Harris. We'd like to ask you a few questions, if you don't mind?"

She watched him, wondering what she was supposed to say.

Unperturbed by her silence, Malden continued. "So how about we start with your name? Could you tell us that?"

"Ashley," she whispered.

He paused, but when her silence remained, he simply nodded. "Okay, Ashley. We can get to last names later. So what can you tell me about last night, Ashley?"

"I didn't..." she started, and then choked on the words.

A moment passed, and he sighed. "Well, what about this? The FBI has your diary, and I'm sorry, but they did have to read it. So we all know what you wrote, and we'll deal with that in a minute. But in the meantime, it might make things go easier for you if you help us find your sister. Get the girl away from your boyfriend before something bad happens."

Her gaze rose, meeting Malden's dark eyes before moving to Harris with numbed incredulity. "What?"

Malden sighed again, but for a heartbeat, Harris' brow furrowed, curiosity flickering through his eyes.

"Your diary," Malden repeated.

"I don't have a diary."

He gave her a tired look.

Trembling, she shook her head. "I don't," she repeated. "I don't have a diary. Or a boyfriend. I don't know what you're talking about!"

Her voice broke as she finished.

"What happened last night, Ashley?" Harris asked quietly.

She turned to him, clinging to the lack of accusation in his tone like a lifeline. "I don't *know*," she cried, pleading for him to understand.

"Is there anything you *do* know that could help us?"

She choked again, the memories hurting more than the quiet urging in his voice. "I just… they… I didn't–"

"Where's your sister, kid?" Malden interrupted wearily. "At *least* help us with that."

Ashley stared at him. "She's dead."

The last shred of cordiality melted from Malden's face as he looked away. Behind him, Harris grimaced.

"You realize you're going to be charged as an accessory to her murder," Malden growled.

Gasping, she struggled to find the words amid the lack of air in the room. "But I didn't *do* that. She fell. I tried to reach her but I–"

"Save it," Malden snapped, and she flinched at his tone. "The FBI has your diary in your own hand, documenting all your plans. You sold the girl out for sex to your drug dealer boyfriend and murdered your whole family. There's blood all over your clothes, for pity's sake. Arson investigators will find out how you burned the house down and between the trafficking, the fire, and the murders, you're not going to see daylight for the rest of your life. So cut the victim act. Where's the girl's body?"

She couldn't breathe. "I didn't do that…"

"Whose blood is on your clothes then?"

Dazedly, she looked down. Dried blood stained the left leg of her jeans.

"Mine."

He scoffed, pushing away from the table and then crossing the room. Behind him, Harris continued watching her. Reaching over, Malden knocked on the door and then stepped back as the officers on the other side opened it.

"Take her to a holding cell while we call the feds and see how soon they can get her out of here," Malden ordered.

The cops nodded and then moved aside as Harris and Malden left. Ashley stared after them, barely resisting when the officers hauled her to her feet.

As they removed her from the room, Malden turned, talking into his phone. Harris jerked his head at the stairs, and his unreadable gaze tracked her as the cops started down the hall.

"I didn't kill them," she said to the older man, trying one last time to make him understand. "I didn't. Please. I didn't..."

Her pleas went unanswered as both detectives walked away.

———◆———

"Okay, thanks," Malden said, and then hung up the phone. "That was Rawlings. FBI will be here in a few hours to pick her up."

Harris glanced across their adjoining desks, and then went back to reading the case file.

"'Great news, Scott! Thanks!'" Malden parodied, and then eyed him skeptically. "Care to share what's up, John? You've been real quiet since we talked to her."

Harris didn't answer, his gaze tracking across the words of the report for the hundredth time. Nine dead. Ten if you counted the little kid, though that was unverified. A drug dealer, a kidnapped girl, and an addict with mental problems who documented her whole plan down to the order and method she'd use to kill each person in the house.

"Anything about that seem off to you?" he asked.

"Besides the fact she looks like she's coming down from a world-class bender?"

A grin flickered across his face at Malden's typical acerbic humor. "Besides that, yes."

"Seems pretty straightforward to me. As much as can be, anyway."

Harris shook his head, setting the folder down. "Did you see the way she reacted when you mentioned the diary? I'd swear she'd never heard of it before."

"You did read the part about mental instability, right?"

"Yes," he answered tiredly. "But I still can't get over this sense she..."

He grimaced, uncertain what he was trying to say.

"Is probably trying to play us," Malden finished. "Junkies'll say anything, John. You taught me that. Remember the guy on Gibson Street? Exactly like her. Covered in blood from that bar fight and still swore on the Bible he'd been home sleeping the entire time."

Harris sighed. "Something just seems off."

Malden gave him a smile. "Come on. Let the feds handle it. She's their mess to clean up anyway."

Harris nodded, though his heart wasn't in it. The addict on Gibson had been one thing. Clear, obvious, simple. This felt like none of those things, and no matter how many times he read the report, he couldn't manage to convince himself otherwise. Something was wrong here.

And he had no idea what it could be.

———————◆———————

The sports car roared down the interstate as though the distance ahead was an insult.

Hours before, they'd left town at the speed of light, and now the highway signs displaying distances to larger cities were finally starting to look familiar. Swiftly calculating based on the miles to Salt Lake City, Cole eased his foot from the accelerator and sighed in relief. It wasn't as bad as he'd feared. They actually weren't that far from Monfort.

From the corner of his eye, a white car in the rearview mirror looked like a cop, and he tensed. The sedan rolled by, and the old man driving it didn't turn from the road as he passed. Exhaling, Cole worked to calm down, while trying not to think about LoJack and all the other tracking devices out there. But those things took time. If he was lucky – insanely lucky – they'd be able to leave the vehicle and get to Travis' before the police had the chance to hunt the car down.

He glanced at Lily. The girl looked perpetually worried. Her life had shattered less than a day ago and thus far the situation hadn't improved. Trembling, she watched the world outside the window as though waiting for it to bite her.

"Lily?"

She flinched, and then looked at him fleetingly before returning her wide-eyed gaze to the highway.

"You knew that man was bad," he said, half-questioning.

She didn't respond.

"What'd he look like to you?"

"Same as the others," she answered, her voice barely audible. She tensed as a minivan passed.

He grimaced, fighting the urge to return the pedal to the floor. Miles from Lily's home, and they still found the two of them. The bastards really were everywhere.

The highway dragged on, with every mile potentially hiding a police car. Eventually, the Rio Dulce river twisted into view to the west, hinting that they were finally nearing town, and when road signs finally started to advertise exits to Monfort, he took the first off-ramp onto the old state highway on the outskirts of the city. In the seat next to him, Lily turned her gaze to the floor, looking for all the world like a smaller version of her sister.

Shaking his head, he pushed away the pain of the memories of last night. He'd gotten the kid out. That was worth something. And like his parents or Lily's father, lingering over Ashley's death wouldn't fix the fact she was gone.

At the intersection of the ramp and the old highway, he paused. Far to the right, a group of storage buildings lurked. He almost turned toward them before realizing that, in the middle of the day, staff would probably be monitoring the property. A bright red sports car wouldn't go unnoticed for long. To the left, a construction site waited. Bulldozers hulked by dirt piles and massive cement pipes, but for the moment, the workers appeared to be elsewhere.

He went left. Service roads, barely more than tracks through the dirt, circled the construction site. Glancing around, he turned off the state highway and, when they were out of the sight of the main road, he pulled over and then shut off the engine.

"Come on," he said to Lily.

She climbed out without a word.

Circling around the car, he took her hand. Giving her what he hoped was an encouraging smile, he started toward town.

Scraggly grass covered the ground beyond the construction site, interspersed with clumps of dry bushes. Their shoes crunched over rocks and dirt as they crossed the seemingly endless distance to the city, and when they finally drew near Monfort, he and Lily were so coated in dust, he doubted anyone would have recognized the kid even if they saw beneath her hood.

Gargantuan mansions edged the town on the northernmost side, and verdant grass surrounded each house, clearly showing where the mottled countryside ended and the property lines began. Tall wrought-iron fences sealed the manors away from the well-kept roads, and ornamental garden work screened the majority of the homes from casual view.

With a hesitancy he knew looked painfully suspicious, Cole crept down the street. His gaze swept windows and yards, searching for the first sign of a glowing person or someone who made Lily squirm. At this time of day, the neighborhood was quiet, and though gardeners occupied several yards, no one looked up as he and the girl walked by.

Travis' house came into view around a curve of the street. An Italianate monstrosity complete with tower, the home had always reminded Cole of nothing more than an enormous version of the Addams family's mansion, albeit with a better paint job. Motioning Lily to stay behind the bushes lining the fence, Cole walked up to the gates and then pushed the buzzer. A moment passed before the intercom hissed.

"Can I help you?"

"Is Travis home?"

"May I tell him who is calling?"

"Cole."

For a brief moment, there was silence, and he struggled not to imagine glowing men rallying behind the manor doors. Then the gates swung open.

Taking Lily's hand, Cole started toward the house, while the little girl watched the gates clank shut behind them. He didn't look back, hoping his nervousness didn't show through. The stone drive swept up to the mansion in a lazy curve, with trimmed bushes lining either side. Even though it was still technically school hours, Travis' truck was parked in front of a garage the size of a middle-class home, next to several other vehicles Cole could only assume belonged to the guy's parents.

At the broad double doors of the entryway, he paused, and then jerked his chin at the bushes nearby. "Stay down," he whispered to Lily. "They feel wrong to you, I want you to run, okay?"

Her brow furrowed. "What about you?"

"I'll be right behind you."

She regarded him, and he knew she could see through the lie. If anything was off when that door swung open, he was probably toast. But maybe he could slow them long enough for her to get away.

"Lily…"

Face set stubbornly, she glared, but she slipped into the bushes.

He drew a steadying breath and knocked. A heartbeat later, one side of the double doors swung open, revealing a butler standing impassively beyond.

"Hi," Cole said.

"You called for Master Travis?" the butler said, the tone somehow a statement while still being a question, with an ounce of accusation thrown in for good measure.

"Um, yeah. Is he here?"

Footsteps thudded on the stairway and before the butler had the chance to speak, Travis' voice echoed through the foyer.

"Cole?"

Jumping down the last steps, Travis crossed the wide foyer and patted the butler companionably on the shoulder. "It's fine, Preston. It's Cole, for Pete's sake. Just leave us alone and go polish something, will you?"

With a conspicuous lack of expression, the man turned and disappeared through the foyer archway to be lost somewhere in the house.

Leaning on the doorframe, Travis watched the butler's retreating back with a grin. Cole's eyes flicked down to Lily questioningly. She shook her head.

"I swear my mom's got that guy wound tighter than a fake Rolex," Travis commented as he turned to Cole. "She should be banned from watching the news. It just makes her crazy." His grin widened. "So what gives? I thought you were out of town?"

"Huh?"

Travis shrugged. "They said at school this morning there'd been some sort of family emergency. Real middle-of-the-night panic kind of thing. So what's the deal?"

For a moment, words escaped him. "My parents are out of town?"

Travis nodded. "Uh, yeah…" he said, clearly confused. "According to the school anyway. I mean, it's not like I went to check or anything, but they asked for volunteers to take notes for you, so I kind of assumed…" He shrugged again. "What? They leave without you?"

Cole didn't answer, trying to process the new information. With Vaughn gone… had Robert and Melissa been killed too? Had they run? They weren't on the same side as the glowing men, whatever that meant, but…

What the hell was going on?

He pushed the thoughts away and forced himself back to the present. Travis wasn't glowing and Lily didn't feel anything off about him, or hopefully she'd already be running. They needed help, and he had to trust someone.

"Can we come in?" he asked.

"We?"

He motioned to Lily and she stepped out of the bushes. Confusion and surprise filled Travis' face in equal measure as he looked between them. Bending slightly, he peeked into the shadows of her hood, and suddenly his expression changed.

"Holy–" His eyes went to Cole. "Dude, is that…" His voice

dropped to nearly a whisper. "Is that the kid from TV?"

Cole hesitated. "It's not what you think."

"My mom's been watching that crap all day," Travis continued, staring at Lily, who was inching behind Cole to hide from the scrutiny.

"Can we come in?" Cole repeated.

Travis tore his eyes from Lily and then he shrugged. "Yeah, sure."

Shutting the door behind them, the guy looked between Cole and the girl again. "So what's the deal? You into kids now or something?"

Cole gave him a flat look. "Very funny."

Travis raised his hands defensively. "Sorry."

"We need your help."

For a moment, Travis looked tempted to make another joke, and then thought better of it. "Um-kay," he answered. He glanced around and then jerked his head toward the marble staircase. "We can talk upstairs."

Cole took Lily's hand and followed as he wracked his brain to come up with a way to explain everything that didn't sound psychotic.

He drew a gaping blank.

Travis' room would have given Melissa a heart attack. Mountains of laundry covered the floor, while posters plastered every square inch of the navy walls. Dirty towels blockaded the bathroom and a massive television occupied a corner, complete with every video game console known to man shoved haphazardly into the shelving below. Speakers hung from each corner of the room, and an enormous brown leather couch took up one wall. Half-buried beneath the spiral stairway leading up to the tower, a few lonely textbooks huddled, nearly obscured by the wrinkled clothes barricading them in.

"So..." Travis prompted as he shut the door.

Halfway to lowering himself onto the couch, Cole paused and glanced at Lily, suddenly uncomfortable with the idea of discussing the nightmare of the past twenty-four hours in front of her. "You got a game she can play? Something nonviolent?"

Travis' brow furrowed, but he headed toward the game systems. "Uh…" he said, clearly struggling to think of one. "I might still have that copy of Penguin Rally my Aunt Mauve forced on me last year."

Digging through the games, Travis retrieved the disc and then inserted it into the console.

"Go on," Cole told her. Lily regarded him suspiciously. "Please?"

She hesitated a moment longer, and then went.

Eyes tracking the girl, Travis came back and sat on the arm of the couch. "Okay, so…" he prompted again, impatience tingeing his tone.

"I watched her family get killed last night, Travis," Cole said, trying to keep his voice beneath the obnoxiously cheery game music.

Travis' eyebrows rose.

"After I went home yesterday, my parents brought over a counselor. You know how they do."

Travis nodded derisively.

"Well, Melissa did her whole mothering act and told me to go to bed, but once I was upstairs, I heard them arguing. The counselor was giving orders and threatening them. He left, I went down to ask about it, and… they attacked me."

"They *what?*"

"Melissa tried to pin me while Robert tried to smash my head in with a bookend."

Incredulity filled Travis' eyes, but the beginnings of a smile pulled at his mouth.

"So I ran," Cole continued, ignoring the expression. "I took Robert's car and went after the counselor, just to get some answers. But when I finally caught up to him, these other guys drove up. Vaughn – the counselor – he shoved me into some bushes, and then the others got out of their cars and started interrogating him."

He paused. "They were looking for me. And then they killed him because he wouldn't tell them where I was, and because someone called and ordered them to leave, so they didn't have any more time for questions.

"Apparently, they'd been looking for her family too," he said, jerking his chin toward Lily. "They wanted them dead, and last night, they found them. And when I overheard that, I couldn't..." He swallowed, shoving down the memories. "So I followed their cars, but I was too late. Their friends had already started."

Cole looked up at Travis. "They killed her sister, the one the news is saying did all this. And her dad, and everyone else. I managed to get the kid away, but not before they'd murdered all the others. But they saw me. I don't think they got a good look at me, but they're still trying to make everyone think I'm a monster in the hope someone will turn us in.

"They want her for something, Travis. When we were escaping, I heard them say they only needed one of the girls alive.

"And now Robert and Melissa are gone too. I don't know what's going on, but we need a place to hide till I can figure this out. That's where you come in. If you'll help."

For a long moment, Travis stared at him. Efforts at humor flitted around his face, but couldn't seem to find anywhere to land. "You realize this sounds insane."

"You have no idea."

Scoffing, the young man looked toward Lily. "And if it wasn't for the kid sitting there, I'd tell you that was the most whacked out dream I'd ever heard."

Travis paused, regarding the girl. "But just so you know, if you *are* some kind of sick pedophile drug dealer with a kidnapping scheme… this is the worst cover story ever."

Cole said nothing, waiting.

"So how'd you get her away from those guys?" Travis asked curiously.

"The racing video games paid off."

Shrugging an eyebrow, Travis glanced back at him. "And those freaks actually tried to *attack* you?"

He nodded.

"Damn."

Travis fell silent, and in his eyes Cole could see the wheels turning. "But you don't have any idea what this is about?" the boy continued.

He shook his head.

A smile pulled at Travis' mouth. "Damn. This is *crazy*, dude."

Cole nodded again.

"Okay," Travis agreed. "Just so we both know that." His grin widened. "So what'd you need from me in all this?"

"A place to hide. They're looking for her, and maybe me too, and whatever they want–"

"Can't be good," Travis finished.

"Exactly. I've got to figure this out, but with Robert and Melissa gone…"

"So we keep an eye out for them, and if we see them again, we go from there. We can't let those bastards catch the kid, right? So you've got to lay low till they make a move."

He glanced at Travis, hearing copious amounts of first-person shooters and spy games coloring the guy's words. "Okay, so…?"

"You stay here," Travis said as though it was obvious. "That's what you were hoping for, right? So yeah, you hide here. Preston never comes in my room and my parents are morons anyway. As long as we keep my mom from spotting the kid, we'll be fine. Meanwhile, I'll scout around town. Oh, but let me guess… the cops are in on it too?"

"Probably."

Travis shook his head. "Bastards," he said dismissively. "They'd have to be for the news to go on about so much 'evidence at the scene', or whatever it was they said. So we hide from the cops, and you lay low till the freaks resurface. Simple."

Cole watched him. "You really believe me about all this?"

"Like I said," Travis answered, grinning. "Worst cover story *ever*. I'll give you enough credit, dude, that if you were going to lie, you'd come up with something more believable than this. She's your long-lost sister or whatever. Not conspiracies for murder and ridiculous midnight escapes. Plus you both smell like you crawled through a swamp so, I mean… really."

Hesitant relief moved through Cole as though uncertain whether it was in the right place. The whole nightmare was one big game to Travis, but that was fine. And if he was willing to accept Cole's story as believable, so much the better. They could keep operating under the assumption it was just spy high jinks and potentially Cole's lunacy.

There was no reason the guy needed to hear the rest.

He looked over at Lily, who was making every effort to appear engrossed in the idiotic rally racing game, while still glancing toward them every few seconds.

"You think we could get a change of clothes?" he asked. "She's been in her pajamas since this all started."

"Yeah, sure. Ellie's got more than enough to spare. I doubt the little brat'll even notice anything's gone."

Pushing off the couch, Travis headed for the door, only to pause thoughtfully. "So… how do you know I'm not in on it? I mean, this could be more of the conspiracy or whatever."

Lily looked back, her eyes meeting Cole's briefly before returning to the game.

"I don't," Cole admitted.

Travis grinned, obviously enjoying the answer. "Cool," he replied, and then disappeared out the door.

Dropping the controller, Lily crossed to the couch, while behind her, the penguin crashed his rally car into the ice walls with a cartoonish display of disappointment.

"You okay?" Cole asked as she sat down next to him.

"We're staying here?"

"Is that alright? You didn't notice anything weird or…"

She shook her head morosely. "Not like Daddy. Not like the bad men. Not like you." She listed the options. "Just… nothing."

"The way that one guy felt?"

"Or the waitress."

Cole glanced back at the door. Four categories then, in their crazy new worldview. Himself, the glowing men he could see, the bad guys she could see, and Travis and the waitress.

At least the latter group didn't seem to be after them. Hopefully.

Studying her feet dangling off the side of the couch, the little girl sighed. "We're not going home anytime soon, are we?" she whispered, only partly questioning.

He wasn't sure what to say.

"And when Ashley goes looking for me… she won't know where I am."

Cole hesitated. "Ashley's gone, Lily."

She turned to him, almost fearsome certainty in her large eyes. "No, she's not."

He exhaled. "She was killed in the fire," he said carefully. "On the cliff, after those men shot her."

Lily's gaze fell away, her determination dimming slightly. She shook her head. "She just doesn't know how to find me. We got separated and now she's lost. That's all."

Frustration rose in Cole, and he struggled to push it back. He'd gone for months after the robbery imagining his parents were still alive. He couldn't begrudge her a bit of the same, especially since her loss was only a few hours old. And she'd have plenty of opportunities to accept the truth. A lifetime of them.

"We just need to stay here a while," he said. "Till we figure out what to do next. Okay?"

She nodded reluctantly. "He's goofy," she said of Travis. "But he doesn't feel bad."

"That's good."

For a long moment, she was silent. "But I want them back," she whispered. "Daddy, everybody… it's not fair. I want them to come back."

Tears slid from her eyes and her brow furrowed as she fought to keep the emotions at bay.

Hesitantly, he reached over, putting a hand on hers. "It's okay to cry," he offered quietly.

Lily shook her head hard. "Ashley's strong. She'd want me to be strong too. Till we find her. Then everything will be alright."

She trembled, holding the pain inside.

Cole watched her, remembering his ten-year-old self reacting so similarly. *Daddy was strong. He'd want the same from me.*

Pushing the memory away, he squeezed her hand. "You have to let it out, Lily. It's hurting you. Ashley wouldn't want that."

A heartbeat passed, and then she looked up, fear behind the resolve in her shimmering blue eyes. "But it's scary," she whispered. "So much… it's just so…"

He pulled her over and wrapped an arm around her.

"I know," he said as the walls around her grief crumbled and she buried her head in his side. "I know."

Chapter Seven

Hours drifted by. The cell bed creaked when she moved, and she could feel every twist of the metal springs through the thin mattress. Steel bars lined the front of the cell, and cement walls surrounded her on every other side. Across the concrete hallway, a narrow window hugged the ceiling, splintering the light with its own bars.

Shadows crept across the floor, tracking the passage of the last few hours of daylight. The cellblock was cold, and in the oversized sweatpants and shirt the police had provided, she shivered. They'd taken away her clothes upon bringing her to the cells, though they'd let her keep her shoes. Two female officers handed her the sweats and then watched her change with dispassionate eyes, before slipping her jeans and shirt into large plastic bags. Evidence, they'd explained. Because of the blood.

In the next cell, a drunk snored loudly, intermittently breaking the silence. Food had arrived a couple hours before, courtesy of a closemouthed officer who'd slid an orange plastic tray through a slot barely tall enough for a child's arm. Though the drunk had thrown his dinner back immediately, where it now sat in cold lumps on the hallway floor, she'd nearly inhaled the meal, trying to fill the gaping hole where her stomach had been.

And time slid by, filled with snores and silence and a tiny ball of fire quivering inside.

Exhaustion pulled at her as she lay on the scratchy mattress, and memories and sleep interplayed through her mind, creating a reality all their own. In her dreams, the police's story was true. Lily was fine. Missing, not dead, and still out there somewhere, waiting to be found. She could almost see the girl, so innocent and peaceful, her blue eyes twinkling as she smiled.

"It's okay, Ashe. I'm right here. I'm safe."

And then she woke up.

Tears traced paths through the dirt on her cheeks. Pushing away from the rough blankets, she drew her knees to her chest and hugged them tightly. Sniffling, she closed her eyes against the pain while snores echoed off the walls.

She wanted to go home. More than anything else in the whole universe, she just wanted to go home and have everything be alright.

The cellblock door clanked and the lock slammed back with a noise that ricocheted down the hall. Nervously, she looked up.

Two officers came down the hallway and stopped at her cell. While one watched her, the other pulled out a set of keys and then swiftly unlocked the door.

"Time to go," he said.

She rose and walked to the doorway warily. The officer tugged a pair of handcuffs from his belt, and then jerked his chin at her.

Hesitantly, she held out her hands. The cuffs clicked around her wrists.

"This way," he said, starting for the exit and leaving his partner to fall in behind.

She followed, while in the next cell, the drunk woke and began yelling for more food.

Malden glanced up as she stepped through the doors, and then returned his phone to his pocket. Pushing away from where he rested against the wall, Harris paused at the sight of her, and she could see him taking in the redness around her eyes. Blinking, she looked at the floor.

"What's going on?" she asked.

"FBI's here," Malden said shortly.

Her brow furrowed in confusion. "Oh."

"Come on, kid," Harris said, his voice kinder than his partner's had been.

She didn't resist as Malden reached over and grasped her arm, while Harris took the lead in escorting her down the hall. Behind them, the other officers turned to the cellblock and shouted at the drunk, who was steadily tearing his mattress apart.

The halls were a maze of taupe and tile, with archive rooms, storage closets and emergency exits providing the only break in the fluorescently lit monotony. Her sneakers squeaked on the linoleum, and by the time they reached the base of the stairwell, Malden's grip was cutting off her circulation.

A voice echoed from the top of the stairs. "So I'm to understand there was no lawyer present when you questioned the young lady before?"

Her heart stopped beating. The world froze, taking with it all the air.

She knew the voice. She'd heard it the moment after her father died.

"No," she begged as her heels dug into the linoleum, dragging Malden to a halt. Eyes locked on the stairway, she backpedaled. "No, no, no…"

"Quit it!" Malden snapped, trying to yank her forward as she fought to pull away.

Confused, Harris turned around and reached for her other arm.

"No!" she cried.

Heat.

Waves of flame rushing over her hands. Her arms. Her body.

And Malden screamed.

Through a curtain of fire, she looked at Harris as the molten handcuffs fell from her wrists. Tumbled back against the stairs, he stared at her, and then his gaze dropped to his partner.

She looked down.

Bubbling, shiny flesh. Blood everywhere. He was still screaming.

"Oh God," she breathed. "Oh God…"

Her eyes rose to Harris as the flames around her died.

The man was coming. Any moment. He'd be here.

"I-I'm sorry. I–"

Harris fumbled for his gun.

She ran.

Sprinklers kicked to life and showered water down. Slipping on the wet tile, she slid and caught herself on the wall.

Bullets shattered the plaster beside her head.

Gasping, she shoved away and raced for the emergency exit at the end of the next hall. Shouting broke out behind her, and then she slammed into the push bar across the door and stumbled into the sunlight.

Claxons blared. Clutching the banister, she launched herself up the steps and out of the stairwell. Glancing back and forth frantically, she took off down the alley behind the station, and then skidded to a stop at the street. From the main entrance, people were calmly leaving the building. Across the road, others milled about in their designated evacuation places. Drawing a ragged breath, she darted out of the alley, ducked around the corner, and prayed no one saw her as she raced away.

Streets blurred. Sirens howled in the distance, though if they were approaching or not, she couldn't tell. Alleys provided short-lived cover and intersections were a nightmare. People stumbled back and then stared in confusion as she rushed by.

Energy fading, Ashley pushed herself to run faster.

The alleys grew cluttered, and the buildings around them older and more rundown. Passersby mostly ignored her, though a few shouted insults for the police. The words were confusing, but barely had time to register. Sirens still rang, growing closer now she was sure.

She was wearing police department sweats. Their logos were on her legs and chest.

The realization cut through her panic, and then made it grow.

She had to get out of sight.

Stumbling to a halt in the middle of an alley, she looked around anxiously. Shops with bars on their windows lined the road ahead, and brick buildings flanked the alleyway. Graffiti covered the boarded windows to her right, while a wind-ravaged sign advertised a date three years previous for the grand reopening of the famous Plaza Hotel.

She rushed toward the building. The plywood over the nearest window hung loose, and her fingers scrambled to push the covering away. Holding the wood aside awkwardly with one hand, she clambered onto the garbage bin beside the wall, and then hoisted herself over the splintered windowsill.

Dust puffed up as she landed and she coughed, fanning it away. Dim shapes resolved themselves from the shadows, becoming cloth-covered furniture and potted plants long since dead. Against one wall, the half-built remains of a front desk rested beside moldering rolls of carpet, while overhead, cobwebs dangled from the grayed crystals of a chandelier. To her right, a wide stairway swept up to a gallery overlooking the first floor. Light slid through gaps in the wooden coverings on the revolving door to her left, making the dust clouds glitter in the air.

Carefully, she eased the plywood back into place. Still waving at the dust, she inched farther into the lobby, and then froze as the floor sagged alarmingly beneath her feet. Picking her way across the room, she clutched the tarnished brass banister and then crept up the steps, her heart pounding as they creaked and groaned.

Atop the stairway, a gaping space for double doors led to a large room, and past the slats on the windows, deep gold sunlight streamed in. Paint tins and old blankets crowded a corner of the room, and beside the doorway, dented food cans lay scattered beneath a broken ladder. Warily, she walked to the windows to peer through a crack between the boards.

The sun was setting, and purple shadows spread over the streets. The last beams of sunlight reflected in shop windows, and lit on the faces of people walking by.

A cop car drove past.

She jerked back, her heart jumping into her throat.

Without pause, the vehicle continued down the street until it disappeared from view.

Closing her eyes, she exhaled and then turned away from the window and sank to the floor. She couldn't stop trembling. Her lungs burned from running and her muscles ached horribly, but above all, she just couldn't stop trembling.

Malden lay on the floor, his skin peeling and blood everywhere. She could hear his screams echoing in her ears.

Nausea rose and she swallowed hard to keep from vomiting. Squeezing her eyes shut, she smashed the memory into the flames, and bore down on the fires with all her might, trying to crush them into oblivion. Flickering and twisting, they fought for a heartbeat and then retreated, fading into an infinitesimal wisp of flame that refused to go away.

She gasped and then choked on the air. She hadn't meant to hurt him. She hadn't meant to do anything at all.

She just hadn't wanted to die.

Tears slipped from beneath her lids to join the dust on the floor.

The stairs creaked.

Her eyes went wide and she rushed toward the blankets against the far wall.

"Well, look what we have here."

Halfway across the room, she froze, the amused voice dragging her terrified gaze back to its owner. From the doorway, a man regarded her, and he felt wrong. So wrong. Like her father, but darker. Like the men in the forest, but still alive.

Trying not to sob, she shook her head, backing up and then running into the wall.

He chuckled as he strolled into the room. "Here I was thinking

I'd have to give up my cripple hunting and go home empty-handed."
The humor left his eyes. "But then I found you."

Frantic, she lunged for the space between him and the door.

"Stupid little bitch!"

Something slammed into her. Nothing slammed into her. But it
sent her back against the wall like a blow from a two-by-four.

She crashed into the plywood and then plummeted to the
ground.

"You're in my territory and *now* you're going to run? You think
I'm just going to let you get away from me like that?"

Scrabbling at the rough floor, she tried to stand. The horrible,
dark mess of energy around him swelled up, and then crushed in on
her like a vice. Circling her neck and cutting off her air, the impossible
nothing lifted her up and pinned her to the wall.

Her legs kicked ineffectually as he came closer, and his face was
all she could see. His eyes drank in her fear and then he scoffed,
stepping back as the energy around him faded. She tumbled to the
floor.

"Come on, bitch. Make it fun for me."

Gunshots echoed through the room.

Paralyzed, she stared as the man's brow furrowed at her. Confusion twisted across his face and he stumbled forward.

Legs giving way beneath him, he toppled sideways to the ground.

By the doorway, two black men stood, guns in hand and a German
Shepherd the size of a wolf at their side. In stained jackets and jeans,
they watched her, no expression touching their dark eyes.

Hysteria bubbled up and it was all she could do not to scream.
The man had… he'd… and then these two men had…

They felt like the boy who'd died. Something missing. A void where something should have been.

The older of the two made a clicking noise, and immediately, the dog started toward her. Momentarily, it paused by the body, sniffing it, and then continued on.

She couldn't breathe. Small, panicked noises escaped between her clenched teeth as the creature stopped beside her, and her eyes couldn't leave the massive jaws inches from her face.

The dog licked her cheek and then glanced back at its master.

In a smooth motion, the older man tucked the gun behind his back and crossed the room. Ignoring the body, he crouched down in front of her, while the younger man made an aggravated noise.

"Are you alright?" he asked.

She was shaking too hard to speak.

"We're not going to hurt you," he said gently.

Annoyance on his face, the younger man covered the distance between them quickly. "We've got to go."

The man in front of her didn't reply.

Muscles jumping beneath the skin of his jaw, he gripped the man's shoulder. "*Now.*"

Looking back, the older man met his companion's eyes.

"Call Bus," he said evenly. "Tell him to get ready to leave." He paused, returning his attention to Ashley. "And that we've got a guest."

She stared at him, struggling to process the words.

Incredulously, the younger man scoffed. "Are you crazy? You saw the news, right? You know who this is?"

Anguish suffused her. They'd saved her. They'd shot the monster. And now they'd leave because of lies on television.

But the older man just gave him a flat look. "Don't tell me you believe that crap."

Ashley blinked, her gaze going from one of them to the other.

Shaking his head, the young man scowled and then took out his cell phone. Ignoring his companion, the older man turned back to her and held out a weathered hand.

"You're safe with us. I promise."

"Who are you?" she whispered.

"My name is Josiah Carter." He gave her a small smile. "Most folks just call me Carter."

"He…" she started, her gaze flicking to the body and then darting away. "How did he…"

She couldn't finish the sentence, but at her words, Carter paused.

"That's not important right now," he said carefully. "What matters is, you're safe. And we need go." His eyebrow raised, and he nodded toward his hand.

Wide-eyed, she stared between them all. The younger man was snapping orders into his phone, and clearly talking over the protests on the other end. Ignoring them, the dog was snuffling through the blankets industriously.

And Carter just waited.

Trembling, she reached out, taking his hand. Stepping back, he pulled her to her feet and then glanced to his companion. Returning his cell to his pocket, the younger man snagged a rucksack from beneath the garbage on the floor and then shoved the cans of food inside. With a nod to Carter, he took the lead out of the room, with the older man a step behind.

The dog fell in beside her as she followed.

At the alleyway, Carter helped her over the windowsill while the other man watched the street as though waiting for it to attack.

"Paint," Carter said.

A can of spray paint materialized from within the younger man's jacket, and without taking his gaze from the street, he tossed it to Carter, who quickly scrawled a swirling mess of rough graffiti across the plywood on the window.

"Carter…"

The older man glanced back and then turned away swiftly, cursing under his breath. Ashley followed his gaze.

A few dozen yards down the street, amid the evening crowd waiting for a bus, a man stood, his cell phone raised. He paused, clicking something on the cell, and then stuffed the phone into his pocket and started across the intersection toward them.

Carter swore. In a fluid motion, he tossed the paint can into an empty stretch of road and pulled out his gun.

The bullet exploded into and through the can, and in the street, people screamed.

"Let's go," he said to Ashley, grabbing her hand.

The men took off down the alley, and she looked back in shock as Carter pulled her after him. Fury creased the other man's face as panicked bystanders clogged his path.

Moving quickly, the two men wove through alleys and roads with a determination that belied their random path. The last shreds of daylight faded as they traveled, leaving dense shadows that could have been hiding anything. Headlights glared in her eyes as cars swept past, and from street corners, drunks and addicts called out, cursing, begging, asking her to come close. Ducking her face away, she strode faster while at her side the dog kept pace, unwavering.

Brick buildings gave way to dilapidated houses with posters warning of guard dogs. No Trespassing signs hung from splintering doors, and chain-link fences circumscribed every yard. Streetlamps flickered intermittently if they glowed at all and, as the neighborhood passed around her, fewer and fewer houses were lit behind their iron window bars.

Empty lots gradually took the place of homes, though occasional concrete foundations showed where buildings once stood. The darkened street curved, and at the end of the next road, she caught sight of the murky river rippling beneath the city lights. A bridge rose to her right beyond the remnants of the neighborhood and the distant noise of traffic mingled with the rushing waters ahead.

The weathered asphalt ended in two pockmarked posts with a No Trespassing sign dangling on a chain between them. The men stepped over it, leaving the rusted metal admonishment swinging and creaking behind them.

Warily, Ashley followed. A gravel expanse separated them from the river and the massive bridge supports plowed deep into its banks. Beneath the concrete structure, a fire burned in a garbage can, with a dark green van parked close by. The dog loped ahead of her as she walked after the two men, their footsteps loud in the silence.

A gun pushed into her back. In the shadows behind the hood of the van, a man rose and aimed a shotgun at her, while another German Shepherd rounded the vehicle and growled.

Ashley froze, her feet skidding to a stop a dozen yards from the garbage bin. Quivering with her fear, the flames began to surge, and desperately, she fought them down while trying to keep from crying.

"Who the hell are you?" someone demanded behind her.

Carter turned around. "It's alright. She's with us."

By the van, the man with the shotgun eased his grip, but the gun behind her didn't budge. Up ahead, Ashley could see dry amusement cross the younger man's face.

Carter just lifted a brow.

The gun disappeared. Footsteps crunched on the gravel behind her.

A girl circled around, her cold gaze not leaving Ashley. Firelight played over the blonde dreadlocks draping past her shoulders, and caught on the gun in her pale hands. A dark jacket hung to her waist and as she tucked her weapon away, Ashley glimpsed another gun stowed in a holster to one side of her chest.

"Got your message," the girl said to Carter. "Trouble?"

"Feral and Blood."

"Dead?"

"Yes and no, respectively."

The girl grimaced, and then jerked her chin toward Ashley. "Who's this?"

Carter glanced over, and Ashley swallowed nervously. A small grin pulled at his mouth.

"Introductions first, eh?" he said kindly. He nodded to the younger man. "Samson you know. The young lady with the weapons is Spider, and the gentleman by the van is Bus." Humor flitted through his eyes. "Most of us aren't fond of common names. So what do we call you?"

She stared. Crossing to Samson's side, Spider raised an eyebrow at him before returning to watching Ashley. Pushing away from the van, Bus circled the vehicle and left the shadows.

The light caught on white hair and bright blue eyes. She gasped softly, crumbling inside.

And then the illusion ended.

It wasn't Jonathan. Besides the hair and eyes, the two men didn't look remotely alike.

Raggedly, she drew a breath. For a moment, she'd thought...

The old man's brow furrowed at her expression, and he glanced to Carter. Swallowing hard, she turned away, her gaze finding the flames in the garbage can.

For a moment, she'd thought the impossible could be real. She wasn't alone, everything wasn't destroyed and, in some small way, she really could go back home.

And then that hope was gone, and stupid, cold reality crashed into the void. She felt like she was falling, though she wasn't moving at all, and everything in her body was far away. Of their own volition, her eyes tracked the embers floating into the night, while in their own dance, the fires twisted somewhere inside.

Carter made a questioning noise. Dully, she looked away from the blaze, recalling what he'd asked.

Only one answer came to mind.

"Ashe," she whispered.

Carter studied her briefly and then nodded. "Is there anywhere we can take you? Someone you can stay with?"

Numbly, she shook her head. Everyone she'd had left had been at the farm, shot and burned and blamed on her, while the rest lay in ashes at a home she couldn't even recall.

The catalog of the dead scrolled through her mind and, trembling, she closed her eyes. It was too big. Dad being gone. And Rose. Jonathan. The farmhands. Lily. The whole world, barely a day before. It couldn't be allowed to sink in. If she let it, she might not survive.

"We'll find you somewhere."

She looked back at Carter.

"We help people hide," he explained. "It's part of what we do. If you like, we can find a place for you with our friends. Somewhere guys like the one who attacked you today won't find you."

She stared at him, questions trying to rise. Guys like the one who attacked her. With nothing. Or who'd killed her dad. With nothing. And these people could hide her. She could be someplace the monsters wouldn't find her.

Her gaze moved to the others. Their faces painted chiaroscuro by the firelight, they regarded her expressionlessly.

"Who are you people?" she asked.

Carter paused. "We're people who'll help get you away from this mess," he said carefully. "If you want us to."

She hesitated. More questions struggled to surface, but faded into insensibility at the look in the others' eyes. They wouldn't answer. Except for Carter, they didn't seem like they trusted her at all.

But they'd get her away from this. They'd put her someplace safe.

Elation hit guilt, and dissolved into a mush she couldn't sort through. She'd have safety. And Dad and Lily, Jonathan and Rose would still be gone. She could be safe.

But not them. Never them.

She struggled to breathe as the pressure of Carter's gaze made her look up. He was waiting for an answer.

"O-okay," she agreed, sounding hoarse to her own ears. "But how…"

"Give us a bit," he said when she trailed off. "I'll make some calls. Most of us like to help each other, so don't worry. We'll find you a place to go."

She blinked, still uncertain she could deserve safety when so many lay dead behind her.

Carter glanced to the others. "You rested up, Bus?"

The old man shrugged. "Much as ever."

"Then let's get out of here."

Shouldering the shotgun, Bus headed to the van and then yanked open the side door, letting the dogs jump inside. Spider glanced to Carter as she and Samson walked past.

"Where're we going?" she asked tersely.

"Gary and Annie aren't too far from here," Samson commented.

"Oh, yeah," Bus called dryly from the driver's seat. "They'd be thrilled to see us again."

A wry grin tugged on Spider's cold expression as she climbed into the van.

"Head south," Carter said. "Wood moved out this way a few weeks back. We can stay with him while I make arrangements."

He paused and glanced back. "You coming, Ashe?"

She flinched at the name and then stared at them. And just like that, someone was helping her. Taking her away from this. Just like that, it could be over.

While Lily, Dad and the others were dead in Montana somewhere. A few dumb little hours' difference, and suddenly she was offered safety like a gift, while they were all dead.

On legs that felt like water, she walked toward the van.

As she neared the door, Carter put a hand on her arm, stopping her. "Hey," he said quietly. "We'll take care of you. Don't worry."

She nodded shakily and then followed the others inside.

Chapter Eight

————— ♦ —————

The van drove through the night, rumbling along the interstate past homes and businesses that had gone to sleep hours before. Empty parking lots drowning beneath streetlamps burned her eyes, while in the abyss between signs of civilization, there was only a sea of stars.

She drifted for a time, her head resting on the side of the captain's chair in the second row of the van. Up ahead, Carter quietly gave directions between crackles from a police scanner below the dash, and in the seat beside her, Spider kept watch on the road without ever looking her way. The dog from the hotel snored softly in the space between their chairs, while the other rested below Samson's sleeping form on the bench behind her. Tala and Mischa, Carter had called them, respectively. Both massive German Shepherds, they nevertheless snuggled like puppies around the bases of the van seats.

Events of the day played back through her exhausted mind, blurring and shifting and losing all meaning as sleep and consciousness vied for control. Lily looked up from the cliff ledge with a smile, while Malden stepped back and avoided the flames. The boy drove them through the night, and for a moment she thought maybe they'd be able to get away.

Moisture soaked her palm where it cushioned her cheek and she jerked back, realizing she was crying. Furtively, she swiped the tears away and then cast a glance over her shoulder, but the others gave no sign of noticing. Swallowing, she rubbed her stinging eyes and returned to watching the world beyond the smoked windows of the van.

The clock on the dash glowed three by the time she heard Carter tell Bus to stop. Leaving the highway, they drove through a darkened town till at last, Bus parked the van in front of an apartment building with a radioactively bright security lamp outside. Blankets hung over many windows in place of curtains, and the electric blue glow of late night television flickered behind several of them. Overflowing garbage bins crowded the side of the building, and weeds clustered the chain-link fence circling the complex.

Turning in his seat, Carter glanced to Spider. "Be right back."

He nodded to Bus, and then the two of them left the van.

"Hey," Spider said, twisting around to nudge Samson. "Wake up."

Scrubbing his face with a hand, he pushed away from the seat. "Where are we?"

"Wood's place."

He regarded the building with a clear tinge of skepticism, but said nothing.

Minutes passed, and then Carter returned. He pulled open the passenger side door, and then reached into the van to disconnect the police scanner beneath the dash. "Come on," he told them.

Drawing a tired breath, Samson dragged a bag from under the seat, while in front of him, Spider did the same. Glancing to Ashley, the girl jerked her chin at the door. "Let's go."

Fumbling at the latch, Ashley pulled the door open and then stepped out into the cold night. Dogs barked in the distance and as they landed on the pavement, Tala and Mischa looked into the darkness, attentive to the noise.

Carter pushed the gate open and, with Spider and Samson behind her, Ashley trailed him along the cracked sidewalk through the sandy yard. The grating of the steps creaked as she climbed the metal stairs, and when they reached the second floor, she shied from the cobwebs filling the gaps in the iron fencing lining the open side of the walkway.

At the last door of the hall, Carter knocked briefly. Cursing rose, followed by the sound of multiple locks being thrown. The metal door pulled back a few inches, revealing a man with scraggly calico-colored hair.

"You know, you could have given me some warning," he sniped.

"Nice to see you too, Wood," Samson said.

The man's eyes narrowed, making them nearly disappear in his thin face, and then he opened the door wider. "Well, get in, already," he said crossly.

Beyond the tight entryway, stained carpet and the smell of stale food greeted them. Trash was piled in the open garbage bin by the door, and dirty plates covered the breakfast bar separating the kitchen from the living room. Seated on a threadbare sofa, Bus grinned at them when they came into the room.

"Love the new place," the old man said.

"Shut up," Wood snapped in reply. Rounding on Carter, he continued. "So how long's this going to be, huh? A day? More? I mean, fine. I owe you for getting me out of Chicago but…"

"We just need a place to crash till we can find her somewhere to stay," Carter said peaceably, nodding toward Ashley.

Wood's gaze slid over her, and the suspicious look he reserved for all the others dimmed. A faintly lascivious smile pulled at his lips. "Oh yeah?"

Eyeing Wood darkly, Spider walked between them, snagging Ashley's arm as she passed. Drawing her along, the girl crossed to the couch, shoved Ashley down next to Bus, and then dropped into the seat beside her. Crossing her arms calmly, she pinned Wood with a catlike stare.

The man's expression melted. Swallowing, he glanced to Carter. "I don't think there's enough space for all of you here," he hemmed, stepping to one side as the dogs pushed past him and then lay down by the patio doors.

"We'll be fine," Carter said. "You still have blankets?"

Nodding, Wood opened the closet by the front door and pulled a stack of bedding from a shelf. Still watching Spider from the corner of his eye, he pushed the pile into Carter's hands.

"Not long, right?"

"Few days tops," Carter replied.

"I guess, then..."

"We'll see you in the morning," Carter told him.

Jerking his head in a quick nod, Wood hurried down the darkened hallway and disappeared into the bedroom at the far end, shutting the door behind him.

Running her fingers between her dreadlocks, Spider sighed and then rose to help Bus take the blankets from Carter. Crossing to the patio window behind the couch, Samson pulled back the edge of the curtain and studied the street while the others spread the bedding on the floor.

Ashley watched them, uncertain what to do.

"You want the couch?" Carter asked her.

She hesitated, and then shook her head. "No, it's alright."

He paused. "Suit yourself," he replied, and then motioned toward a place on the ground.

Nervously, she lowered herself onto the blankets.

With a sigh, Carter sat down in the space she'd vacated.

Spider grinned up at him. "Sure took that fast."

He shrugged. "Old bones."

She scoffed, while Bus regarded him with a raised eyebrow. "Oh, really?" the old man said.

"You had sleep."

"Please," Bus retorted as he headed for the window in the kitchen. Pulling up a chair, he sank down with an exaggerated groan that made Carter smile.

Swiping a pillow from the foot of the couch, Spider tossed it to Ashley, who caught it awkwardly. "Here," the girl said.

"Thanks," Ashley replied uncomfortably.

The girl shrugged, and then pulled off her jacket. Beneath the straps of her white tank top and the black bands of her gun holsters, a broad tattoo showed in dark relief against her pale skin. Wings arched across her back and shoulders, their shape formed entirely of interconnected spider webs.

Realizing she was staring, Ashley jerked her gaze away, but the girl hadn't noticed. Sinking onto the blankets, Spider bundled the jacket into a ball below her head as she lay down.

Pushing the worn pillow into position, Ashley followed suit. Through the blanket and the thin carpet, she could feel the concrete slab of the floor and, surreptitiously, she shifted around, trying to find a comfortable position.

Carter switched off the lamp by the sofa, plunging the room into darkness. The blue-white glow of the security light outside shone past the gap between the patio curtains, silhouetting Samson. In the kitchen, the chair creaked softly as Bus changed position, and then the room was still.

She closed her eyes.

The man who killed her father bent over her. And everyone else in the room was dead. Her throat slashed, Spider stared up from the sodden blankets and Samson hung over the sofa, staining it red. Carter and Bus lay slumped against the blood-splattered walls, their guns dangling from their limp hands.

"I only needed one," the man whispered.

Gasping, she jerked upright.

Shapes lurked in the darkness. Men with guns. Leering faces. Impossible waves of dark pressure and presence, waiting to strike.

And then the nightmare faded. The shadows resolved into furniture and dirty plates reflecting the light from the patio.

From his post by the window, Samson glanced down at her.

"You okay?" he asked, more caution than concern in his voice.

She nodded uneasily, and then lay back down on the hard floor. Tugging an edge of the blanket around her shoulders, she stared at the darkness, trying to convince herself it would be safe to shut her eyes again.

Sleep was a long time in coming.

The soft sounds of an argument woke her.

"... all I'm saying is," Spider insisted quietly, "no one you've talked to this morning has ever heard of the girl. No one."

Ashley kept her eyes closed, barely breathing.

"We don't know everyone," Carter pointed out, his voice equally low. "Especially the ones who have family hiding them."

"Or the sellouts," Spider argued.

"You saw the news," Samson added in a hushed tone. "Mental instability? You know what would prompt that kind of thinking in your average cop. And they flat out said she wanted to have her family killed." Samson made a sound somewhere close to an aggravated growl. "Carter, this screams of someone taking the opportunity to secure a little safety for themselves and you know it."

Carter sighed. "Maybe. But *you* also know how they work. The kid could be caught in the middle of a cover-up as much as anything, especially since she looks like she's hanging on by a thread in the middle of hell."

"Or she's a damn good actress," Spider pointed out.

"And until we know for sure–"

"That could be too late," Samson snapped.

A heartbeat passed.

"There isn't a shred of proof saying she's not a sellout," Samson continued, his voice quieter. "And a ton suggesting she is. We're not the damned Musketeers, Carter. We can't risk everyone over a single kid–"

"We won't," Carter interrupted flatly.

Silence filled the room.

"And if she is a traitor?" Samson asked.

"Then you won't need to worry about what we'll do anymore," Carter answered.

Dishware clinked in the kitchen, and then footsteps passed her on their way down the hall. A door shut and she heard water running in the bathroom.

"I'm going to go check the stuff in the van," Samson muttered.

The front door closed.

Her heart pounding, Ashley opened her eyes. Early morning sunlight streamed past the open curtains, filling the room. From the arm of the couch, Wood was watching her. Seeing her awake, he grinned and then ostentatiously went back to studying the street.

Skin crawling, she pushed back the blanket and climbed to her feet. On the couch behind her, Bus lay sleeping with one arm pillowing his head and the two dogs lounging on the carpet below him. In the kitchen, Spider perched atop a barstool by the window, her eyes on the street and a bowl of cereal in her hands.

The girl glanced over as Ashley quietly entered the kitchen. "There's food in the cupboard right of the sink, if you want any," Spider said.

Ashley hesitated. "Thanks."

Spider returned to watching the neighborhood.

Feeling lost, Ashley took down the box and poured herself a small bowl. Without anywhere else to go, she leaned against the counter and slowly crunched through her cereal, cringing internally as every bite seemed to echo in the silent apartment.

The bathroom door opened and Carter came down the hall.

"Where's Samson?" he asked when he reached the kitchen.

"Getting some air," Spider answered neutrally, not looking away from the window.

Carter paused, studying the girl, and then he turned to Ashley. "Can I talk to you?"

Nodding, she tried not to let her nervousness show as she set the bowl aside. Half the things they'd said didn't make sense – in their argument this morning as much as any other time – but Carter's final statement had been clear. If they thought she'd sold out, they'd hurt her. Maybe kill her. And the worst part was, since she didn't understand what they were talking about anyway, she had no idea what might cause them to think she'd done that.

She could feel Spider's gaze tracking her as she followed Carter into the living room. Ignoring the other girl, Carter cleared away the blankets and then turned to her.

"I want to show you something."

She watched him cautiously.

"Do you know how to fight?"

After a moment's hesitation, she shrugged.

"Okay," he said. He reached over, taking her hand. Besides a small flicker on his face, he gave no sign of noticing her tension. "Hold your fist like this."

Carefully, he folded her fingers into her palm and then wrapped her thumb over them. "Thumb outside. Never inside, okay? You'll hurt yourself if you hold your hand that way."

Her eyes darting between his face and her hand, she nodded.

"Now, this is how I want you to stand…" She could feel Wood eyeing her as Carter shifted her around. "Feet planted this way and your other arm this way. You punch from here–" He patted the side of her back. "–not your shoulders. The power comes from your back muscles as much as anything, alright?"

On the couch, Bus drew a deep breath and opened his eyes. Blinking, he pushed up on an elbow. "We starting a dojo?"

Carter grinned and then held up a hand. "Now," he said to Ashley as the old man climbed to his feet, inched around them and then disappeared down the hall. "Just going slow, I want you to hit my palm here."

Ashley hesitated. They'd argued over her being a sellout, and now he was teaching her to fight. It didn't make sense.

"Come on," he encouraged.

She swung, hitting his hand.

"Good. Now using your other arm, I want you to bring it up like this after a punch to block my counter attack." He demonstrated, and then had her imitate. "Again."

Bus came back in. Seeing Wood studying her, he grimaced and then jerked his head at the other man. "Go keep watch out the bedroom window."

"It faces a brick wall," Wood protested.

"And?" Bus replied.

Grumbling, Wood left the room. With a tired sigh, Bus sank down onto the arm of the couch and studied the street beyond the patio.

"Do it again," Carter ordered her, ignoring the exchange. She repeated the motions. "Again." She complied. "Again."

They kept going, lightly punching and blocking back and forth. Occasionally, Carter corrected her stance or tension, but the interchange never stopped.

"Can you tell me what happened to you?" Carter asked.

She faltered.

With an encouraging noise, he nodded for her to keep going, and swung his fist for an easily blocked punch. Her brow furrowing, she raised her arm and barely deflected the blow.

A few moments passed.

"Can you tell me?" he asked again.

Clumsily, she blocked his punch. To one side, she could see Bus watching them, and she could feel Spider's gaze from across the room.

"Concentrate," Carter said. "Focus on what we're doing here."

She looked back at him. The fighting was a ruse to get her to talk. And yet from the expression in his eyes, she could tell he'd just keep asking till he got what they all wanted.

And if her answers somehow proved what they feared, they'd turn her out on the street. Or worse.

Drawing a tense breath, she swung again, fear-fueled anger making the blow stronger.

"Ashe…"

She hit harder.

He blocked and carefully punched back. She shoved his arm aside and then swung at him with all her strength.

Swiftly, he sidestepped the blow, grabbed her arm and pulled her sharply, sending her stumbling to the ground. She gasped as the hard concrete slammed into her knees and sent pain shooting through her legs. Responding to the feeling, the fires started to rise, rushing to destroy everything for the sake of making her safe again.

Panic shot through her. Frantically, she scrambled to control the flames. Trembling wracked her as she fought the fire back and her fingers dug into the filthy carpet with the effort of holding it at bay.

"Ashe."

"They shot my dad," she snarled through gritted teeth.

Blood everywhere and his body falling. His gasping face, begging her to run.

Her eyes stung. She shook her head, trying to stave off the tears as the flames retreated.

Carter reached down to her.

Brow furrowing, she looked up at him distrustfully.

"Come on," he said.

She shoved to her feet and struggled to keep from wincing as her knees protested. Giving no sign he'd noticed the slight, Carter shifted around and raised his fists to continue sparring.

"Keep going," he told her.

For a moment, she stared at him, and then raised her arms and punched at him. He blocked and then carefully returned the blow.

"What happened?" he asked.

Her fist glanced from his forearm.

"Ashe?"

She swung at him again. He wasn't going to stop badgering.

"They set fire to the barn," she growled.

He punched and then blocked, and his waiting expression never changed.

"I saw it first," she continued furiously. "I just thought the hay had caught fire. And I yelled… I yelled for my dad."

Her arm deflected his blow. His eyebrow twitched for her to go on, but he said nothing.

"Everything was dark. And Dad… he ran outside with us." Her voice caught, and she swallowed, working to hold onto the rage as it began to drain away.

It was hard.

"They pretended to be farmhands. But they'd already killed them. And in the dark, they just… we didn't… and then they shot him."

Moments passed. The thin noise of traffic carried beneath the sounds of their sparring.

"He made me run… me and Lily… and I didn't want to, but Dad, he…"

Her motions faltered. Carter made a quiet noise to keep her going.

"There was this man. Leading the others. He just walked up and… killed him."

She nearly missed blocking the punch, and Carter shifted quickly to avoid hitting her. "Focus," he admonished gently. Swiping a hand across her eyes, she struggled to do as he said.

"I ran. Then this boy drove up. I'd never seen him before, but he told us to get in. He…" The memory surfaced amid the chaos. "He said his name was Cole. And he drove, but the car crashed. We tried to run, but they were coming after us… they just wouldn't stop coming after us… and then there was a cliff."

She stopped and her hands lowered as her gaze dropped to the ground. Wordlessly, Carter pulled the punch, watching her.

"I-I fell," she said haltingly. "And Cole… he tried to help me, but…"

She drew a breath, pushing the stumbling words past the memories. "They shot him too. Like my dad. Like they were nothing. And he had Lily. On the edge of the cliff."

For a long moment, she stared at the carpet as the images played out in front of her eyes. Lily. The screams. The sudden silence. And then her brow furrowed, anger mounting past the pain.

Her eyes met Carter's. "He laughed. The man that–" She exhaled sharply. "He said they just needed one of us. And he laughed."

Fire tried to rise. Reflexively, she crushed it as she turned away.

"I tried to save her," she continued, distantly noticing herself shaking. "To run to her before she–" Her voice choked and she swallowed hard. "But they… they just…"

Loathing joined the anger and the pain, and she shivered harder. "I got away, though. She fell. And I… I got away."

Questions drifted through her eyes as she looked back at him, asking Carter or anyone to explain. "She was eight years old. *Eight.* And he just laughed…"

Her face crumpled into confusion as her gaze returned to the ground.

From the corner of her eye, she saw Carter glance at Spider, but she couldn't bring herself to care what they thought anymore. If this was selling out, they could just go to hell. Angrily, she turned to the window, and caught sight of Bus. Sympathy touched his eyes.

She looked away.

"Hey," Carter said, pulling her attention back. "Come on. No more questions today."

He shifted into a sparring position. She watched him a moment, and then did the same.

Time drifted by, punctuated by the traffic and Carter's quiet corrections. After a while, the front door swung open, and Samson returned. At the sight of them, he said nothing, though the displeasure on his face left his thoughts easy to read. Shrugging off his jacket, and revealing the tattooed coils of barbed wire and chain wrapping the dark skin of his arms, he crossed to Spider's side to watch the street.

A phone rang.

Carter jerked his chin at Bus, silently instructing him to continue the sparring. Stepping out of his way, Carter swiped his jacket from the couch and then retreated to the bedroom.

Wood emerged, grumbling about being shuffled around his own home, but at the twin expressionless looks Spider and Samson gave him, the man paled and swiftly scuttled to the far corner of the room, where he kept his gaze on the road.

Ashley waited till Bus got into position and then cautiously punched toward him. Unsteadily, he blocked her blow.

"Take it easy on an old man!" he cried.

She hesitated and he grinned, throwing a punch harder than any of Carter's. Hastily, she blocked, and his grin widened. Heart pounding, she returned the favor.

He chuckled. "That's better."

Incredulous, she kept going.

"Watch your feet, girl!" he barked a second later. "I could knock you over, you're so loose with how you're standing."

She scrambled backward as he charged toward her. Pulling up sharply, he tapped the top of her head and then winked. "Now, what should you have done?"

Unnerved, she shook her head confusedly.

"Like this." He demonstrated sidestepping and then swinging a leg to trip an attacker. "That's one way, depending on the situation. You want to be able to get away quick, right?"

She nodded, staring at him, and he laughed at the look on her face.

"I've been doing this longer than you've been alive, girl. Even broke my neck once. Didn't notice though. Want to know why?" He winked again. "Neck muscles. Like iron, they are."

She couldn't think what to say.

"So, let's try again. Stand like this and–"

He cut off as Carter walked back into the room. "We'll continue later," Bus told her.

Eyeing the old man, she just nodded.

"That was Shen," Carter said, leaning against the corner of the hall. "She's agreed to take Ashe with her if we can get her out of Nashville."

Ashley's eyes slid toward Wood uneasily. Carter and the rest were one thing, but if this was the caliber of their friends, she wasn't sure what she'd do.

"Shen wants to move?" Spider asked, surprise in her voice. She hopped down from the barstool and came around the kitchen entryway, Samson right behind her.

"A few suspicious characters are lurking about," Carter explained. "She's getting a bit jumpy and thought it was probably time to go. And since Blackjack's busy in Minnesota and Serenity's relocating someone in New York, she called us."

Shrugging her eyebrows expressively, Spider glanced to Samson and then headed toward the living room. Watching them from the corner, Wood's relief practically screamed from his expression, though he wisely said nothing.

"Get Ashe something else to wear, would you?" Carter said to Spider as she passed. "Something a little less conspicuous."

Nodding briefly, Spider continued into the other room.

Carter watched her go and then crossed to Ashley's side. "Shenandoah's a good sort," he said quietly, his voice barely audible over the sounds of the others getting ready to leave. "You don't need to worry about that."

He glanced toward Wood and back again, and then gave her a small grin.

She blinked, feeling as though he'd read her mind.

"Alright?" he asked, and then he patted her shoulder when she nodded. "Good. See you outside."

Following Bus and Samson, he walked out of the room.

"Here," Spider called to her. The girl tossed her an armful of clothes and then jerked her chin toward the bathroom. "Don't leave the sweats in there, either."

Catching the clothing awkwardly, Ashley nodded and then headed down the hall.

Given that she and Spider were close to the same dimensions, the jeans and tank top fit well, though the hooded sweatshirt was fairly baggy. But in light of the way the others dressed, she supposed that was part of the point. The clothes smelled vaguely of being too long in a bag, though, and when she looked in the mirror, she felt like a stranger stared back at her.

Uncomfortably, she ran a hand through her tangled hair, but there was nothing to be done. The dark clothes made her pale skin stand out and blended with her black hair till she looked like an indistinguishable blob with a white face in the middle.

Which, again, was probably the point.

Turning from the mirror, she bundled up the police station sweats and left the bathroom, returning to where Spider waited at the end of the hall. As she came to a stop, the girl regarded her briefly and then reached up, tugging the hood around Ashley's head.

"So people won't see your face," she said, and Ashley couldn't read her tone.

Spider eyed her a moment more, as though weighing what she saw, and then swung her bag over her shoulder and walked out of the room.

"They're dangerous, you know," Wood called from his spot by the patio window. "Probably get you killed, staying with them."

Ashley glanced back. Her skin crawled at the look in his eyes.

Without a word, she followed the others, letting the door swing shut behind her.

Chapter Nine

Machines beeped in the distance and he could hear nurses and doctors conferring quietly at the station at the end of the hall. The lights overhead grew brighter, commencing a relentless assault on the glistening linoleum and mint-toned walls. The hospital was waking up, coming off the night shift, or whatever it was they called it here.

Harris flexed his fingers and returned them to their folded position, elbows on his knees. A dull headache throbbed at the base of his skull, a souvenir from his tumble to the stairs yesterday afternoon. His head had apparently hit a step when he fell, leaving him a goose-egg sized knot and a couple bruises, not that he'd noticed them at the time.

Rhianne slept in the waiting room behind him, curled beneath his sports coat on two cushioned chairs shoved end-to-end. She'd stayed awake all night, waiting for word on her husband, till she finally fell asleep from sheer exhaustion an hour before. On the floor nearby, eleven-year-old Andrew was ostensibly watching cartoons, though no one in the room was fooled. The boy's eyes darted to the door every time anyone walked by.

Nicole's tennis shoes squeaked on the linoleum as she returned from the vending machines at the other end of the hallway.

"Here," she said quietly, handing him the cup of coffee.

"Thanks."

She sank down into the chair next to him, looking far older than her years. But teenagers always did these days. She'd turn fourteen in a few weeks, Harris remembered, and she'd been looking forward to her father watching her test for a red belt in Tae Kwon Do today.

One more thing he'd ruined.

Grimacing, he choked down the cheap black coffee. No one said it. They'd known this could happen, being the family of a police officer. But he could feel it, behind their eyes, behind the soft questions and the things they didn't say at all.

He set the cup down in lieu of crushing it in his fist. Malden had a wife. Kids. He was an elder in his church and the leader of his small group – most of whom had been sitting in the waiting room all night. Harris had none of those things. Was none of those things. Yet he was the one sitting here, while Scott was the one slowly dying of third-degree burns in the ER.

Nicole's hand rested on his forearm, and then crept down to curl into his rough grip. Emotions warred on her face, and he could see her fighting to hold back tears.

He pulled one hand from her grasp and wrapped his arm across her shoulders. "Have you slept?" he asked, guiltily realizing he couldn't remember whether the kids had gotten any rest since their mother received the call from the hospital the afternoon before.

She shrugged wordlessly.

"Come on," he said, rising and bringing her with him into the waiting room. "No more coffee. Get some sleep."

He could see the protests hovering on her lips. "Staying awake won't make things go one way or the other, Nikki," he told her quietly.

She looked away and then let him take her over near her mother. Two of the nameless church members rose and helped move chairs together, and the girl sank down onto the makeshift bed, biting her lip uncertainly.

"We'll wake you if there's any change, honey," one of the ladies said.

Nicole nodded as she lay down.

Harris walked back to his chair in the hall, retreating from the church people filling the room. They didn't know him as more than Scott's partner and they weren't inclined to be rude. But as with everyone else, he could feel the questions behind the kindness in their eyes.

Where were you? What happened?

And he couldn't answer. Because what he remembered was insane.

He'd always trusted his memory; he'd had an excellent one his whole life. But people saw all kinds of things, and remembered even more. Their perceptions could be skewed by everything from the weather to lack of sleep, though especially by their mood. In light of that, he'd trained his memory to be as impartial as he could make it, to recall the world exactly as it was, and to catalog every detail without letting anything influence him.

Then he'd seen a teenage girl go up in flames without suffering so much as a tan, and everything went out the window.

For the first few hours after her escape, he'd been in shock. Barely able to recall anything since the moment they'd escorted her from the cellblock, he'd spent the better part of the night desperately trying to understand how Scott had ended up in the ER and how their prisoner had gotten away. But like a circuit on overload, his mind just seemed to have shut down rather than record the nightmare.

But he was nothing if not stubborn, and somewhere between his fifth and sixth cups of coffee, memory started to return.

She'd looked at him through the fire. The impossible fire covering every inch of her body. And then she'd made the flames disappear, while Scott lay on the floor screaming in pain.

And she'd said she was sorry.

He couldn't stop seeing her face. His wonderful, damnable memory simply wouldn't let it go.

Doctor Patel came down the hall and Harris looked up. With a glance to him, the man continued into the waiting room, where the church people dutifully wakened the family.

Rising to his feet, Harris followed.

Nervousness plain on her face, Rhianne pulled Nicole close and motioned Andrew over as she waited for the doctor's news.

"We've gotten him stable," the doctor said.

Air escaped Rhianne.

"It was touch-and-go for a while, but–"

"Can we see him?" Nicole interrupted.

The doctor hesitated. "We'll let you know."

Harris could read between the simple lines. He knew what Scott had looked like the day before. The kids didn't need to see that. Ever.

"How is he?" Rhianne asked quietly.

"We had to induce a coma. To help stabilize him, you see. At the moment, he–"

From across the room, Harris could see Rhianne trembling as the doctor continued his gentle but direct litany. Words like skin grafts, blood transfusions, and extended physical therapy entered Harris' ears, where they were filed away for later review. But his mind was elsewhere. Back there. In a narrow hall, watching a pale waif go up in flames.

The doctor left. More words came, this time from the church people talking of miracles and hope. Harris glanced up from the erratically patterned carpet, checking on Rhianne. The others clustered around her, patting arms, murmuring comfort.

And he walked out of the room.

He could see Malden on the floor, in the moments after the girl fled. His clothes were ashes, his blood was everywhere, and there didn't seem to be any earthly reason why he was still alive. His screams faded as his nerves gave out, and within the twisted mess of his face, his eyes rolled up into his head, making Harris think he'd died.

And they had the audacity to call anything about this a miracle.

The chair squeaked as he sat down. His hands gripped one another, clenching back into the position they'd held for the past day, because he knew it was that or break something.

"John?"

Rhianne's quiet voice came from the doorway, and he fought back the fury on his face before looking up at her.

She wasn't fooled. Crossing to his side, she lowered herself onto a seat.

"You should get some sleep," she said gently.

"I'm—" He cut off, hating himself for the words he'd been about to automatically say. He was fine. Clearly. And her husband could still die, covered in burns with his skin peeling off. But meanwhile,

John Harris was fine.

Her hand rested on his clenched fists. "Go home, John."

Irrational worry flashed through him, but when he looked up at her, all he saw was empathy in her eyes.

"Please," she said. "Take care of yourself too. For all our sakes."

Guilt gnawing at him, he hesitated and then forced himself to nod. "You'll have someone call if–" He couldn't finish the sentence, and didn't know what he'd finish it with anyway.

She nodded. "No matter what," she said, her voice catching.

He squeezed her hand, and then headed for the elevator.

By the car, he turned on his cell phone and was instantly rewarded with the buzz of missed calls and voicemail from the station. Clicking in the passcode to his mail swiftly, he held his breath, hoping to hear they'd captured the girl, or at least knew where she'd been hiding since the day before. The chief had summarily taken him off the case the moment Malden was injured, with implied concerns Harris would shoot the girl before any explanations could be obtained. Protocol or not, Harris wasn't sure what to feel about the chief's opinion of his own stability. But regardless, it'd left him sitting on the sidelines while others searched for the teenage torch.

The chief's voice firmly requested he come in the moment he received this message, and then hung up without offering additional information.

Harris frowned. That didn't sound good.

Possibilities ran through his mind as he drove to the station and then climbed the steps to the chief's office. They'd found the girl and she was dead. They'd not found her and she'd set someone else on fire. She'd gotten away. She'd not gotten away. The scenarios spun around and, with difficulty, he shoved them all to the back of his mind as he knocked on the chief's door.

"Come in."

He stepped into the office as the squat man behind the desk looked up. Though he was snidely called a leprechaun by those who disliked him, the cops who knew Chief Daly considered him a pit bull and were grateful if they could stay on his good side.

Harris was fairly certain he'd never be on the man's good side again. Not after yesterday.

"How's Malden?"

"Stable," Harris said, not trusting himself to say more. "Did they catch her?"

The chief looked back at his papers. "Shut the door, Harris."

Definitely not good, he thought as he came inside.

"If you recall, we talked about the events of last afternoon soon after the EMTs took Malden to the hospital," Daly said. "And you told me you weren't sure what happened."

Harris nodded, and though he towered over the other man, he couldn't help but feel like a childhood version of himself, suddenly brought into the principal's office.

"I need to know what you remember now."

He hesitated. "I'm not sure what to say, sir."

Daly grimaced and set the papers down. "Listen, Sheldon from Internal Affairs has called a meeting with me tomorrow morning. And you know what that means. He's already started throwing around phrases like charges of criminal negligence – for you *and* Malden. The girl had an incendiary device on her, that much we can ascertain. How it got there is unclear, as is how it got past the both of you. Sheldon wants someone to blame, someone who will satisfy the commissioner and the media hounds at the same time. He's going to let you and Malden hang, John. Now, I don't want that to happen, but you've got to give me something better than 'you don't know what to say', understood?"

Harris exhaled slowly. "What do the security cameras show?"

The chief's face tightened. "Nothing. Apparently, they were damaged by the fire and the sprinklers. We've got the recordings in the system, but the computers can't seem to do anything to clear them up."

"And that FBI agent?"

"No one saw anything, Harris," Daly said, a touch sharply. "You and Malden were the only ones down there. So it's up to you. What can you tell me?"

Looking away, Harris ran a hand over his hair, evaluating his options. They weren't good. "The girl went up in flames, chief."

"The girl," Daly repeated.

"I don't know. I was in the lead, ahead of Malden. When I reached the stairs, all of a sudden I heard the girl protesting, unwilling to keep walking. I turned around, headed back to help Malden bring her on and…"

He could see the flames burst from her hands, rush up her arms and over her body in the blink of an eye. The fire had engulfed her, melting the handcuffs from her wrists, while she just stared between the two cops, her hair stirring as though in a breeze.

Drawing a breath, he jerked himself from the memory. "I can't explain it. There must have been some kind of retardant on her. And fuel. Maybe something she injected beneath her skin. I mean, she was searched when she came in, and she was wearing department sweats, for Pete's sake, but I don't know. Maybe the drunk in the next cell was in on it, or she covered herself in the retardant before she was brought in…"

He trailed off, knowing he was just making up answers. Making it normal, if such a thing was possible. A retardant that protected bare skin and clothes from heat that melted steel like butter? Or somehow made fire vanish as quickly as it came? Or destroyed video evidence? Or…

"We've already talked to the drunk," the chief said, cutting into Harris' thoughts. "He claims to know nothing – which, considering his blood alcohol level at the time, I might be tempted to believe. As for the rest…" He shook his head. "If you remember anything, John, you have to call me right away. Sheldon won't–"

"I know," Harris said, and to his credit, the chief let the interruption pass.

"Until then," Daly continued. "Go home. Get rest. You look like hell."

Wordlessly, Harris rose.

"And I need you back here tomorrow after my meeting with IA," the chief added. "They're undoubtedly going to want to talk to you too."

Daly returned to his papers, but despite the clear dismissal, Harris didn't move. "You never answered my question, sir," he said, knowing he was pushing it and not caring. "Did they catch her?"

"We will," the chief said, and then paused briefly. "And my orders to you still stand."

Feeling more the child than ever, Harris left the room.

Dozens of eyes watched as he left the building, but he ignored them all. The drive home was a blur, and when he finally reached his apartment, it took three tries to get the key into the lock.

The walls echoed with questions, the same ones he'd asked all day. As he lowered himself onto the couch and tossed the keys onto the coffee table, he glared out the windows at the obnoxiously beautiful day. Blue skies. Not a cloud to be seen. If there was any justice in the universe, it would've been pouring down rain, desert climate be damned.

Because this would just make it that much easier for her to get away.

One hand rubbing at the knot on the back of his head, he sighed. City roadblocks. Police patrols throughout the suburbs and the metro area. And they hadn't caught her. In the time it had taken to get everything in place, she'd slipped right past them, and from what he could tell by the chief's statement, neither a sighting nor a clue had been found since. That she'd had help was certain. That her help was essentially anonymous – and presumably as dangerous as her – was equally assured.

And only by a 'miracle' or whatever, Malden hadn't been added to her body count.

Harris leaned back on the cushions, trying to keep breathing. They'd take his badge. They'd sit him on administrative leave – such a nice, vague term. Investigations would follow. Culpability and other such things would be determined. And then…

He didn't know. If the investigations went the way he suspected, firing was certain and prison was a decent possibility. Anything could happen if they tried to charge him in connection with yesterday's events, though at a minimum he'd be treated for mental instability.

The report on her diary came back to him. Maybe the cops just hadn't understood what they'd read at the time.

But regardless, Internal Affairs and the notorious Sheldon wouldn't be happy to leave matters at 'girl spontaneously combusted, case closed'. Hell, he wouldn't be happy leaving it that way. He'd tear the case apart to determine what really happened, if he hadn't seen it with his own eyes.

He'd want to know the truth.

Even if the truth was insane.

Time passed. He paced the room. He watched the clock tick around. He tried cleaning, but ended up breaking two glasses in the sink. He was too awake for coffee, too tired for tea, and the thought of food made his stomach turn. Sleep was a joke, and the idea of flipping on the TV was absurd. The plethora of cop dramas annoyed him on the best of days, and he knew what would be on the news.

The sun sank beyond the skyline and the city faded into purple shadows. Streetlights peppered the scenery, and gradually, windows began to glow in the darkness.

And still, the phone hadn't rung.

Grimacing, he crossed the room, grabbed the keys from the table, and then headed for the door. There had to be something. A blip on the tapes. A piece of evidence they'd missed. Something, somewhere to prove he and Malden weren't to blame.

And he couldn't just keep destroying his apartment, one dish at a time.

His car found its way across town and, in the parking lot, he blinked, barely remembering how he'd gotten there. Shoving the gearshift into park, he climbed out and then thumbed the automatic locks on the key fob. At this time of night, the lot was nearly empty. Cutting across the parking spaces beneath the glow of the streetlamps, he headed for the side door to the station.

The swipe card still worked, and in short order, he was upstairs in the vast array of desks that made up the main office. Weaving through the room, he paused as he reached the place where he and Malden had been stationed.

He drew a sharp breath, and then flicked on his computer. The files were easily located, stored in the customary places on the server, and double-clicking swiftly, he waited impatiently as they loaded.

A window opened. The security tapes started. And it was just as the chief said.

Nothing.

Just… nothing. Static. Minutes and minutes of impenetrable static.

The recording rolled on and greeted him with a black screen once complete. Trembling, he reached out, smacking the playback button again.

Static.

She'd walked away and not a single camera had caught anything. Not a scream, not a flicker of her face. Half a dozen cameras in that hallway, and between the fire and the damned sprinklers, there wasn't a shred of evidence left to exonerate them from this ludicrous fantasy.

The end of the tape. He hit the keyboard again.

He'd never been one for fantasy. He preferred reality, with all its flaws. He'd just tried to make them right. And then this girl came along.

The keyboard was going to break if he kept hitting the keys this hard.

Malden could still die. His whole legacy would be destroyed in the ensuing investigation. Criminal negligence, they were saying now. What would they say when weeks went by and the girl was still free? Would they blame Malden for his own injuries? Or say Harris had done it all?

He couldn't stop seeing her face through the flames. The impossible, inconceivable flames that hadn't burned her and melted metal like it was nothing.

She didn't have an incendiary device. She hadn't been covered in retardant. She'd just combusted. And there wasn't a damn thing he could do to prove it.

The screen flickered.

Harris froze.

Smacking the mouse, he cued up the recording and played it again. Static and copious amounts of nothing, and yet for just a moment, he'd seen something else.

Damn it all, he'd seen her face.

Breathing hard, he gripped the mouse and tried not to throw it across the room. Malden could die. He was going insane. And some little human torch just–

An image of the hallway flashed in front of him, and then disappeared.

"What the hell?" he whispered.

He rewound the security feed. A flash of hallway. A bit of her face.

The tape played again. There was Malden. He could see himself in the corner of the screen.

For minutes on end, he watched the recording over and over, and with every pass, the images grew clearer and the static began to fade. The whole thing was right there, plain as day on the tape the chief said was beyond saving.

But it had taken twenty viewings to see it.

Malden walked down the hall, escorting the girl in her department sweats and handcuffs. A few paces ahead, Harris reached the base of the stairs. And then she skidded to a stop, her back to the camera and her head shaking furiously. She'd been scared of something.

The FBI guy. Harris remembered hearing the man's voice coming down the stairs.

Fire rushed over her. Up her arms, over her body, and oh sweet merciful… Harris wanted to turn away, but he couldn't for fear he'd wake up and find the cleared recording was just a dream.

Malden fell back, thrashing in pain. The girl stumbled away. The flames… they just vanished, no doubt about it. Flames. No flames. Not a burn on her.

She ran. In the corner of the screen, he watched himself fumble for the gun. He should have been faster. He could have crippled her. Shot her leg and gotten answers. He shouldn't have let shock slow him down.

The recording ended.

He hit the mouse again, and then leaned back in his chair, thinking of the girl in the interrogation room yesterday. Her eyes had been like smudges of shadow in her bloodless face, and she barely seemed to understand what was happening. Fear radiated off her in waves, and only conviction of her guilt had kept Scott from seeing it.

"What were you really afraid of?" he whispered to the girl on the screen. "Because if you could do that… you certainly weren't afraid of the police."

Unexpectedly, anger rose up and, dream or not, he turned away from the monitor. He'd almost pitied her. Seen a kid where Scott saw a homicidal lunatic, and thought there might've been more going on than met the eye. She'd looked so much like a victim, after all, and stared at him like a wounded animal in the hunter's sights. But the whole while…

He realized he was crushing the pencil cup; the fine mesh sides were almost completely bent inward. Carefully, he released his grip and returned his eyes to the screen.

The girl went up in flames and then ran, leaving Malden dying. He hit the button to play the recording again.

No, she certainly hadn't been afraid of them.

A shadow fell across the room and he looked up to see a human wall blocking the light from the hallway. The wall approached, calmly moving between the desks and steadily resolving into an identifiable person.

He hesitated. Mr. Brogan. The FBI agent.

"Good evening, Detective," the man said, his constrained voice everything Harris would expect in a fed, though perhaps not one with the dimensions of a Viking.

At Harris' silence, Brogan smiled. "How is the department's investigation coming?"

Harris' face darkened. There was humor around Brogan's eyes, as though he was enjoying a joke, and the expression was the last thing Harris needed right now.

"It's progressing," he said shortly.

"Good to know," Brogan answered, unperturbed. "I'd like the chance to talk with you about that. Is there somewhere we could speak privately?"

"I'm busy. Maybe later."

The humor increased, though Brogan said nothing. His eyes went to the screen and Harris grimaced, cursing himself for not turning the monitor off. And then he froze.

Brogan was watching the tape.

"Interesting recording," the man commented. His gaze slid back to Harris. "Yet you're the only one seeing past the static, am I correct?"

"Who are you?"

"Someone who would like to speak privately."

Harris headed for the nearest interrogation room.

Brogan set his briefcase down on the metal table as the lights flickered on. "I suppose I should start by telling you that I am not with the FBI, though some of my associates once were. I represent a… group… with specific interest in capturing the young lady you detained, for reasons connected to what you experienced yesterday."

Noting the pause for later review, Harris regarded the man. "I'm listening."

"To put it simply, the young lady and those with her are not – for lack of a better word – what you would consider 'normal'."

"Human."

Brogan made a hedging noise. "No, they are technically that. They simply have special skills that they choose to use in the service of their own ends. Doing as they please, or as they deem necessary. The latter of which you saw yesterday afternoon."

"Burning people alive."

"If it suits their needs… yes."

"And how do you fit in?"

"My associates and I work to stop them. Many in our number have, in one way or another, been hurt by her type in the past, much as you have. And thus we try to prevent them from being able to harm anyone again."

"How?"

"Various methods. Whatever is necessary to ensure the innocent remain safe."

Harris paused. The answer truly defined vague, but he wasn't sure it mattered. He needed answers. "Why can't anyone else see the security videos?"

Brogan chuckled deprecatingly. "Fire is only one tool in their arsenal, Detective. Another is remaining invisible to those you would call 'normal' humans – again, when it suits them, and barring the unusual event of someone withstanding their own discomfort long enough to break past the 'static' as you've done. Trust me when I say the latter is rare."

Filing the information away with the rest, Harris' gaze dropped to the table, remembering the girl in a room identical to this one. Invisibility. Fire. And she'd sat there the whole time, giving every sign of just being a frightened teenager.

"So she was setting us up?" he asked, anger beneath his tone.

"Or seeing what you knew. And when it no longer served her purpose to remain…"

Harris' memory went back to the moment before she set Malden on fire.

"But she was afraid of you," he said, his voice only barely making it a question.

A small smile crossed Brogan's face. "We've had some success in stopping her kind before," he admitted. "We are similar to her in skill, Detective, but there the similarity ends. Our goal is to bring an end to what her kind have done. We fight fire with fire, yes, but only to the degree necessary to achieve that goal. Yet most of her allies don't even know we exist, and that anonymity is our best defense and weapon in the war to stop them."

For a moment, he stared at the man, trying to process what he'd heard. He felt like he'd lost sight of the edges of the map hours ago.

"Why are you telling me this?" he asked.

"We want your help."

"Why?"

"Several reasons," Brogan answered. "For one, you are an ordinary human and, to their view, unworthy of consideration. Yet you can see them and therefore, if you choose, you can be a threat."

Harris said nothing.

"And secondly," the giant continued. "There is this."

Flipping open the briefcase, he withdrew two photographs and then tossed them onto the table. Blown-up images met Harris' gaze, both slightly pixilated but easily recognizable.

He stared.

In the nearest photograph, the girl was across a city street, staring directly at the camera. She stood next to a hotel he recognized, though it'd been closed for years. Two men were with her, African Americans, one of whom looked between forty-five and fifty, and the other in his early twenties.

The second image clearly originated from a security camera, and though nearly useless as all cheap video cameras were, the grainy picture nevertheless caught the younger girl, looking very much alive. The young man with her had his face turned from the camera and was blurry to boot. But the logo on the girl's sweatshirt was visible.

A thrill ran through him. Brighton Modisett. The damned prep school was only a few minutes from here.

"Where'd you get these?"

"From associates," Brogan answered cryptically. "The photo of the younger girl we obtained through contacts who *are* actually with the FBI. The other originated from one of our own who, unfortunately, was unable to catch the girl when her companions blew up a spray paint can in the street."

Harris blinked. He hadn't heard about that.

"Regardless," Brogan continued. "I thought you'd like to be the first to know."

For the moment, Harris ignored the last comment, grateful only to have a lead. "When were they taken?"

"A day ago. I'm told the school belonging to that logo falls within your jurisdiction, as does the building by the older girl. Thus far, we haven't turned up anything on the men in either picture and, to be honest, we don't even have the girls' names…"

As he trailed off, Harris looked up. "What're you wanting here?"

"Your assistance," Brogan went on smoothly. "Your Internal Affairs department presumably needs answers for yesterday's events, and I highly doubt they will find any to suit them. As I said, the elder girl and her associates are damnably good at covering their tracks. And when that happens… where do you think Internal Affairs will come?" He paused. "You will never be able to prove what you saw. And so we wish you to work for us."

"Going after the girl?"

"The younger one."

"What?"

"Our previous encounters indicate the younger girl might not be like her sister. She may well be an innocent in this situation, leaving her in greater danger from others of the elder's kind. And yet, for all her brutality in attacking your partner and whatever the news says, the older girl does seem to have some feeling for the child. We believe she and the boy may have been separated unintentionally. And now, they cannot reconnect. But if we were to have the younger child…"

Brogan smiled. "Her sister would come to us. And thus, we could save the younger and stop the elder, all at one moment."

"How can you be sure?"

"Family is important to her kind. Very important. The girl *will* come if she learns we have her younger sister. And then we can stop her."

Brogan watched him. "So, Detective. May I tell my associates we have your help?"

Harris looked down at the photos, the laundry list of violations of the law he was considering scrolling through his head. It was a long list, starting from the major crimes and dwindling down to the relatively minor infractions, all of which would spell the end of his career. Jail was certain. Possibly for life and then some with all the sentences added up.

Just like that, twenty years of an exemplary career would be down the drain.

He'd given everything to the job. He was the job. And the job was keeping the innocent safe. The department would have his badge. He'd probably be fired, regardless.

But even if they didn't, would it matter? Could he go back on the streets with what he knew? What would it be like, the next time he arrested someone, wondering all the while if they would spontaneously combust or do God knew what else? How could he work? He'd be retired or forced to resign within a year.

Because people didn't go up in flames. People didn't walk away after liquefying metal on their skin. *People* didn't do that.

He studied her face in the enlarged photo. Pale. Ghostly. Still looking scared.

What were you frightened of this time? he wondered. The man with the camera, putting you one step closer to being caught?

Because you certainly weren't ever afraid of me.

His gaze rose to Brogan's. "Her name is Ashley," he said. "And yeah. I'll help you."

Chapter Ten

———◆———

Ashley stared out the window as the morning sun crept over the horizon to welcome in another day. On her lap, Tala's head rested, the weight of the dog leaning into the side of her knee. Flopped over her shoes and positioned awkwardly between the seats, Mischa snored softly and dreamed, occasionally twitching as she chased her phantom prey.

The others had traded off driving as the hours passed, and never stopped too long anywhere. When their turn was over, whoever had been driving took the place of the person in the rear of the van and quickly fell asleep on the bench seat till the next driver's turn was done. They never asked her to take the wheel, didn't even seem to entertain the idea, but kept to a schedule all their own with barely a word needing to be spoken.

She'd slept for a while, waking only as the others changed places. The dogs had huddled around her halfway through the night, responding to some unknown impulse of their own. But she was grateful for it. They were oddly soothing and, in the dropping temperature of the night, comfortingly warm.

Idly, she ran her fingers through Tala's dense fur, her gaze on the morning light. The dog leaned into the touch, putting more pressure on her leg and then heaving a satisfied sigh. Ashley gave the animal a tiny smile. She'd never had a dog near her before; never even petted one that she could recall. It was nice. She'd miss Tala and Mischa when this was done.

Her thoughts turned back to their destination as the nascent smile died. In a few hours, she'd leave the only four people in the world she still knew and disappear. A woman she'd never met would take her away and then…

Safety. As the miles passed, she'd started to wonder what the word meant. A place to stay. Somewhere the monsters wouldn't find her. Somewhere to stop for a bit, and try to understand what had happened.

Somewhere that would never be home.

She swallowed, struggling to push the thought away. The past few days had been like a flood, sweeping her along. Forty-eight hours ago, or maybe a bit more, there'd been home. Now it was gone. And in all the changes, she'd just hung on, waiting for it to end and something that made sense to begin.

Even if she was starting to think that wouldn't happen. She didn't like this new world away from the farm, because in it, Lily and her father and everyone she'd loved didn't exist. No one knew them. No one remembered them. Not these people in the van. Not this strange woman she'd be sent off with in a few hours.

Just her.

Other people would have funerals. Memorials. Burials and gravesites and mourners who at least said how sad it all was before they went on with their lives. There wasn't even that. Without even pausing, without even noticing the difference, the world had moved on as if everyone in her whole life had never lived. As though with their bullets and fire, the men who'd destroyed her family hadn't erased anything worth remembering at all.

Her nails bit her palm, driving back the tears. Crying made her feel like she was drowning, and giving into the pain just made everything else more real.

Tala nudged her hand to draw attention to the fact the petting had stopped. Mournfully, the animal eyed her, looking more like a sad puppy than a creature the size of a wolf. Drawing a shaky breath, Ashley ran her fingers through the dog's fur, focusing on the simplicity of the action while the miles sped by.

As the sun inched toward noon, the van left the highway and curved along an off-ramp into Nashville. Around turns and down nameless streets, Samson navigated till he reached a public parking lot at the edge of a quaint shopping district. Spider grabbed her bag as the others climbed out, and Bus woke in the back seat, blinking at the city and doing his best to regain consciousness quickly.

"Stay with Mischa and the van," Carter told him. "We'll call once we check it out."

Bus nodded, scrubbing his face with a hand and then climbing toward the driver's seat.

Carter motioned the others onward, and then fell in beside Ashley as they started down the road, Tala on their heels.

In evenly spaced intervals, flourishing trees shaded either side of the street. Brick buildings lined the road, their awnings and colorfully painted window casements shining in the sunlight. Boutiques and cafés filled the lower levels, with apartments and smaller shops on the next floors, but beneath the modern trappings, the history of the district showed through in the engraved names of long-gone businesses in the buildings' uppermost stonework.

"Shenandoah owns a bookstore at the end of the block," Carter told her, jerking his chin toward the other side of the street. "She's lived above it for over a decade now, and I don't think any of us expected her to—"

Ashley glanced at him as he cut off, and then she looked back at the store. The shop seemed the same as any other, with a handwritten welcome sign and merchandise artfully displayed in the window. On the second floor, another window was raised and white curtains fluttered beside a decorative birdcage with its door open wide.

Samson turned from his vaguely hostile study of the passersby and tracked Carter's gaze. The younger man swore. With a swift glance back and forth, he headed across the road.

"Come on," Carter said, all lightness gone from his tone. Taking Ashley's hand, he pulled her with him as he followed the others into a service drive between the buildings on the opposite side of the street.

Behind the stores, the alley turned, extending the length of the block. Dumpsters lined the brick-walled confines, past due for emptying and supporting more bags against their sides. Ignoring the mess, Samson and the others started toward the rear of the bookstore, and Ashley swallowed hard to see Spider fingering a gun beneath her coat.

"Stay behind me," Carter said quietly.

She nodded, biting her lip as his hand inched toward a weapon as well.

The back door of the bookshop burst open. Half-running, half-falling, a red-haired woman stumbled down the steps. Her gaze raked the alleyway and then caught on them.

"Carter!" she screamed, scrambling up and racing toward them down the alley.

Ashley gasped as guns came out all around her.

Two men stepped out of the shop.

Blood drained from Ashley's face. They felt just like the people on her farm. Exactly the same.

On both sides of her, the others opened fire.

The bullets flew past the red-haired woman, and sped at the two men calmly walking down the stairs.

And hit nothing. A great, clear wall of absolutely nothing, from which the bullets ricocheted harmlessly away.

At her side, Ashley heard Spider swear. Carter clicked at Tala, and the dog surged forward as he continued to fire. Rushing the men, Tala barely made it half the length of the alley before a burst of energy sent her flying back to land in a yelping heap on an over-flowing dumpster nearby.

Sobbing, the woman strained to run faster.

Ashley just stared.

Energy swelled. Clear, crystal, and impossible. It surrounded the men, growing stronger with every heartbeat.

She saw Carter wince and heard Spider curse again. "Shen!" the girl shouted amid the racket of gunfire. "Get–"

The energy smashed down on the woman like a hammer. For a moment, Ashley watched a shell glisten around her, as though taking the blow. Then it shattered, and fragments of iridescent light flew toward the men.

And disappeared.

Like a puppet without strings, the woman crashed to the ground.

The others shouted. Swore. Gunfire echoed all around her. The monsters looked up from the dead woman and cocked their heads at Ashley curiously, while the energy swelled up around them ten times stronger than before.

She couldn't move. She was in the middle of the alley. She needed to move, and she couldn't even breathe.

The energy grew.

Something slammed into her from the side. Carter's weight carried her into the shelter of the garbage bin, while the brick wall behind where she'd been standing fractured and showered debris on the alley.

"Stay down!" he shouted.

She nodded numbly. Across the alley, Spider and Samson crouched behind another dumpster, firing in turns while the other reloaded with ammunition from Spider's bag. Contrary to her promise, Ashley peeked around the garbage bin.

"Bus, get here now!" Carter yelled into his cell before rising and shooting at the men standing idly over the dead woman's body.

The garbage bin across from her launched into the air, taking the others with it. A few yards away, Spider crashed into a pile of garbage bags and then tumbled to the ground. Instantly, the girl rolled to her feet and rushed for the cover of the building's corner.

But in the center of the alley, Samson lay motionless. Blood seeped from gashes on his leg, and his gun rested beyond his outstretched hand.

She stared. A blast tore through the air beside her, narrowly missing Carter. Trapped at the alley corner, Spider screamed for Samson to move.

It was so fast. So very fast. Between one heartbeat and the next, the energy rose around the men again.

Samson opened his eyes. Gasped. Looked toward the monsters. And Ashley could feel the strike coming.

Bolting from the cover of the dumpster, Ashley threw herself at the gun. Her hands wrapped around it, and rolling awkwardly, she flung her arms out and squeezed the trigger till the weapon clicked emptily.

Bullets spun away from the shield surrounding the men.

And the monsters paused.

Lunging from behind the garbage bin, Carter grabbed Samson's shirt and hauled the man with him as he rushed after Spider with Tala running on three legs to follow.

Energy flooded up around the men. Scrambling to her feet, Ashley ran, skirting the corner as the edge of the building shattered in her wake. Debris flew around her, grazing her face and showering the concrete.

The van screeched to a stop at the alley entrance. Racing to the vehicle, Spider threw the side door open, ripped a panel from the floor and then spun, a submachine gun in her hands. She swung up to one side of the door, clutching the overhead railings as Carter hurried Samson inside.

"Get in!" she shouted at Ashley.

Eyes wide, Ashley darted around her and tumbled into the van, Tala coming right behind. In the street, people huddled behind doors and inside shops, and in the distance, sirens howled as police rushed to the scene.

The men came around the corner.

Bus hit the accelerator.

Hanging from the side of the vehicle, Spider unleashed a torrent of bullets at the two men, cutting off as the alley was lost from sight.

Spinning the wheel, Bus sent the vehicle careening around a corner, and then crushed the pedal to the floor. Swinging into the van, Spider dropped into the seat and then yanked the door closed.

She tossed the weapon into the open compartment in the floor and looked back toward Carter and Samson. "Is he…"

"I'm fine," Samson said, his voice tight. He hissed with pain as Carter pulled his coat back, exposing a dislocated shoulder. Grimacing, Samson clenched his teeth, and then let out a muffled yell as the older man shoved the joint back into place.

Watching them a moment more, the girl exhaled and then turned away, emotions flickering swiftly over her face. Rage won. Closing her eyes, she paused, and then kicked the compartment lid closed.

"Sons of–" she muttered.

"Highway in thirty seconds," Bus called, veering around another corner in response to chatter on the police scanner. "Where to?"

"Abbey," Carter said.

"What the–" Samson protested, struggling to sit up and then falling back with a gasp. "Carter, you can't just bring her–"

"Enough, Sam," Spider said without turning around, her quiet voice nevertheless cutting him off. "She saved your life."

The girl looked at Ashley briefly, and then started shrugging off her jacket to check the condition of her own bruises. Carter tied a bandage on Samson's leg and then eased the younger man down onto the bench. Shifting around awkwardly in the tight quarters, Carter climbed to the front, glancing down at Tala as he passed.

"Good girl," he murmured to the dog, who wagged her tail tiredly.

Ashley stared at them. They were so calm. Yet they'd just… and that woman…

"What…" She swallowed hard and tried again. "What…"

The others weren't listening.

"They killed her," she said. "They just…"

Words failed. Directionless, her eyes searched the van for answers and came to rest on Tala. The dog was still breathing, though Mischa licked the other animal's leg and whined.

Images flashed in front of her. Shenandoah. The men. The window. The others had just started across the street at the sight of the window and then…

"You knew," she said, looking up at them. "You knew… those men… you…"

"Of course we knew," Spider said, glancing over at her. "We've been fighting the wizards for years."

Chapter Eleven

"T-the what?" Ashley stammered.

"Wizards," the girl repeated.

Twisting around, Spider winced at the beginnings of a livid bruise beneath her tattoo.

Ashley nodded slowly. Right. That's what she'd thought the girl had said.

"Um…" she tried. "There's, um… there's no such thing as…"

She trailed off, her brow furrowing distractedly. No such thing as what? People who hurt others with impossible nothings? People who burst into flame?

Spider looked at her curiously. "Your parents really didn't tell you anything, did they?"

For some reason, the words made her want to laugh, though she couldn't think why. And meanwhile, the floor kept swimming in and out of focus.

"Are you going to be sick?" Spider asked cautiously.

Bus glanced back in alarm, but Ashley just shook her head, regretting the motion instantly. "No," she managed. "I'm… I'm fine…"

Watching her a moment more, the other girl shifted her shoulders with a pained grimace and then reached down to check the dogs. "So what'd you think was going on?"

The laugh emerged this time, choked and hysterical to her own ears. The impression must have been mutual, because Spider glanced up again, her brow drawing down at the sound.

"I…" Ashley started, swallowing back the fluttering panic. She shook her head, unable to continue.

Spider's gaze went to Carter, who looked between them briefly and then jerked his chin at the other girl. Shrugging her eyebrows, Spider took a deep breath and turned back to Ashley.

"So nobody's told you about Merlin or Taliesin or…?" She trailed off, watching Ashley's face. "Cripples?" she tried again.

Ashley stared.

"Right. And let me guess. You lived on that farm your whole life and just… what? Never left?"

The mildly knowing tone in her voice was annoying, but the irritation was thwarted by how closely the words hit to home. Yet it wasn't entirely true. Sure, for the past few years, they'd stayed with Jonathan and Rose, but not out of a nefarious design on anyone's part. There just wasn't much of anywhere else to go, and vacations weren't possible on a working farm…

And then there were about eight years unaccounted for, before her mother died.

Uncomfortable with the turn her thoughts had taken, she shrugged noncommittally, and the girl shook her head.

"Then your family was what we would consider in hiding," Spider said, her tone fading into seriousness. "And to keep things as normal as possible, some of them don't always tell their kids why."

She sighed, seeing the denial rise up in Ashley's expression. "Okay, look. What you saw today? Those were wizards, and they come in two—" She cut off. "To *them*, they come in two categories."

Ashley's brow furrowed.

Spider shook her head dismissively. "More on that later. What you need to know right now is that they think there are two groups, but they're all just wizards and none of them are your friends. Primary rule: *never* trust a wizard. Keep that in mind, and everything else falls into place."

"Wizards are bastards," Samson muttered. "Bloody fucking bastards."

The girl turned, seeming unperturbed by his words. "Try to rest, Sam," she said quietly.

Grimacing, Samson rolled slightly to one side and closed his eyes.

Her gaze lingered on him for a heartbeat more, and then Spider blinked and shifted back around. Drawing a breath, she continued. "So. We could just say there's two or more sides, depending on your point of view. They're in a war, they hate each other, kill any of them if they mess with you. And we could leave it at that. But," she paused, glancing to Carter, "considering no one ever told you much, it might help you understand what probably happened with your family if you have some background on what's actually going on."

Ashley swallowed uncomfortably.

"To start, one side calls themselves Merlin. The other, Taliesin. Their names come from their basic allegiances, which in turn come from two guys who died about five hundred years ago. The original Merlin and Taliesin were brothers, part of a regular old wizard family, except their mom obviously had an obsession with Arthurian literature and their ancestry tended toward talents nobody else possessed. Wizards are all like that, in their way. Some are better at certain things than others, just like anybody. But Taliesin and Merlin… their gifts were rather freakish by wizard standards, probably because they had a family filled with generations of folks with a liking for magical experimentation. Or so the story goes.

"In any case, Taliesin got it in his head that the current state of staying behind the scenes and letting ordinary humans run things wasn't really ideal. Wizards should *fix* things. Change the world. Figured if they had these abilities, they should take advantage of them. They should set policy and law, not the regular humans who – to his mind – had thus far just screwed everything up. And lots of people agreed and thought it sounded like a great idea."

She scoffed. "Wizards don't have many records of their history, due to everything that came later, but you've got to figure there'd been plenty of folks who'd tried the same thing before. I mean, it's not rocket science. Yet, dammit, *those* losers must have been stupid or less advanced or something. Why else would they have never pulled it off?"

Spider shook her head and then dropped her sarcastic tone. "But not everybody liked that plan. And ultimately, Taliesin's biggest opponent turned out to be his brother. Merlin believed Taliesin would end the wizards up in a position they couldn't sustain. Like his mother, Merlin loved history, and in his opinion, governments that deprived people of any voice eventually degenerated into doing just one thing: using brute force to stay in power. Your regular humans wouldn't remain docile beneath wizard rule forever, and in event of any uprisings, the situation would go one of two ways. Either the wizards would have to make examples of those who opposed them, and then maintain power through further violence, or they'd be eliminated.

"Whichever the outcome, Merlin foresaw his people becoming something he never wanted them to be.

"So, as the story goes, Merlin gathered up what supporters he could, and tried to stop his brother. It didn't go well. In fact, it devolved almost immediately into a bloody civil war. And in not too long, the wizards turned into exactly the kinds of monsters Merlin had hoped to keep them from becoming.

"Nobody really knows how long they fought. Accounts are sketchy, since most records were destroyed in the war. All anybody really knows is that, in the end, it looked like Taliesin had to win. His numbers were greater. Simple as that.

"And then Merlin changed everything. Like I said, his family was freakish. Back in the good old days when the wizards weren't trying to wipe each other off the face of the earth, Merlin and Taliesin's family had long since developed the skill of taking someone else's magic and using it themselves, or binding it away from the original owner, which was something nobody else could even dream of figuring out how to do. So of course, this made them both incredibly dangerous in battle… against one person. And then another. And then another, et cetera ad nauseam. But not a whole group. Not a whole battlefield.

"Until Merlin did it.

"In one moment, he bound the entirety of Taliesin's side. Not just the ones currently fighting either. All of them. Every wizard associated with Taliesin, and their families too. He locked their magic away and left them almost like any human you'd meet on the street. And in a heartbeat, the whole war came to a screeching halt.

Thousands of wizards suddenly had no magic, facing an enemy that still had all of their own.

"No one knows how he did it. He never told a soul. Legend says he bound himself to the spell to keep it going, and tied his family line to it as well. And from then on, that was the way things were. The wizards allied with Merlin kept their powers, and the wizards allied to Taliesin suddenly had to figure out how to live without any magic at all.

"But Merlin didn't think that was enough. At the time, the damage his brother did was too real, and the idea Taliesin might find a way around the spell was too frightening. So he left a mark on the Taliesin wizards – something allowing anyone on either side to tell what allegiance that wizard held.

"If one wizard sees another, they can distinguish them from normal humans with just a glance. They say it's like a perception just beyond sight, telling them if that person is a wizard and on what side. So apparently, the mark around Taliesin made that perception feel like shadow, whereas Merlin just feels like light.

"To hear them, it all sounds ridiculously poetic."

The girl rolled her eyes.

"Regardless, even with their magic bound, the Taliesin wizards could still see their Merlin counterparts, setting them apart from your average, blind human. And so the Taliesin lived their whole lives knowing what they'd lost, and what they were on the outside of."

At the baffled look on Ashley's face, Spider paused. "Okay, slowing down. It's like this. Humans? They aren't too fond of things that don't fit in their world. They've done experiments on this kind of thing, like having a man in a gorilla suit walk past people wrapped up in doing other things. A fair amount of the time, folks won't even notice him, because it doesn't fit into what they expect to see. Wizards go way beyond that. They're human, but if they don't smother it, they basically *are* magic too. But that doesn't work with what humans expect in the world. People blowing things apart without touching them? Walking in one door and coming out another miles away? Please. Can't happen. Doesn't work in 'this' world.

"So folks filter it out. Don't see it. Or them. And generation after generation of doing this has led to remarkable talents in that category. Your average adult human, when faced with something a wizard has done, will show no sign of seeing it at all. On video, it'll just be static. In an audio recording, same thing. Now *kids*, young ones, have the tendency to recognize wizards, but that's only because they haven't caught on to the whole 'don't see things that aren't possible' mentality. And while wizards can repress their magic, making themselves visible by bottling up the energy inside, most don't bother. To their minds, why should they? It's just easier that way.

"But back to what I was saying. For years, Taliesin wizards had no accessible magic and lived constantly aware there was this other group who did. Five hundred years went by, and obviously, that's a long time. Lots of Taliesin families just drifted off, initially giving up on ever getting their magic back and then, as the generations passed, forgetting about magic entirely and thinking their weird tendency to feel an aura of light or shadow around some folks was just an odd family trait. Nothing more to it. And if sometimes others with them didn't seem to see the person with the aura who just walked by, well..." She shrugged. "You drop it. After all, nobody wants to appear crazy."

Spider grinned and then continued, humor fading. "But of course, not everybody gave up. Which brings us to eight years ago, and the lovely world we now live in.

"The descendants of Taliesin and Merlin had become royalty to their respective allies, by virtue of their lineage and their status as possessing the ability to bind magic, and representative councils for the people existed on either side. Between the two groups, though, there'd always been a not-so-subtle hierarchy, wherein Taliesin was eternally second class, if Merlin even acknowledged them at all.

"And then, one night, that all changed.

"News was hard to come by in the first days of their little mess of a war, but rumor has it the Taliesin king got fed up with Merlin 'supremacy' and took matters into his own hands. He went after the Merlin king and assassinated him in effort to break the spell. And while plenty of people had thought to free the Taliesin's magic by doing this in the past, until that night it'd never worked. But then, none of them had been the Taliesin king. Somehow, he killed the Merlin's ruler *and* destroyed the spell, instantly giving thousands of Taliesin their magic back.

"But like before, things didn't go too well."

She shook her head. "Each side turned on one another. Vigilante Merlin attacked whatever Taliesin they found in vengeance for their king, and enraged Taliesin made the first Merlin they saw pay for five hundred years of their magic being bound. And lots of innocent people, just sitting in their homes trying to figure out what'd just happened, instantly became the victims of death squads from the opposing side.

"The regular humans blamed it on gas mains, or gang violence, or holiday decorations causing fires. After all, it was Christmas time, and there were plenty of normal people leaving out candles and then burning their houses down. And wizards are masters at covering stuff up or letting it be explained away. They've all got enough connections from life before everything went to hell that, if they have to step in, it's not too hard to spread the misinformation around."

Past her trembling, Ashley felt a hysterical laugh bubble up again. The stories the police told. Her diary. Boyfriend. Her plan to murder her family and sell her sister to a drug dealer.

Misinformation didn't quite seem the right word.

And then there'd been the gas main at Christmas time.

Her thoughts shied away from the fragmented memory.

Spider sighed. "And so we have the war. Bunches of families went into hiding when it all started, just trying to keep their loved ones safe. Your family probably did the same. And meanwhile, the other wizards just keep fighting. They try to prevent the regular humans from knowing what's going on, mostly because the first wizard who gets caught up by the press or goes to the cops just makes himself a lovely target for the other side. Hiding and stealth are their best weapons, and they're using them to continue their five-hundred-year-old war."

Ashley stared as she finished. Licking her dry lips, she drew a shaky breath. "And they haven't," she tested the word, "'bound' each other again? Or... whatever?"

"It's been eight years. If either side knew how to do that anymore, they would have already." Spider shook her head. "Whatever the hell Merlin pulled off, the continuation of the spell was tied to his family, but the ability to recreate that spell clearly wasn't."

Ashley nodded slowly, as though anything in the past few minutes, hours or days made sense. "And, um... how do you fit in?" she asked, trying to keep her voice calm.

"*We*, darling," Bus called from the front. "Not us. We."

She looked between them. Spider gave her a smile tinged with sympathy.

"They call people like you and the rest of us 'cripples'," the girl said. "Which is a lovely little word we've lately kind of adopted as our own. Makes it something of a joke that way, since depending on your point of view, we're anything but. In translation, though, we're the ones born into wizard families, just without any magic. They say we've got the genes or whatever, but…" She shrugged. "No magic. No distinction between those of us born Merlin or Taliesin either. Just nothing. We can see them, which puts us ahead of your average human, but not the way wizards do. They look like normal people to us, though they say we look like something is missing to them. Like something that should be there inside us, just isn't."

"Bunch of crap, if you ask me," Bus added.

Spider's mouth twitched in a grin at him, and then she turned back to Ashley. "We don't see it that way," she said dryly. "But it puts us at a big risk, because while we can see their existence, we can't tell them – or even ourselves – apart from anyone else. Wizard or cripple, everybody just looks like regular folks to us. And you wouldn't think that would be a serious problem, but then… you saw what happened to Shen."

Anger rippled beneath Spider's expression and with difficulty, the girl pushed it away. "There *is* one thing that sets us apart from normal humans, though, besides being able to see the wizards, magic be damned. We have something… something the bastards can take. It's not magic, exactly. Wizard researchers used to say it's a genetic abnormality. A defect where magic should have been, like somebody born without both kidneys or something. But whatever. Point is, if they hit us with their magic just right, well…"

Spider looked away. "We call the wizards who do that 'ferals'. And they've killed a lot of our kind. They hunt us because when they kill us and take whatever it is we have… it makes them stronger. Boosts their power for a while, like they're hopped up on steroids from hell or something. And it leaves us dead. Like Shen."

Ashley's gaze dropped to the ground, remembering the alleyway.

"Not all wizards do it," Spider allowed, a touch grudgingly. "Maybe not even most. Before the war, killing a cripple for power was considered akin to rape or child molesting. But war's funny like that. Suddenly, the wizards found their lives in danger, their whole society was tumbling down, and dealing with a bunch of ferals just wasn't quite as important anymore. I mean, some still frown on it. Some probably even try to stop it. But you've also got to take into account the ones who say it's despicable, and then look the other way. The ferals are strong, after all." Sarcasm dripped from her tone. "And they make *great* fighters."

Up ahead, Ashley could see Bus' hands flexing, as though strangling the steering wheel.

Slowly, Spider drew a breath. "Which brings us to… well, us. Wizards mockingly dubbed our little group the 'Hunters', and the ferals who've survived run-ins with us kind of picked the name up." She rolled her eyes. "Whatever. It's as good a name as any. We got it from the Merlin, after Carter walked out on them eight years ago. Before the war, he was the cripple ambassador to their Council. Kind of a representative making sure our right not to be killed or whatever was respected. But then everything went sideways, some of the Merlin began turning a blind eye while the ferals tore our people to pieces, and well…"

She shook her head, and Carter shifted slightly, as though

uncomfortable with the turn the history lesson was taking.

"So now we hunt the ferals," Spider said, returning to her original subject. "The four of us, and some others around the country too. We move our people around, help them hide, get them connected with others of our kind for protection, and take out any ferals we can. It's not easy, as you saw today. If they're ready for you, there's not a whole lot you can do. Wizards'll block bullets as easily as anything, and blow you up besides. But if they're not ready for you…" She grinned darkly. "Gun'll kill a wizard if they don't know the shot's coming. Like that guy inside the hotel. We'd been hunting him for a while, tracking him after he took out two of our own a few weeks ago. Let him get enough of a glimpse at us to know there were cripples in the area, and then waited for him to come looking. Didn't expect you to be there, though. Thankfully, he was a cocky enough bastard to drop the magic around himself like he was making some damn point, which gave Carter and Sam the chance to take him out."

Ashley blanched, swallowing hard at the memory. "And you knew when he did? Even if you couldn't… see it… or whatever?"

"Your head wanted to split open from being near him," Bus called back. "Am I right?"

She looked between them.

"Give you the headache from hell when a wizard's doing magic near you," Spider explained. "Doesn't matter what it is. Fighting, healing, pretty much anything short of actually using their magic to *protect* you, and it'll make your brain feel like it's getting sucked out your ears. That thing about us – the lack of magic or whatever – it doesn't like being near wizards using their power. So yeah, while you can't *see* what they're doing, per se, you sure as all hell can feel it."

Barely breathing and not taking her eyes from the other girl,

Ashley crushed the fires inside herself till they nearly disappeared. "Right," she said hoarsely.

"Any time you got a sudden headache around your dad or whoever," Spider said. "I'd bet you money they were doing magic and not telling you. Some families who hid with their cripple relatives were like that, especially if they were Taliesin and started out without magic anyway. Rather than hold up what they could do and their relatives couldn't, the family went on as though their magic wasn't real, trying to hang onto what'd been normal before the world went to hell.

"And it works," the girl continued, glancing at her with sympathy again. "Till that world comes banging down your door."

Ashley looked away, aching from the words and still trying to wrap her mind around yet more things that couldn't possibly be real.

Like the fire. And the forest. And Malden.

Her father, a wizard. The men who came after them, wizards too.

"So they... the others..."

She didn't know how to say what she was asking, but Spider seemed to understand anyway.

"Some or all," Spider answered. "Yeah. Probably."

Ashley shook her head, uncomprehending. "And I'm a..."

Wizard, she answered for herself. The word was wizard. And it made no sense in any rational view of the world.

The litany of impossible things from the past forty-eight hours ran through her head, but she shoved them away, struggling to keep calm in the face of four people with guns who apparently didn't realize she was one of their enemies.

"A cripple," Spider said.

Ashley hesitated. "But you... I mean... there's nothing you see..."

Humor flickered in Spider's eyes. "You think the dogs are just for show?"

Already nearly bloodless, Ashley felt the last traces of color drain from her face. Her gaze dropped to Tala and Mischa, lying curled and snoring between the seats.

"Dogs, birds, cats, you name it… they all hate wizards," Spider said. "Can't stand being near them. Carter had Tala check you out the moment he saw you."

The memory of the dog approaching over the length of the room came back to her. Only after Tala licked Ashley's cheek had the two men holstered their guns.

At Ashley's expression, the girl grinned. "If you were a wizard, that wouldn't have gone quite the same way. Plus, Carter heard the feral talking about cripple hunting. From the sound of it, the bastard thought he'd found himself an easy kill at the end of a long, disappointing day.

"Poor baby," she finished scathingly.

Ashley looked away, feeling nauseated.

"Hey," Spider said, dropping the sarcasm instantly. "Breathe."

She nodded jerkily. In the driver's seat, Bus glanced back, clearly still concerned that she might throw up in his van.

Swallowing hard, her gaze returned to Tala and Mischa. "But they can always tell," she said, her tone inching toward a question.

"Yeah," Spider said seriously. "Against wizards anyway. They act as a defense if we get caught by surprise. But it's not easy. We've lost more than one that way."

Barely registering the last words, Ashley watched the two massive animals sleeping at her feet. Tala had rushed at the men in the alley without hesitation, and it was some kind of miracle she hadn't been killed by the blow that knocked her away.

The dog shifted around, rolling slightly to cover Ashley's feet. They'd lain there the whole time, drowsing like puppies, and never once giving a sign anything was wrong.

But she...

The fires wanted to flicker and twist inside her, to rise and explode as though to show they were real. Trembling, she closed her eyes, trying to restrain the barely restrainable and not blow up everyone in the van just to prove the impossible.

To prove she wasn't crazy. Or they weren't crazy. Or both.

Wizards. It was stupid. Everything was stupid. She shouldn't be having this conversation. Rose was a farmwife, for pity's sake. She'd worked every day in the fields with palms callused to impermeability and skin tanned to leather. Jonathan had been the same. They'd been farmers. Not magical, mystical beings who could wave their hands and make flowers grow and birds sing.

Not that there'd been any birds, really. Lily had never succeeded in attracting a single one, no matter how many birdhouses she made. And Thelma's cats had hated the couple more than anything. Then there was the lack of farm animals. Or the way mice never came into the house, though she'd always been grateful for that. But she couldn't even remember seeing an insect when Jonathan or Rose were around.

She drew a shaky breath, trying to stop the torrent of thoughts tumbling through her mind. Tala and Mischa liked her. She was a fantasy creature whose only skill was murder and destruction through uncontrollable flames, but the dogs seemed to think she was okay. And from what Spider said, that may have been the only reason she was alive.

Nausea turned her stomach and she struggled to just keep breathing.

"There *is* one last thing you need to know," Spider said carefully.

Warily, Ashley's gaze slid back to her.

"There's a third group," the girl said. "The one wizards don't believe exists."

At Ashley's unblinking stare, Spider continued. "You probably saw him outside the hotel. The glowing guy. He's part of the third group. The ones you kill on the first shot or you don't get away."

Shifting around in her chair, Spider sighed. "They call themselves the Blood, that much we've learned. They cropped up around the time the war started, glowing like blazes and more powerful than any wizard we'd seen. As for what side they're on…" She scoffed. "Nobody else's, that's for sure. And though they look practically covered in fairy dust to you and me, they just look like a regular, everyday human to the Merlin and Taliesin.

"And neither side believes they exist.

"When the war first started, before ferals became as widespread and it still seemed like the Merlin might listen, Carter tried to convince them the Blood were real. But cripples don't have magic, remember? So how could we possibly see something the über-powerful wizards couldn't perceive?"

She rolled her eyes darkly. "They refused to believe him. Taliesin had a new weapon, they said. Or the war left Carter unhinged. No matter the explanation, *they* were the wizards, and so what help could a cripple offer? We're the defective ones, remember? Not them."

Shaking her head, she paused and then visibly pushed her frustration aside. "From what we can tell, the Blood are determined to stay under the wizards' radar, though what they're after, we're not really sure. And the Blood know we can see them. They figured that out real quick once the war began. But that makes us a serious liability, meaning whenever they have the chance to do so without being seen, they pretty much categorically try to wipe us out. For our part, we keep tabs on them if we can for safety's sake, and some of our people have succeeded in killing a few. But it's brutal. Because while bullets will slow a wizard down, and even a feral might give up and go home after a couple of rounds fired his way, these guys…"

"Monsters," Ashley whispered.

Spider nodded. "Pretty much."

Ashley turned away. He'd not looked like anything. The man who killed her father. Alone of all the others around him, he'd just… Nothing had been there.

She wondered, had someone seen him glow, if things might have gone differently. They would've had more warning. And her father and everyone else wouldn't have died.

Silence fell over the van. Outside the window, billboards for attractions near the Smoky Mountains swept past, while cars with license plates from all around the country sped by.

Her eyes tracked the vehicles. None of the people looked like anything. Not like the man in the hotel or the ones from the alley. And accordingly, they could just be human.

Or they could be like him.

"You okay?" Spider asked quietly.

Ashley glanced at her, not certain what to say.

"It's a lot to take in," the girl said.

Wordlessly, Ashley nodded and then returned her gaze to the window. Her father had probably known what the men who attacked them were. Or would have, had they not used guns or been tucked behind the grass. And maybe from a distance, he couldn't tell anything about the ones by the barn and the ranch house. Maybe the smoke even obscured the grayish feeling around them.

Or something.

More memories tumbled in. The farmhands patrolling at night. Coyotes, they'd said. The times her father went away. Business. Animals never liked them. No one ever came to visit from out of town. It'd all been so normal.

And every moment of it had been a lie.

She couldn't decide whether to be angry. The feelings were all lost in a soup of confusion and overwhelming amounts of information, any piece of which would make a psychiatrist label her as insane. Everyone she'd known had lied to her. Deliberately. Repeatedly. Every single day.

Until it killed them.

They'd had no warning. But they would have. If they'd told her. If they'd said, hey, there are wizards out there. Mean ones. They want us dead. Don't shout for help if you see the barn on fire. It might be them.

And then nobody would have died.

Water splattered on her hands and she flinched, realizing she was crying. Trembling, she swiped her eyes, anger emerging at the tears where it couldn't at the rest of reality, and she glanced to Spider.

The girl was carefully engrossed in her study of the world on the opposite side of the van.

Blinking hard, Ashley turned back to the window and focused on fighting the urge to cry.

Eight years of lying. Of making her believe everything was happy and normal and safe. Sure, her mother and grandparents had died in a tragic Christmastime fire. But it'd been an accident. Not something that was still hunting them after nearly a decade.

Or something that would come back and kill her eight-year-old sister, the one person that had been spared last time.

Anger struggled back out of the confusion, and started to build. They'd never told her anything. How could people who'd said they loved her spend every day living a lie?

"Hey," Bus said.

She looked up, still shaking. In the rearview mirror, his eyes flicked between her and the road, and from below the seat, he drew out an old towel.

"Rip this up," he said, handing it back to her.

Taking it from him, her brow furrowed in confusion. Old grease stains marred the faded red terry cloth, and threads hung from the frayed sides.

"It helps," he explained. "Trust me."

From the corner of her eye, she saw a smile pull at Spider's lips, though the girl never looked her way. Gripping the towel, she hesitated a moment, and then ripped it in two.

Her brow twitched down in faint incredulity. He was kind of right.

Swallowing hard, she shredded the towel, clutching it and yanking it to pieces, and then shredding the remnants as well. Threads fell like red snow on the dogs, who woke and looked up at her with confusion before choosing to go back to sleep.

And slowly, she poured the anger into the ragged bits of towel till nothing but thin strips, fibers and numbly confused, quivery feelings remained.

Her gaze rose to Bus. He winked at her in the rearview mirror.

"Thanks," she said quietly.

He grinned. "Anytime, kiddo."

She brushed the tattered shreds on her lap into a small pile, and then paused uncertainly.

"Here," Spider said, pulling a plastic grocery bag from the pouch on the back of Carter's seat. Ashley dumped the handful of fabric inside, and Spider bundled it up, not letting any of the threads escape. The girl gave her a small smile and then put the bag away.

Hesitantly, Ashley looked around. "Thanks," she said again.

Spider just shrugged and went back to watching the road. Bus smiled and kept driving. Samson rested, ignoring everything. And Carter never said a word.

Still confused and aching, Ashley turned back to the window. But unlike before, the feeling wasn't quite the same.

She wasn't alone. Even if they didn't know what she was – could never know what she was – there were still four bizarre people with guns who were helping her. It wasn't perfect, or honest in the least, but if she just focused on that, she could almost think she'd be okay.

Chapter Twelve

They drove on through the Appalachian Mountains. Billboards for breweries, wax museums and resorts crowded every available space on the roadside, while souvenir shops clustered at the fringes of towns and cars from everywhere filled the interstate.

And then Bus turned off the highway, and gradually the clutter disappeared.

Following a course Ashley couldn't have retraced if she tried, the old man navigated off the state roads and into the mountains themselves. Houses dotted the valleys between steep hillsides, and cattle clung to the slopes like mountain goats. Eventually, concrete gave way to asphalt, and then to gravel that roared beneath the tires. Trees rushed past only a couple feet from the window, and rusted chain-link fences in the woods were the only sign someone lived nearby.

Gravel became dirt. The chain-link fences ended. The van climbed over slopes and down gullies, and nothing but trees could be seen on either side.

A groan behind her made Ashley turn. On the bench seat, Samson grimaced but didn't wake. The past few hours hadn't been good to him. Sweat dotted his forehead, and his skin looked gray. He'd been growing steadily worse for some time, and the others had long since fallen silent, doing what they could to allow him to sleep.

Her brow furrowing, she shifted back to the front, not knowing what to do. Without more than the rudimentary medical care the others were able to provide, he wasn't going to get better. And from the looks of their surroundings, hospitals probably weren't a possibility.

She glanced around worriedly. Carter's gaze was locked on the window, and he'd hardly spoken since leaving Shen's. With a face colder than normal, Spider watched the middle distance and gave no sign of noticing the others in the van. But she'd stopped looking behind her an hour ago, and fingered the gun in her lap as though finding solace there.

The van stopped. Startled, Ashley looked up. Trees and underbrush filled the space in front of them, while the dirt track serving as a road continued through the forest to their left.

Spider threw open the door, and the other men did the same. Hurriedly, Ashley clambered out at the girl's impatient motion, stepping aside just in time for Carter to climb in and hoist Samson from the seat. Hefting the young man's bulk, Carter grimaced and then gratefully accepted Bus' assistance when he got Samson shifted toward the door.

Groaning, the young man woke. "You don't need–"

"Shut up," Bus told him.

Between them, the older men shouldered Samson's weight and started into the forest, leaving Ashley and Spider behind.

Swiftly, the girl grabbed the bags from beneath the seats and tossed them to Ashley, who caught them awkwardly. Slamming the door behind her, Spider retrieved a few of the bags, shouldered them quickly, and then jerked her head at Ashley.

"Come on," she said, starting after the others.

With the dogs beside her, Ashley followed.

In moments, the van was lost to view, and only forest surrounded them. Straight ruts beneath the bushes gave proof a road had once cut through the woods, though saplings and underbrush had taken its place. The afternoon sun streamed down and shifted as the leaves moved in the breeze. Broken branches crunched beneath their feet, and leaves wet with spring rains swiped their legs. Fallen logs rotting in the undergrowth lay across the invisible path the others walked, and all around, birds called and darted from tree to tree.

Carter paused and whistled shortly, sounding nearly like a bird himself. Alarmed, Ashley looked at him, but the others just kept moving. Brow furrowing, she glanced around. Nothing in the forest had changed.

Warily, she continued walking.

The terrain rolled around them as the minutes passed. Samson hung limply between Carter and Bus, silent and gray. Spider had taken the lead, and now looked torn between the desire to go faster and the realization the others could only move with so much speed.

Men in camouflage rose from the underbrush, guns in their hands.

Heart in her throat, Ashley came to a halt and scrambled desperately after the stupid, useless magical fires that would get her shot.

The others stopped, and Spider turned to the armed men, relief in her eyes.

"All accounted for?" Carter asked.

"Every one," one of the men answered.

Bus and Carter shifted Samson's weight from their shoulders as several of the armed men hurried over to hoist the young man between them.

"I'm fine," Samson protested groggily.

Ignoring him, the men took off through the forest. As they passed, Spider glanced back to Carter questioningly.

He jerked his chin at her.

She followed Samson without a word.

Dumbstruck, Ashley stared at the men. Camouflage covered them from head to toe, complete with leafy branches woven into the jackets and hats they wore. All manner of shotguns and rifles hung from their shoulders, and handguns were holstered at their sides. In the bushes behind them, more dogs waited, eyeing Tala and Mischa but too well trained to move.

And each of them felt like Carter, Spider and the rest. Cripples, they'd said. The ones with magic missing.

"What happened?" asked the man who'd originally spoken.

"Shenandoah's dead," Carter said.

The man grimaced and behind him, a few others looked away. For a moment, the man didn't move, the muscles in his jaw clenching. Then he drew a breath. "And who's this?"

Carter glanced at her. "This is Ashe." He paused so briefly, she barely registered the thoughtfulness that flashed over his face. "New friend we picked up in Utah. One who emptied a gun at the ferals who got Shen, and helped save Samson's life."

She struggled not to look uncomfortable as the man's eyebrows rose appreciatively. "Well," he said. "Nice to meet you, Ashe. Name's Jericho."

"Hi," she said.

"He's in charge around here," Bus chimed in.

Trying not to be impolite, she restrained the urge to look around the empty forest, but Jericho seemed to see it anyway. Chuckling, he gestured in the direction Samson had been taken. "How 'bout we get on with the tour, eh? Van back that way?"

The last was directed at Bus, who nodded.

"We'll take care of it," Jericho said.

With a glance to the others, he twitched his head and then started walking as the armed men headed back into the cover of the trees, their camouflage making them disappear almost immediately.

The dogs still at her side, she followed Carter toward the next ridge. Bus dropped back to walk with her, and he grinned as he took most of the bags from her shoulders.

"What did Carter mean, all accounted for?" she asked quietly.

The old man hesitated, as though deciding what to say. Or, she realized, whether to respond at all. Finally, he bent his head near to hers.

"It's code. Not all our people sided with us. Some went to the wizards for protection. But some of the wizards are ferals, and so to continue protecting their own asses, those cripples now try to infiltrate our hideouts and turn over their own kind to be killed. The Abbey's pretty hidden, but they still get an influx of folks from time to time. Carter was just checking. If Jericho thought somebody around here might be a traitor, he would've said something different. 'Each and every one' means there could be trouble, so keep an eye out. 'All of them' means we've been compromised. 'Every one' means everything's fine."

"How do you keep that straight?" she asked, baffled.

"You get used to it."

She paused. "You're talking about sellouts."

He glanced at her, seeming surprised she knew the term.

"I overheard the others at Wood's," she explained. "They thought I might be one."

His expression cleared and his grin returned. "That was then, kiddo. But yeah, sellouts."

Biting her lip, she kept walking.

Another hill rose ahead. Shifting the bag higher on her shoulder, she climbed tiredly and then blinked as she reached the top. A fence ran along the base of the slope. Barbed wire coiled across the tall chain-link barrier, the length of which stretched far into the forest on either side. The portion directly below them held a gate, set on runners and tied with a padlock and chains.

Walking up to it, Jericho undid the lock and then rolled away the gate, stepping aside and gesturing grandiosely for them to continue once he was done. Bus chuckled at the motion.

Ashley swallowed nervously as she followed the others through. Behind her, Jericho refastened the chain and then came after them, letting Carter and Bus lead the way as the grassy path widened and became a dirt strip between the trees. The track twisted erratically, curving to the left for a hundred yards and then turning right without any apparent reason. Laughter filtered through the air and confusedly, Ashley looked to the others, but the men just kept walking as though the serpentine pathway and ghostly sounds were normal.

And then they came around another turn, the track expanded and turned to gravel, and Ashley's steps faltered.

Log cabins crowded next to mobile homes beneath the trees, and everywhere she looked, birdcages hung. The path branched off into smaller walkways that wound between homes scattered like toy blocks in every available space. Vegetable gardens clustered near each house, and chickens ambled at the edges of the dirt patches. Dogs wandered everywhere, and cats slept on the porches in warm patches of late afternoon light.

And the people. There were so many people, each like the others. Cripples. Dozens upon dozens of them.

Children ran between the houses, filling the air with their laughter. Adults worked around them, hanging laundry, planting in the gardens or repairing their homes. Others sat on their steps, chatting with neighbors. Everywhere she looked, people were living and working as though being secluded in the middle of a forest was the most natural thing in the world.

But then, it probably wasn't any less natural than being stuck on a farm for eight years and never even thinking of leaving.

With difficulty, she pushed the thought away, the sentiment feeling dark and angry in this bright place.

"Welcome to the Abbey," Carter said, a corner of his mouth rising in a grin.

She tried to smile, and then jumped as Jericho clapped her on the shoulder. "Come on," he said, striding past her. "Knowing Magnolia, she's probably gotten a space set up for you already."

"His wife," Bus supplied as he followed the other man.

Uncertain what to think, she started after them, watching the dogs and birdcages. People called greetings and waved to Carter and Bus as they passed, while Spider and the men who took Samson were nowhere to be seen.

"You alright?" Carter asked quietly, falling back to walk by her side.

Feeling overwhelmed, she managed a nod.

"The wizards who hurt your family won't find you here. And even if they tried, they'd run into a hell of a lot more than they bargained for."

She hesitated.

"What?" he asked, seeing her expression.

"Blood," she said uncomfortably. "The man who killed my dad. He was a Blood. The wizards were just working for him."

He paused. "Are you sure?"

She nodded.

Carter echoed the motion, but his attention didn't seem to be with her anymore. They kept walking.

A few hundred feet from the entrance, Jericho left the gravel track and started across a small yard toward a log cabin. Brightly painted cages hung along the porch eaves, and songbirds chirped inside. As they approached, the front door opened and a woman stepped out, a birdseed canister in her hand. Her eyes lit up as she saw them, and swiftly she set down the container. Grabbing up her multicolored skirts, she hurried down the stairs, and embraced Carter and Bus happily.

"I wasn't sure how long you'd be!" she exclaimed, pushing away from them and grinning. "Knowing Jericho, I figured you'd be talking for hours before he let you get away."

Her husband gave her a dry look, though it didn't quite hide his smile.

"And who's this?" she continued, turning to Ashley.

"Maggie, meet Ashe," Jericho told her. "Ashe, my wife Magnolia."

The woman smiled warmly, but after a heartbeat, an under-standing look came into her eyes.

"Well, I've got about a million things to take care of, so if you guys don't need anything, how about I show Ashe where we've got for her to stay? Melody and her husband have some extra room for the two of you, and Blue's inside with Samson and Spider, so unless there's anything else…?" A smile pulled at Magnolia's lips as the men shook their heads. "Then we'll see you at dinner."

The others nodded. Ashley shrugged the bag from her shoulder, handing it to Carter. Bus waved as they walked away.

"Come on, sweetie," Magnolia said kindly. "Let's get you settled, eh?"

Before they could reach the door, it swung open and a tousled auburn head popped out. "Momma?" a little girl called, her cheeks flushed pink from running. "Can Spider sleep in my room? She told me I should ask you."

"Spider's going to be in Bryony's room with Samson," the woman told her carefully. "And Bry is staying with you, remember? We already talked about this."

Frowning unhappily, the young girl nevertheless nodded and then disappeared back into the house. Magnolia sighed. "My daughter, Peony," she explained with a smile. "You'll probably see a lot of her. Or, at least, hear."

Ashley hesitated. "Did she… um, make all this?" she asked, gesturing to the birdcages and trying to keep her tone casual.

"No, that was me."

"They're nice," Ashley said, feeling stupid for being obscurely relieved.

Simply smiling, Magnolia pushed open the door. Color surrounded them as they came inside. Bright rag rugs carpeted the hardwood floor and rainbow-hued afghans draped the sofa and chairs. Along one wall, a fireplace waited, a multicolored runner on the mantel.

Through the open door to her left, she could see half-finished crafts filling the master bedroom, and to her right, hand-painted mugs and bowls of every shade were stacked on the kitchen counter.

Without pausing, the woman led her past the kitchen and into a narrow hallway. From the bedroom at the end, Ashley could hear Peony chatting happily, her voice rarely interrupted by any response. Magnolia cast a frustrated glance down the hall, and then opened a door on her right, revealing a tiny bedroom.

A scrap quilt covered the twin bed and a short dresser sat beneath the window on the far wall. On the floor, a rag rug lay and when she stepped on it, Ashley could feel her feet sink.

"Bathroom is the second door on the left down the hall," Magnolia told her. "We don't usually turn on the generator, but if you'd like a hot shower later, just let me know. We can get the water heater going with no trouble. Blankets are in the closet next to the bathroom if you get cold, and if there's anything else you need and can't find, feel free to ask, okay?"

Ashley blinked. "Thank you."

Magnolia smiled. "Our pleasure. And now if you'll excuse me…" She glanced down the hall again, where Peony was launching into yet another story.

Ashley nodded and the woman disappeared. A moment later, she could hear Magnolia chastising the girl for keeping Samson awake and distracting the doctor.

She turned back to the room. If she stretched out her arms, her fingers would almost reach both walls. But the bed was soft when she sat down, and the blankets seemed like they'd be warm. Homemade curtains draped the window, letting in the late afternoon sunlight. She trailed her hands over the quilt and pillows, feeling as though it'd been a lifetime since she'd last slept on something other than a floor or van seat.

"Hey," Spider said, leaning her head around the door.

Ashley flinched. She didn't know how long she'd been sitting there, lost in thoughts she couldn't recall.

"How's Samson?" she asked.

The girl paused. "Better. Blue's still with him."

Visibly resetting, Spider drew a short breath. "Look, dinner's not for a couple hours and I don't know about you, but those fruit cups from the van aren't quite cutting it. You want to grab something?"

"Okay."

Spider headed for the door, leaving Ashley to follow.

The main path curved along a slope till it ended at the doors of a multistory building that resembled an enormous version of the log cabins behind her. Massive windows arched over its covered entryway, and a broad green roof blended with the trees. Atop cracked stone stairs, double doors stood and, without hesitation, Spider tugged them open and continued inside.

Shadows surrounded them, broken only by the final bits of sunlight pushing through the windows overhead. A stage was set into the leftmost wall, the curtains closed over it, and a gallery circled the second floor to look down on the one below. In a corner, Ashley spotted Carter engrossed in quiet conversation with Jericho and several other men. They didn't look up as she and Spider walked by.

Striding down the darkened hall, Spider pushed back the swinging metal door to the kitchen and then abruptly stopped. Coming up behind her, Ashley looked around, confused.

A large man bent over the oven and then drew out a tray of rolls. Turning, he moved to set them on a butcher's table, when he caught sight of the two of them.

"What do you want?" he said, his tone only making a pretense at civility. He set the tray on the counter, glaring.

"Where's Belle?" Spider asked.

"Home with a sick kid. You didn't answer my question."

Spider paused. Dropping her hand from the door, she stepped into the room. "My friend and I got in a bit ago. We're just here for something to eat."

By the doorway, Ashley didn't move, immobilized by the sudden tension in the air.

"Dinner's in two hours."

"I know that," Spider answered.

A moment passed, and then his mouth twisted into a mockery of a smile. "You all are just something, you know *that*?"

Spider didn't respond, but her eyes stayed on him as she started toward the tray.

"I told you two hours!" he snapped, moving in front of the food when he saw where she was headed. "I swear, you and the rest just think you're gods, don't you? Expecting us to give you whatever you want." He sneered. "Like I'm supposed to kowtow to you for getting innocent people killed."

The girl paused. Ashley couldn't see her breathing.

"But then, your kind don't care who pays for the trouble you cause," he said more quietly.

Slowly, Spider walked up to him till she was only inches away. Her hand reached around his wide bulk to come down on two of the rolls.

Despite his smirk, Ashley could see the man tremble.

Food in hand, Spider turned and strode back out the door,

handing Ashley one of the rolls as she passed.

"Maybe now that your boyfriend's dying, you'll learn how to give a damn," the man called.

Spider stopped. Everything about her became utterly motionless and suddenly, Ashley felt painfully aware of the guns she knew the girl was carrying.

And then Spider kept walking.

At the end of the hall, the girl turned sharply, heading away from the main entrance toward a side door.

"Where are you going?" she called to Spider uncomfortably.

"To shoot something."

With an uncertain glance to the entrance, Ashley followed.

The keypad beside the door surrendered to Spider's rapid jabs, and the stairway behind it emptied into a wide basement, the majority of which was taken up with an improvised firing range. Rags stitched into human silhouettes formed the targets at the far end, and desks that looked like they belonged in an office held stacks of ammunition. Taped to the walls, handwritten signs instructed everyone to use eye gear and earplugs, while piping and metal sheets formed booths where people could stand.

Dropping the roll on the table by the door, Spider strode to the nearest booth, yanked out one of her guns and then emptied it into the center of a target in rapid succession.

The girl exhaled slowly.

Lowering her hands from her ears, Ashley watched her. "You okay?"

Coldly, Spider glanced back, but after a heartbeat, her expressionless stare fractured into a faintly chagrinned smile. "Yeah, I'll be alright."

She set the gun on the ledge and took a breath, closing her eyes. Picking up the weapon again, she walked over to the table and pulled a box of bullets from the roughly organized piles.

"So we know you can fire a gun," Spider said, eyeing her askance with a touch of humor in her gaze. "How are you on aim?"

Ashley didn't say anything.

"Okay," Spider said as though she'd answered. She handed Ashley her gun, and then drew the other from the holster beneath her jacket. Checking the boxes again, she pushed one toward Ashley and then quickly showed her how to load the weapon.

"Keep it pointed down and away from you, me and everything, understand?" Spider told her. "And always assume it's loaded. No matter what. Even if you know it's not."

Ashley nodded.

They crossed to the booths, where Spider continued her instruction, showing her how to hold the weapon and stand, and finally allowing her to fire at the targets after ensuring Ashley understood everything she'd said.

Her shots missed entirely.

"You're milking it," Spider said when Ashley pulled out her earplugs. "Hard grip, remember? In a fight, you're going to be crushing that sucker, so get used to it now. Try again."

Ashley glanced back at the table. "I don't want to waste your bullets."

"Blue reloads them for us when he's not patching people up. It's fine."

Not really knowing what that meant, but taking the reassurance at face value, Ashley reloaded the weapon and then fired again.

A few shots hit the target.

She lowered the gun and then tugged the earplugs away, staring at the bullet holes in faint shock. It felt weird, knowing she'd just done that. Shot at something and had it work.

The memory of her father dying suddenly surged back. She set the weapon down sharply, hands trembling. A gun will kill a wizard…

And if she'd had one that night, it would have.

Her eyes found the target again.

"You alright?" Spider asked.

Distantly, she nodded, and then pushed the earplugs back in and fired. The gun clicked at her when the bullets were gone.

She glanced to Spider.

"Feels good, doesn't it?" the girl asked.

Ashley nodded again.

"Want to keep going?"

She shoved the earplugs back into place and then reloaded swiftly.

Two hours later, Spider called it quits and motioned Ashley away from the booth.

"Can you tell me what that man meant?" she asked the girl as Spider pulled open the drawer for earplugs and safety glasses.

Spider shook her head tiredly and tossed her gear inside. "He's just an old coward. One who thinks killing ferals is what makes them attack us, and that everyone who stays out there and not here deserves their fate."

Ashley wasn't sure what to say. She set her safety glasses in the drawer, and then held out Spider's gun.

"Keep it," the girl said, her attention on the ammunition boxes.

Startled, Ashley's brow furrowed.

"I've got others," Spider said. "And it might've helped if you'd had one earlier. Though you did pretty good anyway." She glanced over, amusement in her eyes. "Plus this way, wherever you end up, you can protect yourself. Even if it's just from creeps like Wood."

The girl went back to sorting through the boxes.

Ashley looked down. "Thanks," she said quietly.

Spider shrugged.

Uncertainly, Ashley paused, wondering how to carry the weapon.

"Back of your jeans works in a pinch," Spider said, her eyes still on the boxes in front of her. "We can get you a holster too, though."

Hesitantly, Ashley reached around and tucked the weapon away.

Spider's gaze flicked to her briefly and a small smile tugged at her lips. She shut the drawer and then pushed the boxes back into their stacks. "Come on," she said, her expression taking on a sarcastic cast. "Dinner's probably ready."

They headed upstairs. Emergency lights provided the only illumination in the massive room, making the space surreal. Leading her deeper into the building, Spider wound through the darkened hallways, emerging finally into an empty sunroom overlooking a broad patio.

Bright against the darkness, a bonfire burned on the lawn, lighting the people seated on a ring of logs around the blaze and in a large pavilion to one side. Windows and glass doors separated her from the porch and festivities, and made the firelight waver strangely in the carpeted space. Beyond the bonfire, a river she hadn't seen from the building's other side shimmered with the flames and moonlight.

Spider pushed open a door, and then closed it after Ashley. Crossing the patio, the girl paused at the stairway, scanning the crowd.

"What?" Ashley asked.

"Blue's not here."

The girl's brow furrowed. "Listen, I'm going to go check on Sam. Will you be alright?"

Ashley nodded. She didn't have much choice. The alternative just made her feel ashamed, like some helpless person the others had to carry.

"Okay," Spider said, still looking distracted. "See you later then."

The girl jogged down the steps and then disappeared back up the path toward the houses. Ashley watched her go, nervous and hating herself for the feeling.

She made her way down the wide stairs to the lawn. People were hard to distinguish in the harsh firelight, though it would have helped if she'd known more than a handful of them anyway. The shifting crowd parted and she spotted Bus sitting on a log by the fire, a group of children surrounding him. Unbidden relief moved through her, and she worked to ignore it while still heading quickly toward the only person she recognized.

Bus was telling them a story, the gist of which she grasped only too easily. A feral was chasing him, intent on taking his life. In rapt horror, the children listened as he described the wizard's crazed expression and the way it taunted him as it hounded him through the streets.

At the edge of the group, Ashley sank onto a log, trying not to interrupt. He'd run into the first store he'd seen, Bus told them. He'd just been trying to get away. But the store turned out to be a pet shop, and as he ran, he'd slammed headlong into a stack of cages, each of them filled to bursting with mice. The cages scattered, their tiny occupants flying to the four corners of the room. And as the wizard came in, even with his magic, he couldn't hope to get past the crowds of people suddenly screaming and jumping as the furry terrors scurried up their pant legs.

The children erupted in laughter and questions, but at the sight of Ashley, Bus waved them off. "You need to get food before your parents eat it all," he told them seriously, and at his words, most of the kids grinned and clambered up, rushing for the pavilion and the dinner waiting inside.

"Do you want me to bring you some?" Peony asked, still sitting beside him.

"How old do I look to you, kid?" he retorted indignantly. "You think I can't fight those grownups off? It's little things like you that got to worry. Now scoot!"

Giggling, Peony pushed off the log and ran after the others.

Once the little girl was gone, Bus winked at Ashley and motioned her closer. "So how you doing, Ashe-girl?"

She shrugged. "Is that story true?"

The old man affected a hurt expression. "You calling me a liar?"

Ashley shook her head and he smiled. "I might've embellished a bit," he admitted. He glanced around. "So where'd Spider get off to?"

"She went to check on Samson."

His eyebrows moved expressively. "Blue said it'll be a while before he can walk again. And Spider's really not going to like hearing that. Close as anything, those two. Been looking out for each other since he found her on the street when they were kids. Couple ferals had her cornered in an alley, but she'd already taken one of them with a shard of glass and her bare hands by the time Samson showed up and shot the other."

Bus shook his head. "She'd pay money for it to be her in there rather than him, no questions asked." The old man sighed, pushing the thoughts away. "So how're you settling in?"

"Okay," she said. "It's nice here."

He nodded amiably. "I always like it."

"Did you guys build this place or something?"

"Nah," he said, chuckling. "Bought it. Few decades back, it was some kind of resort. The company who owned it went belly up and, after the war started, Carter and most of the folks here pooled funds to get it, add the mobile homes and keep it all running."

He paused. "You could probably stay, if you'd like."

Surprised, she looked over at him.

The old man shrugged. "If you'd like," he said again.

Uncomfortably, her gaze fell to the firelight on the grass. She'd avoided thinking about it. Couldn't really in the midst of all the information she'd received over the past day. But things had changed after Spider told her the truth of what was going on. Yesterday, she'd been a girl whose family had been brutally killed. Today she was a wizard in a war, whose family had been brutally killed by monsters in whom no one but these people believed.

A wizard who, if the others learned the truth, would be cast back on the streets. Or shot. If she didn't accidentally kill them all first.

Her gaze strayed to the people milling around the fire. Hastily finished with their meals, the children ran between clusters of talking adults, their rowdy play undercutting the quiet conversations. By the pavilion, she could see Magnolia, her gray-speckled brown hair slipping from the loose bun at her neck as she threw back her head in a happy laugh.

Ashley turned away. She didn't know what to do. She wished things were different. That her family hadn't been killed, or that she could've been a cripple like the others believed.

It might've been nice to stay.

"Ashe?"

Blinking, she pulled herself from the thoughts and glanced back to the old man, who was eyeing her curiously.

"Sorry," she said. "Just… thinking."

His brow furrowed. She cast around quickly for another subject to distract him.

"So, um… would you mind telling me why everybody likes, you know, different names? I mean, did cripples always do that or…" She balked as his eyebrow raised. "Unless that's just your name. Or it's personal. I don't mean to be rude, I just–"

She cut off as he grinned.

"You sure took to it easy enough," he told her.

Ashley shifted uncomfortably, and he nudged her shoulder companionably. "Just teasing, kiddo. Not all of us are as lucky as you were, having a family who'd watch out for us. Most of us have to do what we can for our own protection, sometimes first and foremost from those who knew us before."

Her brow drew down in confusion, and he sighed. "Families went weird after the war. All of a sudden, people had to make life or death decisions constantly, and so priorities got shifted, sometimes not in the best ways. Cripples can't defend themselves. At least, not how the wizards would consider 'traditionally'. And when you're on the run, people who don't seem to offer much defensively can start to look like a liability. Or, because of other things, an opportunity.

"Some people's families abandoned them. Others turned on them. Samson's Taliesin relatives looked the other way while his vicious bitch of a sister went after him and his twin brother for power, and only Samson got away. Spider's Merlin group kicked her out on the streets to die when the war started, even though she was barely twelve at the time. My own family would readily let me stay wherever they're hiding, on the sole condition that it's only me. Everyone else I care about can go to hell, because it's not about compassion in their eyes. Just duty."

He scoffed. "There's a thousand stories like ours, one for every cripple you meet. And so we break with the old. We keep ourselves safe from the ferals or the sellouts in our own backyards by losing those identities. Nobody knows Bob Smith or Julie Brown. All those folks are gone. And we protect our own – most of us, anyway. Most of the time.

"So," he continued, "if your wizard family is attacked, they can't give you up. If your relatives get desperate and decide to go feral, you're nowhere to be found. Because that person doesn't exist anymore. You're someone new.

"The thing you've got to figure, kiddo," he told her, "is you choose who you belong to. Who you want to be. It's not blood or birth. It's a choice. This is our way of setting ourselves apart, as much as anything. Saying we're not like them. And we never will be."

She paused. "But Carter didn't change," she said, half-asking.

"There's a few others," he acknowledged. "But no, he didn't. For him, well known as he was, there just wouldn't have been much point."

He fell silent for a moment. "The name suits you, though," he said finally.

Ashley hesitated. "Thanks."

Bus nodded and then sighed, clapping his hands on his knees. "Better go get some food before it's all gone," he said. Pushing to his feet, he paused and then rested a hand on her shoulder. "Glad you're with us, kiddo."

She watched him walk away. By the pavilion, Peony and the other children ran up, begging for another story, while Magnolia hurried over to shoo them away. Bus laughed, and then glanced back to Ashley, pointing to the buffet and raising his eyebrows questioningly.

Awkwardly, she managed a nod.

Bus dished up plates of food. Escaping her mother's grasp, Peony giggled madly as she dashed off. Turning her gaze back to the bonfire, Ashley swallowed hard and tried not to think about the fact that, even though so much had changed, she was somehow still living a lie.

———•◆•———

Magnolia sat with them through dinner, and the conversation drifted from gardening to van repair, never settling on any topic for too long or delving deeper than small talk. Content to let her contribute if she chose, the others would merely smile at her from time to time, sharing humor at something said and making space for her easily.

She stayed to help clean up, letting Magnolia take drowsy little Peony back home. With the dishes put away and the food stored, Bus walked with her to the darkened cabin, and after leaving her by the porch, he waved as he headed toward Melody's.

Ashley pushed open the door, and then stopped.

"If they're working together now, there's no—"

Jericho's angry murmur cut off, and he looked up as she came inside.

Carter turned around. On the end table, an oil lamp between the two men's chairs provided the only light in the dark house.

"Sorry," she said.

"It's alright," Carter told her.

Looking between them uncomfortably, she shut the door. "Goodnight," she said, heading for the hall.

"Goodnight," Carter replied.

She disappeared into her room and shut the door. A moment passed, and then she heard Jericho begin talking again, his words too low to make out.

A few steps brought her to the chest of drawers, and reaching up, she tweaked the curtains shut. The thin fabric diffused the moonlight, still leaving her enough to see by. Hesitating a moment, she took out the gun, laid it on top of the dresser, and then pulled off the jeans and baggy sweatshirt she'd worn for the last few days, leaving the tank top as a stand-in for her nonexistent pajamas. She lay down, but her eyes wouldn't stay closed. Words kept spinning through her mind, filled with fragments of conversation from the past day.

Wizards. Cripples. Ferals. Blood. Merlin, Taliesin and the utter lack of gray area in between. Wars and murderers and monsters chasing her because they only needed one.

Whatever that meant.

So many lies. Her life was a lie. Being here was a lie. She'd given them Lily's pet name because it was all she could think of at the time. And now, a few days later, Lily felt like the only thing that'd ever been real.

Choose who you belong to. Bus' words rose from the morass. Who you want to be. It's our way of saying we're not like them. Never will be.

She closed her eyes.

To those around her, she was the deceived girl. Lied to and misled, naïvely accepting of the untruths that'd filled her life. And she was the broken one. Shell-shocked and hurting, and nothing more than a child needing protection.

But then, that was all they'd ever seen.

Choose who you want to be.

Her gaze found the gun atop the dresser, its dark metal outlined by the moonlight.

She'd wandered since the fire, since the moment Lily died. In all the chaos, she'd been swept along and tossed about like a dandelion in a hurricane, and never had really come back down. She'd been shattered, left in pieces by the loss of the life she thought she'd been living.

We hunt them. We take them out. Spider's words joined the noise.

Everything she'd known had been a lie, except for one little girl with bright blue eyes whom the wizards had killed as though she didn't matter at all.

We're not like them. Never will be.

Her hand reached up, wrapping around the gun, and she sat up in bed, holding it gently.

She'd always been Ashe to Lily.

And she wasn't helpless. Or broken. She refused to be.

She couldn't wield magic, or change what'd happened before. But in all this great mess, she could make a life out of what remained true. She was Lily's sister. Even if everything else was gone, through a simple name, something of Lily would always be with her.

Her fingers ran over the gun.

And she had one tiny power she could control.

She'd seen his face. And since the Hunters tracked his kind, maybe that was enough.

Because a gun would kill a wizard if they didn't know the shot was coming.

Down the hall, she could hear Carter and Jericho still talking. Setting the gun aside, Ashe rose and grabbed her jeans from the rug. Pulling them on swiftly, she headed for the door.

The men looked up as she came into the room.

"Carter," she said. "If I asked you, would you help me find the man who did this? The Blood wizard who killed my family?"

Jericho's brow rose, but Carter just glanced to him and then met her gaze seriously.

"Yes," he answered.

"Would you help me kill him?"

Jericho grimaced. Carter simply watched her. And then he nodded. "Yes."

She trembled, realizing she hadn't been breathing. "Thank you."

Carter nodded again.

She turned and headed back down the hallway, only to stop with her hand on the doorknob.

Arms crossed and leaning on the bathroom doorframe, Spider watched her. With a shrug of her shoulder, the girl pushed away from her support, and a small smile curved across her face.

Without a word, she disappeared back into the bedroom at the end of the hall.

For a moment, Ashe's brow drew down at the look in the girl's eyes, and then she continued into her room and shut the door.

The bed squeaked faintly as she sat down. Her gaze rested on the gun nearby.

She had only one power she could use. One single thing she could do.

And she refused to be broken anymore.

Chapter Thirteen

———◆———

I f he played one more video game, Cole thought he would lose his mind.

A week had passed since he and Lily found themselves hiding with Travis, and the time had not gone well. When he'd been stuck with Robert and Melissa, he'd often fantasized about having the freedom to do nothing but relax all day.

But in reality, the lack of activity was starting to drive him insane.

Lily wasn't doing much better. Most of her days were spent pacing the room or making origami crafts from whatever paper she could find. A small mountain of flowers, pinwheels, and cranes now littered the tower room upstairs, but even the girl looked like one more folded creation was likely to leave her screaming.

They both wanted answers. Direction. And one week into this, lightning still hadn't struck to provide him with either.

People with superpowers were after them. He couldn't seem to come up with a solution for that.

On the wall, the obnoxious alien clock struck three, and for the hundredth time, he resisted the urge to throw something at it.

Nearby, Lily scowled and flung her head back on the floor cushion, glaring upside-down daggers at the trilling, tentacle-laden abomination.

The door swung open as Travis came into the room. Tossing his bag down and sending textbooks spilling across the floor, he flung himself onto the bed. "Dude, this is just getting creepy," he announced.

Cole waited for more, but nothing came. "What is?"

"That cop was back."

Lily's exasperation with the clock melted. She looked between him and Travis in alarm.

"What cop?" Cole asked warily.

"I told you about him."

"Uh, no. Pretty sure you didn't."

"There's a cop poking around the school, asking about you and the kid. He showed up a few days ago, and then he was back today."

"You didn't tell me this, Travis," Cole said, trying to keep a rein on his temper.

"Oh. Sorry. But yeah, it's creepy, right?"

"What was he asking?"

"Who knew you, that sort of thing."

"Did he talk to you?"

"Eh, I told him I hadn't seen you since your parents went on vacation."

At his expression, Travis scoffed. "Relax. If I'd said I didn't know you, it would've taken him five seconds to figure out I was lying. Everyone at school knows we're friends." He leaned back, balancing one foot on the other and folding his arms behind his head. "Don't worry. I know what I'm doing."

Cole saw Lily grimace as she went back to the moronic penguin video game, but thankfully the boy didn't notice. Running a hand over his face, Cole exhaled and then shoved to his feet. Crossing to the window, he tweaked back the curtain and scanned the street. Nothing moved and, in a neighborhood like Travis', there weren't even cars parked by the curb.

He let the curtain fall back into place.

Cops at Brighton Modisett. Too close was an understatement. If he knew where else to go, they'd already be leaving.

Days upon days of thinking had left him with nothing but a headache and no options he could see. Neither of them had relatives to help them and, try as he might, he couldn't let himself rest easy in thinking he was the only one who could see Lily glow. Wherever they went, they ran the risk of someone recognizing her, either from the light on her or the pictures still occasionally playing on TV. And with all signs pointing to the cops being in league with the people chasing them, recognition would equal a fast track to falling into their custody.

As much as he hated it, without a direction, logic said they might as well stay here. Except that nothing was happening here, beyond the exponential growth of Travis' belief that this was a game. And since he and Lily didn't exactly fancy spending the rest of their lives in this room, he was starting to think they were going to *have* to just leave if they wanted to get anywhere in solving this psychotic mystery.

Except he didn't know where to go. And thus he ended up back at the beginning, cycling through the same thought processes that had yet to accomplish anything.

A buzzing sound pulled him out of his frustration and he turned around, looking for the source of the noise.

"What's that?"

Rolling off the bed, Travis sighed and headed for his cluttered desk. "Nothing," he said, yanking open a drawer and shoving papers aside. "Just the old phone you had."

Cole stared at him, speechless.

"Here we go," Travis said, pulling the cell from the bottom of the drawer.

"You told me you were going to get rid of that," Cole said, flabbergasted.

"I am. Justin's going to pay me for it tomorrow."

"That's not the same thing!"

"But this way, if anyone comes looking they'll just–"

"You were supposed to throw it out," Cole snapped, crossing the room and snatching the phone out of Travis' hands. Glancing down, he hesitated, the numbers on the display looking vaguely familiar.

"Who is it?"

"I'm not sure."

"Well, don't answer–"

Cole thumbed on the phone. "Hello?" he said warily.

Travis threw up his arms in incredulous exasperation.

"You're a moron for keeping this phone, you know that?" Robert snapped.

Cole paused. "Nice to hear from you too."

The man was silent, and Cole could almost hear him grinding his teeth. "I take it they haven't found you yet."

"I'm hanging up."

"Wait! I... I'm sorry."

Cole hesitated, still itching to end the call. His eyes flicked to the alien clock. "You've got ten seconds," he told the man, watching the tentacles tick around.

"The bastards paid us to keep you, okay? Said they'd spare us if we watched you. But I knew they'd turn on us. Why'd you think I kept so damn many guns around? And they did. I barely made it out after you left, thanks to Melissa. That stupid bitch couldn't even come up with a convincing cover story for our friendly neighborhood spy. But they're still going to be looking for you. Me too, since I know who they are. So I figure we can help each other."

"Bullshit." The word popped out before he could stop it, and he glanced to Lily uncomfortably.

"Look, they screwed me over too, okay? You think it was easy watching you for all those years, worrying you'd get shot or run off and leave us with nothing? But I'm no fool, alright? Not like that harpy they set me up with. She never was a great thinker, and she sure as hell didn't think fast enough to get herself out of there."

"Is she dead?"

"I don't know. Probably. Now that you know it's all a sham, there's no point in keeping us around. We've seen too much, plain and simple."

Cole glanced to Travis. The boy was watching him in disbelief from across the room, and tapping his wrist as though to indicate the time.

"Who are they?"

"Not on the phone. Dammit, we've already been too long. They're probably tracing us already, since you kept this line."

"You called me."

"I figured you'd do something stupid, left on your own."

"Goodbye, Robert."

"Dammit, wait! Look, Sunrise Campground near highway eighty-nine. Can you get there?"

Cole hesitated. "Yeah," he said, suddenly understanding the familiarity of the phone number. Robert loved the campground and used to call home from the nearby ski resort before he'd acquired a cell.

"Good. Lot twenty-three. I'll find you."

The call ended.

Cole set the cell down on the desk, staring at it.

"What the hell were you thinking?" Travis burst out.

Cole ignored him. Ninety-nine percent of what he'd just heard was gibberish, and the last time he'd seen the man, Robert had tried to smash him over the head with a bookend.

He glanced at the glowing girl watching him from across the room.

"Are you listening to me?" Travis snapped. Striding to the desk, the boy snatched the phone as though to stop Cole from making another call. "I was going to get rid of this for you! And now they've probably traced the call and everything. I can't *believe* you answered the phone! Are you insane? Haven't you seen–"

Travis kept ranting. Cole barely heard him.

They needed answers. And a week of waiting had gotten them precisely nothing.

"Is their house still empty?" he asked.

"And you just picked up the line like– what?" Travis' ears caught up to his tirade. He sputtered and then regrouped. "Yeah, I checked this morning."

Cole nodded. Every day for the past week, Travis had stopped by the hill overlooking Cole's old neighborhood and used his ludicrously expensive binoculars to see if anyone came by the Smith's home.

But the driveway stayed empty and the darkened house never changed.

"Can I borrow one of your trucks?"

Travis groaned. "You've got to be kidding me."

Cole waited.

"No, seriously," Travis continued. "Be kidding me. Please. You can't honestly think anything he said was the truth."

"Probably not. But I still need to find out for sure."

The boy stared at him.

"He knows what's going on, Travis. I can't just sit here."

"The cops are going to be waiting! He's setting you up!"

Cole shifted uncomfortably. "Maybe," he allowed, and then glanced to Lily. "That's why you and Lily stay here. I'll go see what he has to say and if it's safe, I'll let you know."

Lily dropped the controller and surged to her feet. Crossing the room, she glared up at him. "No," she said flatly.

Determination trembled through her, covering the fear in her eyes.

"Lily–"

"What about the bad men? The other ones?" she said, her gaze darting to Travis as she tried to hide her meaning. "Huh? What then?"

"I'm trying to look out for you here, Lily. If it's a trap–"

"Then don't go."

"It's not that easy."

"Then take me."

Arms folded, Travis regarded him with satisfaction. "Can't argue with the kid, huh?"

Frustrated, Cole turned away. "What if he knows a way out of this?" he asked, directing the question at Travis because it was easier than fighting with Lily. "We can't just stay in your room forever."

"Then take me," Lily repeated, biting off the words.

"I'm trying to keep you safe!" he snapped, his tone harsher than he intended.

Her face crumpled, though anger still held back the fear. "But what about you?"

Cole hesitated.

"We stick together," she continued, her voice trembling. "We have to."

He grimaced uncomfortably.

"So you can't leave without me."

"This is stupid, Lily!" he protested as a last ditch defense against agreeing. "If those men are there…"

"You'll protect me. And I'll protect you."

Behind her, Travis looked like he'd laugh if he wasn't so aggravated with Cole for still planning on going. Shaking his head, the boy paced away from them.

Cole looked back down at the girl. "One condition," he said softly. "You see anything wrong – and I mean anything – you run. You don't wait for me. This is part of me protecting you, Lily. You've got to promise."

For a moment, she didn't move. And then reluctantly, she nodded.

"Promise," he ordered.

"Promise," she repeated.

"I still don't like this."

Lily nodded, but her hand found his and she worked her fingers into his grip. She trembled as she clung to him.

Cole sighed. "So what about the truck?" he asked Travis.

"You're both idiots," the boy said flatly.

"Okay."

Infuriated, Travis scoffed. "And what if it is a trap? What then?"

"Then you'll be the only one who knows the truth. And you'll have to tell the world, so they don't get away with making us disappear."

Despite the melodramatic wording, he could see the wheels start turning in Travis' head. A heartbeat later, the boy shook off the fantasies.

"That doesn't justify being a moron," he insisted. "You're just going to walk in there and *hope* he's not playing you. What kind of plan is that?"

"You have a better idea?" Cole replied, starting to feel the minutes ticking away. "A sniper rifle Lily could use, maybe?"

Travis thought briefly. "I got a Taser for my birthday."

Cole paused. "Okay."

For a moment, the two of them stared at each other, and then Travis rolled his eyes. Still grumbling about stupidity, he headed into his closet to dig out the Taser.

"And what if something happens here?" he asked when he returned, slapping the compact device down into Cole's palm. "How am I supposed to reach you? I'm guessing you don't want to keep the phone?"

"No."

Travis grimaced. "Fine. Use mine. I'll get another one and call you if something comes up." He paused. "And you can take the Toyota. It's in better shape anyway."

He pulled out his cell and keys, and tossed them both to Cole before heading for the door. Cole followed, still holding Lily's hand. The girl's grip on his fingers was marginally crushing.

Downstairs, the sound of Travis' younger sister watching cartoons drowned their footsteps, and as they rushed past the kitchen, Travis' mother never glanced away from directing the dinner preparations. Edgily, Cole watched the kitchen door over his shoulder as he waited for Travis to check the garage and almost theatrically make certain the coast was clear.

At the truck, Lily clambered onto her seat and buckled the belt swiftly, her every motion daring him to change his mind about her coming. He shook his head and thumbed the control clipped to the visor, watching in the rearview mirror as the garage door slowly climbed the rails.

"You're being a moron," Travis told him, leaning on the wall.

"You told me."

Travis scoffed.

Cole glanced over at him. "Thanks for your help."

Rolling his eyes, the boy looked away.

A grin pulled at Cole's mouth as he put the truck in reverse. Stonework grumbled beneath the tires as the truck rolled down the drive and then pulled out onto the wide, empty street. Breathing a sigh of relief at simply doing something, he headed for the interstate.

———◆———

Cautiously, Cole eased the truck down the narrow campground lane. Tents and RVs dotted small clearings beneath the trees and, around a few picnic tables, children ran.

He glanced to Lily. Over the bottom of the windowsill, she watched the forest and campers, her fingers digging into the ledge between the door and the glass.

"Anything?" he asked.

She shook her head.

Lot twenty-three came into view, and he slowed the truck to a crawl. On the other side of the road, another clearing sat unoccupied by campers, though a beat-up old station wagon gave proof someone planned to return.

"Get down," he said to Lily. "We're almost there."

Silently, she slid into the footwell and pulled her legs up tight, hugging them to her chest.

Drawing a steadying breath, he drew closer to the lot. Surrounded by spring wildflowers and shaded by the trees, the clearing sported nothing more than a gravel drive and a picnic table, with Robert nowhere to be seen.

He stopped the truck. "Stay there," he told Lily quietly.

Watching the motionless campground, he climbed out. In the distance, he could hear highway traffic, interspersed with birdcalls.

Robert stepped from behind a tree on the far side of the lot, gun in hand.

Cole froze.

"You came alone?" the man demanded.

Resisting the urge to check if Lily remained hidden, he kept his eyes on Robert and wondered why the man thought he would tell the truth anyway.

"You never answered my question," Cole said.

The man's lip twitched humorlessly. He walked away from the trees, keeping the gun level at Cole's chest. Craning his neck, he looked over the hood of the truck to check the passenger seat, missing the small girl huddled in the footwell.

"Fine," Robert said, glancing around warily. "But not here. I don't know where you got that truck, but leave it. We're taking my car."

Cole shook his head. "No. I came this far. Now tell me what the hell is going on."

Robert grimaced. "You always were a little punk, you know that?"

Eyes narrowing, Cole paused, and then shrugged casually. "Alright, well if *that's* all you had to tell me…"

He reached for the door handle.

"Damn you, kid!"

One hand still on the door, Cole waited.

A flurry of anger and frustration passed over Robert's face, and then suddenly, it faded. Shaking his head, he scoffed like a man staring over the edge of the abyss, wondering if he should just jump in.

The sound made Cole's skin crawl.

"You won't believe me," Robert said. "No one will. They make sure of that."

"Who?" Cole asked slowly.

Robert's gaze returned to him. "The wizards."

Cole paused. A glowing girl was sitting in the footwell and Vaughn was killed by men with superpowers. And now his fake adoptive father believed in wizards. As explanations went, it was about on par with everything else. Which meant insane. He just needed to find the point where this all translated into something *not* crazy.

"Okay."

"You don't believe me," Robert scoffed.

"The freaks who killed Vaughn ripped the door from his car without touching it."

Robert froze. "Edmund's dead?"

"Lots of people are dead, Robert," Cole said shortly. "Now what's going on?"

But the man wasn't listening. His gaze skittered across the ground as though searching for answers there, and Cole couldn't tell from his face whether he was elated or terrified.

Carefully, he glanced to Lily, jerking his chin slightly. Hoisting herself on the edge of the seat, she peered over the dashboard, and then dropped back into the footwell, her eyes wide. She pointed to Cole.

"Like you," she mouthed.

Cole's gaze slid back to his adoptive father.

"They were real," Robert said in amazement.

"Who?"

The man tore himself from his gravel study. "I don't know."

Cole reached for the door handle again.

"Don't go!"

"Then tell me something worth the gas to get out here."

Familiar anger returned to the man's expression, but after a moment it gave way to whatever motivation made him call in the first place. Swiftly, Robert scanned the campground as though expecting monsters to appear from the wildflowers, and when that didn't happen, he motioned with the gun toward the picnic table.

Cole glanced into the truck cab, meeting Lily's worried gaze. Fingering the Taser in his pocket, he followed the man.

"Gun where I can see it," Cole ordered as he eased onto the wooden seat.

With exaggerated indulgence, Robert set the weapon on the table. "You are *such* a little–"

"Whatever it is, you've told me already. So how about you start explaining what you meant by wizards instead?"

Robert glared. "I meant *wizards*. Magical people. Hocus pocus. The whole nine yards."

At Cole's silence, the man scoffed. "Your mommy and daddy were wizards. Your dear 'counselors' were wizards. People with magical powers, determined to keep that information from the rest of the world. You and me are what they call 'cripples' – the bastards. Means we don't have magic. Can see them, but can't tell the difference between a wizard and a human to save our lives. Which is the problem."

Cole's brow furrowed.

Robert made a frustrated noise. "You are such a–"

"Said it already. Get to the point."

The man drew a breath. "Look. I need your help. And you need mine. The wizard bastards who set this up – the whole thing with Melissa and me and all of it – they don't give a shit about me. I was just there to keep you happy in your perfect little suburban life."

Images from his time with the Smiths flashed through Cole's mind, and it was all he could do not to laugh.

Eyes narrowing, Robert seemed to see the impulse. "Whatever, brat. I did the best I could with that harpy and the damn neighbors watching our every move. You got a hangnail, the wizards came pounding on our door, wanting to know what we were doing wrong. It was always 'keep him happy', 'keep him complacent', and you–"

"Why?" Cole interrupted.

"Hell if I know. All I do know is that eight years ago when the damn war started, three wizards showed up at my door and offered me a deal. They'd keep me safe, keep the other wizards away, and set me up with a great life, if I'd just play daddy to some orphaned ten-year-old. What the hell, right? People were dying every day, and I get this sweet deal just for watching you? How was I going to argue?

"So I went. Had to put up with that bitch, Melissa, which was a test, I'll tell you. 'Don't draw attention', 'make the wizards happy'… if it wouldn't have gotten me killed by the bastards, I'd have shot her in the first week. But I made it work. Kept you in line and kept everything going smooth, till that harpy had to screw it up by not mixing your drink right."

He hadn't thought he could get more confused, but Cole's brow furrowed deeper.

"The cocoa, moron," Robert explained. "Melissa's 'special recipe'. God knows what she put in there, but it always knocked you out."

"I never drank it. I usually just poured it down the drain."

Robert scoffed. "Figures. She was such an idiot. Swore to me it was working every time." He shook his head. "And then you go and prove her wrong by ruining everything."

Scowling, the man looked away. Cole stared at him, trying to figure out where to start in the mountain of questions he'd just amassed. "War?"

"Merlin and Taliesin trying to wipe each other off the map, like the world wouldn't be better with them both gone."

"Okay," Cole said, picking up the next question immediately. "Merlin and Taliesin?"

"Sides of the wizard groups. Some old bastards five hundred years ago they all think are so special. Merlin bound up Taliesin's magic, and his followers' too, and left them all useless till about eight years ago when the Taliesin king knocked off the Merlin one. And voila," the man said dryly, "we have ourselves a war."

Filing the information away as psychotic, Cole went for another question. "And some of them wanted you to keep me happy… why?"

"I told you, I have no idea. They didn't say and I didn't ask. We were just supposed to watch you and keep you cheerfully oblivious to the war."

"And they'd kill you if I wasn't."

Robert made a motion as though the statement was obvious.

Cole ignored him, running through the conversation again and trying to remember each crazy detail. "Because you're a… 'cripple'?"

"Person who came from a wizard family, but doesn't have magic," Robert translated. "It's a damned insult. Magic's a talent, they say. Like being good at the piano or painting or whatever. But because you, me, and damn near fifty percent of their population are born without it, they call us 'cripples' and treat us like crap. It's a narcissistic double standard created by self-righteous cretins who should just wipe each other out and spare the world any more trouble."

The man went on grumbling, but Cole was only half listening. "But what was that about 'telling the difference'?"

"There's three groups. You, me and others like us. The wizards and all their crap. And then the lovely little regular humans who don't have a clue."

Cole stared at him, waiting for the vituperative explanations to begin. Smirking, Robert complied. "No, kid. You're still human. They all are. Talent, remember? You don't bleed green or anything.

"But as a part of their 'talent', the bastards don't blend well with regular humans, meaning people have trouble seeing them when the wizards don't want to be seen. Being wizard-yet-not, you and I don't have that problem. We see them just fine. But it means they don't like us much, probably because we keep them from just being all-powerful demigods and leaving us mere mortals behind."

He paused. "We do have something though, and some of them

hunt us for it. I don't know what it is, but if their magic hits you right…" Robert shrugged his eyebrows illustratively. "No more you. Then they take it, and grow stronger." He smirked. "So watch your back."

Cole glanced away, remembering the man by the strip mall. The hungry look in his eyes. Suppressing a shudder, he turned back to Robert. "So which side are the glowing ones on?"

Robert's expression wrinkled into confusion. "Glowing ones?" he repeated as though Cole was the one who was insane.

He hesitated. "The guys who killed Vaughn glowed."

"Wizards don't glow, kid. They feel something different about each other, like shadows on the Taliesin and light around the Merlin. But they look the same as anybody to us."

Cole said nothing. So he was crazy. Hit his head too hard. And accordingly, an eight-year-old glowed in the dark and healed him from near-fatal bullet wounds.

Right.

"Which side were the ones you dealt with on?" he asked, dropping the topic momentarily.

"I don't know," Robert said dismissively. "I think Melissa'd caught on after a while, and definitely knew more than she'd say, but the selfish bitch was too busy protecting her own skin to let me in on anything."

Cole let the blatant hypocrisy pass. "What about the ones you didn't think were real? Who're they?"

"Whoever the hell the wizards wanted to keep you away from. We were supposed to watch for anything suspicious, people getting too close. Why do you think Melissa was so obsessed with everyone you met? But we didn't have details. All I know is I never saw anyone.

But obviously, they were out there."

"And why do you need me?"

"Because they do."

Cole tensed and Robert scoffed. "I'm not turning you in for protection. I'm not stupid. You know what's going on, so they don't need me anymore. Wizards aren't nice, kid. I'm a lot better to them dead than alive and able to talk. One hit with their magic and they'll be stronger and have my silence at the same time.

"But they spent a hell of a lot of energy keeping you happy, which means they won't just kill you now. So this is what I figure. I might've been out of the loop for eight years, but I've still heard rumors of some cripples who help people like us hide. They're a tight group; nobody talks about them unless they trust you or you have connections. But I'm working on it. If I can contact them, then they can get us both out of here. And in the meantime, if the wizards catch up to us, you can act as a diversion while I escape."

Cole's eyebrows rose. "And I'm just supposed to let them grab me while you scurry away?"

Robert glared. "What're you going to do on your own, kid? You know how to get in touch with this group I'm talking about? You know where the safe hiding places are?" He sneered. "You have an armory of guns to defend yourself with?"

Cole paused. "What's to stop you from just shooting me once you've gotten in touch with these people? You won't need me anymore."

"Idiot," Robert said. "You're not worth anything to me dead. So what? I get a place to hide. That doesn't make the wizards not exist. That doesn't mean the war suddenly ends. God knows how long it'll take the bastards to wipe each other out. And in the meantime, I'd like a little insurance to give me a chance of getting away."

Cole's thoughts went to the girl curled up in the footwell. To say Robert was untrustworthy was an understatement, but his plan had benefits. They gained a chance at safety with people who might know what was going on, assuming they were real. And if things went wrong and the bad guys showed up, Cole could provide a distraction while Lily escaped. It wasn't perfect, but it was something.

And meanwhile, she could see wizards. He almost laughed at himself for even thinking the word. *Wizards* were after them. It would seem idiotic, if not for the events of the past week.

"Saying I agree," Cole hazarded. "Are we staying here? In a public campground?"

"I have a cabin. Melissa, the wizards and all their damn spies never knew about it. Keep half my gun collection up there. It should be safe till I can get in touch with this group."

Cole hesitated. In Hollywood…

"Who were the spies?"

"The lady next door, the man with the terrier down the street, and the school janitor," Robert said as though it didn't matter. "They watched everything and reported to the wizards if there was a problem. We didn't have any other way of reaching the bastards either. *Security*, you understand. Kept us from giving them up to their enemies."

"And were they all wizards?"

"Who knows? We can't tell, remember?"

"Were there any others?"

"Why?"

Cole shrugged.

"You've been in contact with someone, haven't you?"

He paused. "A guy from school."

"Son of a–" Robert slammed his fist on the table, making the gun jump. "Idiot! What the hell were you thinking? That's where the truck came from, isn't it? Did this guy know where you were coming today?"

He considered it briefly. "I don't think so."

"Well, we've got to get out of here. You screwed up everything! How could you–"

"I don't think he's a spy," Cole said, hoping it was true.

"And how're you supposed to know? Can't see them, remember! And you just…"

With skill born of years of practice, Cole ignored him. If Travis wanted to betray them, he'd had a week to do it. And Lily hadn't seen anything. Which raised another issue.

Cole's eyes slid to the gun, but the man wasn't paying attention.

He snatched the weapon from the table.

Robert froze in mid-rant, and then a baleful smirk slid across his face. "You sided with them, didn't you? Your friend's a wizard and he sent you to see what I knew."

"That's not what's going on here," Cole said cautiously, easing himself away from the picnic table.

"Oh, really."

"I have a way of spotting wizards. I just didn't want you to shoot her."

The man's eyes narrowed.

"A bunch of guys killed Vaughn," Cole continued. "And yes, they glowed. They put him through the trunk of his car without laying a hand on him either. And then they went after her family. Killed them all."

He paused. "I got her away. But she saw something weird about every one of them who just looked like a regular person to me. So she sees wizards. And if you try to sell her out for your own protection, I will personally make sure the wizards kill you. Understood?"

Robert's smirk deepened.

Cole tightened his grip on the gun.

"Fine, kid," Robert sighed. "Show me your wonder girl."

Hesitating a moment longer, Cole backed toward the truck and opened the door. From the footwell, Lily looked up at him worriedly.

"It's okay," he told her, praying he was right.

She climbed out.

The blood drained from Robert's face and he swore, half-rising. Cole made a cautioning noise. Slowly, the man lowered himself back onto the seat, never taking his eyes from Lily.

Wrapping her hand in his own, Cole led Lily toward the table. Easing onto the bench, he cautiously set the gun beside him.

"What *is* she?" the man asked.

Indignation broke through some of the fear in Lily's eyes.

"She's a girl, Robert," Cole said dryly. "Her name is Lily."

"But she's *glowing...*"

"I noticed."

The man wouldn't stop staring.

"Robert!" Cole barked after a few seconds passed.

Blinking in stupefaction, Robert tore his gaze from the eight-year-old and tried to focus.

"The..." He gestured to the girl.

"Lily."

"She sees wizards?"

Cole nodded.

"But can they see that glow thing around her? I mean…"

"I'm pretty sure you're the only one besides me who's noticed it."

For a moment, Robert studied the table in shock, and then suddenly, a wide smile spread across his face.

"This is brilliant, kid!" he cried. "This is… She can see wizards!"

Cole watched him, wary of this latest shift of emotion.

"Anyone who comes by, we can tell instantly if they're a threat. And they… they really can't see anything around her?"

"No one's reacted to it yet."

"This is incredible. This is…" Robert trailed off, and then he smiled again, a disturbingly excited light in his eyes. "Lily. It's Lily, right?"

She glanced to Cole, her unease clear, and then she nodded at the man warily.

"Lily," Robert continued. "How'd you like to stay with me for a while? Me and Cole, I mean. Would you like that?"

She regarded him silently, but he continued as though she'd spoken. "You'll love it. I have a cabin in the mountains, with lots of trees and birds and everything. It's beautiful. Wouldn't that be nice?"

The girl looked to Cole, alarmed.

"Oh, he can come too," Robert said hastily. "Don't worry."

"We'll both go," Cole told him. "And if she's ever out of my sight for more than a bathroom break, I call my friend and tell him to go see the neighbors."

Robert's gaze snapped back to him.

"Agreed?" Cole said.

"You don't want them catching you either."

"I'll take my chances."

Robert studied him for a long moment. "Fine."

"Come on," Cole said to Lily, jerking his head toward the truck.

"I have a car."

"We'll follow you."

"You're such a—"

"Said that already, Robert," Cole snapped. "Are we going?"

The man sneered, and then swiftly stifled the expression and tried to replace it with a smile when he saw Lily watching him. Turning, he headed for the opposite lot and unlocked the station wagon sitting there.

Cole walked back to the truck, and held the door open for Lily to climb in. Circling around to the driver's side, his eyes never left his adoptive father.

"He's mean," Lily said after Cole shut the door.

"You just figured out all there is to know about him."

Glancing over, he met the kid's eyes, and then followed the station wagon away from the campground.

Chapter Fourteen

"So who's this?" Spider asked, scrawling a symbol into the riverbank with a stick.

"Samson," Ashe said.

"Perfect. This one?"

Another symbol followed.

"Serenity," she answered, naming one of the other Hunters.

"How about this?"

The series of interlocking symbols made her blink.

"Bus says someplace isn't safe…?"

"You need to get faster at that one," Spider said.

"I'm working on it," Ashe replied tiredly.

The girl gave her a brief smile and then swiped the symbols away with her foot before drawing the next one.

Ashe ran a hand through her dark hair, trying to concentrate. For the past month, Spider had slowly but surely been teaching her to recognize the graffiti that comprised the language she and the other Hunters used to communicate on the streets. Elaborate interconnected designs showed directions, instructions and warnings, with each sign changing in relation to the overall tag of the person drawing it. Myriad symbols for safety, danger, and each of her friends' names now burned behind her closed lids every night, interspersed with endless images of the firing range. Over the recent weeks, she'd reached the point of being able to hit a target with decently reliable consistency and distinguish in an instant many of the cryptic paint-drawn calling cards.

But a few were still taking time.

"Okay, so what about this one?"

"Run."

At her tone, Spider glanced over at her.

"Sorry," Ashe said. "Keep going?"

Pausing a moment longer, the girl nodded and drew another.

"Safe house."

She appreciated the effort the others were putting into making certain she was ready to be away from the Abbey with them. If they became separated, the symbols could save her life.

It was just that everything was taking so long.

Ever since she'd asked Carter to help her hunt down the Blood who'd killed her family, time had seemed to crawl. She hadn't been so silly as to think they'd locate him immediately, but every passing day made the whole thing seem more and more like a stupid child's fantasy.

Find the bad guy. Take the bad guy out.

Helped if you had any clue where he was in the first place.

Irritation surged and, with difficulty, she tried to calm down. The training, the planning and all the hours Carter spent on the phone searching for any sign of the Blood wizard had gotten her through a lot. Countless nightmares and sleepless hours when all she could do was sit in bed shaking and hugging her knees had been pacified by the knowledge that soon, they'd be after him and this would finally end.

But it'd been weeks, and life hadn't stopped in the meantime.

Between calls to other Hunters around the country, Carter fielded questions and requests from everywhere. People needed moving. Hiding. Helping. Rumors reached them of a previously unknown cripple wanting relocating in the west, but no one recognized him or any of the connections he claimed. After a fourth person mentioned the man, Carter finally sent a few people to investigate, albeit with three attack dogs and enough weapons to start a second war.

If it was a trap, no one wanted to be caught unprepared.

Meanwhile, more violence raged up north, the area where most wizards apparently stayed. Ferals had increased almost exponentially in the past month and new reports of wizard battles arrived all the time. And while the idea of Merlin and Taliesin killing each other didn't bother anybody, word of cripples being caught in the crossfire left the Abbey silent for days.

And in the midst of it all, the Blood were mysteriously absent.

The others attempted to make her feel better, reminding her of how things took time. She tried to stay positive, appreciative, and not let them see how she trembled every time another call came in, only to prove to be nothing.

"Ashe?"

Spider's voice broke into her thoughts and she blinked, realizing she'd been staring at the symbol on the ground without speaking.

"Blood in the area," she answered quietly.

Glancing up, she caught the other girl's expression and then grimaced ruefully. "Sorry."

"Break time," Spider said. She twitched her head toward the main building. "Come on."

Scratching the symbols out with her foot, the girl tossed the stick aside and then headed up the riverbank with Ashe a step behind. In the kitchen, the rotund and middle-aged Belle greeted them cheerily, bidding them to sit down and share in the latest gossip she'd heard from the outside world. Biscuits and preserves appeared from storage bins, and by the time the two girls extricated themselves from the hearsay, an hour had gone by.

"You knew that would happen," Ashe said as they headed back for the riverbank.

"I was hungry," Spider replied, shrugging defensively.

Ashe grinned. Skidding down the steep slope, they landed in a shower of rocks on the water's edge.

"Feeling better?" the girl asked.

Humor fading, Ashe shrugged. "He's still out there," she said softly.

"Growing more desperate every day," Spider finished. "Even if he just wants you for bait, time's ticking for him too. He'll get sloppy." She paused. "And then we'll find him."

Ashe drew a slow breath and nodded. The others had debated the meaning of 'only needing one' over the past few weeks, concluding primarily the Blood must want her to draw someone or some group out of hiding. The theory held merit, though she didn't know of anyone still alive who'd be looking for her anyway.

Retrieving her stick from the shore, Spider glanced at her briefly and then sketched a symbol on the ground.

Ashe's brow furrowed. After a moment, she shook her head.

"Bus' design," Spider told her. "Means 'nice place, bring food'."

Looking at her askance, Ashe raised an eyebrow.

"He hasn't had a chance to use it," Spider continued, a half-smile on her face. "I think he's saving it for after the war."

Sidestepping to a clear stretch of dirt, the girl drew another symbol on the riverbank.

The sun was climbing past mid-morning when a shadow fell across their practice and made them both look up. Standing on the grassy edge of the drop-off to the river, Carter shaded his eyes from the glare of the sunlight on the water.

"I think we may have found him," he said.

A shiver ran through her, starting from her middle and spreading outward in a wave. Crushing down the fires by habit, it was all she could do to keep breathing at the news.

"Blackjack called from Ohio. Elsa's in a panic because she saw a Blood meeting up with a couple lowlifes outside a bar in her neighborhood. The description was a bit disjointed, but from what we can tell, it sounds like your guy."

Words escaped her and she swallowed hard. "So…"

A smile pulled at his mouth. "Go tell Bus we're heading out."

She had to stop herself from running back up the slope.

As the others continued down the main path, she diverted through the space between two mobile homes. A narrow track led deeper into the woods, and for a few minutes, she only heard birdcalls and leaves moving in the breeze.

Clicking sounds cut through the forest ahead. She walked into a small clearing just as Bus let out a holler of victory and the rumble of an engine coming to life replaced the noise she'd heard before. Stepping back from an old truck, Bus clapped his younger companion on the shoulder and then caught sight of her by the trees.

"Hey there!" he called cheerfully. "Take a look."

Biting her lip, she came closer and dutifully looked over the engine.

"Great," she told him, her tone distracted despite her best efforts.

He glanced at her as he grabbed a rag hanging nearby. "What's up, Ashe-girl?" he asked, wiping his hands clean.

"They found him."

Bus' eyebrows rose. "Carter say when we're leaving?"

"Soon."

"We'll get the van ready."

Motioning to the young man with him, Bus tossed the cloth at the truck and then headed for the other vehicles hunkered beneath the trees. A brown van waited at the edge of the junkyard, rusted on the outside though Bus assured them it was solid internally. For the past month, he'd been making modifications, welding in new storage areas and reworking the engine.

Leaving them to their work, she hurried back to the Abbey, half-jogging as she threaded her way toward the cabin. The living room was empty when she came in, though at the end of the hall, the door to Bryony's room was shut and she could hear Spider and Samson talking quietly inside.

A pang of discomfort hit her. Trying to ignore it, she continued into her tiny room and pulled out the bag beneath the bed. Over the past weeks, she'd acquired a few more articles of clothing from castoffs others at the Abbey didn't need. It wasn't much, but she'd never before appreciated the marvelous relief that simply having something clean to wear could provide.

Such as it was, her small wardrobe fit into the bag easily, and her gun remained tucked into the holster beneath the worn leather jacket Jericho had given her. With everything else in the room belonging to Magnolia and her family, it only took minutes before every trace of her presence had been packed away.

At the edge of the room, she hesitated, her hand lingering on the doorframe as she scanned the tiny space.

It wasn't home. It never would have been.

She shoved away from the door and headed outside.

From Melody's cabin, Carter and Bus emerged, carrying their own bags and a few extra besides. Tossing her an empty sack, Carter jerked his head toward the main house and then began heading in that direction.

"Food," he told her succinctly as she caught the bag.

She followed him to the kitchen, knowing Belle would happily have food to share.

But time slid past. Things took too long. The sun was crossing the sky too quickly and when they finally emerged from the kitchen, she felt like the day had already passed them by.

Even if it'd only been half an hour.

People waved to them as they headed for the gate, calling out wishes for safe travel and goodbyes. A cluster of children raced up to Bus, playfully trying to keep him from leaving before he managed to chase them away. Tala and Mischa emerged from wherever they'd been hiding, and the burrs stuck in their dense coats made Carter shake his head.

Leaning on a crutch, Samson stood on the cabin porch, his free arm around Spider's shoulders and her forehead resting on his chest. As the others passed, the girl turned swiftly and followed them, not looking back.

Pretending they saw nothing, Carter and Bus continued to the end of the gravel path, where Magnolia, Jericho and a handful of people stood waiting. At the sight of them, the woman smiled, and wrapped Ashe in a hug as soon as she came near.

"Take care of yourself, sweetie," Magnolia said.

Ashe nodded.

"Was good to have you here," Jericho told them all.

Carter and Bus agreed, and shook hands with their friends who'd come to say goodbye.

It only took a few moments, and then suddenly they were leaving the Abbey behind.

At the edge of the dirt path, Ashe glanced back. Children ran between the houses as the adults went back to what they had been doing. A dog chased off a few chickens from where he'd been sleeping, and birdcages swayed in the breeze.

And in the distance, she could see Samson standing on the porch, unmoving.

She turned away and followed the others down the narrow trail between the trees.

———◆———

Over the bridge guardrails, Ashe watched the river and ignored the rush hour traffic hurrying home for the evening.

"See the wall there?" Bus called from the front, glancing back at her and then pointing to a rugged stone wall running along a service road by the riverbank.

"Yeah?"

"We call that one Seagull."

Ashe nodded, studying the scene and trying to burn the place and its corresponding code word into memory.

"You sure you're remembering all this?"

She looked back at him. "Seagull, the stone wall by the river near the bridge," she said, listing the locations and trying to keep the annoyance from her tone. "Tumbleweed, the abandoned lot behind the gas station off exit one-twenty-three. Angel, the northeast sanctuary door of the cathedral on East Seventeenth on the south side of the river. And Pepper, the service entrance to the sandwich shop on South McLane."

"You forgot the pawn shop. What's that one again?"

Biting back her frustration, she started to reply when Spider rolled her head across the headrest and saved her the trouble. "Bus, relax already. She's got it."

Spider raised an eyebrow at him and reluctantly, Bus gave in and turned around. Without another word, the girl rolled her head back and resumed staring out the window.

Glancing to Spider, Ashe tried not to let her gratitude show. Ever since they'd hit the suburbs, the old man had been drilling her relentlessly on the Hunter's pre-arranged meeting places, in case they became separated. In an emergency, she'd head to the nearest one, waiting for the others or leaving messages about where she'd gone.

It wasn't that the information wasn't useful. Like everything else, she knew it could save her life. It was just that Bus seemed to take any slip of her memory personally, despite the massive amounts of detail he was trying to force into her brain.

Cutting across two lanes, Carter sent the van up an exit ramp and into the city. Commercial districts passed, filled with stores whose signs were so crammed on top of one another, she could hardly read them. Cars crowded the parking lots around them, and stoplights seemed to interrupt Carter's driving every few feet.

"That—" Bus began, pointing toward a strip mall before catching himself.

"Another one?"

Faintly chagrined, he nodded. "Shoebox."

"I'll remember," she assured him.

Hesitating a moment more, he went back to watching the road.

A small grin twitched her lips, and she hid it quickly.

Past banks and houses, schools and churches they drove, winding through the city till at last Carter pulled the van to a stop by a curb and sighed. "This is why I let you drive," he told Bus, rubbing his eyes tiredly.

The old man clapped him on the shoulder sympathetically and then set to work detaching the police scanner from beneath the dashboard.

Ashe tugged up the hood of her jacket and then jumped out after Spider and the dogs. Across the street, teenagers lounging on a porch watched them, and down the road, music pounded from a house converted into a bar. Old trees cast long shadows on the cars lining either curb, while a few blocks away, traffic rushed by yet another stoplight.

Shouldering her bag, she followed Spider up the steps from the curb and past the sidewalk, and then thanked Carter quietly as he held open a chain-link gate. A yellow cottage stood atop a small rise, its walls bordered by scraggly bushes and creeping ivy.

Pulling back the screen door, Carter knocked and was instantly rewarded with the sound of a tiny dog yapping madly.

"Every time," Bus muttered, shaking his head.

Letting the screen close, Carter sighed.

A moment passed. From the opposite side of the street, the

teenagers studied them.

The door swung open. "Oh!" cried an old woman. "You–"

She cut off as a small, fluffy dog charged the door, barking furiously. "Mitzi! Quiet!" she commanded, though the dog paid no mind. "Quiet!"

At her helpless look, Carter opened the screen and stepped inside. Torn between fierce determination and cowardice, the little animal retreated, still barking for the world to hear.

Bus groaned quietly and followed.

"You got here sooner than I expected," the old woman said, sounding flustered as she herded the dog toward the basement stairs. Shutting the door on the noise, she exhaled in relief and put on a pleasant smile as she waved them all farther inside.

Spider closed the door behind her, but Ashe barely noticed. A time capsule surrounded them, as different from the neighborhood outside as another reality. Floral wallpaper covered the walls, edged by dark mahogany trim. Pale rose carpet absorbed the sound of their footsteps and thick satin curtains shrouded each window. In the living room, a vintage couch and loveseat occupied two walls, and from beneath the lacy shade of a gold-plated lamp, the porcelain forms of a shepherd and shepherdess dangled.

And on every wall, pictures hung. A much younger version of the old woman smiled out at the world from the arm of an equally youthful man, and though the scenery and decades shifted from image to image, the subjects remained.

A lifetime, chronicled in gilt frames.

"I don't believe we've met, dear," the old woman said to her. "I'm Elsa."

Blinking, Ashe dragged her gaze from the walls and introduced herself.

"A pleasure," Elsa replied. "Well, I've got the bedroom down the hall set up for the girls," she continued to the others. "But I'm afraid you boys will have to take the living room. There's some blankets in the hall closet…"

Stepping aside, she waited for Bus to precede her. Glancing to Carter, the white-haired man worked to keep a straight face as he dutifully headed for the designated closet.

"You kids must have had a long drive. I can brew some tea before dinner if you'd like? Or I might have coffee. I… where's Samson?" Elsa asked suddenly, glancing around.

"He needed to stay behind," Carter told her. "Is there a place I can set these bags?"

Distracted by the question, she nodded and showed him another closet as Spider slipped down the hall toward the bedroom. Ashe followed.

A twin bed and a lower trundle sat in the small room, matching quilts covering them. Spider glanced between the beds. "You want that one?" she asked, motioning for the twin.

"Doesn't matter."

Shrugging, the girl dropped her stuff by the trundle and busied herself with sorting through the ammunition in her bag.

Hesitating briefly, Ashe set her own bag down and then headed back to the living room. The kitchen adjoined the room by way of a dining area, and beside the polished white sink, Elsa was instructing Carter on how to prepare the salad. Ignoring them, Bus nudged aside the thick curtain by the back porch and studied the yard, while Tala and Mischa flopped onto the floor nearby. The dull thud of music from the bar undercut the quiet, and occasionally someone outside would shout.

Ashe glanced around, uncertain what to do, and then crossed to where Bus was standing. "So what now?" she urged softly.

"Dinner."

She paused uncomfortably.

"Take it easy, girl. Carter's got a couple things going right now, but don't worry. We'll find your monster."

Her brow furrowed in confusion.

"Look around," Bus said quietly. She surveyed the quaint decor, still lost. "We're damn near the heart of wizard territory. And yet…"

He saw the understanding come into her eyes as she glanced at Elsa.

"She seems so…" Ashe trailed off, unable to find the right word.

"Oblivious? Trust me, she's not. At least, not underneath. She's just determined to pretend the war isn't happening, even if it gets her killed."

Impatience churning, Ashe watched the woman. "Is there anything I can do to help?" she asked finally, working to set the frustration aside.

"Keep watch on the front. And for the love of everything holy, don't freak if you see anything. Elsa won't handle it well."

Taking a breath, she started to nod and then froze, suddenly realizing that if the Blood showed up, she wouldn't see anything at all. She wouldn't know them from the kids across the street, while they could spot her in the window and tell instantly what she was. And then there was the issue of wizards coming by, and protecting her friends while not giving herself away.

Heart picking up speed, she made herself keep breathing. She hadn't thought this through. In all the training and planning, this fundamental issue simply hadn't crossed her mind.

Her eyes slid back to Bus, but he was studying a car driving down the neighboring street. How could this not have occurred to her? She'd been so focused on hunting the Blood down, and yet…

Nauseated and working to hide the feeling, she headed for the kitchen window.

Meatloaf eventually emerged from the oven, and accompanied a meticulously prepared salad to the table. Carter gave Ashe a humored smile as he passed, careful not to let Elsa see. Upon joining them in the living room, Spider was instantly assigned to setting the table, to which she wordlessly complied. China plates and antique silverware appeared and, unfolding a napkin and laying it on her lap, Elsa smiled. "It's so nice to have you all back again."

Carter made a noise of agreement and sat down.

Glancing up, Elsa caught sight of Ashe. "Oh, do come sit at the table, dear," she called.

Ashe glanced to Carter. He hesitated and then looked back at Bus, twitching his head toward the front window. Elsa made a movement as though to call him over as well, but at a soft sound from Carter, she bit back her protests with a look of faint displeasure.

"Yours will reheat," she told Bus.

He thanked her and then tweaked back the kitchen curtain, watching the road.

"So I was talking to Serenity," Carter started after a few moments.

"Carter, no," Elsa said sharply, setting down her salad bowl. She paused and then took a breath to calm herself. "We've been over this."

He said nothing else, and Spider kept her eyes on dinner. A minute passed in silence.

"You told Blackjack you saw one of the Blood," Carter said.

Elsa's fork clattered onto her plate and she turned to him angrily.

"One of them killed her family," he said, nodding toward Ashe.

Elsa's eyes darted to her and away. For a moment, she seemed to struggle with herself. "He was horrible," she allowed, her quiet voice carefully controlled.

"Does he know you're here?"

Annoyance flickered and then was smothered. "I wouldn't think so."

"You mean you don't know," Bus called from the kitchen.

The anger returned and she gave him a glare before burying the expression beneath deliberate good manners. "I will not discuss this again."

Silence fell, broken only by the faint clink of silverware.

"What'd he look like?" Ashe asked softly.

Elsa looked up from her meatloaf, defensiveness at the ready before the question sank in. The expression dwindled into a mixture of fear at the memory, and pity.

"Tall," she said after a moment. "And big. But not fat. More like a giant than a man. He was white, and had reddish-brown hair. He was riding in a black sedan, but not driving it, and stopped to speak to a few other men outside the bar before he left."

"Wizards?" Carter asked, his attention on the meatloaf.

The old woman gave him an irritated look which he pretended not to see. "Surely not. Mitzi would have warned me."

Spider closed her eyes briefly, and then kept eating.

"When did you see him?" Carter asked.

Elsa hesitated. "Once yesterday," she admitted. "And again today."

"Then you're staying away from the windows and keeping that dog downstairs, while we watch the bar to see if he comes back tomorrow," Carter said with finality.

"Now, I can't stay hidden the whole time," Elsa protested. Carter's gaze slid to her and she flustered. "Norman is coming by in the afternoon to help with the garbage, and he'll be concerned if I don't answer the door."

"Norman."

"He lives down the street," she explained. "And you needn't look at me like that. I've known him for thirty years. He was a great friend to George before he passed on, and he stops by every other day to take out the garbage, bring me groceries, that sort of thing. He's terribly protective, and just the most thoughtful man – but not more than George was, of course."

She paused. "Though he might be surprised to see you all here."

"We'll stay out of his way," Carter assured her.

Elsa returned to her dinner, missing the quick look he gave Spider and Bus.

Dinner completed in silence, and Elsa thanked Ashe after she helped wash the dishes.

As Ashe left the kitchen, Carter stopped her momentarily. "You take first watch," he said, keeping his voice low. "Back window. I'm going to keep an eye on the front."

She nodded, glancing toward Elsa, who was watching them with thinly veiled suspicion as she put the dishes away. Biting her lip briefly, Ashe walked to the bookcase and then drew a random novel from the shelf. Flipping it open, she carefully pretended to read by the backyard window, and from the corner of her eye, she saw Carter smile.

Cautiously, she studied the neighborhood, while glancing to the book intermittently. Sunset gilded the grass and leaves, and threw long shadows in which nothing moved. Overhead, birds darted between the trees, making their own dinner of the early evening insects.

But her heart was pounding. If a wizard appeared, or even one of the Blood, she still had no plan.

She hadn't felt this helpless in weeks.

A warm weight brushed her leg and she looked down. Bumping her hand, Tala signaled her ever-present need for attention before leaning on Ashe with her deep brown eyes on the yard.

Relief hit her. Tala could spot the wizards, and nobody would think anything of it. And if someone came near and the dog didn't react, she'd assume it was one of the Blood and call for Carter.

It wasn't much of a strategy, but she couldn't think what else to do.

Digging her fingers into the dog's coat, she watched the sun slip behind the houses and silently begged the animal not to leave.

Chapter Fifteen

He'd had some success, and Harris supposed he should be pleased. Over the past few weeks, he'd determined with reasonable certainty the identity of the boy from the security camera outside the café. With only one person missing for a month from the school, it hadn't been hard to narrow down the suspect list. He'd tracked the boy's friends, retraced his movements from the day before he vanished, and discerned the obvious fact that something strange was going on.

On the flipside, he'd yet to catch anyone, see hide nor hair of the younger girl, or find the boy anywhere.

So really, success was a debatable word.

Following their discussion, Brogan had summarily taken care of IA, though in Harris' opinion, his solution left a lot to be desired. Memory returning, the ostensible FBI agent recalled voices in the hall prior to the explosion, and thus claimed the girl had an accomplice who must have taken out the cameras and arranged her escape. As cover stories went, it lacked a certain finesse, since now Harris' claims of the girl being a human torch automatically left him looking insane.

He'd been dropped on leave faster than he could say psychosis, and now was required to attend counseling sessions twice a week.

It was insulting. And damned inconvenient.

They'd taken his gun and badge, as he'd expected, and to the department he became something of a pariah. For their part, Malden's family quickly learned of his apparent breakdown through the grapevine, and now treated him with kid gloves the likes of which he'd never seen.

On some level, he supposed Rhianne and the kids' reactions were to be expected. Due to heavy doses of painkillers and general trauma, Scott couldn't remember the afternoon of the fire, and Brogan's story contained no trace of anything abnormal. In light of that, the most rational conclusion seemed to be that stress had made Harris lose his mind.

Except that now every conversation began with questions of how he was feeling and whether the counseling was going well.

Yet for all the problems, he still had the gun his father left him, so he wasn't defenseless. And a day after losing his badge, a replacement had shown up by courier, courtesy of the giant, and bearing the implicit message that breaking the law was little of Brogan's concern.

He'd left the package on the table, and had yet to bring himself to take the badge from the box. Crossing the line was one thing. Being reminded of it so openly was another.

Of the giant, he'd seen almost nothing. Within a week of meeting him, Brogan headed east with a vague statement about securing additional support. A few of his associates remained in Monfort though, with the understanding that if he were to find anything,

Harris was to contact them immediately.

Which was fine. He preferred the solitude. But a life as a private investigator had turned out to be amazingly annoying compared to that of a police detective, and being an unsuccessful one was starting to make him crazy.

His target wasn't the issue. He wanted to find the little girl alive as much as anyone, and he tried to convince himself, as Brogan asserted, that locating her would draw the older girl in. But he also knew that the longer this took, the more chance there was that Ashley would send someone else up in flames. He had to find her soon, if only to stop his conscience from making him lose more sleep than he was already. And from slowly eating him alive.

Though it didn't help that his current best lead in accomplishing that goal was a teenager with a spy complex so blatant, he may as well have been wearing a sign.

Resting his head against the car window, Harris tweaked the volume on his police scanner and resisted the urge to sigh as Travis Braun slipped into the electronics store for the third time this week. Without department resources and all manner of useful things, tracking what exactly the boy purchased would have been difficult, if not for the store's bags having the transparency of tissue paper.

Minutes passed. The boy emerged and promptly glanced around surreptitiously. Harris rolled his eyes.

Walkie-talkies again. The prior two models hadn't cut it apparently. Who did the boy think he was kidding?

The kid pulled from the parking lot, and Harris waited a few moments and then followed him away from the store. As leads went, the kid wasn't very helpful. But with the other boy's parents gone and no other friends on hand, Travis was the best link he had to the car thief, Cole.

He exhaled as the truck turned a corner. As much as anything else, the boy was a mystery. Cole Smith, son of the thoroughly unremarkable Robert and Melissa Smith, was a young man with no criminal record, history of drug use, or even a detention to his name. Over the weeks, Harris had wracked his mind for explanations of Cole's involvement, though none stood out above the rest. The parents were in it with him. He'd murdered them before leaving. Cole was dead and the parents were actually in control.

Or Ashley'd used the boy, in which case all this was pointless because while Harris was sitting here trying to find them, the whole family could've already been killed.

He'd exhausted every avenue he could explore, trying to determine which theory rang true. But the teachers at Brighton Modisett had been closemouthed as clams, owing to tiny things like the law and the school's reputation of educating those for whom impropriety simply wasn't conceivable. From the security guards at the neighborhood gates, he'd gained equally little insight. Most of his attempts at unofficial questioning invariably degenerated into mention of their applications to the police force and not-so-oblique requests for recommendations if they happened to provide any help.

It was maddening.

Winding his way through town, Travis pulled to a stop on a hill overlooking Cole Smith's neighborhood. It was a daily ritual, and as with each time before, Harris came to a halt behind the bushes, and waited as the boy scanned the suburban terrain.

Minutes passed. He was taking longer than usual. Pulling out his binoculars from behind the seat, Harris studied the teenager, using the foliage as a screen.

Dropping his own binoculars, Travis cranked the engine and drove away.

Brow furrowing, Harris waited and then crept his car toward the spot where the boy had parked. He looked out at the neighborhood, watching Cole's house.

Nothing. No lights. No cars in the drive. Same as every prior day.

Lowering his binoculars, Harris watched the kid roll through a stop sign and roar toward the city, leaving a cloud of dust in his wake.

After endless weeks of tracking the would-be spy, any anomaly was worth noting. And though Harris couldn't see any change, the kid had clearly noticed something.

He lifted his cell and placed a quick call to the security guard station.

"Louis here."

"Harris. Have you seen any sign of that boy I asked you about? Cole?"

"Nope," came the cheerful response. "Promise I'll call if I do, though."

He thanked the man distractedly and hung up, still studying the house.

Something spooked Travis, and that something hadn't been Cole. Or anything at the house. Or anything the virtually useless guard saw. Yet something had changed, and for the life of him, he couldn't tell what it'd been.

Uneasily, he drove after the pretentious little spy who remained his only lead.

Inside the cabin, something crashed to the ground.

Sitting on the picnic table, Cole glanced toward the house. From her perch on the porch steps, Lily sighed but didn't bother looking away from her pile of woven grass blades.

The back door slammed, and a moment later, Robert stalked off into the forest, grumbling furiously.

So that call hadn't gone any better than the last fifty. The mysterious cripples were still nowhere to be found.

Taking a deep breath, Cole shook his head and returned to cleaning his gun. After a week of arguing, Robert had finally shut up about Cole keeping the weapon he'd snagged at the campground. No matter how rabidly myopic the man could be, even he'd had to concede that two armed people would stand a better chance of protecting them against wizards than one.

Not that they'd seen wizards. Or any other human beings besides each other for the past month. And while he'd hated Robert before, it was nothing compared to how infuriating he found the man now.

First had come the attempts to slip off with Lily, thwarted primarily by the fact the girl wouldn't stray more than a few feet from Cole's side. Then came the fake identification cards, bought and paid for by Robert, but then summarily locked up to keep them from even touching the IDs without his permission. The final straw had been the refusal to part with any more information about the wizards or their war. Information was power apparently, and Robert knew ignorance kept them dependent upon him.

Cole wasn't certain he'd ever hated the man as much as when Robert went close-lipped about everything. In light of the elaborate setup of the past eight years of his life, and Lily's entire family being murdered with no explanation as to why, Robert's smirking silence had almost been too much to bear.

Lily had finally screamed at the man, and threatened to run away if he didn't tell them all he knew. The surge of anger out of her had taken Cole by surprise as much as Robert, though when he'd asked about it later, she'd just looked defiant.

"Ashley's out there in this," she'd said. "And if I can find out what's going on, and why people hurt our family, maybe I can help her."

He hadn't had the heart to argue.

Bit by bit, they'd learned about cripples, the wizards and all that went with that world. The details, paid for by minutes on end of Robert's vitriolic tirades, painted a spotty picture of a situation where, but for seeing a few people glow, Cole possessed a million vulnerabilities and absolutely no advantages. No magic, but it could kill him instantly. No way to recognize wizards, but they could easily identify him. No defenses, except for the dubious benefit of getting migraines around magic, and the chance of maybe getting a lucky shot with a gun. And while Robert ranted about the world being unfair, Cole kept returning to the same thought over and over again.

In Robert's world, he was useless.

And yet Vaughn had died to keep him hidden.

Branches snapped as Robert marched back out of the forest, and Cole suppressed a grimace. He knew that look only too well. The man wanted to attack something, hurt something. Life went better when he stayed away long enough to cool down.

"And just what the hell do you think you're doing?" Robert snapped at him. "You cleaned that thing twice already. I'm not letting you have any more bullets just because you polish it up nice."

Cole paused, weighing potential responses. With ammunition at a premium and Robert paranoid as hell, the man had let Cole empty what ammo the weapon held in practice, and then forbidden him a single bullet more. That Cole hadn't ever learned to shoot didn't seem to enter the equation, nor did the fact that defending them from wizards might require him to know how. Robert only cared that Cole might shoot him instead, and thus banned him from even approaching the locked cabinet where the bullets were stored.

The buzz of his phone saved him the trouble of replying, and without taking his eyes from the man, he pulled the cell from his pocket.

"Hey, Travis," he answered.

Glaring angrily, Robert headed for the house, belatedly trying to produce the semblance of a jolly smile for Lily. The girl ignored him.

"Dude," Travis said breathlessly. "Your mom is back."

Cole blinked. "What?"

"Your *mom*. That neighbor you told me about just showed up. The old lady pulled into her driveway and when she got out, Melissa climbed from the back seat. She stopped at the neighbor's, but she's got bags so I'm guessing she'll be back at your place any minute."

"You sure it was her?"

"What do you take me for?"

"Sorry," Cole apologized distractedly, his mind whirling.

"What do we do?"

"Stay there. I'm coming to you."

"Are you sure–"

Cole hung up.

He stared at the ground without seeing it. For all his ranting, Robert hadn't produced a single scrap of information on why the wizards worked so hard to keep Cole from knowing about them. Their motivations hadn't interested the man, just their protection.

But his comment from the campground had stayed with Cole. While Robert knew nothing and didn't care, Melissa was a different story altogether.

And now she was back.

"What happened?"

Lily's quiet voice broke into his thoughts. Pushing up from the porch, she glanced back at the house nervously and then walked over to him.

"Cole?" she persisted when he didn't answer.

"Melissa's back," he told her, keeping his voice low and hoping Robert wasn't near the open cabin windows.

Lily bit her lip. "What do you want to do?"

"I need to go back there."

The girl paused. "We," she corrected.

He hesitated, reluctant to drag her into what would undoubtedly be a dangerous situation. But the only other option was leaving her with Robert, and he wasn't so stupid as to believe either of them would still be here when he got back.

"We need to," he agreed. "Can you distract Robert for me? I need to get something."

Her eyes darted to the gun, and unease moved across her face.

"Lily, please?"

She drew a small breath, pushed aside the discomfort and then nodded resolutely. Turning on her heel, she marched into the cabin.

At the sight, an amused smile pulled at his mouth, and he buried it swiftly for fear she might see. Climbing from the table, he tucked the gun behind his back and followed.

Inside the cabin, Lily made a beeline for the rear bedroom and then paused outside the closed door. In the next room, Robert could be heard attempting yet another call to the elusive cripples. She glanced questioningly to Cole.

He hesitated and then shook his head, motioning her away from the door. "Just knock something over if he starts to come out," Cole whispered.

She nodded and backed up beside the broom propped by the back door.

Cole hurried to Robert's jacket on the couch. Patting down the pockets, he found the man's Swiss army knife and swiftly fished it out before heading for the cabinet. Trying to keep his hands steady despite the adrenaline racing through him, he pulled out the narrow metal toothpick and attacked the lock.

He could hear Robert talking. The words were unintelligible. And the damned lock wouldn't budge.

Cole grimaced. He hadn't attempted to pick a lock since he was twelve and had been trying to run away. And he hadn't succeeded then either.

As symmetry went, it was infuriating.

The lock gave.

Exhilaration ran through him like electricity. Beyond the cabinet doors, ammunition sat beneath a manila envelope. Ignoring the envelope for the moment, he scanned the piles, spotting the magazine Robert had taken from his weapon. Noting with mild shock that Robert had actually reloaded the thing, he grabbed it and then shoved it into the gun. Snatching the manila envelope, he ripped it open and then drew out their IDs.

Paul Wood. Hannah Wood. He grimaced at the names Robert had bought, but it wasn't important. They had to go.

"Come on," he whispered to Lily as he shoved the cards into his pocket.

Lily nodded and followed him across the room. At the front, he glanced back. Robert was still on the phone. From his excited tone, it sounded like things were finally going well.

He hesitated, but there was nothing for it. Either they went now or not at all.

Quickly, he motioned the girl ahead of him and then jogged down the steps. Near the dirt track edging the cabin property, the pickup sat behind Robert's station wagon. Thumbing the key fob, he pulled open the door and then climbed inside.

"What the hell are you doing?" Robert shouted, coming out the front door. "Get back here!"

The engine turned over. Robert rushed down the steps, fumbling for the gun in the old western style holster he kept at his waist.

"Go!" Lily cried.

Cole yanked on the gearshift and smashed the pedal to the floor. Spewing dirt, the tires caught and the truck raced onto the path as gunshots cracked through the air.

"Get down!" he ordered the girl.

He needn't have bothered. She'd plastered herself to the seat the moment Robert reached for his gun.

In the rearview mirror, he caught a glimpse of the man running after them on foot. More gunshots echoed through the forest, though nothing hit the pickup. Curving sharply, the path followed the steep downward slope of the tree-lined hillside, and in moments, Robert was lost from view.

Drawing a shaky breath, Cole loosened his grip on the wheel. "You okay?" he asked Lily.

Pushing up from the seat, she peered through the rear window.

"Uh-huh." She paused. "We're not going back there, are we?"

The plea in her voice was easy to hear, and he shook his head. "You think he'd let us?"

She echoed the motion, certainty on her face. "Not you. Me..." She scowled.

He suppressed a smile at her disgusted expression. For weeks, the man had tried to coax Lily into thinking him a wonderful person, while remaining oblivious to the disrespect he showed everything else. Candy appeared for her, obtained from God knew where, and endless invitations for games assaulted her at every turn, all conveniently designed to draw her away from Cole. After the first week, she'd begun feigning deafness, if only to make Robert stop talking to her.

"Do you think Melissa will know why..." She trailed off, gesturing illustratively when words failed.

"You're glowing?"

She nodded.

"Maybe. We have to get the chance to talk to her first."

"What're you going to do?"

A frown flickered over his face. That was the million dollar question. "Let me think about it."

She grimaced and then nodded, obviously wanting an answer but reluctantly willing to give him time. Turning to the window, she watched the trees go by.

The dirt track wound down the hills and eventually reached a rough concrete road. Bouncing along, Lily glanced to him from time to time, saying nothing.

And slowly, the fragments of a ridiculous plan began to come together.

He took out his cell and hit redial. "Travis?"

"Dammit, you didn't let me finish!"

"Sorry, I–"

"That cop is still following me! I think I saw him when I was checking your place, and now he's practically sitting outside my house!"

Cole swore and then winced. Lily just stared at him, waiting to hear what was going on.

"He's freaking me out! Every time I think I shake him, he turns up somewhere else! Grocery stores, gas stations, school… he even followed me to church! I'm going nuts here and–"

"Okay," Cole interrupted, trying to think. "Where's he now?"

"Down the street, sitting in the Ulbright's driveway like he owns the damn–"

"Fine. Look, does Ellie have a cell phone?"

"Yeah, so?"

"Can you get it?"

"I guess…"

"Do that." He checked the clock on the dash, calculating distances swiftly. "And then wait half an hour. Call the cops. Tell them you've seen the little girl on TV over by Pendleton's grocery store, that she's with a guy matching the description of that drug dealer, and that she looks like she's been crying. Or something. Make it dramatic enough to get the cops' attention."

"Yeah… yeah…" Travis said, latching onto the idea. "Bastard'll rush over there and leave me alone."

"He'll be back when he finds out it's a trick, so for Pete's sake, don't call till it's been at least half an hour. We need some time before he comes looking for you. Then head to that new hotel construction site north of town. You know the one I'm talking about?"

"Yeah."

Cole paused. "And one other thing. Does Preston still have that World War Two memorabilia? The old guns and stuff?"

Travis' curiosity was clear. "I think so…"

"Get some of it. Guns especially. Bring them with you."

"You want *guns*? Dude, what the hell are you–"

"It's not what you think," Cole said, painfully aware of the handgun resting between him and Lily on the seat. That would require some hefty explaining if Travis caught sight of it. "Trust me. Can you get them?"

"I guess…"

"Thanks. I'll call when we get closer to town."

"Alright," Travis said uncertainly.

Cole hung up. Lily's questioning gaze burned into him, impossible to ignore.

"It's not what you think either," he said.

She shrugged equivocally, her eyes flicking to the gun and then back to him again.

He grimaced and kept driving.

Forty-five endless minutes later, he pulled up a few yards from Travis' bright blue truck at the construction site. Beyond mounds of dirt, a bulldozer rumbled and workers shouted, but the space around the trucks was empty. Looking incredibly shifty, Travis climbed from his pickup and scanned the area.

Grabbing the gun from the seat, Cole shoved it into the back of his jeans and pulled his t-shirt down over it before the boy came up to the window.

"He took the bait," Travis said by way of greeting.

"Did you bring the guns?"

"I'm really not sure why you–"

"Travis."

The boy grimaced. "Yeah. But Preston keeps his stuff pretty organized. He'll know they're gone."

"I just need them for an hour or two."

"What're you planning?"

Cole glanced to Lily. "You're going to play delivery guy," he told Travis. "Take the guns to Melissa's. Tell her Robert ordered them before they left for vacation, and you need payment. She hates attention, so if you make it serious enough – threaten collections or something – she should let you past the security guards."

"What then?"

"Lily and I will be hiding in the back of the truck. If you can get us past the neighbors and the security guards, I can take it from there."

Travis looked skeptical. "That's it?"

"You have a better idea?"

The boy shrugged. "We could slip over the wall or something. I think the–"

"Security cameras mean anything to you?"

He looked deflated.

"You're running point on this one, Travis," Cole said, resorting to action-adventure mode at the guy's expression. "You've got to pull this off, or we're done."

"As a delivery guy," Travis said flatly.

"As our only way inside," Cole said. He paused. "You going to be cool with this?"

"Yeah," Travis sighed.

Cole nodded gratefully. "The code to call the house from the gate is one-seven-two-one-three. And did you bring Ellie's phone?"

Travis pulled it from his pocket.

"Ditch it here. They might try to trace the call."

The thought seemed to enliven the boy. Disassembling the phone, he tossed the pieces to the road.

Cole climbed from the pickup, Lily following. Pulling back the tarp covering the bed of his blue truck, Travis waited as Cole hoisted himself over the edge and then helped Lily in. A few moments of shoving around the sandbags near the wheel wells provided them with a space in which to hide, shielded from anyone who might glance at the mesh tailgate.

The tarp closed back over them and Travis hooked it down before returning to the driver's side. The truck rocked as the door slammed.

"Back again, eh?" Cole said to Lily.

Rolling over slightly, she gave him a flat look. "You sure this is going to work?"

"I hope so."

The engine came to life, and then the truck bumped out of the construction site and back onto the road. Plastic crunched briefly as the cell phone shattered beneath the tires.

Minutes passed in silence. Beneath the tarp, the warm spring air slowly became stifling.

And then they stopped. The keypad beeped as Travis typed in the number.

"Hello?"

Instinctively, Cole tensed at Melissa's voice. The slightly peevish sound was like fingernails on the chalkboard of his spine.

"I have a delivery for Robert Smith," Travis said, his tone radiating official business.

The phone clicked as she hung up.

Travis paused. Cole could almost feel the confusion radiating from the boy. Barely breathing, he waited.

Beeping noises came as Travis dialed again.

"Yes?"

"I have a delivery."

"Robert Smith doesn't live here anymore."

"Ma'am, Mr. Smith ordered this vintage World War memorabilia nearly a month ago, cash on delivery. Now I've been patient in trying to get this to him, but if I don't get paid for this stuff, I'm going to drag somebody into collections, do you get me? I have three lawyers on retainer for this kind of thing, and unless you want me calling them right now, I'd suggest you–"

A beep sounded and then the box clicked off again.

Travis swore in irritation. "She do this a lot?" he asked the guard.

"I think I'm going to need to see some ID," the rent-a-cop replied coldly.

The gate creaked as it swung open and Travis chuckled. "After I get back, eh, buddy?"

He raced the truck past the gates and into the neighborhood.

"Damn, that was awesome!" Travis cried through the open rear window.

Cole winced, hoping no one else heard.

A few moments later, the truck came to a stop and then backed up, jostling them as it crossed onto the driveway.

Travis opened his door and slid out. "You're next to the garage," he hissed as he drew out the box of memorabilia. "Neighbor's by the rosebushes in her backyard."

He slammed the door and headed for the front of the house,

whistling obnoxiously.

Cautiously, Cole unhooked the tarp and sat up. Surrounded on three sides by the house and garage, only the edge of the neighbor's yard was visible. But he knew her rosebushes weren't far.

Travis knocked loudly on the front door, and a moment later, Melissa answered.

Hurriedly, Cole hoisted Lily over the tailgate and then followed her to the ground. Ducking below the truck, he rushed toward the back door.

They hadn't changed the locks, though he couldn't think why he'd worried they would. Shutting the door carefully, he motioned Lily to stay out of sight and then headed for the living room entryway. In the foyer, he could hear Melissa arguing with Travis, trying her usual method of controlling the situation by biting the head off of whatever threatened her perfect world.

"I will personally see you in court if you continue this nonsense," she spat. "I won't tell you again–"

"And I'm telling *you*, I got three lawyers on retainer, lady. You think it's going to take much for me to get them here?"

"You–"

She cut off as she saw Travis' gaze go past her. Swiftly, she tossed a glance to the kitchen and then froze, the anger on her face melting to shock. "Cole?" Her gaze darted between him and Travis. "How…"

Cole didn't take his eyes off her. "Wait for us around the corner past the gate," he told Travis.

Looking undecided, the boy hesitated and then did as instructed. He shut the door behind him, but neither Melissa or Cole broke eye contact at the sound.

"It's so nice to see you home again," she said saccharinely.

She lunged for the phone.

The gun appeared in his hand as if by reflex and, fingertips on the receiver, the woman froze.

"Don't," he ordered.

Melissa eased away from the phone, flickers of a pleasant expression still struggling to materialize. "What's going on, honey?"

"How long do we have till the spy next door stops by?"

Shock flashed through her eyes, buried swiftly. "Spy?" she asked, feigning incredulity.

He cocked the gun.

"A few seconds," she answered.

"Tell her everything is fine. And that you need to go to the grocery store in a bit to replace the food gone bad."

A sneer tugged at her lips.

He held out a hand to Lily. The girl took it, and he pulled her from behind the kitchen wall.

Blood drained from Melissa's face and he could tell she wasn't breathing. But alarm only partly filled her expression. The remainder was reserved for a wary sort of fear.

"She feels like you," Lily said quietly.

Melissa swallowed. Cole didn't take his eyes from the woman.

"You know what glowing people can do?" he asked.

She didn't look away from the little girl, and he could read the answer on her face.

"Tell the spy everything is fine."

A knock sounded on the door. Carefully, he backed behind the kitchen wall. Keeping one eye to the living room entryway, he retreated with Lily into the shadows of the pantry.

The front door opened.

"Ethel," Melissa said, and the discomfort in her voice made Cole tense.

"What's going on?" the old woman snapped as the door shut behind her.

"I'm sorry?"

"Who was that?"

"Oh, just a delivery boy," Melissa said, chuckling gaily. "Robert ordered something a month back and–"

"What did he want?"

"Just money," Melissa answered, the happy note falling away. "It's fine, Ethel. Really."

A whimper suddenly escaped her, and for a moment, breathless silence filled the house.

"If you're lying to me..." the old woman growled, her voice barely audible.

"I wouldn't... you know I wouldn't... please..."

Melissa gasped as the old woman stopped whatever she'd been doing.

"You're not answering that door again, understand? Not unless it's him."

Footsteps clicked on the foyer's tile floor.

"I–" Melissa began nervously. The footsteps stopped. "I need to go to the grocery store."

"What?"

"The food's all rotten," she continued, pleading. "I... I don't have anything to eat."

An exasperated noise escaped the old woman. "Order a pizza."

"But you said–"

Melissa cut off with a squeak as the neighbor stalked back toward her.

"Fine," the old woman sneered. "And I'll follow. You're not getting away like the other one."

"N-no," Melissa agreed. "Thank you. Thank you, Ethel."

The door slammed.

Warily, Cole eased out of the pantry and crossed to the living room doorway. In the foyer, Melissa was leaning on the wall, head bowed and cradling one arm. At the sound of his steps, she flinched, as though she'd forgotten he was there. Red-eyed, she stared up at him.

"You ruined *everything*," she said.

"I've heard." He jerked his chin toward the neighbor's house. "She a wizard?"

Melissa nodded. Taking a breath, she seemed to forcibly push her fear and pain behind the mask of propriety she'd worn ever since he met her. With rigid self-control, she walked to the couch and lowered herself down.

But she wouldn't look at him.

"Who are they?" he asked.

She didn't answer.

Pulling Lily with him, he strode to the opposite couch and sat down across from Melissa, keeping the gun in plain view. His gaze twitched to the front bay window, but only a thin strip of the yard was visible between the closed curtain panels.

"Melissa, answer me."

Her gaze flicked from the ground, to him, to Lily in the space of a heartbeat. Her nose wrinkled slightly as though irritated. "They're wizards who work for the Taliesin Council."

"What do they want?"

She went back to studying the carpet, looking like nothing more than a recalcitrant child.

"Melissa!" he snapped. He drew a breath, reining in his temper. "They set this up. They enlisted you and Robert. They did all this… why? What's the point?"

His hand wrapped around the gun at her silence, and annoyance twisted her expression.

"To keep you happy and oblivious, so they'd always look like the good guys," Melissa said, spite dripping from her words. "So when they finally told you about the war and their world, they'd come off as the great saviors who'd given you such a peaceful life. And you'd love them for it. Be so thankful. Then whatever they wanted, you'd do without question."

Her eyes rose to meet his, and for the first time, he could see the real hatred behind the pettiness and cowardice she held inside.

"Because you'd never know that in reality, they'd been the ones who'd killed your mommy and daddy all along."

Chapter Sixteen

———◆———

From the edge of the Pendleton's parking lot, Harris watched the cops milling around. Police cars lined the fire lane of the grocery store, but for the past twenty minutes, nothing appeared to have changed.

The little girl was gone. If she'd ever been here in the first place.

He could hear the dispatcher and the officers talking on the scanner, but their conversations hadn't amounted to anything. The clerks had been questioned to no avail, and he was fairly certain the security videos wouldn't show anything. Even if the girl had been here, her sister's kind were too good at hiding to let something like a security camera give them away.

As he knew only too well.

He ran a hand over his hair, trying not to surrender to the desire to punch the steering wheel. From the moment the call came in, his gut had said something wasn't right, but he'd been too frustrated with a month of finding nothing to listen.

It was strange, though, how the alert appeared just after the bizarre behavior by his would-be spy.

Brow furrowing, he picked up the cell and thumbed through the recent calls till he reached the security booth's number.

"Louis?" he said when the guard picked up. "Are you *sure* nothing's changed in the last hour?"

The guard scoffed. "There was an asshole delivery boy came through here not ten minutes ago, but other than that…"

"Delivery for whom?"

"Mr. Smith. Thought they weren't home, but I guess they got back before my shift. Haven't seen the kid though."

Harris' hand tightened on the phone. "Brown-haired white kid driving a blue truck?"

"Uh, yeah. Why?"

He dropped the phone and yanked the car into gear. "That little…"

As he drove up to the walled neighborhood, Louis hit the button to open the gate immediately. "Detective?" he called from the booth. "Should I dial 9-1-1? Is he here?"

Cursing internally and willing the gate to open faster, Harris ignored him.

The man blanched. "Uh, what does this mean about my recommendation?"

Harris smashed down the pedal and darted through a gap barely wider than the car.

At the end of the Smith's block, he pulled to a stop and climbed out. A few houses down, he could see the closed curtains of their home. Their car wasn't in the drive, but with a garage that size, it might never be.

Hating the ambiguity, he darted across the neighbors' yards, heading for the Smiths. He looked like a criminal, but there was nothing to be done. With the damage Ashley's kind could do, stealth was the only defense he had. One hand hovering near his weapon, he paused against the gray siding, listening for shouts or cries.

Nothing.

He crouched, inching around the front and then peering cautiously through the gap between the curtains on the bay window.

His heart hit his throat.

Cole was in there. With the kid. And a gun.

Heart pounding, he eased away from the window and then retreated around the corner of the house. If Cole was like Ashley, Harris didn't stand a chance. Neither did any officers he'd call. And he couldn't just burst in there. He and the kid would probably get killed.

With hands shaking much more than he would have liked, he fumbled out his cell and dialed Brogan's men.

———— ◆ ————

"What?" Cole said.

Melissa sneered. "What's the old poet say? 'Shot him down like a dog on the highway'?" Her mocking expression grew. "Or hallway, or whatever."

He nearly lunged across the coffee table at her.

"Don't," Lily said, and Cole couldn't tell if she was talking to him or Melissa. But the woman's mocking expression faded all the same. "What do you mean?" the girl continued.

"They arranged it," Melissa said, still striving to appear in control despite her obvious discomfort with the little girl. "The kidnapping, all of it."

"Why?"

His voice sounded rough to his own ears. Alien.

"They want you for something," she said, shrugging. "I don't know what."

At his expression, she looked defensive. "I don't! The Council killed your parents and kept you alive. That's all I know."

He could feel his heart pounding. "The Taliesin Council?"

She scoffed, reading his tone. "What? You think you're going to do something about it? Maybe get a little familial revenge?"

His gaze flicked to hers. Beneath the derision and the makeup, he could see her pale.

"They won't let you," she assured him. "They want you for something, but they're not going to put up with you trying to hurt them. They'll make you wish you'd never crossed them. Trust me."

"Does Ethel know where they are?"

She stared at him. "Does it *matter*? What're you going to do? Go over and beat it out of her? She's a *wizard*! It doesn't matter what they did. It doesn't matter what they do now. You can't fight them."

When his expression didn't change, she looked around incredulously, and her eyes came to rest on Lily. "And what about the kid, huh? Your little glowworm there?"

"She can hide."

Melissa gave a gasp of laughter. "She can die is what she can do!"

She stared at him, and then shook her head when her words had no effect.

"You think your little Blood wizard means you can fight them," she said, her hysteria fading into something darker. "You think you can use her as a weapon to get what you want. One little girl." Melissa scoffed. "Imagine a room *filled* with wizards, each with fifty years more magical experience than she has. You think one little kid can stand up to that? You think they won't turn her into a pillar of ash for trying? They'll make you listen to her scream. They'll burn her alive slowly just for you, and watch you beg them to kill her before the end."

She reached down and rolled back the sleeve of her loose blouse. Lily's grip on his hand clenched. Blackened burns and blood-encrusted welts covered Melissa's arm, continuing up beneath the fabric of her sleeve.

"Or do you think I'm lying?" she asked quietly.

Cole didn't take his eyes from the woman, but his thoughts were elsewhere. In a bedroom, listening to wizards kill his mother. And on a cliff beneath an inferno, where another girl he'd tried to save had died.

He wanted to punch something, even though it wouldn't help. Yet.

"They demanded I tell them all I knew about you," Melissa continued distantly, studying her arm. "But I didn't have everything they needed. And when they weren't satisfied…"

"What about the others?" Cole interrupted, trying to keep his voice calm.

Melissa's brow furrowed in confusion.

"The ones who glow like her. Why are they after me?"

And Lily, he added silently.

"They want you for something too, I guess."

"You don't know?" At her silence, he continued. "But you've seen them before. People who glow, I mean?"

She hesitated. "Once. From a distance, back in Kansas City. But the Council moved us that night."

Cole remembered. He'd been eleven and out of the blue, Robert and Melissa decided they needed to move. Overnight, they'd forced him to leave everything he owned, saying it wasn't worth keeping. He'd been furious, but as usual, they didn't care. And by the time a few years had passed, so many instances of hurt and disregard had occurred, the move had lost all significance.

"They were there?" he asked.

"A few."

"Who are they?"

Melissa shrugged. "I overheard one of the wizards call them the Blood. That's why I know what the kid is. And how she's probably setting you up for them."

She risked a nasty look at Lily, whose eyes narrowed angrily. Melissa's spiteful expression disappeared instantly and she turned from the girl as though the exchange hadn't happened.

Cole squeezed Lily's hand, willing her not to say anything about her family.

"I think it's time we head for the store, don't you?" he asked the girl, not taking his eyes from Melissa.

Lily growled in agreement.

"And then what?" Melissa said. "There's no one to protect you out there, Cole. Her kind won't help you, whatever the girl's said. The wizards are too strong for that."

He said nothing.

"Just go back," she continued, a hint of begging in her voice. "Tell them you're sorry. Tell them anything. Who cares if they killed your mom and dad? For all you know, your parents brought it on themselves. You can't throw everything away over that. Just do what they want so this can end."

For a moment, Cole stared at her.

"Get the car," he said, barely trusting himself to speak.

"Cole–"

"Now!"

She hesitated, and then rose to her feet, the picture of primness and self-control. But her hand shook as she reached for the keys on the console table.

"You're making a mistake," she said stiffly.

Pulling Lily after him, he didn't answer. Gripping the keys, she crossed the foyer and opened the door.

Two black sedans stopped by the curb.

Cole's eyes went from the cars to Melissa's startled face, and then he was moving. With Lily's hand in one fist and the gun in the other, he raced through the kitchen while, behind him, he heard Melissa slam the door.

As though that would stop them.

He yanked the back door open, and then jerked to a stop. Lily crashed into him.

"Put the weapon down, son," a man said, his gun pointed at Cole's chest.

Three men strode in from the living room and before Lily could do more than shriek, two of them ripped her away from him and the third shoved him into the doorframe.

His head cracked against the wood and stars scattered across his vision. The gun went skittering away as his arms were twisted back, and handcuffs locked around his wrists immediately. Behind him, he heard Lily scream.

The migraine from hell surged through his head.

"You don't want the kid to see you get hurt, do you?" the wizard holding him growled into his ear. "So just stay calm and come with us, cripple boy."

His gaze went to the neighboring yard. Ethel the spy wasn't there.

They hauled him through the living room. Melissa was nowhere to be seen. But past the front door, he spotted Lily struggling in the grip of one of the men.

"Cole!" she screamed, clawing at her captor in effort to reach him.

The man yanked open a car door and shoved her inside.

Cole's heart hit his feet.

A wizard pushed him into the other sedan's back seat, and instantly he twisted around, trying to see the girl past the glare of the sunset on the windshield. Two men climbed into the car with her, and he heard the engine turn over.

He'd never felt more helpless in his life.

The car doors opened ahead of him and the wizard swung into the driver's seat, with the man from behind the house joining him on the passenger side.

Neighbors gawked at the sedans pulling away from the curb. The security guard stared when the driver flashed him a badge and spat something about being from the FBI. The gate swung open immediately. Through it all, Cole watched the other sedan, trying frantically to think how to help the girl and keep them both alive.

Taking out his cell, the driver glanced between the phone and the road, and then punched in a call.

"We have them." The wizard waited, and then handed the phone to the man next to him. "He wants to talk to you."

"Brogan?" the other man said. "Yeah, it's Harris. Yeah. Both the boy and younger girl. Cole Smith."

A pause.

"Hey," the man called to him.

He didn't look away from the rear window, straining to determine if Lily was still alright. The glare kept obscuring everything but vague glimpses of shadow. But the car was still behind them. If they turned off, he didn't know what he'd do.

"Hey!" Harris repeated sharply.

Balefully, Cole glanced to him, and then blinked as the man snapped a photo with his phone.

Harris punched a few buttons, and then raised the cell to his ear again. "You get that?" He paused. "Yes… yes, I said Cole." His brow furrowed in alarm, and he looked to Cole as though seeing him for the first time.

Suddenly even warier than before, Cole watched him between glances to the other sedan.

"Yeah," Harris said slowly. He flinched as though startled. "No, I hear you. I will. I *will*."

The last came out sharply, as though to convince the person on the other end.

Looking vaguely stunned, Harris lowered the phone.

"Brogan's sending men to meet us," he told the driver, still eyeing Cole. "He said you'd know where."

The wizard nodded. Seeming bewildered, Harris hesitated and then turned back around.

Skin crawling, Cole returned to studying the other vehicle.

No one was glowing, though that might not mean much. Yet they weren't with the Taliesin Council, because they didn't seem to know who he was.

Or, at least, they hadn't. He wasn't sure what'd just changed.

He needed a plan, and he had nothing. But there had to be a way out of this. Somehow.

Struggling to focus past the adrenaline, Cole kept watching the other sedan as they headed onto the interstate.

———— ◆ ————

By the clock on the dash, it had been fifty minutes. By Cole's estimation, it had been a million years. His neck was cramped from watching the other sedan, though he still couldn't see Lily inside. And meanwhile, he had no plan.

At least, no good ones.

The exit ramp jostled the car, and his heart hit his throat as the second sedan didn't follow. They were leaving. They were taking her. He yanked at the handcuffs frantically.

Pulling onto the ramp, the second sedan continued after them.

He exhaled. Time was skewed. It'd only been a few seconds. And he still hadn't come up with a plan.

Feigning a heart attack had occurred to him. Or somehow making the car crash. But the latter didn't help Lily and the former wouldn't be believable anyway. Drawing attention to the car by crashing didn't mean that the men holding her would stop either. And then he'd be stuck.

The sedan climbed a small rise and pulled into a gas station. Abandoned and overgrown, the old station was decaying in privacy behind a screen of pine trees and scrub brush. Jouncing over the pot-holed lot, the sedan came to a stop beside the rusted pump shelter.

When the other car followed, Cole glanced ahead and then froze.

Two white vans waited on the other side of the parking lot, advertisements for handyman services painted on their sides. On the racks atop the vehicles, ladders and brooms were lashed down, and security fencing could be seen inside the rear windows.

Blood wizards leaned against the rear doors, and straightened as the sedans stopped.

Harris climbed from the car and started toward the Blood, calling out questions to which Cole couldn't make out the words. In the front seat, the driver turned around.

"Don't fight," he advised. "I'd hate the kid to have to watch you die."

Winking coldly, the man rose from the car and then pulled open the back door. Grabbing Cole's arm, he hauled him out. Tugging at his handcuffs, Cole twisted, trying to find Lily.

Growling a warning, the man shoved him toward the vans. "What'd I say?"

A few yards back, the other sedan sat. The men inside stepped out, and one reached for the handle of the rear door.

Three cars raced into the parking lot. Pain like a jet engine roared through Cole's head. The vans crumpled as though hit by giant sledgehammers.

All hell broke loose.

Ducking, the Blood returned the favor, and suddenly, two of the cars skidded sideways and crashed into the trees. A second impact followed, shattering the windows and sending ballistic glass strafing inward upon the screaming occupants.

Cole blanched, recognizing Ethel inside the car.

Grabbing his arm, the wizard hauled Cole down beside the sedan. Pain rushed toward them and punched into the vehicle, spinning the car on its axis. The rear wheel slammed into the wizard, propelling him into Cole and knocking them both sideways. His handcuffed wrists still tangled in the other man's grip, Cole crashed down, his head cracking painfully on the concrete.

Roaring filled his ears and red lights scattered across his vision. Dizzily, he looked up to see the wizard trying to tug him to his feet, and then agony shot through the air, blinding him for the heartbeat it took to pass by.

The man was gone. Gasping, Cole rolled to one side, trying to rise.

Dead eyes met his gaze. Lurching away, Cole stared at the wizard. Blood drenched the man's face, originating from head wounds too deep to be survived.

Nausea hit him and he scrambled back till he bumped into the car. Blasts shook the ground and he could hear people shouting.

He forced himself to breathe. To think. His hands were bound. He needed the keys.

Inching around, he closed his eyes briefly and then fished through the dead man's pockets till metal met his questing grasp.

Swiftly, he pulled his hand out and scooted away, scanning the area. Pinned down on either side of the parking lot by the magic slicing through the air, both the wizards and the Blood were sniping at one another from whatever cover remained. But the other sedan was still a few yards away.

And the men who'd been beside it now lay on the concrete, blood pooled beneath them and their clothes stained red.

He couldn't see Lily anywhere.

Rising, he glanced around quickly and then darted toward the other sedan. Blasts of energy shredded the air behind him, surging by in a Doppler shift of pain.

He reached the car. Lily was inside, trapped behind the fence separating the front from the back of the vehicle and hauling on the door handle frantically.

"It won't open!" she shouted at him.

Spinning, he fumbled for the latch and yanked the door open, cursing all child locks as he moved. The girl scrambled out.

"Here," he said urgently, turning so she could take the keys.

The handcuffs clattered to the ground.

Metal screamed behind them. He shoved Lily to the concrete as siding from the gas station scythed over them and impaled itself on the trees nearby. The Blood shouted, and he could see the wizards trying to find a way to reach the two of them first. Several lay dead as evidence of the effort, along with all the Blood's allies.

Except for Harris. Behind the corner of the gas station, the man crouched. Pale-faced, he was staring at the wizards, and when he caught sight of Cole, his eyes went wide.

Swiftly, Harris took aim.

"Go!" Cole yelled at Lily.

They took off. Bullets pelted the trunks beside them as they rushed into the forest.

One hand clutching Lily's, he tugged out his phone and smashed down the redial. He pressed the cell to his ear, glancing back as he ran.

No wizards yet. And the phone just kept ringing.

"Travis?" he gasped when the ringing stopped. "We need help. How fast can you get out of town?"

"I-I'm trying to find you right now," the boy answered, sounding distracted. "I thought maybe I could follow those guys who arrested you, but... I'm not sure where I lost them."

Cole choked, almost tripping over his own feet. "Wait, what?"

"I thought they took an exit past this old gas station a few minutes ago, but now I can't see the cars anywhere. I mean…" The boy seemed to refocus. "Dude, hold on. How're you calling me?"

Incredulous laughter nearly burst from him. "We're not far from the gas station. But don't go back there. Is there somewhere you can meet us?"

"There *was* a service road north of there," Travis said uncertainly. "Maybe. I mean, I was pretty sure there was one. Is that where you are?"

"Close. But don't go to the gas station. Just get back to that road. We'll meet you."

"Okay, but… where the hell'd the cars go?"

"It doesn't matter. Just call when you get close."

"Yeah. Right. Okay."

The call ended and Cole shoved the phone into his pocket. Behind them, the sounds of fighting were growing fainter, though by distance or one side winning, he wasn't sure.

But the forest was empty. So far.

His pulse pounded through the lump on his head, and blood from it caked the side of his face. Lily's grip was sweaty in his own and in the fading light, the ground was becoming difficult to see. Hoisting her over a fallen log, he took a breath and kept running.

The road appeared through the trees. In his pocket, the phone buzzed.

"I'm here," Travis said. "I think. Was there an earthquake or something? I mean, there's all these trees down on the highway and–"

"Where are you?"

"Just turning off the intersection. I'll– oh, there you are."

A blue truck flashed between the trees, and Cole rushed from the cover of the forest. Travis came to a stop.

"Dude, what the hell happened to you?"

"Just drive," Cole ordered, lifting Lily into the vehicle and then swinging in after her. "Fast. Now."

Startled, Travis pressed the pedal to the floor.

<hr>

"Okay," Travis said, dropping the keycard onto the table as the motel room door swung closed behind him. "The clerk took cash, so we should be good for a while. Now you want to tell me what's going on?"

On the edge of the bed, Cole looked up, and Lily made an angry noise. Perched on her knees on the lumpy mattress, the little girl shifted around slightly and then went back to dabbing the gash on his head with a wet washcloth.

"We've got some bad people after us," he said.

"I noticed," Travis answered dryly. "You just got arrested and then escaped police custody, so you care to elaborate?"

Cole glanced to Lily. The little girl grimaced and then headed toward the bathroom sink to rewet the cloth.

"I just found out that the people Melissa and Robert were working for killed my parents."

Travis paused. "Huh?"

"I'm adopted. Clara and Victor Jamison were my real parents and eight years ago, a group of people murdered them and then kidnapped me. They're determined to get their hands on me again, and they'll kill anyone who tries to stop them."

The boy blinked.

"They tortured Melissa," Cole said. "Then left her as bait. And they'll kill Lily to get me to do what they want."

"Which is?" Travis sputtered.

"I don't know."

Scoffing, the boy ran a hand through the tangles of his hair. "But I thought they killed the kid's family to get to her?"

"Maybe it was something similar," Cole said. "A different group wanting the same thing. I don't know."

Lily returned from the sink and climbed back up onto the bed. He hissed as she pressed the cold cloth to his head again.

Brow furrowing, Travis looked away, his gaze straying to the muted television across the room. The late night news played video of the gas station with captions about vandals with explosives and the police wanting anyone with information to call their hotline.

"So what do we do now?" Travis asked, ignoring the images.

Cole hesitated. He hadn't had a lot of time to think this out, but it didn't matter. He knew what they had to do.

"We need to disappear. Lily and me."

Travis hesitated, and then let out a baffled chuckle. "What? Wait a minute, I can help. I mean, you can't just–"

"You saved our lives, Travis," Cole said seriously. "Multiple times. If you hadn't been there with the truck…" He let the rest go unspoken. "But it goes both ways. They're killing people to get to us. You got to let me watch your back too."

Travis looked down, the desire to argue clear on his face.

"Please, Travis."

A moment passed. "So that's it then," the boy said.

He glanced up from the carpet.

Cole shrugged. "We couldn't have done it without you."

Travis nodded and then chuckled ruefully. "Right," he agreed.

"Yeah."

Seconds crept by in silence, and then the boy pulled out his wallet and keys. "Keep the truck," he said, tossing the keys onto the bed. "And this should last you a while."

He handed Lily some bills, and Cole saw several hundreds from the corner of his eye.

"I'll take the bus home," Travis continued. "And then wait a couple days. Tell my parents I gave the truck away. They won't care."

He grinned.

Cole hesitated. "Thanks."

"It's been fun," Travis answered with a candid shrug, and then he paused awkwardly. "Or… you know… whatever."

Cole nodded.

Pushing to his feet, Travis headed for the door. One hand on the handle, he glanced back. "You'll call if you're ever back around though, eh?"

Nodding again, Cole didn't know what to say.

The boy echoed the motion, a hint of regret flashing over his face. And then he left.

"What now?" Lily asked into the quiet.

Cole didn't answer. He knew they needed to go. To get away from the war and everything it'd done. It was the smart thing. The safe thing.

But it felt like saying his parents' deaths were fine. Like agreeing with Melissa. Like Clara and Victor Jamison just meant nothing.

Like running away.

Lily's hand found his own. "It'll be alright."

He glanced down. She gave him a hesitant smile.

And he sighed.

He'd find a way to make the wizards pay for what they'd done. He'd find something, do something, to be strong enough to face them. It'd happen.

Even if it took time.

And would never fix the fact they'd taken his parents away.

Drawing a breath, he squeezed her hand and then rose to make certain the door lock was secure. It wouldn't stop wizards, but at least it'd give the two of them some warning.

And tomorrow, they'd head west, away from the wizards, the Blood, and the war. They'd run.

For now.

Chapter Seventeen

———◆·———

By the porch window, Ashe blinked and then rubbed a hand over her eyes when the fog didn't clear. She'd just been watching the yard for a few hours this afternoon, in between pretending to read, but it felt like a lifetime when the only change had been the occasional bird eyeing her quizzically from the deck railing.

On the couch, Elsa crocheted an afghan while watching the latest in an endless stream of daytime television shows. The woman hadn't left the spot since Ashe woke earlier that morning, and seemed determined to hold onto her illusions by willpower and soap operas alone. In the kitchen, Bus studied the street while Carter talked quietly with Spider, making plans for the next steps they'd take.

Because the Blood wizard hadn't returned. And it was nearly four in the afternoon, and thus long past the time Elsa said she'd seen him on the previous days.

For her part, the old woman seemed to be growing more and more content as the hours passed. Her peaceful world was resuming. Seeing a Blood wizard had simply been an anomaly, and therefore nothing that required any more of her concern.

Sighing, Ashe leaned forward, peering around the edges of the yard to see if anyone was sneaking along the sides of the neighboring houses. It'd become apparent from the comments she'd overheard that hoping the Blood would return had been one of the better options available. Very few cripples remained in this part of the country after years of war and ravaging by ferals, and consequently the Hunters had limited sources upon which to draw for information. Going into the city to track the man down was riskier by far than simply hiding here till he returned, but it was starting to look like that was what they'd be forced to do.

Bus made a warning noise and instantly, Carter and Spider fell silent. "Someone's coming," the old man said. "Could be a wizard."

Elsa paled, looking torn between fear at the approaching person and the tremors in her tranquility. For their part, Spider and Carter drew their guns.

The doorbell rang. From her prison in the basement, Mitzi erupted into furious barking.

Carter glanced to Mischa and Tala, but the dogs were silent.

"Elsa?" came a voice from outside.

Rising hastily, the old woman shuffled toward the door. "Oh, put those away," she said, waving her hands ineffectually at the guns. "For pity's sake, it's only Norman."

Carter nodded to Spider, who turned and motioned for Ashe to follow her into the other room. Ashe's brow furrowed in confusion.

"You don't want to make yourself popular, girl," Bus said from his post by the window. "Human or wizard."

She blanched, suddenly remembering the news. The arrest at the train station. She hurried after Spider as Bus quickly turned down the police scanner.

As the bedroom door shut behind her, she could hear Norman come in. His surprise at the others was apparent in his tone, though she heard Bus attempting to allay it with a story of being an old friend, road-tripping with his buddy across the country.

By the closed bedroom door, Spider adjusted her grip on the gun, listening intently. Warily, Ashe drew her own weapon, barely breathing as she waited.

A minute passed. The front door shut.

"All clear," Carter called quietly from the hall.

Putting the gun away, Ashe followed Spider back into the living room. The girl eyed Carter questioningly and a hint of exasperation crossed his face, making his opinion clear. In the kitchen, Bus grimaced and then turned back to the police scanner, letting the static bursts of intermittent voices fill the room again.

Without a word, Ashe headed for the porch window, grateful to see Mischa trail after her. Ignoring them all, Elsa sank onto the couch, her attention returning to her crochet.

Bus made an alarmed noise, but the front door swung open before anyone could move.

"Elsa, I forgot to ask if–" Norman started, pulling his key from the lock.

His brow furrowed at the sight of the two girls.

"My granddaughter and her friend," Bus said, rising to block his view.

By the window, Ashe ducked her head, letting her hair fall around her face.

"Oh," Norman said. Clearly still thrown from finding Bus and Carter in Elsa's home, he paused, taking in Spider's appearance.

Blinking briefly, he extended a hand to the girl.

"Nice to meet you," he said, trying to sound pleasant.

"Likewise," Spider said easily, stepping in front of Ashe and motioning to the door. "You live down the street?"

"Yeah. Past thirty years. You know, Elsa never mentioned you."

"Eh, you know how it is with old friends," Bus said. "Years go by."

Norman nodded distantly, his gaze sliding to Carter and away.

"You were going to ask me something, Norman?" Elsa prompted.

"I was just planning on heading to the store and wanted to know if you needed anything."

"Oh no, I'm fine. Thank you so much, though, for checking."

He nodded again, seeming unconvinced. "So you're sure you're alright?"

"Norman," Elsa said patiently. "Don't be rude. These are my friends. They just stopped by for a quick visit on their way through town."

The man glanced over them again, leaning slightly to look past Spider at Ashe.

Blanching behind her curtain of hair, she snatched up the book and turned to set it on the shelf. When she looked back, his gaze had moved on to the others.

"I'll come by tomorrow then," Norman said, starting toward the door.

"Looking forward to it," Elsa said, escorting him.

"Right," the man said uncomfortably. "Okay."

Elsa shut the door behind him as he left.

"You didn't tell us he had a key," Carter said quietly as she returned to the couch.

"Of course I did."

"Elsa."

"Well, I meant to," she amended primly, taking up her crochet again. "Anyway, Norman's just protective. I don't see why you have to be so worried."

"You know why."

"It's fine, Carter," Elsa said, her voice becoming firm, and Ashe could see the woman trying to make herself believe the words.

Not answering, Carter walked into the kitchen and joined Bus by the window. Swallowing hard, Ashe followed, while Spider wordlessly took up position where she'd been.

"Are we still okay?" Ashe asked.

Pulling back the curtain slightly, Carter didn't answer. Bus just rose and headed for the living room, leaving the two of them alone.

"Carter?"

He glanced at her, and she could see him evaluating the factors. If they missed the Blood wizard returning, it could be months before anyone spotted him again.

But if Norman had recognized her… if he called the police…

With the exception of Elsa, every person in this room was probably wanted for murder in one city or another, even if their faces hadn't been plastered all over the news like hers had been.

"We'll find him," Carter said gently, his hand resting on her shoulder.

Air escaped her.

"Get your stuff," he continued. "I'll call Serenity and Blackjack before we leave. Check if their people have seen anything."

Trying to be comforted by the gesture, however useless she suspected it'd be, she forced herself to nod. She walked back into the living room, and Bus gave her a sympathetic look before reaching for his bag.

Carter cursed. "He's coming back again."

"What *is* it with this guy?" Bus asked, shoving his bag under the couch and then rising. Ashe ducked behind the hall corner while, by the window, Spider shifted slightly, clearly wanting to reach for her gun.

"Elsa," Norman said as he pushed open the door. "There's just one other thing."

Ashe stopped breathing as his gaze slid past her. He recognized her. She was certain of it.

He continued into the living room. Carter followed, glancing between the man and the open door.

"You're being rather rude, Norman, just barging in here," Elsa protested, rising from her seat.

"I just need to ask you something. I'm planning on bringing food to the senior center for the Fourth of July, and I was wondering if you would–"

"Norman!" Elsa cried.

He spun to face them, an old pistol clutched in his shaking hand. Everyone in the room froze.

"Think about what you're doing, buddy," Bus said carefully.

"Shut up," Norman snapped. He sidled between Elsa and the others, half-turning his head to the old woman as he continued. "I don't know what they've told you, Elsa, but these people–"

He cut off, his hand jerking in alarm as the police scanner squawked. Ashe flinched at the motion, and then felt the blood drain from her face as the scratchy words filled the room.

"All available units, please respond. We have a report of a hostage situation at 1512 East Pine. At least four suspects, potentially armed, holding a seventy-year-old white female. Suspects are a white teenage female wanted for homicide in Montana, black male approximately fifty years old, white male approximately–"

"You son of a bitch," Bus growled.

The gun twitched toward him.

"I'm taking her out of here," Norman said, his voice trembling. "I'm not going to let you hurt her."

"Norman…" Elsa started fearfully.

"Quiet." The gun moved toward Ashe. "Get away from the door."

Barely breathing, she slid from the hallway into the living room. Nervously, her eyes went to Carter, and she saw him nod slowly to the old woman.

Elsa slumped to the floor. Startled, Norman turned to her, taking his eyes from the room.

Bus slammed into him. Clutched in Norman's hand, the weapon swung toward Spider and the girl hit the ground.

The pistol fired, the sound deafening in the crowded living room. Smashing his elbow into the man's side, Bus sidestepped and then sent the weapon clattering to the floor.

Norman choked. Hand outstretched, he stumbled toward his pistol, and then froze when he saw Carter's gun.

"Don't," Carter said quietly.

Scowling, Spider shoved up from the carpet and then crossed the room, retrieving the pistol while Bus patted Norman down.

Carter glanced to the kitchen window, his gun still leveled at the other man, and Ashe followed his gaze.

Her breath caught.

Four wizards stood outside the bar.

Panicked, she looked to Carter. His eyes narrowed and then he swore as the men started for Elsa's house. "Go! Out the back. Now!"

Bus and Spider didn't hesitate. Tossing the pistol behind the couch, Spider headed for the porch door and yanked it open. Taking Elsa's hand, Bus hurried the old woman outside.

Ignoring Norman's objections, Ashe rushed after them, Tala and Mischa on her heels.

"Mitzi!" Elsa cried.

With a fluid motion, Carter ripped open the basement door, and then strode across the room. Grabbing Norman by one arm, Carter spun him around, jabbed the muzzle of his gun into the man's side and then forced him out onto the deck.

"What do you want?" Norman protested as Carter muscled him down the stairs. "Money? Just let Elsa go. Whatever you want—"

"Shut up," Carter growled.

Unlatching the chain-link gate, Bus held it wide as the others hurried into the utility easement between the yards. Sirens shrieked in the distance, coming closer. Scooping the little dog into her arms, Elsa hesitated at the gate, her gaze going back to her house.

"Elsa…" Bus urged.

Clutching the animal, she left the yard.

"Which house is his?" Spider asked.

Norman made a protesting noise as Elsa pointed. "The blue one."

Three houses down, Carter shoved open the gate in the tall wooden fence surrounding Norman's property. "Go," he told Elsa. "They're after us, not you."

Releasing Norman, he propelled him through the entrance after the old woman.

"Get her inside," Carter ordered. "Keep her away from the windows and don't answer the door for anyone. Her life depends on it."

An explosion thundered from the yellow cottage, punctuated by the sound of shattering glass and wood. Elsa cried out and staggered back toward her home. Dumbstruck, Norman caught her.

Carter motioned the others to run. "Go!" he barked at Norman.

As she started after Spider, Ashe caught a glimpse of the old man hurrying a sobbing Elsa toward his house.

They ran down the easement and skirted the opening to the street. Police sirens blared in the neighborhood behind them, joined by the howl of fire engines racing to the scene. Darting across the road, they cut through the space between two houses and swiftly scaled the fence separating the yards.

"Split up," Carter said, pausing for the dogs to leap the barrier. "Head for Pepper."

Spider jerked her chin at Ashe, and then clicked her tongue at Mischa before taking off. Ashe followed, looking back to see Carter and Bus disappear around the corner with Tala.

She ran after the other girl, dodging between the houses and parked cars lining the streets. From one road to the next, they emerged into a business district, but Spider didn't slow, veering between two buildings and then across the parking lot behind them. A gap in the fence cordoning off the lot gave them entrance to the next street, and a space in the row of office buildings that followed let them into the alleys behind.

Heart pounding, Ashe glanced back as they dashed between the brick buildings. The sirens were growing fainter, trapped by the need to check the neighborhood before moving on. Smoke from Elsa's house billowed into the sky, but the clouds were growing thinner with every moment. Mischa panted heavily at her side, and the sound of her own breathing drowned the rush of traffic in the streets.

Spider raced around the corner, Ashe on her heels.

Energy slammed into her, propelling her back into a dumpster, and Mischa yelped as she crashed down beside her. Gunshots rang out, the bullets pelting the brick walls.

Dizzily, Ashe pushed up from the concrete, blood dripping down her face. Darkness swirled across her vision and then pulled away.

A wizard had Spider by the throat. His other hand gripping the girl's wrist and his knee crushing her chest, he pinned her to the ground, and as she fired desperately at his defenses, his mouth curved into a smile.

Magic rose around him. Above him.

And swung down.

Ashe screamed at the fires inside.

White heat turned the air to flame as it raced over her body, her arms, her hands. Ripping past Spider, the magic slammed the wizard and threw him backward. Shoving to her feet, Ashe strode down the alley, her eyes locked on the man.

Burned and bleeding, he tried to rise.

Fire met him.

He couldn't even scream. Flames tore into him, raking his body till only a blackened corpse dropped to the ground.

Trembling, she lowered her arm.

A click sounded behind her.

She stopped breathing. Slowly, she turned around.

Her gun aimed at Ashe's chest, Spider stared. The girl's face was bloodless. Her hands shook. Red marks from the wizard's grip shone brightly against the pale skin of her throat.

But her expression never wavered.

"Spider..."

The girl made a warning noise, the weapon twitching in her hand. Wordlessly, she backed away, not taking her eyes from Ashe. Reaching for Mischa, she fumbled till she found a grip on the dog's collar and then tugged the limping animal with her.

At the corner of the alley, she paused, and Ashe could read the threat in her eyes. Her fingers tightening on the gun, Spider watched her a moment more, and then disappeared behind the corner of the building. Her footsteps pounded on the pavement as she raced away.

Ashe blinked.

She…

A shiver shook her.

Spider just…

In dazed incredulity, her gaze dropped to the concrete. The blackened corpse waited by her feet and she flinched, backing away.

They'd left. Spider. But with her went Carter. Bus. Jericho and Magnolia and Peony and Belle and…

Ashe gasped as names tumbled through her head like pebbles preceding an avalanche.

It'd happened. It'd finally happened. Every safe person, every safe place had evaporated in a heartbeat, and in their place, the whole great world opened like a maw, full of nothing but emptiness and waiting to swallow her whole.

Because of what she was. Because everything about her had always been a lie.

A choked sound escaped her. Unsteadily, she turned, her feet leading her away from the body and the direction Spider had gone. She trembled as she reached the end of the alley, the broad street suddenly seeming a thousand times more threatening than before.

Nervously, she started across the road. Her feet moved faster.

Faster. Air grated on her lungs as she ran.

Wizards would be coming. And with them, the Blood.

The city blurred. Alleys sped by, broken by parking lots and main thoroughfares. Racing past a busy street, she darted around the buildings on the opposite side and then skidded to a stop. A steep embankment rose like a wall before her, topped by train tracks. Frantically, she cast a glance back to the traffic and then rushed for the slope, pulling herself up by tree roots and scrabbling at the shale from the railroad. She dashed over the tracks and then slid down from the rise, her hands scraping on the gravel as she tried to control her fall.

Athletic fields stretched in front of her, with office buildings covered in security cameras on their far end. A soccer team played to her left, their shouts punctuating the noise of traffic from beyond the railroad.

Swallowing hard, she glanced to her right. A wall of scraggly brush and a chain-link fence separated the field from the rear of a cemetery.

She took off.

Her scraped hands stung as she jumped the fence, but she ignored them. Heart pounding, she dropped down amid the bushes and trees, and checked around warily. No shouts rose. Even the traffic sounded distant here. At the heart of the cemetery, a line of cars waited by a maroon pavilion on a hill, the late afternoon light silhouetting the figures within.

She hesitated, watching them. They were too far away to make out any details, which meant she would be indistinct as well. Biting her lip, she edged around the graveyard, sticking to the brush and ducking deeper into the foliage when she reached the cemetery's adjacent side.

The well-tended lawns of a massive office complex lay beyond the trees. Cameras watched from the enormous buildings dotting the grassy swaths, while gardeners riding noisy lawnmowers carved checkerboard paths through the fields.

Behind the cover of the brush, she sank to the ground. The sun would set soon. In the darkness, it'd be easier to cross that vast space.

And go somewhere.

Her eyes stung. The vast, unknown sprawl of the city seemed to contract around her, drawing in upon places she could no longer go. Places where her friends would shoot her if she came close.

Sniffling, she struggled to push the thought away. Reaching up gingerly, she touched the cut on her forehead and then flinched when it stung. She'd hit something besides the dumpster when she fell, but unlike the gunshot wound all those weeks ago, the gash hadn't healed and she had no idea why.

She pulled up her knees and hugged them to her chest. The fires gave way, crushing down into nothing with more ease than ever before.

Fires. But more like energy now than flame. Like light as much as heat.

And by her command, by her thought alone, they'd burned that wizard alive.

Shivering, she swallowed down the memory. She didn't know if she'd meant to kill him. She didn't know if it mattered. He was still dead.

She was still responsible.

But he'd been about to kill Spider. He'd worked for the men who murdered her family. He'd been after her.

And she'd just killed him. Like the men in the forest, and the way she wanted to kill the Blood wizard.

If she still could.

Closing her eyes tightly, she fought back the tears. Everything wasn't lost. The Hunters might be gone, but she could go after him on her own. After all, the Blood wizard was in this city somewhere, and now he knew she was here too. He'd come looking.

And maybe she'd see him first.

Drawing a ragged breath, she rested her aching head on her knees and tried desperately to believe the words. To believe she hadn't lost everything along with her friends.

It wasn't easy.

In the cemetery, cars pulled away from the pavilion and wound their way down the hill. Minutes drifted past, and then three grave-diggers climbed the slope and set to work atop the rise.

"You know, if you're going to hide, you might want to try not running away in a straight line."

Her breath caught and she looked up to see Spider watching her through the branches.

"Though, as covers go," the girl continued, her voice slightly raspy from the bruises around her throat, "it's not bad."

She glanced to the trees, but Ashe could hear the double meaning in her words. Returning her gaze to Ashe, Spider studied her briefly, and then pushed aside the branches and slid into the small hollow between the bushes. She held back the tree limbs for Mischa to follow, and then lowered herself to the ground as Mischa limped over to lay at Ashe's side.

Spider said nothing, watching the dog.

"So what are you?" she asked finally.

"Wizard," Ashe answered quietly.

"How'd you get past them?" She jerked her chin at Mischa.

"I don't know."

Spider's eyes narrowed. Ashe looked away.

"I'm sorry I lied to you," she told Spider.

The girl paused. "You were pretty convincing."

Ashe exhaled, struggling to know what to say. "I wasn't… I'm not…" She stopped and took a deep breath. "I didn't know what I was. Not until you told me about the wizards after what happened at Shen's."

"Why didn't you do anything?" Spider asked, anger breaking through her calm for the first time. "You could've saved her! You–"

She cut off, clearly fighting to control her emotions.

"I didn't know!" Ashe repeated desperately. "The first time… the *only* times I used magic… Spider, I killed people. I couldn't stop it. So I thought if I let even the tiniest bit out, anybody near me would die. You. Carter. Everyone. I…"

She looked down, sick at the thought that she could have helped Shen. "I didn't know what it was."

"So back there…?"

"He was going to kill you."

"But if you hadn't been able to control it…"

Ashe didn't answer.

Spider paused, taken back.

"What about everything you told us?" the girl continued after a moment. "Your dad? Your sister?"

"It was true. I just… I didn't know how to talk about the other parts."

Spider waited.

"Wizards killed my family. But when they shot him, my dad did something. Pushed us away somehow. And then the Blood wizard came. He just looked like a human to me, but he…" She grimaced, forcing herself to keep talking past the memory. "He killed my dad without even touching him.

"We escaped because of what my dad did, though. And then Cole showed up. I don't know who he was or why he was there, but he was a cripple like you. I didn't realize it till I met Carter and Samson, but that's what he was. He helped us like I said, but then…

"They shot me. Through the leg. Cole tried to help me, but then they shot him too. He fell. Lily was with him. I couldn't run to her. Couldn't save her and next thing I knew…" She shook her head. "I woke up in the middle of a forest fire with my body covered in flames. The wound in my leg was gone. And the men who shot me were dead. But the Blood wizard hadn't been there, and I didn't know what I'd done. What was happening. I thought it was a dream."

Ashe took a deep breath, determined to be done with secrets. "I got arrested when I reached town. But the Blood wizard followed me to the station, pretending to be an FBI agent. When I heard his voice, I panicked, and suddenly, fire was all over me again." She paused. "One of the cops was killed."

Brow furrowing, she drove the memory aside. "So I ran. I was hiding when that feral found me. I had no idea what he was. What wizards were. He was just a monster trying to kill me, and then Carter stopped him."

She looked back at Spider. "I swear I didn't know anything about this. And once I did…"

"What?" the girl asked when she trailed off.

"I was afraid you'd shoot me. Or leave. Or turn me over to them.

I don't know."

For a moment, Spider studied her. "You look like a wizard to me. Like nothing but a regular human, I mean. And the dog reacts to you like a Blood – again, like nothing but a human. You convinced Carter to hunt the Blood, even though that's about the most dangerous thing we could do. So what? You're a new one of them?" She paused. "Is this some kind of trick?"

Ashe hesitated. "You wouldn't ask that if you thought it was."

"I don't know what to think."

Wordlessly, Ashe looked away.

Silence fell between them. Distant sounds of evening traffic mingled with the rustle of wind through the trees, and over the soccer field, bright lights flickered to life and slowly began blazing like the sun.

"You could've just let him kill me," Spider suggested, almost conversationally.

Ashe blinked, confused.

"Rejoined the others with a story of how the wizards attacked and only you got away. And they would've believed it. I mean, you're getting there, but…"

Ashe looked down, feeling a bit defensive of her rudimentary shooting skills.

"And your cover would've remained intact." Spider paused. "But you didn't."

For a few seconds, the girl sat silent.

"Hurt like hell what you did, though."

"Sorry."

Spider chuckled, picking at the detritus by her legs. "Yeah, well, given the options."

Ashe watched as Spider slowly shredded a leaf.

"I really thought he was going to kill me back there," the girl said quietly, her humor gone.

Spider glanced up. "Thanks."

Hesitantly, Ashe shrugged.

The girl returned to her destruction of the leaves for a while, and then finally sighed. "We should get back," she said, brushing the debris from her lap. "The others will be wondering if we got out or not."

Uncertain she'd heard correctly, Ashe blinked. "But…"

"We'll find a way to tell them."

Ashe stared.

Climbing to her feet, Spider scanned the cemetery and then pushed the branches aside, letting Mischa precede her. When Ashe didn't move, she glanced back. "Unless you'd rather stay here?"

Faintly stunned, Ashe shook her head and rose. Ducking beneath the branches, she followed Spider from the brush. Sunset lit the western sky, casting lengthy shadows from the tombstones and trees. On top of the rise, a mound of dirt covered the new grave, the workers and the pavilion long since gone.

"This way," Spider said.

In the fading light, the two girls headed back into the city.

Chapter Eighteen

———•◆•———

The fishbowl windows of the sandwich shop glowed in the darkness, clearly showing empty seats and a tired clerk inside. Staying out of the pool of light cast on the sidewalk, Ashe and Spider slipped around the building and, as they reached the alley at the back of the shop, Carter and Bus rose from the shadows behind a dumpster.

"Son of a bitch," Bus swore, his blue eyes raking over them and taking in the dried blood on Ashe's face and the bruises around Spider's throat. "What happened to you?"

"Ran into a bit of trouble," Spider replied. "It got taken care of."

The old man looked between them when the girl didn't say anything more. "You sure you're okay?" he persisted, directing the question mostly to Ashe.

She attempted to smile, and failed miserably. Her stomach wouldn't stop doing flip flops, and she could feel the pressure of Carter's gaze. For the first time since Shen's, she felt like the word 'wizard' might as well have been branded on her forehead.

"Bus," Spider said.

He grimaced, dropping it.

"Where to?" the girl asked Carter.

"Twitch's."

Bus blinked. "That boy still alive in there?"

"Last time Serenity got him to open the door," Carter answered.

The old man shook his head. Glancing to Spider, he motioned for her to go ahead. The two of them started off, and Ashe could hear the girl checking if Bus had any extra bullets she could use for her gun.

Ashe jumped as Carter's hand rested on her shoulder.

"You alright?" he asked quietly, concern in his eyes.

Not trusting herself to speak, she nodded.

He squeezed her shoulder. "Scary?"

She hesitated, and then shrugged.

Carter smiled. "Come on."

Wordlessly, she followed him away from the shop.

Keeping to alleys and dimly lit streets, they wound through the city. A bustling college campus slowly surrounded them, and through the gaps between buildings, she could see coffee shops and bars aglow in the night. Police cars patrolled the streets, following unpredictable patterns and forcing the Hunters to duck continually into hiding. Students roamed the sidewalks in packs, and if they paid attention to the four of them, it was only to glance over curiously before wandering on.

Frat houses and sororities appeared, bordering brick streets with old trees hugging their sides. From within shrouds of spring leaves, streetlamps glowed on roads that rose and fell with the terrain as it drew closer to the river.

At two buildings no different than the others, Carter turned, cutting down a narrow gravel drive. An unpaved parking lot waited at the end, its width barely enough for the cars wedged inside. Unkempt bushes and trees encroached on it, obscuring the view of anything beyond, and without pausing, Carter crossed it to pull aside the branches and let the others skirt through.

Tugging past the grasping twigs, Ashe stepped onto the shattered concrete of another parking lot. Years' worth of weeds spread like a forest from the cracked surface, continuing to the base of an enormous building. Five stories of brick stood at the center of the lot, while security lamps mounted on its corners streamed white-blue light onto the concrete. Weathered plywood was bolted over each window, and No Trespassing signs plastered the first floor. Graffiti adorned the walls, seeming more the work of bored college students than cripples, and except for the security lights, the whole building looked as though it'd been abandoned for years.

Or not, she realized as they came closer. Atop the building, small security cameras turned, their tiny green lights blinking as they tracked the four walking across the lot.

A broken cement step led to a thick metal door, the only entrance she could see. Carter banged on it twice, and then stepped back, waiting.

Nothing happened. Minutes drifted by. Through the dense walls of foliage surrounding the parking lot, only a whisper of late night traffic could be heard.

"You sure he's still in there?" Spider asked quietly.

Carter didn't answer.

A soft clank came from beyond the door, and then another. Several more followed, making their way down the length of the metal.

The noises stopped. A moment passed. The door crept open, and a white face behind enormous glasses peered out.

"Carter?" the man said, his thin voice turning the word into a question of whether the people in front of him were real.

"We need to come in, Twitch," Carter replied carefully.

The man's white skin grew even paler, and on the edge of the door, his skeletal fingers fluttered. "A-are you sure?"

"Yes."

Behind the scuffed surface of his glasses, his eyes flitted across the four of them, as though hoping they would disappear.

"Twitch."

At Carter's voice, he winced and then reluctantly inched the door back, leaving them just enough room to slip by. A narrow entrance waited beyond, lit by a single low-watt bulb dangling from the ceiling. Through the door to her left, Ashe could see a card table and folding chairs inside what appeared to be a tiny apartment, although except for the space by the closet and the efficiency kitchen, boxes lined every inch of the walls.

She glanced around. It wasn't just the apartment. Boxes were the predominant feature everywhere. Through the gaps in the metal stairway, she could see more of the cardboard shapes behind the steps, while the hallway to her right was blocked entirely.

Behind her, Twitch shoved the door closed, and furtively busied himself with throwing the locks. When the last was in place, he turned, his glasses reflecting the dim light. Wild tufts of hair stuck up from his head in haphazard fashion, and his bony shoulders were hunched, making him almost half Carter's size.

"Y-you changed," he said, his gaze darting to them and away. "You...with that one." He pointed a trembling finger to Ashe and then jerked it back as though expecting her to bite. "And not the big one."

"We need a place to stay, Twitch," Carter said.

The man quivered, his eyes going wide and distant. "That's bad… Bad things come…"

"We'll be gone soon."

Blinking rapidly, the man processed the information, and then glanced to the door. "Upstairs then. Upstairs is safer. Upstairs…"

Still muttering the word to himself, he scuttled between them and then gave a startled cry at the sight of the dogs. Skirting around the animals, he clutched after the metal banister and then scaled the steps as though trying to flee.

Closing his eyes, Carter shook his head and then motioned them to follow.

The second floor hall was completely black, and before she could take a step beyond the stairs, Bus grabbed her arm with a wordless warning noise. Invisible in the darkness, she couldn't see his face as she looked toward him in confusion.

Twitch's footsteps preceded them swiftly, effortlessly navigating the space. In the distance, a red glowing panel appeared as he pulled a hatch aside. His narrow fingers danced over it, and suddenly the buttons shifted to brilliant green.

A doorway opened. The darkness thinned to red-toned gray, and the dim shapes of boxes could be seen lining the path to the door.

Warily, Ashe followed the others out of the hall.

The second floor had been destroyed. At least, by the definition of anyone sane. The space ahead was nearly the width of the building, with only a few rooms on the far ends spared the demolition. Throughout the center of the level, every wall had been torn down, leaving only the barest framework of metal struts to support the floors above. Holes peppered the ceiling, through which dense braids of cords and wires hung. The multicolored spaghetti of cables twisted across the carpet and tile to scatter at the massive bank of computers lining the leftmost wall. Sleepy orange lights blinked on each workstation, and reflected opaquely on the monitors above them. Black-and-white images of the parking lot flickered across the screens, interspersed with news channels showing crime scenes around the country. In the heart of the mess, a rickety folding chair stood, one bent leg supported by a dog-eared book.

Ashe stared as Twitch darted across the space, hopping like a leprechaun through the gaps between the cords. On the far side of the room, he pulled aside another hatch and flittered his fingers over the red buttons to charm them into green. Impatiently, he waved at the others as a door swung open at his side.

Eyebrows drifting up in disbelief, Ashe followed Bus across the room. More steps met them behind the door, and though the way to the first floor was blocked entirely by boxes, the path upward was comparatively clear. On the levels above, small windows in the stairwell doors revealed more glowing red panels, one by each door lining the halls.

Ashe froze as, in the shadows of the corridors, small forms skittered along the walls. Shuddering, she forced herself to keep moving, praying she didn't step on anything.

On the top floor, Twitch hurried to the first door by the stairs and tapped out a key code faster than Ashe could follow. Shoving open the door, he stepped aside and then motioned tensely to the room with his eyes on the floor.

Boxes were everywhere. There was barely space for two people to stand.

"Twitch," Carter said. "Is there another room we can use? One with fewer boxes?"

Flustered, the man looked around. "I... I..."

He turned and scuttled down the hall.

More red panels lined the corridor. In the dim light, she glanced at them, and swiftly, Bus grabbed her arm as though to stop her from touching anything. In a furtive look back, Twitch caught sight of the motion.

"Rats," the little man warned. "Rats' rooms. Don't go in the rats' rooms. Rats don't like it if you go in their rooms."

Ashe stared at him, and then turned the incredulous expression on Bus.

"The doors are wired," Spider explained shortly, walking past them both as she followed the scurrying man.

Bus patted her hand with a tense smile and then kept going. Blanching, Ashe trailed after them, sticking squarely to the center of the hall.

An exit sign flickered at the end of the hallway, and immediately before it, Twitch pushed open another door. Compared to the rest of the building, the apartment inside was relatively clear, with only a few boxes stacked along the back wall. Cans of food formed a small mountain to one side, with cracked plates and bowls nearby. Through the bedroom door, she could see more computers, a smaller version of the command center downstairs.

In front of the door, Twitch paused, shuffling from one foot to the other as though reluctant to let them in. His eyes darted across the group in small circles, going first one way, blinking rapidly, and then swinging the other.

"Would you prefer some of us slept elsewhere?" Carter asked after a few seconds. "So there are fewer people in here?"

Twitch nodded, the motion quick and jerking.

Carter glanced at them.

"Ashe and I can take the room down the hall," Spider said. She looked to Twitch. "You mind if we move some boxes?"

Relief and reluctance warred in short spasms across Twitch's face. "Okay…"

Without another word, Spider headed back to the room, Ashe and Bus coming after her.

The boxes were heavy, but with the work of two people, they could be moved. Gradually, the jumbled mess became towering stacks by the walls, as though the three of them were shoring up the building by cardboard alone. Squares of cleaner carpet emerged beneath the dusty containers, and as Bus helped Spider shift the last of the stack, Ashe gave in to her curiosity and pulled back the corner of a box to peek inside.

Dozens of random magazines were stacked within and bore mailing labels ranging from doctor's offices to libraries, with random homes in between.

"You want to see if Twitch will spare some food?" Spider asked.

Shoving the box flap back in place, Ashe turned quickly. "Sure."

With a last, alarmed glance to the boxes, she followed the others out of the room.

Scrounging food from among the cans in Twitch's apartment, they passed the dinner in silence and, when they had finished, the little man shifted back and forth, impatient for the girls to leave. At Spider's request for blankets, he scurried into the other room, returning with a bundle of scratchy, stale-smelling material that he shoved into Ashe's arms before running back to his bedroom and shutting the door.

Spider took half the pile. "Sleep well," she told Bus and Carter dryly.

Wordlessly, Ashe followed her down the hall. In the apartment, they spread the blankets on the floor, trying to stir up as little dust as they could. Once the bedding was laid out, Ashe disappeared into the bathroom, discovering with relief the crazy place had running water. Having washed away the blood on her face, she returned and then paused as Spider lay down.

"Um..." she began, glancing around. In addition to the planks, dense black paint covered the windows.

"Don't worry," Spider said tiredly, pillowing her head with one arm and then wrinkling her nose as she tried not to sneeze. Waiting a moment, she continued when the urge faded. "Twitch'll keep as good a watch as we ever could. He's got police scanners and news feeds for half the state wired into that hodge-podge of his, on top of all the cameras outside."

"And bombs on the doors," Ashe added, still feeling shocked by the last.

"Well, yeah."

"Isn't he... isn't *somebody* worried he'll blow up the building? I mean, if someone bumps the wrong door..."

"You see why we don't stay here unless we have to."

"But how'd he even do all this? I mean..." She trailed off, wanting to put into words how ridiculous this place felt, as though describing the insanity would tame her panic at staying in a partly demolished building lined with bombs.

Spider scoffed. "Hell if I know. Serenity told me his rich wizard daddy paid him lots of money to go away and stop embarrassing the family. Blackjack said he worked for a bank and embezzled millions. Twitch won't say what's true, and you're putting a lot more faith in him than I would if you'd trust what he told you anyway.

"Take the break for what it is," she finished with a smile. "We'll be heading out soon."

Nodding mechanically, Ashe flipped off the light and then carefully lowered herself onto the blankets, still stirring up enough dust to promptly make her sneeze. Grimacing, she lay down and pulled the itchy blanket over her shoulders.

Her eyes popped open. Scurrying noises rushed through the walls, and faint cheeping followed. Heart pounding, she lay motionless.

A few feet away, she could hear Spider breathing deeply as she slept. Nothing bothered the girl. And that nothing included the thought of rats sniffing at her in the darkness, or swarming over her in her sleep.

Skin crawling, Ashe cringed as the scurrying continued. Every itch made her think the rats had reached her, and each twitch of skin made her want to swat the area nearby.

Minutes passed, creeping into hours. The noises would fade, only to return when she closed her eyes. Shuddering, she tried to force herself not to care. So what? Rats weren't the worst thing in the world.

A cheeping sounded near her and she sat bolt upright, scanning the darkness. Swallowing dryly, she gritted her teeth, cursing herself for being afraid and ordering herself to go to sleep.

She didn't move.

This was stupid. She'd fought a wizard today. She was hunting the Blood. And she was scared of rats? It was ridiculous.

It would really help if Tala or Mischa were around.

Latching onto the thought, she hesitated and then rose in the darkness. Drawing a breath, she inched her foot out, coming down only onto dusty carpet. Step by careful step, she made her way across the floor, commanding herself not to make a noise if she landed on anything.

Dim red light filled the hall, emanating from the small panels and the distant exit sign.

And at the door to the stairway, Carter paused.

Blanching, she ducked back instinctively, and then her brow furrowed in confusion. It was Carter, not a monster. But from the look on his face, something was deeply wrong.

Nervously, she peeked around the corner again.

He was gone.

She glanced back, but Spider hadn't moved. Biting her lip apprehensively, she hesitated and then rushed toward the stairs. Small forms scurried away in the dim light, making her heart jump, and her hand caught the door an instant before it closed. Slipping through the gap, she stood motionless, listening as she let it shut behind her.

A moment passed. Another door closed far below.

She hurried downstairs, past door panels glowing red in the darkness. Worried she'd be trapped on the stairwell if Carter reset the door after passing through, she moved faster till finally a green panel came into view.

Warily, she pulled open the door to the second level.

The room was empty, save for the tangled mess of tripwire cords. Brow furrowing, she paused. He hadn't been heading for the monitors, which meant Twitch must not have seen anything through his cameras.

Her eyes went to the door panel across the room. Like an electronic breadcrumb, it also glowed green.

Weaving between coils of cable, she crossed the room and opened the door. The hall was dark, but faint light showed from the floor below.

A door shut downstairs. On the metal stairway, Ashe froze.

"Thank you for seeing me," came a man's voice.

Her brow drew down. Smooth and cultured, the sound was familiar but not. Like a dream on the edge of memory, it flitted away before she could grasp it.

"You said it was an emergency."

Carter's voice was colder than she'd ever heard, and guarded.

Heart pounding, she glanced around nervously, and then crept down the steps, praying they wouldn't creak. At the first floor, she slipped around the boxes beneath the stairs and into the darkened space behind them.

"So I did," came the reply. "Those were your companions on the police bands earlier, I assume?"

At Carter's silence, he continued. "But then, you wouldn't be here if it wasn't. The similarities were too strong."

"Get to the point or get out, Cornelius."

"I came to talk about one of those mentioned by the police."

"Forget your point. Just get out."

"The young lady from Montana. I need to see her."

Ashe's heart climbed into her throat.

"It's not her," Carter replied.

"Really."

"Oh, go to hell, Cornelius."

She could hear footsteps approach the apartment door.

"I have to find her, Josiah," Cornelius said, a tinge of urgency in his polished tone.

"So find her," Carter replied carelessly. "But she's not with me. Bryony's the only brunette in my crew. She's the daughter of an old friend of mine, and she's been with us for over six months. Hell, we haven't even been to Montana in three years, but she's been mistaken for that other kid for weeks. It's made life crazy."

"And may I meet 'Bryony'?"

Carter's laugh made Ashe's skin crawl. "Oh, I don't think that would go well. The rest of my crew aren't as… *understanding* as I am."

"If you're sheltering her, you have to let me see her."

"Or what? You'll go feral on me?"

"That's not fair."

"No," Carter said, his voice becoming heated. "Eight years ago wasn't fair. Watching women and children of my people get butchered isn't fair. Fighting battles your people are too cowardly to accept isn't fair."

The anger in his voice grew cold. "Having you stand by and do nothing before the Council was never fair. But then, we're not five years old anymore, so why are we discussing fair?"

"You can't let that go, can you?" Cornelius asked. "Your theory of–"

"It isn't a theory killing my people out there!"

Cornelius exhaled furiously. "But it's not *possible*, Josiah. Cripples seeing wizards we cannot? Magical beings no one has ever heard of? There isn't a shred of proof–"

"No. There's just our word and the lack of faith your kind has in it."

An incredulous noise escaped Cornelius. "And what? You think cripples are the only ones dying? You think I haven't lost countless innocents to traps using your people as bait? This is not about faith, Josiah. This is about not chasing ghosts in the middle of a war! Please! Let this go! Your people will be better served if you give up these fantasies–"

"My people are served by me protecting them from you, the ferals, and the Blood roaming the streets. My people are served by each of those your Council dubbed 'Hunters' giving their lives to stop the ones you ignore. And right now, my people will be served by you getting the hell out of this building and not coming back."

Carter emerged from the doorway. Behind the boxes, Ashe held her breath, trembling.

"You have to let me talk to that girl," Cornelius insisted from inside the room.

"Why?" Carter tossed back.

"Because she's one of the Children."

Carter froze.

"Because she and her sister are the last of the Children," Cornelius continued when Carter didn't turn around. "Taliesin found Patrick. He's dead."

Slowly, Carter looked back at the other man.

For a moment, Cornelius was silent, and when he spoke again, the barest hint of pleading touched his voice. "I know you're still loyal, Josiah, whatever our differences may be. So you have to let me talk to her. You have to let us protect her. If the Taliesin–"

"It's not her," Carter interrupted. "I told you. Bryony's the only brunette with my crew."

A pause followed his words.

"I see," came the careful reply. "Well, if you should see her... this is where to find me."

Silence greeted him. In the room, Ashe heard a door open, and a faint tingle of magic ran over her skin as the air pressure shifted. By the apartment doorway, Carter winced slightly.

"It was good to see you again, Josiah," Cornelius said.

The door closed.

Carter crossed the room, and then emerged, a small scrap of paper in his hand. For a moment, he regarded it, his face unreadable. And then he sighed, shoving it into his pocket as his gaze rose to the stairway. Beneath the steps, Ashe shrank farther into the shadows.

He headed upstairs.

She left the dusty space, her eyes on the second floor landing. Creeping forward, she peeked around the edge of the apartment door.

The room was empty.

Her gaze went back to the stairs, and for the barest heartbeat, she considered just turning around and slipping out the front exit to escape the incomprehensible look she'd seen in his eyes.

But the door panel glowed red, and there wasn't anywhere else to go anyway.

Heart pounding, she followed him through the building again.

At the fifth floor, she paused, and then looked around the corner of the doorway, uncertain where he'd gone. The light in the room she shared with Spider suddenly came on and she heard the girl exclaim in confusion.

"Where's Ashe?" Carter asked.

His voice made her tremble. As guarded as it'd been downstairs, it now held something more. A mixture of urgency and pain she couldn't understand.

She slipped out of the stairwell and walked over to the room.

"I don't know," Spider said. "She was here. I–"

The girl cut off as Ashe stepped around the door. Carter turned, and Spider's gaze flashed between them.

"Carter…" Spider started, tension in her voice.

He glanced back at her. Spider stared at him.

"We… I was going to tell you," the girl began.

"Go wait in Twitch's apartment," he ordered her quietly.

She hesitated.

"Spider."

Her eyes went from him to Ashe and back, and then she nodded. She crossed the room carefully, pausing as she passed him.

"She saved my life, Carter."

He nodded. Echoing the motion briefly, she left.

Gripping the doorframe behind her, Ashe held her breath, waiting. Down the hall, she heard Spider close the other door, but for a long moment, Carter didn't look up from the ground.

And then he chuckled ruefully.

"Ashley." He glanced over at her. "It's Ashley, isn't it?"

Cautiously, she nodded.

"I should've recognized you," he said. "Though, in my defense, the last time I saw you, you were seven. And you hid behind your mother."

Her brow drew down, and he gave her a small smile. "I'm not going to hurt you." He motioned her into the room, and warily, she released the doorframe.

"So I guess you heard him?"

Ashe hesitated. "Why didn't you tell him I was here?"

Carter sighed. "He's a wizard."

"Never trust a wizard," Ashe finished.

"Almost never," he said, nodding to her.

Her gaze dropped to the floor.

"Truth be told, I needed to hear it from you first," Carter continued. "I'm not going to hand you over to some wizard at the drop of a hat, even if he is my cousin."

"Hear what?" she asked nervously.

"That you're a wizard."

She couldn't breathe. She nodded again.

"And why you didn't say anything."

"I was scared."

He looked at her seriously. "I told you, I'm not going to hand you over to them. Not unless you want to go."

She shook her head quickly. "I don't know them. I don't..." She trailed off. "I just want to find the Blood who killed my family."

He grimaced. "And that's something they won't help you do."

"Because they think it's a fantasy," she said, half-asking.

Carter nodded.

"But will you still help me?" she tried. "Even if I'm... one of them?"

He looked at the floor and then chuckled again, shaking his head at a joke she couldn't see. His gaze rose to meet hers and hope fluttered up inside her at the look in his eyes.

"Do you have *any* idea who you are?" he asked softly.

Her brow furrowed in confusion.

An explosion rocked the building.

Clutching at the doorframe, she stared at Carter as the man stumbled, trying to keep his feet. Eyes wide, he looked to her for a heartbeat, and then rushed for the door, holding her back to keep her from following as he scanned the hallway.

Spider raced from the room at the end of the hall, and in the apartment, Ashe could hear Twitch howling.

"Blood!" the girl yelled, drawing her gun.

The building shook hard. Spider crashed sideways into the wall. Behind her, Bus grabbed the doorframe, one hand clutching a sobbing Twitch.

Gasping, the girl started forward again.

The ground beneath her buckled.

"Spider!" Bus shouted.

Frantically, the old man snagged her hand and yanked her back as the floor where she'd been standing crumbled.

"Go!" Carter shouted as the building groaned. "Get to Seagull!"

Spider nodded. With a glance to Bus, she rushed for the exit behind them. Calling to the dogs, the old man brought Twitch in tow.

Gun in one hand and Ashe's arm in the other, Carter headed for the stairs.

Smoke filled the stairwell. Orange light flickered on the first level far below.

Carter swore and pulled her after him, racing down the steps. Gunfire popped in the distance. Shouts echoed beyond the hallway doors. Explosions made the stairs lurch and pieces of the building pelted the ground.

His grip on her arm was unrelenting.

Smoke from the fire surrounded them and the first floor was an inferno, but Carter didn't hesitate. Coughing hard, he held her behind him and pushed open the door to the second level, checking quickly around.

Nothing. Pulling her with him, he rushed across the space.

A figure stepped from the hall ahead.

Carter's bullets ricocheted away, shattering the monitors on the far side of the room.

And the man smiled.

Calmly, he walked toward them through the red-lit shadows and the falling debris, towering larger than life, more giant than man.

Just as she remembered.

Energy surged around him. Carter's eyes went wide.

Her magic rushed outward, surrounding her and Carter, and then shuddering hard as the giant's power smashed down.

She gasped, uncertain what she'd just done. But the Blood wizard simply chuckled.

"Hello Ashley."

Carter shoved her behind him.

"My name is Mason Brogan," the giant continued as though Carter wasn't there. "Pleasure to meet you."

More bullets ricocheted away.

"My people are killing your friends as we speak," the Blood told her calmly, "so if you don't wish this one to die, I'd suggest you tell him to stop shooting at me."

Trembling, she stepped past Carter, pushing his hand aside.

Brogan smiled. "That's–"

Her magic slammed into him.

She could feel his defenses buckle. Feel them crack. And then energy a dozen times stronger than before rushed out of him and hit her.

The blow threw her to the ground as the protection around them vanished. Gasping, she rolled to the side, looking for Carter. He lay next to her and in the dimness, his eyes met her own.

"Kill him, Ashe," he whispered. "Whatever it takes."

She stared at him as Brogan's footsteps crossed the room.

"Do it!" Carter ordered.

Shaking, she pushed up from the ground and backed away. Eyes locked on hers, Carter nodded.

Ashe's gaze went to the giant.

He began to smile.

She let the fires rise.

"You can't kill me, little girl," Brogan said, energy like an electrical storm rushing up around him and crackling from his fingers and hands. She could feel the magic inside him, like a river of power coursing through his veins.

He chuckled. "You don't even know what you're up against."

Lightning struck out at her.

And from her shields, it rebounded away.

Fire covered her. She met his eyes through the flames.

"Yes I do," she whispered.

Her hand flung toward Carter.

The room exploded.

Boarded-up windows blew outward as the blast wave rolled. Brogan crashed back through cinderblock and drywall. The ceiling over him crumbled, pouring down in a torrent while the girders of the building snapped and howled.

She spun, fires vanishing as she rushed toward Carter. Shoving to his feet as her shield around him disappeared, he grabbed her arm and raced for the door.

Something moved at the corner of her eye. Carter slammed into her, driving her to the side.

A gunshot rang through the room.

Carter clutched her arm, staring at her as his brow drew down. Horror spread through her.

"No," she gasped. "No!"

Choking, he stumbled, and then crashed to his knees.

Her head shaking, she grabbed him, trying to haul him up as her eyes went to the far side of the room.

Bracing himself on a shattered wall, Brogan climbed to his feet. Blood drenched him, but his mouth still curled into a smile.

She trembled. Heat twisted through her, like white light spreading beneath her skin. She could feel the energy inside Brogan, rising from deep within his veins to strike. She could feel the source of it, like a cord just at the edge of reach.

Carter's blood covered her hands.

She could feel everything.

Electricity burned the air as it screamed toward her.

Magic surged around her, faster than thought, faster than him. Reaching across the distance, it drove down to the root of his power and twisted, choking it in her own.

She tore it from his body. Gasping, he stumbled as his magic roared into her, shrieking through her bones.

Her gaze met his.

Brogan's eyes went wide.

She flung the magic back in his face.

Fire and electricity slammed into him, engulfing his body as it smashed him through the concrete and metal of the walls. Smoking girders and burning drywall rained down, but in the wreckage, the Blood wizard didn't move.

Not knowing what she'd done and not caring, she grabbed

Carter, taking in his graying skin and the blood soaking his chest at a glance.

He coughed wetly. "You have to go…"

"No." Desperately, she tugged at him. "I'm not leaving without you."

Coughing again, effort twisted his face as he staggered up. "Get to Seagull…"

Ashe nodded frantically, pulling his arm around her shoulders to take some of his weight. "Seagull," she agreed.

The hallway was a million miles away, and the stairs an eternity. Limping and lurching, she dragged him toward them both.

Wizards rushed up the stairway.

Fire consumed them before they could scream.

In the first floor hall, they charged her.

Flames flowed from her hand, and she barely noticed as the wizards died.

The doorway was all she could see.

Metal flew backward and, hauling Carter with her, she stumbled into the night. Behind them, the windows gushed smoke and the building sagged, crumbling from its wounds. On the concrete, the security lights lay shattered and their glass crunched beneath her shoes.

Tears ran down her face as she set fire to the trees, burning them from her path. Carter's breathing was growing fainter, and his trembling had begun to fade. His feet stumbled forward with her own, and gasping, he slowed as they rounded the corner into an alley.

"Ashe," he whispered.

"No."

"Ashe, please…"

She looked over at him, her muscles quivering with the effort of supporting his weight.

He sank down, and she couldn't hold him. Tumbling to the concrete, he gasped and then coughed. "Have to go on."

"No. You're coming with me."

His head shook weakly. "They'll be coming."

"I'm not leaving you."

He coughed again. "It's… an order…" His fingers fumbled at his pocket, and he winced with effort as he drew a scrap of paper from inside. Awkwardly, he shoved it into her hand.

"Go…" he said. "Have to protect you… tell Merlin about the Blood… make them believe…"

Clutching the scrap of paper, she shook her head. "No, please, Carter…"

Blurry with pain, his eyes rose, meeting hers, and his hand came to rest over her own. His mouth curved into a kind smile.

"… would have done anything for you…" he whispered. "My queen."

The smile faded. His gaze drifted beyond her.

She stared.

Beneath his hand, she trembled, and her brow drew down in numbed disbelief. She gasped softly, her body forcing her to draw in air.

Sirens called in the distance.

She looked up at the dim alley and the apartment buildings lining the street. Along the road, people emerged from their homes, drawn by the fire if not the magic and filming the blaze on their cell phones.

Her gaze dropped back to Carter.

Unwillingly, her fingers slipped from beneath his and, for a moment, her hand hovered beside him. And then she pulled away.

Shakily, she rose, the scrap of paper crushed in her hand.

The people on the street couldn't see her. And because of her, perhaps they couldn't see him.

But survivors of the fire would be coming.

Tears fell as she closed her eyes.

Choking back a sob, she swallowed hard and then drew a shuddering breath. She had to go. She had to leave him.

It was an order.

Trembling till she thought her bones would break, she forced herself to turn.

Amid the chaos and commotion, no one saw the dark-haired girl in the alley as she slowly walked away.

———— ◆ ————

Gray sky greeted the sun as it rose, and on the stone wall at the edge of the river, Ashe watched it with eyes that had long since run dry. Blood covered her clothes, though she'd washed her hands by the riverbank a while before. The stretch of service road running along the river was empty at this hour, but she wasn't really worried about people seeing her anyway.

One of the benefits of being a wizard.

Boats drifted past, water sloshing against their hulls, and on the bridges in the distance, she could see early morning commuters speeding toward the skyscrapers towering over the riverside. Seagulls swooped down on the river, welcoming the morning with their cries.

Quiet footsteps sounded on the gravel behind her, and then came to a halt.

She glanced back.

Spider stood at the edge of the road.

Ashe looked away, and let the magic around her fade.

Seconds passed. Gravel crunched. The girl hoisted herself up onto the wall, and her legs dangled by Ashe's over the side.

"Where's Carter?" she asked softly.

Ashe closed her eyes.

A moment slid by.

"How?" the girl whispered, her voice tight.

Eating at her slowly, the words took a long time to arrive. "The Blood wizard shot him. He was trying to hit me."

Spider drew an uneven breath. "Did you kill him?"

"Yes."

The girl nodded in reply.

"Is Bus…" Ashe trailed off, afraid to know.

"He's helping Twitch. He's fine." Spider paused. "They all are."

Silence fell, interspersed with bird cries.

"We need to go," Spider said quietly.

Ashe nodded. "You should."

Spider looked over at her. "What about you?"

Ashe shook her head. "I'm going to find the Merlin," she said, her eyes on the water.

"Why?" The girl's tone was incredulous and encompassed a thousand reasons for not going in the single word.

Answers flitted through Ashe's mind as the river swept by. Cornelius. Her father. Eight years of unanswered questions, on top of the others she couldn't even recall.

Being called a queen.

But none of them compared to the truth.

"Carter told me to."

The girl's brow furrowed. "Why would he–"

She cut off as Ashe looked away.

"What're you going to do?"

Ashe drew a breath. "I'm going to convince them the Blood are real. I'm going to finish what Carter started."

For a moment, Spider said nothing. And then she nodded.

"We're going back to the Abbey. Samson's there and…" She trailed off. "People will need to know. But… if you get into any trouble…"

Spider glanced at her.

"You too," Ashe said.

The ghost of a humored expression flitted across the girl's face, as though to question how that would be possible.

With difficulty, Ashe managed a smile.

Her humor fading, Spider turned and slid down from the wall. One hand on the stonework, she took a breath and then glanced up again. "See you around."

The sound of seagulls above her, Ashe watched as Spider walked away.

Her gaze drifted back to the water. Overhead, the gray clouds brightened, giving way to the sun. From her pocket, she drew out the scrap of paper, rereading the address amid the bloodstains.

And she sighed.

The Blood were still out there. Brogan hadn't been the only one. And while she wasn't sure if they would still be coming after her, it didn't matter.

She'd be coming for them.

Climbing down from the wall, Ashe let her magic rise around her, hovering just on the edge of flame and obscuring her from human view. Gravel crunching beneath her feet and skyscrapers catching the morning light before her, she walked into the city.

<h1 style="text-align: center;">Epilogue</h1>

———◆———

"**O**kay," Harris said resignedly. "Thanks for your… time."

He grimaced as the secretary hung up before he could finish. Forcibly keeping himself from slamming the phone onto the Formica tabletop, he set the cell aside and then drained the last dregs of his coffee. It was his seventh refill. He hadn't slept all night.

And the kids had vanished. Ashley's kind had escaped. Brogan's men were dead.

Just like that, everything was gone.

In the hours since the impossible bloodbath at the abandoned gas station, he'd done everything he could to keep from accepting that fact. He'd gone back to the house. In the space of an evening, it'd been put up for sale and the Smiths had disappeared. He'd tried to find Travis. The boy hadn't been seen since the day before. He'd called the school. They claimed no child named Cole Smith had ever attended their institution. From the aftermath of the battle, he'd even scavenged a cell from one of Brogan's men and tried dialing the giant. There'd been no answer all night.

And slowly, the realization that his whole search might be over had been spreading across his world with suffocating clarity, despite how little he wanted to believe it.

Rubbing his burning eyes, he sighed and then motioned to the diner waitress for another coffee. Ignoring her raised eyebrow at his request, he returned his gaze to the tabletop and eyed his stack of notes balefully. They were largely useless now, seeing as how everyone to whom they pertained was either dead or gone, and it was only because he knew how utterly childish the action would be that he kept himself from dashing them to the floor as he pushed the pile aside.

"Don't tell me you're giving up now, Detective."

Harris glanced up.

Dressed in a well-tailored suit, a middle-aged business man with graying brown hair regarded him with a small smile. Hands in his pockets, he casually stepped aside as the waitress came up and deposited a coffee mug on the table before scurrying uncomfortably away.

Harris' eyes narrowed.

The man's smile grew. Calmly, he lowered himself into the opposite seat of the booth.

There was something familiar about his face, though Harris couldn't place it.

"Mr. Brogan spoke highly of you," the man continued. "I wouldn't expect you to surrender so easily."

"Who're you?" Harris asked.

The man chuckled self-deprecatingly. "My apologies, I'm being rude. I'm Mr. Brogan's employer. My name is Victor Jamison."

Want to know what happens next?

Read Ignite

Book Two of the Kindling Trilogy

Available Now

Loved the book?

If you've enjoyed Kindling, please consider leaving a review on Amazon.com, Goodreads.com, and other book-related sites.

Hear about all the new releases!

Join Skye Malone's mailing list at

www.skyemalone.com/mailinglist

Other titles

The Awakened Fate Series

The Touch Me Series

The Kindling Trilogy

About the author

Skye Malone is a fantasy and paranormal romance author, which means she spends most of her time not-quite-convinced that the magical things she imagines couldn't actually exist.

A Midwestern girl who migrated to the Pacific Northwest, she dreams of traveling the world — though in the meantime she'll take any story that whisks her off to a place where the fantastic lives inside the everyday. She loves strong and passionate characters, complex villains, and satisfying endings that stay with you long after the book is closed. An inveterate writer, she can't go a day without getting her hands on a keyboard and can usually be found typing away while she listens to all the adventures unfolding in her head.

Connect with Skye

Website: www.skyemalone.com
Twitter: www.twitter.com/Skye_Malone
Facebook: www.facebook.com/authorskyemalone
Instagram: www.instagram.com/authorskyemalone

Acknowledgments

There's really no way to repay people for all the good they do for you during the creation of a book. Thanks alone seem insufficient for the hours of reading, editing, discussing and then re-discussing everything that goes into a novel. I will do my best, however.

Much gratitude goes to my beta-readers, Lynn Nguyen and Neil Peterson, for their time and input. The value of extra eyes scrutinizing your work really cannot be overstated.

To my mother and my sister, Mary Ann and Keri, I owe more than I can say. You've supported my dream of becoming a published writer since before I had a single story to my name, and your belief in me has never wavered. Thank you for reading and rereading this book time and again, and for having faith in me through every twist and turn the road to publication has taken.

Deep and rather speechless thanks goes to my partner, Avery. You've sat with me for hours, discussing every little plot point and question I've had in this story, and there is no way this book would have come into the world without your help and support. For reading, for editing, and most importantly, for being my best and dearest friend, thank you.